The Magic Jukebox

The Magic Jukebox

Changes, True Colors, Wild Thing

Judith Arnold

ISBN: 1940547083
ISBN 13: 9781940547084

Table of Contents

Changes

Book One

One

It was love at first sight.

Diana had never believed such a thing existed outside the pages of romance novels, but the moment she spotted the object of her affection standing by the wall across from the bar at the Faulk Street Tavern, she was infatuated. Smitten. Over the moon.

"Oh, God," Peter said, his voice as dry as burnt toast. "Can we leave?"

Of course they couldn't leave. Not before she'd crossed the room, planted herself in front of that magnificent specimen and indulged in a few up-close-and-personal minutes. Maybe she'd run her hand along a curved surface. Maybe she'd touch the buttons, two neat, vertical rows of red. Maybe, if she dared, she'd press one of those buttons and see what happened.

Ignoring Peter, ignoring the niggling voice inside her skull warning her that he considered a mildly grungy watering hole like the Faulk Street Tavern so far beneath him that he'd need rappelling equipment to descend to its level, ignoring the certainty that if she spent more than five seconds here he was bound to be royally pissed, emphasis on *royally*...Ignoring everything but the target in her sights, she strode across the room. The dark pine plank floor was suspiciously sticky in a few spots. The booths lining one wall were crowded with patrons drinking, chattering, laughing, arguing. Most of the tables were occupied, too, and the long bar was insulated by a two-deep layer of people, mostly men, mostly clad in jeans or work pants, and flannel shirts layered over thermals. A few sported duck-billed caps.

Working-class, she thought as she moved through the room. No problem, as far as she was concerned. Peter was such a snob, though.

A waitress carrying an empty tray passed Diana en route to the bar. "You okay, hon?" she asked.

Other than being madly, wildly in love, Diana was fine. "Thanks," she said with a nod.

"There's an empty table over there." The waitress tilted her head in the direction of one of the tables. "Grab it if you want it. Tables don't stay empty long here on a Saturday night."

"Thanks," Diana said again. She glanced toward the door, trying to signal Peter to claim the available table. He remained where he was, his arms crossed, his handsome face twisted into a scowl.

Diana detoured to the table herself, tossed her jacket over one of the chairs, and then continued to the wall, to her destiny.

It was gorgeous. Utterly, heart-stoppingly gorgeous.

A Wurlitzer jukebox.

Her expertise didn't run to jukeboxes, but a few had passed through the galleries of Shomback-Sawyer Antiques in the five years Diana had worked there, and she did know a thing or two about antique furniture.

This jukebox, while not exactly a piece of furniture, was a beauty. Burnished wood rose to a dome of gold-hued, marbleized veneer which ended in a graceful crown trimmed in red glass and chrome. Beneath that crown was a semicircular window, cloudy with age, behind which stood a stack of vinyl records. A horseshoe of mesh fabric covered the speakers, surrounding what looked like a stained-glass depiction of two peacocks, the male's long tail curving down to cushion the female. Those red buttons, for selecting songs, stood in two straight columns on either side of the peacocks.

None of the buttons was labeled. Diana wondered how someone could choose a song.

Not that it mattered. Surely the jukebox didn't actually work.

She tried to recall what the concierge at the Ocean Bluff Inn had said when she and Peter had asked what people in Brogan's

Point did in the evenings. "Besides what we have here?" The concierge had gestured with a generous sweep of her arm, encompassing more than just the inn's charming lobby but the entire sprawling complex of buildings, gardens, multiple dining rooms, tennis courts and a path down to the beach. "There are plenty of places in town. Being an antiques buff, you ought to check out the Faulk Street Tavern. It's an easy walk from here, less than half a mile away. It's got an antique I think you're going to fall in love with."

So they'd checked out the tavern, and now Diana knew why. She was more than merely an antiques buff, and this was more than merely a jukebox. The concierge, a cheerful, chatty woman named Claudia, was right: Diana had fallen in love.

"Okay. You've looked at it. Can we leave?"

She'd been so transported by the jukebox, she hadn't even noticed Peter abandoning the entry and crossing the room. Now he stood so close behind her she could feel the warmth of his chest against her back. "No, we can't," she said. "This is an amazing piece. I want to spend some time with it."

Peter rolled his eyes. He was an elitist—well bred, well educated, well groomed, and overly condescending when confronted with anything, any place or anyone he considered inferior. Apparently jukeboxes weren't worth his time. Or they might be, if they were in a museum. In a dive like the Faulk Street Tavern, no.

"I need to learn more about this," she said, wondering whether the piece was truly an antique or whether the locals just fed tourists a phony story about it, like all those shops down the road in Salem which sold "genuine" witchcraft paraphernalia. Diana knew some people did practice witchcraft, but she doubted most of the ticky-tacky souvenirs sold in Salem had anything to do with that.

"What do you need to learn?" Impatience tightened Peter's voice. "You're not going to buy it for Shomback-Sawyer."

"If it's for sale, I might."

"Oh, this baby ain't for sale." A man sidled up beside her and Peter, and she felt Peter growing exponentially more annoyed, as

5

prickly as a porcupine under siege, its quills quivering. She reached for his hand with her own and gave it a reassuring squeeze. He had no reason to feel threatened by the man who had joined them at the jukebox. The guy looked to be in his forties, maybe older, his face grizzled and his chin hidden beneath a stubbly beard salted with gray. He was thin, his gangly torso clad in a heavy cotton shirt with *Frank* stitched in red thread above the chest pocket and *Kreske's Auto Supplies* imprinted on the pocket itself.

"Do you know anything about this jukebox?" she asked the man. Peter tightened his grip on her hand just the slightest bit. *Oh, for heaven's sake,* she wanted to snap at him. No need to go all caveman on her. She was talking to the guy, not inviting him back to her room for the night.

"Just that it's a fixture here, and it ain't goin' nowhere. Gus would never allow it."

"Gus?"

"Owner of this bar. Nobody can remember a time before the jukebox was here. 'Course, anyone who could would probably be dead by now." He edged closer to the jukebox and gripped its polished golden flanks with both hands.

Diana almost yelled at him not to touch such a treasure, but then she conceded that he knew a lot more about it than she did. That gave him certain rights. "So it's always been here?" she asked.

"Long as I can remember. Were you planning to play something?"

"Does it actually work?" If it did, Shomback-Sawyer could make a fortune on the piece. Two fortunes. Diana might just buy it herself. She loved its shape, the grain rippling through the wood, the beautiful stained-glass peacocks. If it actually played music, too…

"Wouldn't be much of a jukebox if it didn't," the man said.

"But there's no listing of the songs." She gestured toward the buttons. "How do you even know what song you're requesting?"

He laughed, revealing a mouth full of crooked teeth. "You don't," he said.

"You don't know what's playing?"

"Well, you do once it starts playing and you can hear it." He shrugged and dug his hand into the pocket of his twill work pants. "You don't get to choose, though. You just put in your money and press a button or two, and you take your chances. It don't play nothin' new," he added. "Nothin' more recent than the invention of the iPod. Just old songs and really old songs. Some folks say it plays what you need to hear."

"What you *need* to hear?"

He nodded. "I don't *need* to hear nothin'," he added, "so I'm prob'ly safe." He removed his hand from his pocket, a quarter pinched between his thumb and forefinger. "Ten cents apiece, three for a quarter," he said. "Same price as when I was a kid and every diner, restaurant and bar had a jukebox." He inserted the quarter into the coin slot and poked a few unlabeled buttons. "Let's see what we get."

The cloudy window in the machine brightened, resembling an upside-down smile. Diana heard a couple of clicks, a mechanical hum, and then the velvet-smooth voice of Frank Sinatra singing "New York, New York." A loud chorus of hoots and boos arose from the bar, although everyone—including the man who'd paid for the song—seemed amused. "Don't think I need to hear *this*," he joked.

"It's a good song," Diana conceded.

"If you're a Yankees fan, maybe."

She grinned. She might not be a baseball fanatic, but she knew Frank Sinatra's rendition of "New York, New York" was the song played at every Yankees home game, just as Neil Diamond's "Sweet Caroline" was played at every Red Sox home game. In this pictur-esque seaside town an hour north of Boston, fans of the Yankees—the home town team's arch-rivals—were undoubtedly a rarity. The people carousing at the Faulk Street Tavern surely preferred "Sweet Caroline."

The stranger grinned back at her. "If *that's* what the jukebox wants to tell me, I ain't listenin' to it. Have a good one." He nodded at Peter, an acknowledgement Peter probably didn't deserve, given that he hadn't even bothered to say hello, and then strode back across the room to rejoin his buddies at the bar. They continued their hooting and guffawing over the Yankees theme song, even as they slapped him on the back and handed him a bottle of beer.

Enthralled, Diana turned back to Peter.

"Can we go now?" he asked. He looked, if anything, even more annoyed. And sulky. And miserable.

"We've got to listen to all three songs," she argued, trying to thaw him with a smile. "The man put in a quarter. I snagged a table. Let's have a drink and hear the other two songs. Then we can go. All right?"

Peter eyed the bar warily. "Do I have to have a drink? I'm not sure this is the kind of place where they wash the glasses."

She refused to let his attitude irk her. They'd come to Brogan's Point to assess the Ocean Bluff Inn as a possible wedding venue. Peter favored a mansion they'd visited in Newport, but Brogan's Point was easier to reach from Boston, and their money would go a lot farther at the Ocean Bluff Inn than it would in Newport. Not that their families couldn't afford any venue Diana and Peter decided on, but she was a practical sort. If they booked a less expensive venue, she'd feel free to spend a little more on the band or the food.

She was glad she'd talked Peter into spending the weekend in Brogan's Point. The inn was truly lovely. The facility had several different event rooms, ranging in size from intimate to ballroom-grand. It also boasted plenty of guest rooms for attendees who wanted to stay overnight, and a breathtaking garden surrounding a gazebo that overlooked the ocean. Weather permitting, they could have the actual ceremony in the gazebo.

They'd ordered tasting menus for dinner earlier that evening, sampling a variety of possible hors d'oeuvres, appetizers and entrees. The chef wanted them to try some desserts, too, but after all the crabmeat tartlets and apple-and-brie quiches, the tuna tartare and caviar blini, the fillet mignon and poached salmon, they'd been too full.

Peter might loathe this bar, but he'd liked the inn—maybe not as much as the place in Newport, but enough not to veto it out of hand. While they'd stuffed themselves with bites and nibbles from the catering menus, he'd been the open-minded, courteous fiancé with whom she'd agreed to spend the rest of her life.

When he got the way he was now, however, stuffy and grouchy and arrogant, she wanted to hurl the dazzling three-carat diamond solitaire he'd given her at his nose. He had a perfectly sculpted nose. Michelangelo could not have improved on it, nor could Dr. Kafavian, her mother's favorite plastic surgeon. But the rock currently glittering on her left ring finger, if properly thrown, could give Peter's pretty nose a nice, bloody gash.

She didn't want to hurt him, of course. He was her husband-to-be, and she was fully prepared to gaze at his nicer-than-hers nose across tables in kitchens, restaurants and even seedy bars like the Faulk Street Tavern for the next fifty years. But honestly, when he got this way, he pissed her off. Maybe even royally.

"Just one drink," she cajoled, leading him to the table and nudging him into one of the chairs. She removed her jacket from the other, draped it over the chair's ladder-back and gazed around the room in search of the pleasant waitress she'd briefly spoken with on her way to the jukebox.

"Somehow, I doubt this place is going to have a decent wine," he muttered.

"Then get an indecent wine. Or a beer. Or a martini. They probably can't botch that."

He mumbled something—she was pretty sure he was complaining about the likely uncleanliness of the glasses, although if he ordered a beer he could drink directly from the bottle and not have to worry about the bar's hygiene. She hoped that once they were married, he would loosen up and be less judgmental.

She and Peter had known each other since childhood, and they'd started dating toward the end of high school. Even as a teenager, Peter had tended toward superciliousness. He came from an old Boston-Brahmin family and had upper-class tastes. He liked his clothing tailored, his cars expensive, his wines vintage and his scotch single-malt. He was fortunate enough to be able to afford it all, not only because of his family background but because he'd graduated from Harvard Business School and landed a ridiculously well-paying job at a private equity firm. He appreciated the good things in life. More than appreciated—he expected them.

Diana wished he could occasionally forget he was the scion of a top one-percent family and perhaps understand the appeal of a rattly pick-up truck, a greasy hamburger, and a joint like the Faulk Street Tavern. At least it was called a tavern, not a bar. Why couldn't that be enough for him?

Frank Sinatra belted out the final notes of "New York, New York," accompanied by a flourish of trumpets and a lot of jeers and catcalls from the tavern's patrons. Diana found herself chuckling at their enthusiastic negativity, but a part of her mind focused on the music itself. Or, more accurately, the jukebox. That an apparently antique machine could produce such decent acoustics impressed her. The sound quality wasn't quite like listening to an MP3 file through her high-end earphones, but if the jukebox was really as old as she thought it was, its speaker seemed awfully good. "That sounded great, don't you think?" she asked Peter. "The trumpets, and his voice. It sounded almost stereophonic. I don't think stereo had been invented when that jukebox was built."

Peter shrugged, clearly uninterested. His gaze darted around the room, searching for a waitress. Evidently he wanted to get this drink over with so he could return to the more elegant environs of the Ocean Bluff Inn.

The waitress arrived at their table just as the second song began on the jukebox: a bright, bouncy tune, sung by a man in falsetto, about how someone made him feel like dancing. To Diana's surprise, quite a few people left their seats in the booths and at the tables and filled the empty floor space at the center of the tavern.

"I didn't realize this was a dancing club," Diana said to the waitress.

The waitress grinned. "People react to the songs. What can I get you folks?"

Peter waited for Diana to order. She asked for an Irish coffee—something sweet to make up for the dessert she'd skipped at the inn—and he grudgingly requested a Sam Adams lager. As soon as the waitress departed, he leaned across the scarred oak table and muttered, "After this drink, we're out of here."

Diana sighed. She wished that when he'd leaned across the table it would have been to ask her to dance. Or to admit the song was catchy. Or just to crack a smile and concede that remaining at the Faulk Street Tavern for as long as it took to enjoy a drink wasn't sheer agony for him.

But he remained scowling, his arms once again folded across his chest, his cashmere sweater smooth and much too tasteful in this room full of people in flannel and denim and leather. Lord, he could be such a pill. Most of the time he was a fine man, smart and clever, honorable and respectful, but every now and then he'd slip into curmudgeon mode. His temper could flare into a major blaze in a fraction of a second. Once they were married, she'd have to figure out a way to get him to lighten up and mellow out.

The waitress was back sooner than Diana expected; the service was quicker here than at the Ocean Bluff Inn. She set three square napkins on the table, then placed a mug peaked with whipped cream like a snow-capped mountain in front of Diana, and a beer in a sweating bottle and a V-shaped glass in front of Peter. His glass had tiny flecks of ice on the rim but it appeared clean. Diana wondered whether he would pour his drink into the glass or drink it straight from the bottle. Drinking from the bottle would protect his tender digestive system from whatever imaginary contamination the glass might contain, but it was so *déclassé*.

Her mug looked clean enough. She took a sip—hot coffee, cool whipped cream and soothing whisky, a blend of bitter and sweet that simmered down her throat. It was, in fact, the most delicious Irish coffee she'd ever tasted. She smiled at Peter, but he was too busy frowning at the beer bottle and glass to notice.

The song ended, and the crowd at the center of the tavern thinned as the dancers drifted back to their seats. Diana followed a couple with her gaze as they walked arm-in-arm toward the bar. The woman was plump, the man husky, and both were clad in plaid flannel and blue denim. She couldn't see their faces, yet from their posture alone, the way the woman's arm snuggled around the man's waist, his arm looped over her shoulders, and her head leaned gently into the hollow of his neck, Diana could tell they were in love. She allowed herself an envious sigh, then wondered why she envied them. She and Peter were in love, too, weren't they?

When the couple reached the bar, a man stepped out of their way. Tall and lean, he had on black jeans, a Henley shirt and a denim work shirt over it, his sleeves rolled up to expose strong forearms. His face was an intriguing arrangement of planes and hollows, shadows and light. He had a hard chin, a long nose—definitely not a pretty nose—and dark, dark eyes. His hair was dark, as well, thick and wavy and in desperate need of a comb.

His eyes met hers just as the third song began to emerge from the jukebox. It was an old song, from before her time, but she recognized it anyway. Her Uncle Martin loved British rock from the Sixties and Seventies, and when Diana's family visited him on Martha's Vineyard, he'd serenade her with his favorite songs. This one was David Bowie. *Changes.*

The man with the dark hair and the darker eyes was staring at her. She stared back, unsure why. Unsure why she couldn't seem to look away from him. Unsure why he was gazing at her with such intensity.

The song's familiar, stammering refrain filled the air: *Ch-ch-ch-ch-changes.*

Every other sound fell away. She heard no other voices. No clinks of glasses touching, no thuds of bottles being set on tables, no scrape of chair legs against the wooden floor. She heard nothing but the song—and she saw no one but the man.

"Diana!" An instant after the last soulful wail of a saxophone at the end of the song faded away, Peter's voice intruded, forceful and demanding. "Diana!"

She flinched and swung around in her chair, as if by ending, the song had released her from a spell. Peter was studying her, his brows dipped into a deep frown. "Where the hell were you?"

"Right here." Her voice sounded odd to her. She took a hot sip of her Irish coffee, as if that would wash away the fog in her throat, in her brain.

"Finish your drink." He waved impatiently at her mug. "I want to leave."

You've wanted to leave since the moment we arrived, she thought with a strange blend of irritation and...fear. Fear that something inside her was wrong, something had become unhinged. Something was falling apart.

Had the bartender added a dangerous extra ingredient to her drink?

"All right," she said, nudging the mug away from her. "Let's go."

But even after she'd stood, donned her jacket and let Peter lead her out of the tavern, she knew she'd left a piece of her soul behind.

—⚏—

Gus handed Nick a glass of beer before he could ask for one. His hand automatically curved around the icy surface, chilling his palm. His mouth tasted the bitter foam before it had even passed his lips.

Who the hell was that woman? Why did locking gazes with her make him feel as if someone had plunged a stiletto right through his heart? Clean and painless, yet it left him dead. Or reborn. Transformed, in any case.

She wasn't beautiful...except that she was. Long, tawny hair fell in gentle waves around a narrow, angular face. Her eyes were too large, too round, and even in the bar's dim light, even with a good thirty feet separating her from him, he could see that they were hazel. Damn, he could see her eyelashes.

He could also see the guy with her. And the diamond solitaire, as big as the frickin' Rock of Gibraltar, glinting on her left ring finger.

Given the size of that ring, Nick felt safe in assuming that, one, she was engaged, and two, Nick—a man who never would, or *could*, give a woman a ring like that—wasn't her type. The guy with her was clean cut and dressed in clothes that reeked wealth. Her outfit pegged her as upper-class, too: tailored trousers, a soft, pale sweater beneath a tweedy-looking jacket, a colorful silk-looking scarf coiled around her neck.

The folks Nick hung out with wore faded wool scarves their mothers or wives or girlfriends had knitted for them four Christmases ago. But then, the folks Nick hung out with didn't dress like they'd just stepped off a sixty-foot yacht. If they'd stepped off a boat, it was a trawler, and they wore waders and smelled of fish.

He'd wager a year's salary that the woman whose too-big eyes had sent that stiletto straight through him from all the way across the room didn't smell like fish.

"It's the song," Gus said.

Nick snorted. "Don't start in."

Gus chuckled and poured some vodka into a martini glass. It flowed in a smooth, clear thread from the spout plugged into the top of the bottle. Gus never had to measure. She knew the exact amount of every ingredient in every drink. "I'm not starting in," she said. "Just saying."

Nick swiveled around to face the bar, to stare at Gus rather than the woman with the blinding engagement ring adorning her left hand. The only jewelry Gus wore was a loop of braided leather around her wrist. She was tall and athletic in build, her red hair fading to gray and chopped in short tufts that looked almost, but not quite, masculine . She'd been running the bar since Nick was in diapers, and it felt somehow disrespectful to argue with her. But all those legends about the jukebox, the weird songs that came out of it, the weirder effect they had on people…

Nick didn't believe that shit. Real life had laid too many scars on him. The only things he believed in were hard work, good sex and paying for your mistakes. And an occasional cold beer.

Not magic. And certainly not jukeboxes.

Two

Nick's Monday morning routine was to rise around six and head over to the Community Center to work out in the gym. Free membership was a perk of his job, and during his time in detention, he'd discovered that vigorous physical exercise kept his brain functioning as well as his body. After his workout, he'd shower and walk down the street to Riley's for breakfast. Rita, his favorite waitress there, always topped off his travel mug with coffee before he left.

From Riley's, he'd stroll down to the concrete and stone sea wall constructed along the edge of the beach, designed to keep the ocean's waves from sweeping across Atlantic Avenue, damaging the cars and buildings and leaving behind a residue of sand, shells, and seaweed. The abutment had served its purpose for more than fifty years, failing only a few times when huge nor'easters had roared up the New England coast.

Nick liked standing by the retaining wall, leaning his arms on the thick concrete ledge and surveying the beach below. Beyond it stretched the eastern horizon, a seam separating the blue-gray Atlantic from the dawn-pink sky. It didn't surprise him that ancient navigators, gazing west from the shores of Europe, believed the earth was flat. How could it not be, when the horizon was so straight?

They were wrong, of course.

The folks who believed the Faulk Street Tavern's jukebox had some sort of supernatural power were wrong, too.

Just because that damned David Bowie song was still humming through his head, a two-day ear worm that refused to wiggle its way out of his skull, didn't mean anything except that the music he'd listened to all day yesterday—head-banging heavy metal, whiny C&W tunes about runaway dogs and bitchy women, or maybe runaway women and bitchy dogs, and finally a ninety-minute megadose of Pearl Jam—had failed to eradicate the Bowie song from Nick's brain. He didn't even like the song. All that stammering. The melodramatic melody. The sobbing quality of Bowie's voice. Nick had vague memories of his parents listening to David Bowie years ago, and memories of his parents were something he'd just as soon avoid.

The coffee from Riley's was helping, though. The coffee and the blustery March wind gusting off the water were doing more to clear that god-awful tune from his head than all the music he'd blasted yesterday. Above the water, a pair of gulls flew circles around each other in an airborne dance. Beyond the jetty to the south, the silhouette of a fishing boat, cables and masts vivid against the pale morning sky, headed out toward that flat horizon. "Don't fall over the edge," Nick murmured, as if the boat could hear him. As if there was an edge to fall over.

In the distance to his north, he spotted a jogger running along the beach, heading toward where he stood. As the figure drew nearer, he could see she was a woman, gliding across the sand at the high-tide line. Running on dry sand could strain a person's ankles and calves, but along the tide line the sand was damp and solid, supporting a jogger's footfalls. Still, the wind was stiff and the air chilly, so the jogger had her challenges. She wore black running pants that clung to her long, slim legs, and a radioactive-orange jacket. She'd be visible in that thing even if she ran at midnight. Her hair was pulled back into a ponytail.

Tawny hair, sunlight turning the strands gold. A sharp, angular face. Way-too-big hazel eyes.

Once again, he couldn't look away. There was no jukebox out here, no David Bowie song, so he knew none of Gus's idiotic superstitions were at play. Yet he was transfixed by the woman as she jogged closer. Captivated. Unable to keep from staring at her.

His gaze tracked her as she sprinted past him, running parallel to the retaining wall. Street level was about five feet above the beach, so she'd have to look up to see him. But her face remained forward, her eyes aimed at the sand ahead of her as if she could visualize an actual path instead of just a stretch of beach.

She continued south toward the jetty, and he decided she looked almost as good from the rear as from the front. Those stretchy black running pants did wonders for her ass.

The sun caught the diamond on her left hand.

So she was taken. He understood that. No law said a guy couldn't look. And admire. And maybe enjoy a pleasant if frustrating twinge of lust.

Even if she weren't wearing an engagement ring, he'd never have anything to do with her. She wasn't his type. Too patrician. He could tell she was from a different universe, not just by her obviously expensive jewelry but by her bearing, her polish, the way she could jog the length of the beach without popping a bead of sweat. Sure, the air was cold, but Nick could work out in an industrial freezer and still wind up drenched in perspiration. Rich people had more refined sweat glands, he figured.

She had to be a tourist. He knew most of Brogan's Point's residents, even the wealthy ones who lived in the sprawling mansions on the north side of town, past the Ocean Bluff Inn. Those rich folks were the people he often hit up for donations to subsidize the youth programs he ran. He'd give talks, write proposals, sit through excruciating teas and cocktail parties where funds were being raised. He didn't hate affluent people, or even resent them. He did his best not to gag on the Prosecco or the sherry they served, and he tried not to make a mess with the finger sandwiches, which never seemed to be the right size for his fingers. He was grateful to those rich citizens. But he knew they weren't *his* people.

The beautiful jogger wasn't *his* people, either. She was just a wealthy woman passing through town, one of those iconoclasts who vacationed in Brogan's Point during the off season. Maybe she preferred beaches when they weren't mobbed with riffraff—the public beaches here in town were usually jam-packed from Memorial Day through Labor Day. Or maybe she spent those prime summer

17

beach months someplace nicer—Nantucket, or Kennebunkport. Or the Riviera.

She reached the jetty and halted, hands on hips. He could see the rise and fall of her shoulders as she panted. After a minute, she lifted one hand to her head and pushed back her hair. Then she turned.

And saw him.

The only music he heard was the caws and mews of the sea gulls swooping down toward the jetty, no doubt looking for some unlucky clams to smash against the rocks and devour. But just like two nights ago at the Faulk Street Tavern, the woman stared at him and he felt…punched in the gut today. Not stabbed, punched.

He took a sip of coffee to keep from doubling over and grunting like someone on the wrong end of a fist. The coffee was still blessedly hot. Thank God for insulated travel mugs.

Her gaze pinning him like a laser sight on a rifle, she sauntered up the beach's slope to the retaining wall. Her feet sank into the powdery white sand above the high tide line, but that didn't slow her down. He saw now why she'd tried to smooth her hair. Multiple strands had escaped from the elastic, and the wind off the water had tangled them into a silky mess.

She halted just a few feet below where he stood. He contemplated leaping down from the retaining wall to join her on the beach. But then he'd have to walk all the way to the jetty to get back up to the street. It would be easier to reach down and haul her up the wall. She was so slim, she couldn't weigh much.

"That coffee smells amazing," she said.

Definitely not what he'd been expecting her to say. He wasn't sure what he *was* expecting, but he was surprised she could smell the coffee from a distance, with the travel mug's lid screwed on tight and the briny fragrance of the ocean heavy in the air. "It *is* amazing," he said.

"Where did you get it?"

"Riley's, just up the street. Best coffee in Brogan's Point. Maybe in the world." Why were they talking about coffee? Then again, why not? Discussing coffee with her seemed natural, easy, like something they might do every morning. "I'll buy you a cup," he said.

"Oh, I…" She gazed around, then patted the zippered pockets of her glow-in-the-dark jacket. A faint laugh escaped her. "I don't have any money with me."

"You don't need money. I just said I'll buy you a cup."

"Do you think that's a good idea?"

His gaze snagged on the huge diamond sparkling on her left ring finger. Then he shrugged. "Riley's coffee is always a good idea. Give me your hands." He set his mug down on the sidewalk adjacent to the retaining wall, then braced himself and reached down to her.

She eyed the wall dubiously, and then his hands. Her shoulders rose and fell again, another deep breath, and she lifted her arms.

He was right; she didn't weigh that much. She bent her legs and used the treaded soles of her running shoes against the stones, half walking up the vertical surface as he lifted her. As soon as her hips reached the ledge, she twisted and sat on it, then swung her legs over.

He took a step back, giving her space. Standing, she dusted off her cute little bottom with her palms and shot him a wary glance. "I should probably go back to the inn."

"You're staying at Ocean Bluff?"

She nodded. "They have coffee there."

"Not as good as Riley's."

She bit her lip and averted her eyes, indecision radiating from her. "I really shouldn't."

He could have said something to reassure her. He could have introduced himself, provided references, assured her she would be safe with him. He could have lied and told her he was noble of spirit and pure of soul.

Instead, some crazy impulse seized him and he sang, so softly no one but she could possibly hear, "Ch-ch-ch-ch-changes."

—ༀ—

This was crazy. She didn't even know him—and she needed a shower.

Something peculiar had happened to her Saturday night, when that song had spilled from the jukebox at the Faulk Street Tavern and she and this man—this total stranger—had engaged in a staring contest as intense as a round of steamy sex.

That was a totally inappropriate thought. She gave her head a brisk shake and turned to view the ocean. The early morning sun hovered just inches above the horizon, painting a streak of splintered light across the waves.

Crazy.

Her whole life seemed crazy at the moment.

Her decision to stay on in Brogan's Point was definitely crazy. She and Peter were supposed to drive back to Boston yesterday, but she'd sent Peter off alone. "I need more time here at the Ocean Bluff Inn. I think it's the right place for our wedding, but I want to be sure."

"I liked the mansion down in Newport better," Peter had argued.

"I hated that place." Resembling nothing so much as a downsized version of the Palace of Versailles, it had been much too opulent for her tastes, all that Louis XIV furniture, the murals of fat cherubs prancing across the walls, the gilt moldings and frenetic floral patterns on the rugs. People—not least of all the bride and groom—would be rendered invisible, surrounded by such hectic décor. "Besides, I'd like to check out some of those antique dealers we passed on the drive up here," she'd told Peter. "I might find some gems for Shomback-Sawyer."

"We can stop at a few of those places on the way home." Peter had busied himself draping his shirts neatly on hangers inside his folding suitcase. He'd been so eager to leave, he'd started packing right after breakfast.

She had been even more eager to stay, to visit the antique dealers, yes, and to absorb the atmosphere of the Ocean Bluff Inn. And also to figure out what had happened when she'd heard the David Bowie song emanating from that wondrous jukebox Saturday night.

She hadn't dared to mention the last reason to Peter, however. She'd been as enthralled by the tavern as he'd been appalled by it.

Throughout their stroll back to the inn after they'd left the place, he'd muttered about its low-rent ambiance, its even lower-rent customers, and the fact that his beer had been too cold. Or maybe too warm. Or both. Whatever. Something had been drastically wrong with his drink, and he'd found the entire outing horrid.

So she'd sent him on his way yesterday, after they'd argued and then lapsed into a frosty truce. He would eventually forgive her for staying on in Brogan's Point. He'd stew and mope for a while, and then get over it. How long could he resent her for spending a few extra days in this quiet North Shore town and bringing in some new business for Shomback-Sawyer? If she transported some treasures back to the antiques dealership, she might even earn a bonus. Not that she or Peter needed the extra income, but money was the sort of thing that impressed him.

After he had departed, she'd asked Claudia at the inn to line up a rental car for her and enjoyed another delicious tasting-menu meal in the inn's Sunrise Room, an octagonal, glass-walled dining room facing east, overlooking the ocean. It would be a beautiful space for a wedding reception, and she'd assured herself that was why she'd wanted to dine there. But as she'd worked her way through mouth-watering bites of portobello caps stuffed with gruyere, butterflied shrimp, and asparagus spears wrapped in bacon, she hadn't thought much about the wedding at all. She'd thought about whether she dared to return to the Faulk Street Tavern.

She'd decided it would be best not to tempt fate, even though she had no idea what heading back to the tavern for another Irish coffee had to do with fate. Instead, she'd spent Sunday night in her spacious room at the inn, sprawled out on the king-size bed she no longer had to share with Peter. She'd watched television, read, and gone to sleep. In her dreams, a dark-haired, dark-eyed stranger had floated in and out of view, staring at her.

Now, here he was, with his black, dark waves of hair and his penetrating brown eyes. Here he was, wearing faded jeans and a battered leather jacket which looked gloriously lived in, its surface laced with creases. He'd clasped her hands and hoisted her over the sea wall. He'd spoken to her. He'd asked her to have a cup of coffee with him.

He'd whispered the refrain of the song the jukebox at the tavern had been playing when their gazes had met and fused.

He extended his right hand to her. "Nick Fiore," he said. Did introducing himself mean he was no longer a stranger?

Whether or not it did, she couldn't ignore the gesture. Shaking his hand, she said, "Diana Simms."

"So. Coffee?"

She opened her mouth to say no. But what came out was, "Thank you. I'd like that."

He motioned with his head toward a street perpendicular to the road that bordered the sea wall—Atlantic Avenue, she believed it was called. "It's just a short walk. I don't know how tired you are from your run."

"I'm okay."

He dug his hands into the pockets of his jacket, a move that kept him from taking her hand, if indeed that was something he'd considered doing. He had been forward enough to invite her for coffee before he even knew her name, after all. And he'd held both her hands for the few seconds it took to hoist her up off the beach and over the wall. Her own hands still felt the warmth of his, the strength of his grip.

That warmth was enough to make her hesitate. This was crazy, *crazy*. She halted on the sidewalk as soon as they'd crossed Atlantic Avenue. "I should...shower," she finally said. She wasn't about to announce her concerns about her sanity to him.

His mouth curved in a crooked smile, as if smiling was something he didn't do that often. "You smell fine. You look fine, too."

"My hair's a disaster."

His reluctant smile gave way to a low chuckle. "Riley's isn't the Ritz. Trust me—you're better groomed than most of the people in there." He lowered his eyes to her body, then back to her face. "Nobody's even going to notice your hair. They'll be blinded by your jacket."

She laughed, too. Yes, this was crazy—but since he'd gotten her to laugh with him, he'd earned the right to have a cup of coffee with her.

They ambled up the street in silence, until he paused at a storefront and swung the glass door open. It emitted a tinny jingle as a bell perched above the hinge announced their arrival.

The coffee shop was packed. At eight a.m. on a Monday morning, this was obviously the place Brogan's Point's wage-earners started their day. Men in heavy work clothes and thick-soled boots perched on the stools along the counter like sparrows on an electrical wire. The tables and booths held clusters of men, some in suits and others in denim or canvas work apparel, and women in skirts, pant suits and scrubs. Waitresses circulated with thick porcelain plates containing aromatic omelets and home fries, bowls of oatmeal and glass coffee decanters. Conversation blended with the clink of silverware against plates and the thumps of mugs against Formica tabletops.

No empty tables, Diana noted with a mixture of disappointment and relief. Maybe they'd be forced to leave, and she could jog back to the inn and regain her mental stability.

"In the back, Nick," a waitress hollered to Nick as she scurried past with a couple of empty dishes. Diana took some small comfort in the understanding that he'd given her his real name, and that he was apparently a regular here. The crowd offered her a layer of protection, too. What could happen in a coffee shop with so many witnesses?

Nick beckoned her to follow him past the packed tables toward the rear of the diner, where, sure enough, a booth stood empty. He gestured her toward one of the banquettes and slid in across the table from her, then tugged a couple napkins from the chrome dispenser at the wall end of the table and laid one in front of her. Beside the dispenser stood salt and pepper shakers and a cylindrical jar of sugar. That seemed so quaint. Even the more humble coffee shops Diana patronized in Boston usually had bowls on every table containing packets of plain sugar, raw sugar, brown sugar, and a variety of no-calorie sweeteners.

With its maroon leatherette banquettes and checkerboard-tile floor, Riley's seemed frozen in another decade, another century. All that was missing from their booth was a table-side jukebox.

Thank heavens for that. Diana dreaded to think what would happen if someone slipped in a quarter and David Bowie's voice, crooning about changes, rose above the din of chattering customers and waitresses. The effect of his song emerging from a jukebox had been bizarre enough when the length of the Faulk Street Tavern had separated her from Nick. With him just the width of a table away from her, who knew what would happen if they heard that song again?

Despite the crowd, a waitress materialized at their table almost immediately, carrying two laminated menus. "Back again?" she teased Nick. "You just can't stay away, can you."

"It's because I'm in love with you, Rita," he teased back. "If only you'd marry me, we wouldn't have to keep meeting like this."

She laughed and fanned the air with her hand, waving off his flirtation.

"I'll just have another coffee," he told her, then nodded toward Diana. "She'd like a menu."

"No, thanks," Diana said. "Just coffee for me, too."

"You should eat something," he argued. "You just ran, what? Twenty miles?"

"More like two."

"That's worth a couple of slices of toast, at least. One slice per mile."

She shook her head. She had planned to eat breakfast at the inn. But who was to say that an expensive breakfast at the inn would taste better than a piece of toast at this greasy spoon? Given how wonderful the coffee smelled…"All right," she conceded. "Just one slice, though."

"Whole wheat, rye, white, sourdough, seven-grain, English muffin," the waitress recited. "You look like someone from the city, so don't order a bagel. Ours are pretty lame. Can't compete with a good Boston bagel."

Diana laughed. "I don't want a lame bagel. Sourdough, I guess. Just one slice."

"The order comes with two." The waitress pivoted and strode away.

Diana glared at Nick. "You'll have to eat one slice."

"Demanding, aren't you." But he was smiling. Not a crooked smile this time, but a warm, gentle smile that eased the harsh lines of his face and brightened his eyes.

Was that why she was here with him right now? Because she'd known that somewhere inside him, that smile was waiting for her to set it free?

She was engaged to be married. She was in the preliminary planning stages for her wedding. She shouldn't be thinking about Nick Fiore's smile and his soul-melting brown eyes.

But she couldn't very well get up and leave. The man had done nothing wrong. He'd been a complete gentleman, he'd invited her to have coffee with him, and she'd accepted. Perhaps he'd forced the toast on her, but she could forgive him for that.

It was herself she was having trouble forgiving—for having accepted his polite invitation and letting her mind stray in danger-ous directions. She thought about how inviting his smile was, how mesmerizing his gaze. How his rough-hewn features came together into the sort of face a woman could study for a long time without ever getting bored.

She thought about sweaty sex.

She needed to make things clear, for her own sake if not for his. "Nick, I'm really not sure why I'm here," she began—a statement as lame as the bagels in this café were alleged to be.

"You're here because of the song."

"The David Bowie song?"

He nodded.

Before she could question him further, the waitress returned, holding a tray laden with their order. The bread was sliced thick and toasted to a golden brown. It shared the plate with a huge slab of butter. The waitress distributed knives, teaspoons, and a lidded stainless-steel pitcher of milk. "You want any jam?" she asked.

"No, thank you." Diana glanced at Nick. He was going to have to eat one of the chunks of bread; he might want jam.

"We're good," he said to the waitress. She gave him a sweet smile. She had to be at least a dozen years older than him, but the soft shine of her eyes told Diana she appreciated Nick in a way that transcended their friendly banter. Diana couldn't blame her. He was definitely worthy of appreciation.

Feeling her cheeks grow warm, she lowered her gaze to his hands. Those hands had hoisted her off the beach as if she'd weighed less than air. He had long fingers, sharp, bony knuckles, and an unfashionable watch on a leather strap buckled around his left wrist. No rings. Specifically, no wedding band.

He nudged aside the travel mug he'd been carrying and wrapped his fingers around the bulky mug the waitress had brought him. Diana found herself wondering what those fingers would feel like brushing against her cheek or wandering through her hair.

She was *engaged*, damn it. She had to stop thinking about him that way. This whole situation was nuts.

But he'd ordered her toast, and she couldn't very well not eat it.

She dabbed the tip of her knife into the butter and spread a thin layer across the crisp surface of her bread. "That other slice is for you," she told him. "Call me demanding if you want, but it's too much for me to eat."

"You just ran a marathon. You need fuel."

"I ran from the Ocean Bluff Inn to the jetty. That is *not* a marathon."

"So, what do you think of the OB?"

It took her a minute to realize he was referring to the Ocean Bluff Inn. She wondered if revealing where she was staying had been a wise idea. Now that he knew where to find her, he could track her down there. He could insinuate himself into her room, into that vast king-size bed with its smooth sheets and its fluffy duvet.

Oh, for God's sake. No more thoughts about sex. She absolutely forbade her brain to go there. "It's lovely," she said, referring to the inn.

"And you're from Boston?"

He could have guessed that from her discussion of bagels with the waitress. Admitting it to Nick wasn't revealing any secrets. "Yes."

"Just passing through town? Or are you planning to stay for a while?"

"I'm planning—"*a wedding,* she ought to say, but didn't "—to stay for at least a few more days. There are so many little antique dealers in the area. I want to explore."

"You're into antiques?" His face was blank. She couldn't tell if he was impressed or put off.

His opinion shouldn't matter. "It's my job. I work for an antiques dealership in Boston. Shomback-Sawyer Antiques. While I was here, I figured I could check out some of the local dealers and see if I could find any treasures for our clients in town."

"While you were here," he echoed, his tone casual, his hand reaching across the table to snag the second slice of toast.

"Yes."

He was waiting for her to tell him why she was there. And she *should* tell him. He could probably figure it out, anyway. His gaze slanted toward her left hand, where her engagement ring glinted in the light from the fluorescent ceiling fixture.

Yet she couldn't bring herself to speak the words. He was still a stranger—maybe not a total stranger, since she knew his name, but a stranger nonetheless—and for some inexplicable reason, she couldn't bring herself to say she was in Brogan's Point because she thought the Ocean Bluff Inn would be a beautiful venue for her wedding. She couldn't even bring herself to think about a wedding, about her engagement, about Peter. Merely gazing across the table at Nick Fiore created sensations inside her that she never felt when she was with Peter.

It was a terribly disloyal thought. But her voice stuck in her throat, the words *I'm planning my wedding* refusing to emerge. She felt the way she had at the bar Saturday night—as if she were under a spell that robbed her of free will. Saturday night the spell had made her stare at Nick across a room of drinking, dancing, carousing bar patrons. Today it silenced her when she ought to tell him she was engaged to be married a year from June.

Then again, he probably couldn't care less that she was engaged. If she told him, he'd congratulate her, wish her well, maybe joke that he'd bill Peter for the cost of her coffee and toast. Surely he hadn't bought her breakfast because he was interested in her. Just because her hands still tingled when she recalled the strength of his fingers gripping her, pulling her up over the retaining wall at the beach, didn't mean that brief contact had affected him in any way.

Nothing was going on here. Nothing but two people sharing a cup of coffee and an order of toast. Nothing but two strangers who, last Saturday night, had glanced at each other when a silly old David Bowie song played in a beautiful antique jukebox.

"Do you work?" she asked, glad her voice finally seemed to be functional again.

Her voice, perhaps, but not her brain. Nick frowned as if she'd spoken in Swahili. She realized her question, emerging from a prolonged silence, was a complete non sequitur, lacking any sort of context.

"I mean," she explained, feeling her cheeks grow warm again, "do you have to be at work? Am I keeping you from your job?"

He smiled. "If I show up at my office at ten instead of nine, no big deal."

"Your office?" She did her best to filter any hint of judgment from her tone, but Nick certainly wasn't dressed like someone who worked in an office.

"That's a room where I sit at a desk and look important." He laughed. She loved when he joked. His laughter smoothed his edges just enough to make him irresistibly handsome. "I coordinate programs for at-risk kids," he continued. "I spend half my life raising money and the other half dealing with the police, the state's Department of Youth Services, the schools and the kids themselves. My office is in the community center. I think it used to be a utility closet before someone crammed a desk in there and told me to set up shop. But I don't spend much time at my desk, so…" He concluded with a shrug.

"Wow." His career sounded much more important than selling antiques to wealthy Bostonites. "You're—what? A social worker?"

"Something like that," he said vaguely.

"That's wonderful."

Another quick, self-deprecating laugh.

"No, really." She wanted to lean across the table, give his shoulders a shake, and tell him not to downplay the value of what he did. Actually, she just wanted to lean across the table and grab his shoulders. She deliberately leaned back, pressing into the banquette's stiff upholstery. "I trade in dusty old stuff rich people want to decorate their houses with. You save lives."

"I wouldn't go that far," he said, not quite convincingly. His modesty was sweet, but Diana would bet a whole lot of pricy antiques that he *did* save lives.

She munched on her toast, buying time as she sorted her thoughts. She hadn't been wholly honest with Nick Fiore, and she wasn't sure she could be. But she couldn't keep avoiding the truth that sat between them, invisible but as real as the mugs of coffee steaming on the table, the stainless-steel pitcher of milk, the glass cylinder of sugar. She dared to lift her gaze to him and found him watching her, his smile gone, his expression quizzical. Was he as bewildered as she felt? As churning with questions?

"Did…did something happen Saturday night when the jukebox played that song?" she asked.

That he didn't ask her what the hell she was talking about indicated that he also believed something had happened. "I don't know," he finally said.

"Something *did* happen."

He sighed and studied his coffee. The steam rose in a lazy curl of vapor. "Yeah," he said, then raised the mug and took a sip.

"What? What happened?"

"I don't know." He sighed again, his eyes not meeting hers. She followed their angle and realized he was staring at her diamond ring. "You're right. I really should get to my office. All those lives waiting to be saved," he added, his smile fleeting and sardonic. One final swig of coffee drained his mug, and he shifted in his seat to pull his wallet from his hip pocket.

Minutes later, after Nick had paid the bill and traded a bit more flirtatious banter with the waitress, Diana found herself outside Riley's, blinking in the glaring morning light. During their time indoors the sun had risen fully and the air, while still blustery, had warmed a few degrees. "Do you need a lift back to the inn?" he asked.

She would love a lift back to the inn. She would love a little more time in Nick Fiore's company, trying to fathom what the song they'd heard at the tavern Saturday night had done to them, what it meant, why she felt so disoriented, and why her raising the subject had caused him to stand abruptly and announce that he had to get to work. She would love to grab his shoulders—not to shake them but to pull him toward her, to feel the warmth of his body against hers. She would love to figure out why, after he'd clearly guessed that she was engaged—his obvious scrutiny of her ring implied as much—she couldn't speak the words, couldn't tell him the truth, couldn't admit that she wanted something she couldn't have, something she shouldn't want.

"I need to run," she said, meaning it literally. "Thanks for the coffee."

Before he could stop her—as if he'd even want to—she spun and jogged down the sidewalk, back toward Atlantic Avenue and the retaining wall and the beach. Back to the inn. Back to safety.

Three

Gus Naukonen wiped the bar down with a wet cloth. Once a week, she'd treat its glossy mahogany surface to a complete waxing and buffing, but most days a good scrub with water and cleanser was all it needed.

She loved this time at the bar. Mid-afternoon, open but quiet. A couple of older women sat at a booth, sipping chardonnay and catching up on gossip. Ronnie Marzetto, who'd retired and passed his lobster boat down to his son-in-law a year ago, worked his way through a beer, a bowl of peanuts and a crossword puzzle at another booth. Carl Stanton slouched on a stool at the far end of the bar, nursing a coffee.

Carl drank too much. Gus knew it. Carl knew it. She'd cut him off after his third whiskey and told him hiding in a bar and guzzling the hard stuff wasn't going to solve his multitude of problems. "On the house," she'd said, filling a mug with coffee for him. She'd brewed it hours ago, and now it was as dark as tar and smelled burned. But Carl wouldn't know the difference. He just needed to sober up before Gus called his long-suffering wife and asked her to come and pick him up. Gus had already made him hand over his keys.

At least he was a quiet, mellow drunk. Gus felt sorry for him. Out of work, and his wife was sleeping with Bruce Bauer, and everyone knew it. If Carl Stanton was Gus's husband, she'd probably be sleeping with someone else, too. Not that Bruce Bauer was anyone's idea of a heartthrob. It was one of those frying-pan-fire situations.

Gus didn't judge.

Beneath her feet, she felt subtle vibrations as Manny Lopez moved crates of liquor around in the basement. Manny was thick and sturdy, his torso as solid and round as a beer keg, his arms as solid as granite, his legs as thick as the trunks of the centuries-old pines lining Forest Road. Yet he was a teddy-bear, always smiling, light on his feet despite his massive build. When he wasn't literally doing the heavy lifting, maintaining her inventory, lugging boxes of bottles up the stairs and bins of glassware and plates to the industrial dishwasher in the kitchen, he was mopping the floor, backing up Gus and the other bartenders during surges in traffic, and breaking up the rare fight.

People didn't come to the Faulk Street Tavern to get into fights. It wasn't that kind of place.

It was Gus's kind of place. Tranquil. Homey. A bar where a person could relax and get a generous drink at a reasonable price. Not a bar where crap was tolerated.

The front door open with a familiar creak of its hinges. During peak hours, of course, no one would notice that creak, but in the mid-afternoon lull, Gus could hear every sound. The lullaby-soft murmur of the women's voices as they sipped their wine. An occasional sniffle from Carl—either he had post-nasal drip or he was crying; Gus did him the courtesy of not searching his face for tears. The slap of her rag as she gave the bar a final swipe. Another thud and gentle rattle of glass from below. And the front door's hinges.

She smiled, expecting to see Ed Nolan sweep through the door. He usually dropped by around this time. "Just checking to make sure everything's copacetic," he'd say. "Had a fender-bender up on Wayne Road, and I'm in no hurry to get back to the station house and do the paperwork." He always had an excuse for visiting the tavern during his shift, and Gus always pretended those excuses mattered to them both. Ed would never admit he'd stopped in because he wanted to see her.

However, when the door arced wider, the person who stepped into the nearly empty bar wasn't the tall, handsome cop who could make her body sing in the wee hours of the morning, after she'd shut the tavern for the night and crawled into bed with him. It was a young woman.

Gus knew who she was. She didn't recognize every person who entered her establishment, especially on a busy Saturday night, especially an out-of-towner. But she remembered this girl, with her softly waving honey-colored hair, her slim figure, her delicate features and big, goo-goo doll eyes. This was the girl the jukebox had bound to Nick Fiore.

She was dressed in a tweedy brown jacket, a white sweater, a colorful silk scarf coiled loosely around her throat and skinny jeans that showed off her slender legs. Gus was six feet tall and raw-boned, so any normal-size woman tended to look graceful to her. But this woman was particularly well put together. Petite and elegant, she carried herself like someone who had spent more than a few precious years of her childhood in ballet classes.

Gus recalled her own mother signing her up for ballet classes at the Brogan Point rec center, back when she'd been a kid and the lessons had been dirt cheap. After a few sessions, the teacher, a skinny woman with a beak nose, a Russian accent and a spine as straight as a flagpole, had urged Gus's mother to sign her up for basketball, instead.

Gus was still grinning at the memory when the young woman neared the bar. As she'd walked across the empty dance floor, she'd kept pausing and glancing over her shoulder at the jukebox, which sat idle at the far end of the room.

When the girl reached the bar, she turned back to Gus. Her cheeks and the tip of her nose were pink, probably from the brisk late-winter air outdoors. Her brows dipped in a slight frown. Silent, she stared at Gus as if not really seeing her. She might have been looking at the row of bottles standing along the shelf behind Gus, or at her reflection in the smoky mirror behind the bottles.

"Can I get you something?" Gus asked.

Her voice seemed to jolt the girl. "Oh." She blinked, then smiled shyly. "It's really too early for a drink."

The stale old joke about how it was five o'clock somewhere drifted through Gus's head. She let it pass. "I've got soft drinks.

Coffee, tea, soda, lemonade...." The woman still seemed to be in something of a stupor. "A glass of water?"

"That would be nice. I'll pay for it," the woman added.

Gus snorted and turned to fill a glass with ice and water from the tap. "On the house," she said, placing a square cocktail napkin beneath the glass as she set it down. No sense letting the glass sweat all over the bar just minutes after she'd wiped the surface clean.

"I feel bad, taking a stool and not ordering something."

"Especially when the place is so crowded," Gus said, waving her hand at the nearly empty room.

The young woman glanced behind her, laughed, and then stopped laughing as her gaze alighted on the jukebox. She turned back to Gus. "You're going to think I'm insane, but...can I buy that jukebox?"

Yeah, Gus thought she was insane. She hooted a laugh. "Buy it?"

The girl looked earnest. "I work for an antiques dealer in Boston," she said. "I'm sure that's an antique. I'd pay you a very generous price—"

"Sorry," Gus cut her off. "It's not for sale."

"It's an amazing piece."

No kidding, Gus thought.

"Can you tell me about it?" the young woman asked. "Do you know anything about its provenance?"

There was a fancy word. Fortunately, Gus's vocabulary was up to the challenge. "All I can tell you is, it was here when my husband and I bought the place."

"Really?"

"Standing right there. We never moved it. For all I know, it was standing there when this was just an empty lot, and they built the tavern around it."

The girl's frown intensified, and then she realized Gus was joking. She allowed herself a small laugh. "It's gorgeous."

Gus couldn't argue that. "Yeah."

"So beautiful. The woodwork, and those gorgeous peacocks... Just amazing." She smiled and gave Gus a direct stare. "Are you sure

I couldn't write you a check right now and take it off your hands? There would be a lot of zeroes on that check."

Gus liked checks with lots of zeroes on them as much as anyone else. But the jukebox? No way. She shook her head. "Sorry."

"You must have it serviced, right? What does the service guy tell you about it? Has he ever mentioned its age or vintage?"

"It hasn't been serviced since we bought the place. We had a guy come in then. He showed us how to open the money box and get the coins out. He said to contact him if we wanted to change the records inside. It was all records, vinyl. Back when we took over this place, CD's didn't exist, let alone MP3's."

"So what do you do when you want to change the records? Does someone from Wurlitzer take care of that?"

Gus tossed the cleaning rag she'd been using into a hamper at the far end of the bar. Swish—three points. She'd definitely been better suited to basketball than ballet. "I've never changed the records. The songs keep changing on their own. At least that's what it seems like. Who knows? Maybe there are a few hundred records inside there. Only vinyl records. The jukebox never plays any songs more recent than around the mid-80's."

"It changes the records on its own?" The girl's frown returned, even more intense.

Gus shrugged. "It plays what it wants. People slide in a dime or a quarter, punch some buttons, and then whatever comes out comes out. Folks around here think it plays whatever song someone needs to hear."

"Someone *needs* to hear?" At Gus's nod of confirmation, the girl shook her head. "That doesn't make any sense."

"Lots of things in life don't make sense." Gus busied herself emptying trays of clean glasses from the dishwasher rack onto the shelves beneath the bar.

"But you empty the coins?"

"Donate them all to charity. The local food bank, a battered women's shelter, the American Cancer Society."

"That's very generous." The girl traced her finger around the rim of her glass. Her nails were manicured, the polish reminding Gus of pearls. "What do you mean, it plays whatever song someone needs to hear?"

Gus stopped fussing with the glasses and leaned on the bar. Compared to the girl's hands, her own were large and blunt, the nails cut short and unpolished. The last time she'd had a manicure was the day before her wedding, thirty some-odd years ago. After that, she'd worked alongside Joe running the tavern until she'd had the boys, and then she'd been a barkeep and a mother, and then a barkeep and a widow. Who had time for manicures?

Fortunately, Ed Nolan wasn't a fussy kind of guy. He seemed to like her hands just fine.

"You were in here Saturday night," she said, deciding that the poor girl needed a bit of direction. She might be an antiques expert, she might have gorgeous hands—and that diamond ring adorning her left ring finger was probably worth as much as the jukebox's charity earnings over the past ten years. But she seemed bewildered. Gus decided to enlighten her. "You were sitting over there—" she gestured toward the table where she'd seen the girl"—and the jukebox played 'Changes.'"

"Yes. The David Bowie song." The girl laughed sheepishly. "My parents and my uncle listen to a lot of classic rock."

"That song was talking to you," Gus explained.

"It certainly felt that way." The girl still looked sheepish, perplexed but fascinated. "So it was telling me to make changes?"

"What do you think?"

"I think the whole thing is bizarre."

Gus lined up her shakers and strainers. "The song says, 'Turn and face the strange.'"

"It does? I never really listened to the lyrics. Just that stuttering thing he does. Ch-ch-ch-ch-changes." She rested her arms against the bar, apparently growing more relaxed in Gus's company. "Do you know all the lyrics to all the songs?"

"Just the ones that leap out at me. That one did. Probably because it hit Nick the same moment it hit you."

"You know Nick?" Her cheeks grew redder—and the color couldn't be blamed on the chilly March air. They were indoors, and the radiators were working.

"He's a local. I'm a local." Gus let the woman finish the thought for herself: *you're not a local.*

"Does he need to make changes, too?" the woman asked.

"I guess you'd have to discuss that with him." Gus noticed movement at the door and heard the familiar whine of the hinges as it swung open. There he was—Ed in his uniform. He'd made detective nearly a dozen years ago, but he still worked as a patrolman a lot of the time because Brogan's Point just didn't have much call for police detectives. That was fine with Gus. She liked the way he looked in in navy blue, with his thick leather holster and his shiny badge.

"Hey," he called out, striding into the tavern. "I was in the area and thought I'd see how things are going."

"They're going fine," Gus said as he approached.

"Not so fine for Carl." Ed angled his head toward the moping guy at the end of the bar.

"He's drying out."

"Have you got his keys?"

She dug into her apron pocket and produced the jangling key ring. Carl peered up from his coffee and scowled. "Those are mine," he said, his voice slurring.

"Don't worry," Gus called down the bar to him. "I'm taking good care of them."

"I should probably let you get back to work," the girl said, inching away from the bar.

"This *is* my work," Gus assured her. "Giving people who come in here drinks. Even if it's only water."

The girl reached into the leather purse dangling from a strap on her shoulder. "I must owe you something."

"Not for water. Come back later and buy a drink."

"I would," the girl said dubiously, "but I'm afraid the jukebox will play some other song and send me another message I don't understand."

"You've already heard your message," Gus said. "Let it sink in. Maybe you'll understand it in time."

The woman nodded, although she didn't look entirely convinced. She took a few steps toward the door, then turned back and extended her right hand. "I'm Diana Simms."

Most customers didn't introduce themselves. Either Gus knew them or she didn't. This gesture was a surprise—a pleasant one. "Augusta Naukonen," she said, shaking the woman's hand. It was so small and fine-boned, Gus had to take care not to bruise it.

"Everyone around here calls her Gus," Ed piped up.

Gus released Diana Simms's hand and the girl took another step toward the door, then hesitated and asked, "So you think the song was sending a message to Nick, too? Is he supposed to change?"

"Like I said, you'll have to discuss that with him," Gus told her.

Diana had the prettiest frown Gus had ever seen—and she'd seen it several times now, so she felt qualified to judge it. "I guess I will," she said on a sigh, then turned and walked to the door.

Gus watched her leave, then turned to Ed. "Do I need to keep an eye on her?" he asked.

Gus shook her head. "No. She's just trying to puzzle out the jukebox."

Ed snorted. "That jukebox. It makes people crazy."

"Either that, or it makes them sane," Gus said.

He smiled. "You make me crazy," he murmured before leaning over the bar and planting a kiss on her lips.

Four

A s days went, this was not Nick's worst. He'd met with the town
manager at ten-thirty to discuss next year's budget, enjoyed a
fruitful phone conversation with the high school principal about
the after-school tutoring program he'd established there, reviewed
the schedule at the community center gym, met with two drop-outs
he'd been counseling and got them signed up for GED classes, and
talked to someone in the state's Department of Youth Services about
a local girl with substance abuse issues who belonged in therapy and
not the juvenile justice system. "Find me a good rehab program
her family can afford," he'd argued. "You can litigate her DUI later.
First, let's get her detoxed."

All in a day's work.

He tried not to think about the atypical way his day had begun.
He tried not to think about Diana Simms, with her eyes the color of
the ocean. He tried not to think about the damned song playing in
a never-ending loop inside his skull.

Changes? Sure, he could use some changes in his life. A higher
salary would be a nice change. A little less caffeine, a little more
exercise. A new shower curtain for the bathroom in his house. What
he'd really like would be to install glass sliders above the tub, but
he'd need an upward change in his salary to afford a glass-sliders
change in his bathroom.

None of the changes he'd welcome had anything to do with
Diana, though—not given that her life was in Boston and her finger
was adorned by that blinding diamond engagement ring.

At around six o'clock, he left his cramped, windowless office at the community center, locked up and headed for his car, calculating how bad the traffic would be if he detoured to the big-box home repair store down on Rte. 1 to look at shower curtains before driving home. Not that the shower curtain was a major change, but maybe if he bought a new one, he could silence the song he'd heard playing on the jukebox at the Faulk Street Tavern Saturday night—and continued to hear playing in his mind ever since.

He climbed into his car, started the engine and turned on the radio. Bass-heavy Metallica blasted through the speakers, and he let it surge over him, praying that it, too, might drown out the David Bowie song. He turned the radio's volume up so high, he didn't hear his cell phone ringing.

He felt it vibrating against his thigh, however. Pulling it from his pocket, he peered at the screen, turned off the radio and cursed.

He should just ignore the call. But it was hard to ignore your mother—even when she had left scars across your psyche that would never fade. Sighing, he thumbed the connect icon and lifted the phone to his ear. "Yeah?" His voice emerged as a growl.

"Don't be like that," his mother said. "It's been ages since we talked."

He took a minute to subdue his reflexive anger at the sound of her voice. "I've been busy," he said.

"One of the shutters fell off in front of the house. A living room window. I thought maybe you could stop by and rehang it."

Sure. There was nothing Nick wanted more than to do freaking repairs for his mother. "Like I said, I'm really busy."

"Nick." Her voice took on a familiar wheedling tone. When he was a kid, the syrupy sweetness of her voice had made him feel loved, made him feel as if she would keep him safe and protect him from his father's wild temper. Not anymore. Now, when she said, "I'll make you dinner. You can come, hang the shutter, and I'll make manicotti. You love my manicotti," all he could think of was that he loved her manicotti a hell of a lot more than he loved her.

Still, she was an older woman, living alone. Her body was worn down by time, loneliness and the abuse his father had inflicted on her. The old man had specialized in discreet punches and slaps, leaving bruises no one could see, and emotional abuse that left bruises no less real, even if they were also invisible—the fear, the caution, the constant anxiety that one wrong word or gesture might change the abuse from emotional back to physical.

Nick had a master's degree in social work. He knew about domestic violence. Growing up, he'd had a front-row seat in the boxing ring of his home. So from a clinical standpoint, he could sympathize with his mother.

But he'd fought in that arena, too. He'd fought harder than his mother ever had. His sympathy had limits.

"Hire a handyman," he spoke into the phone. "Someone who knows how to hang shutters."

"I can't afford—"

"I'll pay for it," he said, thinking again about how much he'd like his salary to ch-ch-change. "Look, Mom, I have to see someone right now. I've got to go."

"Call me," his mother whined. "Come visit. I'll cook something nice."

He rolled his eyes, muttered good-bye and tapped the disconnect icon. And cursed again.

He was in no longer in the mood to shop for a shower curtain. Nor was he in the mood to drive home and listen his mother's plaintive voice alternating with the Bowie song on that audio loop in his mind. He wasn't even in the mood for a blast of Metallica.

He tore out of the community center parking lot, his tires spitting loose pebbles behind him. Instead of heading west toward his house or south to the shopping district on Rte.1, he steered to Atlantic Avenue, the road paralleling the retaining wall, the beach, and the ocean beyond. The sky to his right was fading to dark as he cruised north, the last light of dusk bleeding out of the day. Although the evening air was cold, he rolled down his windows and let the sea breezes whip through his car.

A cigarette would have helped—if he still smoked. A glass of something strong—if he wasn't driving. A mother he could trust—if he could swap his own mother for a better one.

The houses along Atlantic Avenue were tightly packed, barely a sliver of space between one and the next. Land was precious this close to the shore; a large yard would spike the already prohibitive costs of ocean-view properties even higher. Further north, Brogan's Point featured plenty of mansions owned by gazillionaires. Along the stretch of the Atlantic Avenue closer in to town, though, single-family homes nestled shoulder to shoulder with triple-deckers, summer rentals, and rambling old houses transformed into quaint bed-and-breakfasts that catered to New Yorkers and folks from Western Massachusetts who came to enjoy a long seaside weekend in a town they could reach in just a few hours.

He kept heading north until he reached the driveway to the Ocean Bluff Inn. The entry was flanked by short stone pillars topped with lantern-shaped lights. As he steered up the winding drive to the imposing white clapboard structure spread across the grassy ocean-view bluff for which it was named, he slowed the car, took a few deep breaths and shook his head, hoping to clear it.

He cleared some of the anger, some of the static. But the damned David Bowie song remained.

Why had he driven to the inn? Diana probably wasn't here. Or if she was, she might be with her fiancé, that clean-cut dude who'd been with her at the Faulk Street Tavern on Saturday night. That proper gentleman who'd planted a massive chunk of crystalized carbon on her ring finger.

Nick was an idiot to have driven to the OB. Seeing Diana made no sense.

Except that not seeing her made even less sense.

He shut and locked his car—the oldest, shabbiest vehicle in the guest lot—and walked to the front steps, his footsteps crunching on the crushed shells and sea-smooth pebbles that paved the path leading to the building. He climbed three shallow steps to a broad veranda furnished with a few heavy wooden Adirondack chairs and rockers. It was still too early for the inn to put lightweight wicker furniture on its front porch; winter hadn't released New England from its grip yet. The green tips of daffodils and crocuses were beginning poke through the soil and a few trees were dotted with leaf buds, but no one would be shocked if the region saw a few more inches of snow before spring officially arrived. Winter usually took its time departing from Massachusetts.

Nick crossed the porch to the heavy oak door, swung it open and stepped inside. He was immediately embraced by the heated indoor air. The inn's lobby was small and welcoming, the walls painted a soft white and adorned with framed seascape paintings and photos of old sailing ships, the hardwood floor covered with thick patterned area rugs. Along one wall ran a counter of polished oak—the hotel equivalent of Gus's bar, he thought with a wry smile. A bowl of apples stood at one end of the counter, an urn holding brightly colored flowers at the other. Halfway between them, a clerk in a dark blue blazer and khaki trousers was stationed. The clerk eyed Nick curiously, then asked, "Can I help you?"

"I'm looking for..." Nick paused, hearing a woman's voice emerging through the arched doorway leading to a parlor off the lobby. Diana's voice. "I think I found her," he said, moving toward the doorway.

Diana stood in front of a window in the parlor, her back to Nick, a cell phone pressed to her ear. "No," she said, her voice tight with tension. "I'm sorry you feel that way, but—" She listened for a moment. "I will when I'm ready," she said. Another pause. "Peter. Don't be this way. It's not—I'm fine. Really. Right. Okay. I'll call you tomorrow." She lowered the phone, jabbed her finger against the screen and muttered, "Screw you."

This must be the evening for unpleasant phone calls—and Nick shouldn't have eavesdropped on Diana's. She'd hidden herself inside this small parlor, which was furnished with overstuffed chairs and a sofa, a floor-to-ceiling bookshelf stacked with weathered hard-covers, and a fireplace with an ornately carved mantel. Maybe she'd hoped for privacy. But if she'd truly wanted privacy for her phone call, she should have gone to her room. The parlor was a public space, sort of.

Nick gave her a moment to simmer down, then cleared his throat. She spun around and gasped. "Oh!"

"Sorry—did I scare you?"

"No." Even from across the room, he could see the tension seeping out of her spine, her shoulders relaxing as she let out a long breath. "You just startled me a little. What are you doing here?"

Good question. "I…was pissed off," he said.

Her huge eyes clouded with concern. "At me?"

He gave her what he hoped was a reassuring smile. "No, of course not. But I thought…" God, this was going to sound odd, no matter how he expressed it. "I thought seeing you would cheer me up."

"And instead, you found out that I was pissed off, too." She slid her phone into her purse. "I guess you overheard that argument."

"Just the tail end." He smiled again. "Maybe you're pissed off, but you're cheering me up." It was true. Simply standing in the same room with her eased his tension, deleted his mother's phone call from his memory, and muted the Bowie tune.

Diana took a step toward him, then halted. The room wasn't large. One more step and she'd be close enough for him to touch her.

"You want to grab some dinner?" he asked.

It didn't seem like that complicated a question, but she took a full minute to mull over her reply. "I was going to eat here at the inn," she said. "I've been doing these tasting menus.…" She bit her lip, then shrugged and smiled. "The hell with that. Let's go somewhere else. You must know some good local restaurants. That place where we had coffee this morning—"

"Riley's. Great for breakfast, not so great for dinner. You like seafood?"

"I'd better, if I'm spending time in Brogan's Point."

"I'll take you to a good local place. No atmosphere. Lobster right off the boat."

"It sounds perfect. Let me run up to my room and grab my coat." She neared him, then moved right past him, denying him the chance to take her hand or brush a stray lock of hair back from her cheek. Just as well. He had no business wanting that kind of contact, that connection. She was a visitor, a Boston woman. Already taken.

"Go ahead," he said. "I'll wait down here."

He followed her into the lobby and watched her walk up the grand stairway to the second floor. The main building had four floors, so he assumed there must be an elevator somewhere. But Diana was a jogger. It figured she would take the stairs.

Five minutes later, he watched her descend that double-width stairway like a debutante—one wearing tailored slacks, a wool coat and a colorful silk scarf rather than a gown, but just as regal, just as elegant. Just as beautiful.

She was smiling.

And she wasn't wearing her diamond ring.

Five

"I love this place," Diana said.

The Lobster Shack was the antithesis of the Ocean Bluff Inn's fancy dining rooms, and of any Boston restaurant she'd ever dined at with Peter. It was located in a small converted warehouse across Atlantic Avenue from a wharf lined with commercial fishing boats, back in port after a day's harvest. The restaurant's walls were paneled in splintery shingles draped haphazardly with woven ropes and trawling nets. Its tabletops were unvarnished planks topped with butcher paper. Its lighting was uneven, some bulbs in the ceiling fixtures emitting a glaring silver light and others a softer amber glow. The lobsters were served boiled to a bright red, accompanied by a cup of drawn butter, a saucer of coleslaw and a basket of greasy French Fries. The waitress had brought glasses along with their bottles of beer, but she hadn't bothered to pour the beer, and when Nick took a slug straight from the bottle, Diana decided not to bother with her glass, either.

He looked ridiculous wearing a plastic bib with a cartoon drawing of a smiling lobster on it—ridiculous but adorable. She'd donned a bib, too. He was a lot more adept than she was at cracking lobster shells with the hinged metal nutcrackers the waitress had provided for them, but then, Diana wasn't used to eating lobster this way. Peter always argued that eating boiled lobster straight out of the shell was too sloppy and uncivilized. To make him happy if they were dining out together, she would order a "lazy man's" lobster, the meat already removed from the shell.

Breaking the shell and wrestling the steaming pink and white flesh out with a tiny fork was challenging and messy, but it was fun. It also kept Diana and Nick too busy to talk about anything other than how delicious the lobster tasted. Prying chunks of succulent meat from the claws required her full attention. It distracted her from thinking about her argument with Peter an hour ago.

He'd phoned her while she'd been staring blankly at some of the inn's catering menus and wondering why none of the elaborate descriptions of the food tweaked her appetite. She ought to have been starving, since she hadn't eaten lunch. The thick slice of toast she'd consumed with Nick that morning had filled her up, and once she'd hit the road, she hadn't wanted to stop for food.

She'd gone to three antiques dealers Claudia had suggested to her, all of them located on a winding country road leading northwest out of town. The first two had been stocked with glorified trash—as she and her colleagues at Shomback-Sawyer always joked, these were the sorts of shops that ought to have signs reading, "We Buy Junk—We Sell Antiques" hanging above their doors. The third dealer had operated out of a barn not far from the New Hampshire state line, and it was there that Diana had scored a major coup, purchasing a pair of authentic Tiffany lamps for eighty dollars apiece. They were dusty and their bronze bases were crusted with dirt, but they were genuine. Given the price the dealer had charged her, he apparently hadn't known how to tell a real Tiffany lamp from a reproduction. But Diana had rubbed enough crud from them to spot their Tiffany Studios stamps and numbers. The dealer had rolled his eyes when she'd asked him to pad them with yards of bubble-wrap. She'd offered to pay extra for the wrapping, and he'd pretended he was doing her a big favor by charging only twenty bucks to wrap the lamps and nestle them into a sturdy box.

She'd driven about a mile back toward Brogan's Point before pulling off the road and phoning her boss. "Really? The lamps had Tiffany stamps?" James Sawyer had said.

"Stamps and numbers. They aren't the most magnificent specimens I've ever seen, but they're the real thing."

47

"In that case, stay up on the North Shore as long as you want. Maybe you'll find some more treasures for us. Use the company card. Good job, Diana."

After stashing the lamps carefully in her room at the inn, she'd strolled down the hill toward town until she'd found herself at the entry to the Faulk Street Tavern. She'd gotten lucky with the lamps; maybe she'd get lucky with the jukebox, too.

She hadn't, and she'd left the bar bewildered and strangely edgy after her conversation with Augusta, the tall, lanky bartender who had implied that the jukebox was somehow magical. *Turn to face the strange,* she'd recited, song lyrics that must have lodged themselves in Diana's soul on Saturday night. Her day had certainly turned strange.

And then Peter had called and turned her day from strange to infuriating. He wanted her to come back to Boston. He didn't like her "wasting time"—his words, not hers—in Brogan's Point. He'd decided he didn't like the inn at all. He wanted to have the wedding at that ostentatious mansion in Newport. He thought Diana was too stubborn. Her parents were worried that she hadn't come home with him. He didn't care that James Sawyer had urged her to stay on at Brogan's Point and check out some more antique dealers in the area. She needed to come home. *Now.*

She'd ridden an emotional rollercoaster all day. From the high of discovering the Tiffany lamps hidden in that gloomy barn full of mediocre Depression glass and not-quite mint-comic books to her bewildering conversation with Augusta at the bar, to her phone conversation with Peter…to this moment, eating the simplest, freshest, most delicious lobster she'd ever tasted and wearing a plastic bib. If Peter saw her in this bib, in this eatery, he'd probably break off the engagement on principle. No future wife of his ought to be seen in public wearing a plastic lobster bib.

"So," Nick said, leaning back in his chair. His hair was tousled, his cheeks and chin wearing a day's growth of stubble. His eyes were unfathomable, so dark. She had to avert her gaze so as not to be drawn in by their beauty. "You took off your ring."

Right. She was wearing the bib, and she *wasn't* wearing her engagement ring. She'd been so angry with Peter after his phone call, she'd taken it off and hidden it inside a pair of rolled socks in a drawer when she'd gone to her room to fetch her coat. She hadn't considered whether Nick would notice.

How could he not notice? The stone was three carats, as ostentatious as the Newport venue where Peter wanted their wedding to take place.

"I was annoyed," she said, hoping that was enough of an answer to satisfy Nick. She didn't want to think too much about the implications of her not wearing her ring while she ate dinner with an irresistibly attractive man who wasn't her fiancé.

He remained silent, gazing at her.

His silence forced her to acknowledge that, in fact, she did want to answer the questions he was too polite to ask. Something in his piercing gaze, something in the angle of his head and the set of his jaw and those strong, rugged hands of his, hands that just that morning had lifted her off the beach and into his world, compelled her to open up to him. "My fiancé can be kind of...domineering. That was who I was talking to when you showed up at the Ocean Bluff Inn. And he was...well, being domineering. It ticked me off. So I removed my ring." *It doesn't mean I broke off the engagement,* she wanted to say. But the words wouldn't come.

"You must feel ten pounds lighter," Nick joked.

Despite the fury inside her when she thought about Peter's imperious attitude, his judgmentalism and his downright bossiness, she laughed. "It's a silly ring, isn't it."

"Silly isn't the word I'd use for it. That ring could pay for my after-school tutoring and rec programs for a year."

"Well, it's much bigger than anything I would have picked out. But Peter didn't want me to pick it out. He likes to make the big decisions." And even the smaller decisions, she thought indignantly. Like when she should go back to Boston. And how she should eat lobster.

Nick tilted his head slightly, as if viewing her at a different angle might clarify things for him. "You don't strike me as the sort of person who wants other people making big decisions for you."

"I make my own decisions," she said. "It's just..." She sighed, nudged back her plate, and took a sip of beer. "Peter and I have been together forever. We grew up together. Our parents are close friends. I know the way he can be."

"Generous to a fault," Nick joked, flicking his fingers at her naked left hand, where her too-generous ring should have been.

She laughed, then faltered. Peter could be generous, and he could also be mean, especially when he didn't get his way. She had learned, after the many years they'd known each other, that life was a lot easier if she simply let him get his way—or at least *believe* he was getting his way—most of the time.

That understanding stirred a mix of emotions inside her, worry and anger and guilt. "I shouldn't talk about him behind his back," she said. "It seems disloyal."

"When is the wedding going to happen?"

Never. The word rose up into her mouth like a neat, round bubble, just waiting to pop. Startled, she swallowed, forcing the bubble back down. Of course she was going to marry Peter. They were planning on their wedding a year from June. The families had discussed it. Everyone had cleared their calendars and worked out their schedules. An engagement announcement had run in the *Boston Globe*. All she and Peter had to do was reserve a venue—if they could agree on one.

She realized Nick was waiting for a response. He appeared curious and probing, as if he could see more than she wished to reveal. "I don't know," she admitted. "We haven't set a date yet." Feeling even more uneasy, she plunged her hands into her lap, as if that would make her less keenly aware of her ringless finger. "What can you tell me about the jukebox?"

He gazed at her for a moment longer, then accepted her change of subject with a crooked smile. "At the Faulk Street Tavern?"

She nodded.

"It's been there forever. Some people think it's magic."

"I don't believe in magic," she said, wishing she sounded more certain.

"I don't either." He shrugged. "They say it tells people what they need to hear."

Apparently Augusta had told him the same thing she'd told Diana. Or else the legend of the jukebox was beyond Augusta's control, and everyone in Brogan's Point knew about it. "Did any of the other people in the bar need to hear David Bowie on Saturday night?" she wondered aloud. Perhaps Peter should have listened more closely to the song. It wouldn't hurt him to change his overweening attitude and become more open-minded. But he hadn't seemed to be paying attention to the music that night, any more than Diana had paid attention to the other songs the jukebox had played. She couldn't even remember what they were. She just remembered people singing along, and then filling the dance floor at the center of the room, and then... *Changes*.

Nick drank some beer, his eyes never leaving her. "Here's the way I understand it—and again, this assumes you believe in magic and all that. The jukebox plays a song that someone in the bar needs to hear, and that person hears it in some special way. They know the song is sending a message to them. That's what I've been told, anyway."

"And you *don't* believe that?"

He shrugged again. "Magic? I don't think so."

"But that song, 'Changes'—it was talking to us, wasn't it? You sang it to me this morning at the beach."

He opened his mouth and then shut it. Magic or not, he seemed to acknowledge that the song had connected them somehow. "Maybe it just happened to play when I was in a reflective mood on Saturday night. I can't really think of much in my life that needs changing. Nothing important, anyway. I'm happy. Life is good."

"You told me you were pissed off, and you thought seeing me would cheer you up."

"It did. It does."

"But you were pissed off."

"That was about…someone else. Someone I can't change. I can only change myself—if I need to change. Which I don't."

She was tempted to quote the Shakespeare line about protesting too much. "Who's the someone else?" she asked, figuring she deserved to know as much about him as he knew about her. "Have you got a fiancée, too?"

He snorted, then shook his head. "No fiancée. I was pissed off at my mother."

She smiled. "Forgive her. Mothers can't help but piss us off sometimes. I'm sure your mother loves you."

"I'm not," he retorted, then shook his head. His voice was gentle even though his eyes were hard and cold when he added, "Forget it. It's not worth talking about."

That alone convinced her his problem with his mother *was* worth talking about. But she wouldn't pry. It wasn't her business.

The waitress appeared at their table. She handed them foil-wrapped wet-wipes and stacked their dishes, somehow managing not to spill the precariously balanced pieces of empty lobster shell piled on their plates. "You folks want any dessert?" she asked.

Diana had devoured an entire lobster and more French fries than she should have. "I'm full," she said.

"Just the check," Nick said.

"My treat?" she asked. She earned a good living, and she believed in equality. It irritated her that Peter would never let her pay for their dates, even though once they got married his money would be hers and her money his. "The man pays," he would declare, as if it were one of the Ten Commandments, whenever she pulled out her wallet at a restaurant.

She hoped Nick wasn't that rigid. More important, she hoped he understood that this wasn't a date.

"Next time," he said, implying that he was indeed more open-minded than Peter—and also implying that there would be a next time.

She should have been concerned. Maybe she should have spelled out that, the absence of her ring notwithstanding, she was engaged to Peter, and any encounters she had with Nick had to take that fact into account. But she was too pleased, too wickedly, inappropriately thrilled by the thought of a next time with him, to say anything.

Once the bill was settled, they left the restaurant. Night surrounded them, cool and dark. Lights along the wharf etched the sailing boats in silhouette. The clang of chains and metal hooks against masts sounded like bells as the boats bobbed in the water. The sea air had a briny scent, salty and lush. "Boston Harbor doesn't smell like this," she pointed out.

"That's a harbor. This is the ocean." He folded his hand around hers and headed toward the wharf. Once again, she thought about saying something, reminding them both that his holding her hand implied nothing, that they were only friends, could never be more than friends...

Except that deep inside her, she didn't believe that. She didn't believe his holding her hand implied nothing. She didn't believe they were only friends.

Did this mean she was turning to face the strange? Did it mean *she* was changing?

They strolled in silence to the end of the wharf, where the breeze was stronger, the ocean's fragrance thicker. Her hair tangled in the gusts and he shifted slightly, angling her so the wind would blow her hair away from her face. When one thick lock snagged on her nose, he caught it and brushed it back, tucking it behind her ear.

Her ear tingled. Her scalp. Her hand, enveloped in his. Her entire body. The wind was chilly but she was warm. Too warm. She shouldn't be feeling this way, not about Nick Fiore. She should say something, tell him not to pivot to face her, tell him not to give her hand a quiet tug, pulling her closer to him. Tell him not to lean in, not to lower his head until his lips were a breath away from hers, then less than a breath away. Then touching hers.

She should say no. But her mind scrambled. Her heart pounded. Her soul said *yes.*

She reached up with her free hand, steadying herself as the heat of his mouth on hers caused her legs to weaken and sway. She might have been standing on one of the boats rather than the dock; the earth seemed to rock beneath her feet. But Nick was solid and secure. The world could be churning with wild waves, hurricane tides, whitecaps and undertows, but as long as she clung to him, she would be safe.

Through the worn leather of his jacket she could feel the firm bone and muscle of his shoulder. The tips of his hair grazed her knuckles, cool and silky. He slid his arm around her waist, embracing her as if he knew she needed protection from the storm, as if he feared that one powerful wave might sweep over them and carry her off.

It occurred to her that he wasn't the solid ground she was counting on. He was the powerful wave, carrying her off. He was the storm, surging around her, inside her.

His mouth clung, coaxed and conquered. When her lips parted in a faint moan, his tongue stole inside, claiming her. She'd never experienced anything like this before. She'd kissed, of course, and been kissed, but she'd never been so totally, utterly turned on by a single kiss.

Her brain tried to inject some rationality into the moment. *You hardly know him. He's a stranger. This is wrong. You're engaged.*

No. It was right. Maybe later, when she thought about it, she'd decide it was wrong. But at that instant, standing on the wharf with Nick, his arms holding her, drawing her against him, the warmth of him enveloping her as the heat of his kiss burned through her body and deep into her soul…

Nothing in her life had ever felt more right.

Six

H oly shit.

He shouldn't have started this kiss—but now that he had, he couldn't stop it. She tasted so good, so sweet, better than any dessert they might have ordered at the Lobster Shack. Better than any woman he'd ever kissed before.

One kiss, and he was rock-hard. It took all his willpower to keep from arching his hips into her, letting his body find the heat of hers. He didn't have any willpower left to stop kissing her.

So he didn't stop. He tasted, sipped, nibbled, nipped. He ran his hand up her spine to the nape of her neck and dug his fingers deep into her hair. He'd wanted to touch her hair the moment he'd seen her at the Faulk Street Tavern Saturday night, the moment the song had started to play and his gaze had met hers. He'd imagined her hair feeling like honey, because it was the color of honey. But of course it didn't. It felt like strands of satin.

Her hair was amazing, but so was the rest of her. He knew she was slim—he'd easily lifted her over the retaining wall that morning—but wrapping his arms around her informed him of how slender her waist was. He remembered how tempting her ass had looked in her stretch-fabric running pants, and he decided that, as soft and seductive as her hair was, he needed to explore more of her.

He ran one hand down her spine to the small of her back, then lower, cupping one tight, round cheek.

Mistake. He'd thought he couldn't get any harder. That one touch proved that he could.

She made a tiny sound—a sigh, a groan, a feline purr. God, he wanted her. All of her. All night long. "Come home with me," he whispered against her mouth, trying to remember when he'd last laundered his sheets. If she was half as crazed with lust as he was, she wouldn't notice the sheets. She definitely wouldn't notice the dingy shower curtain.

"I can't," she murmured.

He could practically hear tears in her voice. He could practically feel them in his eyes. Not because she was denying him what he craved, but because she was reminding him of everything that was impossible about this, about them, about letting one blazing kiss lead them where they both wanted to go.

Maybe she didn't want to go there as desperately as he did.

Christ, maybe she was kissing him only to get back at her domineering fiancé. The guy had pissed her off, so now she was extracting her revenge by tangling tongues with Nick. It was possible.

Slowly, reluctantly, he loosened his hold on her. The fingers that had arched so naturally around her butt now curled into a fist as he let his hand drop to his side.

She lowered her eyes. Her lips were swollen, glistening with moisture. *I did that*, he thought with a combination of satisfaction and irritation. He'd kissed her—and himself—senseless, and now she was saying no, and he was…*Pissed off* didn't come close to what he was feeling.

"I'm sorry," she mumbled.

"Yeah."

Her gaze shot up to his face. She appeared startled by his anger. Wasn't she as frustrated as he was? Wasn't she as exasperated that the domineering fiancé, the asshole whose ring she'd deliberately removed, was preventing them from going the distance? Or was she just playing Nick, fooling around a little before she put her ring back on and became the dutiful bride-to-be?

Instead of firing back at him, she brought her hand to his face and caressed his cheek. Her fingers felt cool against his skin, which was practically steaming from the lust burning inside him—and her touch was so gentle, her expression softening from surprise to wistfulness, that he felt his fury drain away. "Nick," she said.

He waited, watching her, wishing she would keep her hand pressed to his face forever. Or else press it to his throat, his chest, his dick.

"I can't start something with you when I'm engaged to someone else."

Something? Were they pursuing *something?* He'd thought they were just going for a hook-up. No complications. No meaning attached to it. No thinking allowed.

Which was ridiculous, and wrong. Casual hook-ups had been fine when he'd been younger, but he was thirty now. He liked to know the woman he was making love to. He liked waking up with a woman as much as he liked sleeping with her.

Diana was right. This was *something.* Damned if he knew what. But whatever it was, he couldn't just blow through it, have some fun and move on.

And if it wasn't a casual hook-up, if it was *something…*Well, there was a fiancé in the picture. Nick might not be the noblest guy in the world, but he didn't make a habit of fooling around with women who were publicly attached to other guys. He had at least that much integrity.

"Sorry," he said, apologizing for having forgotten the existence of her fiancé when he'd kissed her, and ruing the fact itself. Yes, he was sorry she was engaged. If she weren't, they might be in his car right now, speeding back to his house, him flooring the gas pedal and her running her hand up and down his inner thigh.

"I have to work this out," she said. "I have to…I don't know, try to make some sense of everything."

By the time she made sense of everything, she'd probably be back in Boston, with her antiques and her family and her fiancé's family. And her fiancé.

It would probably be for the best, too, Nick thought, although his body wasn't convinced. Just looking at her gave him a hard-on. Remembering how she'd felt in his arms, her hair spilling through his fingers, her lithe body pressed to his, made him think that her refusal to go home with him was not even remotely for the best.

They walked side by side up the wharf to the parking lot by the Lobster Shack, no longer holding hands. Neither spoke. Diana seemed lost in thought, and Nick wouldn't have been able to string three words together if he'd tried. His mind was as dense as shoreline fog. Only one word managed to break through the thick, gray mist: *Sorry. Sorry, sorry, sorry.*

The drive back to the inn passed without conversation. She sat next to him, her face pinched, her arms wrapped around her middle in a self-protective hug. He thought about turning on the radio, but while a dose of loud, clashing rock would give his brain a needed jolt, it would probably scare her. Even worse, he might turn on the radio and hear David Bowie singing that freaking song.

There was nothing wrong with the song. He couldn't blame it for what had happened between him and Diana. What should have happened. What wasn't happening.

Not a word shattered the silence until he eased the car to a halt in front of the inn's broad porch. Only then did she speak: "I'll see myself in, thanks."

Apparently she took him for a gentleman, assuming he would have gotten out of the car, opened her door for her, and walked her up the steps to the porch and inside. He wasn't always the epitome of courtesy. With Diana, he would have been. But she didn't want him to be.

She unfastened her seatbelt and turned to him, once again wistful, her eyes shimmering in the gloom of the car's interior, her lips still rosy, still way too tempting. The word *sorry* was replaced in his mind by the word *desire.* And then the word *hopeless.*

"I have to think," she said, as if that explained everything.

He nodded. He wasn't going to say *desire* or *hopeless.* And he sure as hell wasn't going to say *sorry.* He'd already said that. It wasn't worth repeating.

He waited to start the engine until she was safely inside the building, the heavy front door swinging shut behind her. Then he coasted down the driveway, back out to Atlantic Avenue, and a couple of blocks south to Faulk Street.

On a Monday night, the bar wasn't that crowded. The place was busy enough for Gus to earn a nice profit, but not packed the way it had been on Saturday night. A slow song he didn't recognize, layered with syrupy violins and soulful singing, filled the air, and several couples rocked back and forth on the dance floor, arms wrapped around each other, feet barely moving. Lucky people, he thought. They were holding their lovers, rubbing body parts, getting it on as much as it was possible to do while fully clothed and in a public place.

He crossed directly to the bar. Gus was pouring something pale and frothy from a blender pitcher into a bowl-shaped glass. She handed it to a waitress, then acknowledged Nick with a squint and a pointed critique: "You look like hell."

One thing about Gus: she didn't mince words. "Thanks. I wish I could say the same about you."

She smiled. "Bad night, huh. What can I get you?"

He wasn't sure. He'd had a beer with dinner, but he could manage another drink without jeopardizing his driving skills. He eyed the whisky bottles arrayed along the mirrored wall behind her.

"He'll have coffee," Ed Nolan's voice reached him from behind.

If it were any other cop, Nick would have figured the guy was intervening because Nick was acting dull and dazed. But Nick didn't have a buzz on—what was the opposite of a buzz? Was it possible to be too sober? And Ed Nolan knew Nick as well as Nick knew himself. Ed knew what Nick could handle, what he couldn't, what he needed.

He wasn't sure he needed coffee, but he probably needed Ed.

"Two decafs," Ed told Gus. "This boy looks shit-faced."

"I'm not drunk," Nick said.

"I didn't say you were." He took the two steaming mugs from Gus and beckoned Nick to follow him. They settled into an empty booth just steps from the jukebox. If Nick had been thinking more clearly, he would have grabbed the banquette that faced away from the jukebox. But Ed took that seat and Nick wound up with a clear view of it, its peacock decoration glowing, its glossy veneer reflecting golden light from the ceiling lamps.

He steered his vision to Ed. Tall and broad-shouldered, Ed Nolan projected strength and vigor, even though he was closing in on his sixtieth birthday. He had a square face, blunt features and a thick head of slate-gray hair.

Ed was as close to a father as Nick had ever had. Nick was as close to a son as Ed had ever had. Ed's daughter was somewhere out west, San Francisco or Seattle, drifting around, selling jewelry at craft fairs or something. His wife had died when Maeve had been a teenager, and she hadn't taken it well. Ed knew a thing or two about screwed-up teenagers.

"Drink," he said, nudging one of the mugs closer to Nick. "You heard what I said to Gus. It's decaf. It won't keep you up all night."

The coffee wouldn't. Memories of kissing Diana would. Nick drank. The coffee was scalding and bitter, the exact opposite of Diana's sweet, soft lips.

"So," Ed said, cupping his beefy hands around his own mug. "What truck ran you over?" Although he'd lived in Brogan's Point for years, he still talked like a kid from Revere, the proudly working-class town abutting Boston to the north. Ask Ed where he grew up, and he'd say, "Ra-*vee*-ah."

"A truck named Diana Simms," Nick told him.

Frowning, Ed rummaged through his memory and came up empty. "She from around here?"

"She's from Boston. Staying at the OB Inn."

"Nick, Nick, Nick." Ed shook his head and clicked his tongue. "You're messing around with tourists?"

"I'm not messing around with her." *Unfortunately*, he added silently. "It's that damned jukebox. She and her boyfriend were here Saturday night. So was I. The jukebox played 'Changes' by David Bowie. Nothing's been the same since then."

"Her *boyfriend?*"

"Her fiancé," Nick said grimly.

A normal person, someone who wasn't devoted to Gus, some-one who didn't live in Brogan's Point and hadn't heard about the legendary powers of the jukebox, would have told him to forget about Diana, take a cold shower and get on with his life. But Ed wasn't normal, at least not by that definition. "Are you sure the song wasn't for her and the fiancé?"

"I'm not sure about anything," Nick conceded. "But I think *she's* sure it wasn't for her and the fiancé. She sent him packing and stopped wearing her engagement ring." At least for tonight. Tomorrow it might be sparkling above her ring-finger knuckle once more. "What is it about that frickin' jukebox, anyway? Everybody else was dancing and drinking and having fun while that song played. Me, I felt like I was drugged or something. I couldn't move. I could only stare across the room at her. And she could only stare across the room at me."

"Who knows?" Ed shrugged. "The jukebox has never spoken to me, not like that."

"It didn't speak," Nick muttered. "It sang."

"The way Gus explains it, it only speaks to someone who needs to hear what it's saying. Maybe you need to make some changes."

"I thought of that," Nick said. "But I don't know what I should change. I'm in a good place right now. Work is good. My friends are good. No complaints." He drank some more coffee. "Maybe *she* needs to make some changes. The whole fiancé thing. Maybe she shouldn't marry him."

"You'd like that?"

Nick opened his mouth and then closed it. Sure, he'd like her not to be engaged. If she hadn't been engaged, they could have been at his house right now, in his bed, trying out every position he knew. But Ed was asking something more. "I hardly know her," he admitted. "Would *I* want to be her fiancé? Hell, I don't know. Is she desperate to get married? I don't know. She's a city girl. She buys and sells antiques. What do I know about antiques?"

"You drive one," Ed joked.

Nick indulged him with a smile, then grew solemn again. "I don't know what I want—except *her*. I want her."

"Maybe what the song was telling you was that if you want to get her, you have to change."

"Change what?" Nick leaned back in his chair and spread his arms wide, as if to say, *I'm perfect the way I am.*

Ed shrugged again. "Court her. Let her know you're serious. Let her know *you.* I don't suppose you told her about your background."

He sighed. "Yeah, right. I'm going to tell a classy antiques dealer from Boston about that."

Ed tipped his head and raised his bushy gray eyebrows, as if to say, *Why not?*

Here was why not: because a woman like her wouldn't want anything to do with a guy who'd been convicted of attempted murder, who'd wound up in the justice system, who'd been shipped off to juvie detention until he'd aged out. Who'd been rescued by a good-hearted cop, someone who'd believed him even if the judge hadn't, someone who'd helped him get scholarships and loans to attend UMass and then to earn a master's degree in social work. Someone who'd helped him establish a position in town as a youth counselor, offering guidance and support to kids as screwed up as himself, rescuing them the way Ed had rescued him.

Diana came from the kind of world where a ring with a diamond that took up half her finger was considered "silly." A world where antiques were bought and sold, not driven.

"I remember a time," Ed said, "when you decided you couldn't hack college. Somewhere in the middle of your sophomore year, I think. You were holding down two jobs, you were drinking a lot—"

"Not that much," Nick objected.

"Enough to cause problems. Your course work was challenging. You felt alienated from your classmates—all those nice kids whose only run-ins with the law were speeding tickets. You called me up and said you were dropping out, you didn't belong there, you couldn't do it. Remember that?"

Unfortunately, Nick did. "I'd drunk too much that night."

"And a hell of a lot of other nights," Ed needled him. "Do you remember what I told you?"

Nick sighed. "Something wise, I'm sure."

"I told you that if you wanted something, you had to go after it. You had to fight for it—even if that sometimes meant you had to fight yourself. You wanted that degree, Nick. You wanted to prove something—to yourself and to the world. You wanted to overcome the shit you'd been through. You wanted to transcend it. So you fought. You fought all the obstacles and you fought yourself, and you got the degree."

"I kept drinking."

"Saturday nights, maybe. Not weeknights."

Nick sighed again. "Getting my degree was a valid goal. Nailing a pretty antiques dealer who's engaged to someone else? I'm not sure that's worth fighting for."

"You don't want to nail her, Nick. You want to *have* her."

"Christ. When did you turn into Yoda?"

"I've always been Yoda," Ed joked. "You want her? Fight for her."

Seven

"James?" Diana sat inside the rental car, staring through the windshield at the compact Cape-Cod style house sitting squarely on a scraggly lawn that showed no signs of spring revival. The house's roof sagged slightly, its clapboard siding was in desperate need of fresh paint, and the asphalt driveway leading to its one-car garage rippled with cold heaves and cracks.

Diana had just emerged from the house, raced to her car and punched in her boss's number on her cell phone. Her heart thumped with excitement. Another find. Another score—or it would be another score if James gave her his approval.

"Don't tell me you found some more Tiffany lamps," he said.

"Even better. The concierge at the inn where I'm staying told me about a friend of hers whose grandmother had recently died, and the friend was planning to empty her grandmother's house so she could sell it. She's got a liquidator coming in on Saturday. But Claudia—the concierge—gave me her friend's number and said I should see if she'd let me look around first. If we come up with a better bid than the liquidator, she'll cancel that Saturday appointment and let us clean the place out, instead."

"And we would do that because…?"

"It's like a pirate's treasure chest, James. There's plenty of junk, but…my God. It's amazing! The grandmother was a packrat."

"A hoarder?" Diana could practically hear him grimacing and shuddering through her cell phone. "We don't deal in old newspapers."

"No old newspapers. But lots of rare books in mint condition. She's got this amazing Stickley oak sideboard. A gorgeous roll-top desk with a patent and date stamped in it—1878—in excellent condition. There's a crank gramophone that actually works, with a gorgeous morning-glory horn. She's got a collection of music boxes to die for—and they all work, too. A couple of rugs—I think they were Turkish, but Eugene would have to appraise them. Oh, and a mirrored vanity table…" She sighed. She'd loved that vanity table. She'd imagined herself sitting on the tufted satin stool, gazing into the triptych mirror, grooming her hair with the sterling-silver-handled hairbrush sitting on the marble-topped table and then spritzing some perfume behind her ears from the cut-crystal atomizer next to the hairbrush. "James, we have to make a bid on this."

"The whole lot?"

"I know, that sounds kind of crazy. But I'm telling you—this is a phenomenal find. Even if we had to toss half of what we got, we'd make a mint on the other half."

"I don't like to buy entire lots, Diana. We're not liquidators. We've built a reputation on our selectivity—"

Diana didn't make a habit of interrupting her boss. He was revered among antique dealers throughout the country. He often appeared on TV shows, sharing his expertise. He had hired Diana shortly after she'd graduated from college, at least in part because her parents and grandparents had purchased more than a few big-ticket items from Shomback-Sawyer over the years, and he'd trained her. He'd sent her to seminars. He'd brought her along with him to estate sales. Five years after joining his staff, she still had a great deal to learn, and she made it her practice to keep her mouth shut and absorb his wisdom, not to question him.

But this time, this house…She just *knew* that if James was with her, he'd be bidding on the whole thing, if only to get his hands on that sideboard. And the gramophone. And the vanity.

"Lenore—that's the granddaughter—wants the entire house cleared out," Diana explained to James. "Everything has to go so she can sell the place. She's on a tight schedule. There must be at least fifty thousand dollars' worth of antiques here, probably closer to six figures. She said the liquidator offered her eight thousand for everything. He's not an antiques dealer. He has no idea what she's got."

James said nothing. Diana wasn't sure if his silence was a result of his crunching numbers or keeling over in shock.

"We could easily get it for twelve grand plus moving costs," she said. "Maybe even less. But we have to act fast."

"You ran that number past her? Twelve thousand dollars?"

"No, but she seemed to think getting eight thousand was a good deal. Why would she object to getting fifty percent more?"

James sighed. "This is not like you, Diana."

"What's not like me?" she asked hesitantly. Was he going to chew her out? Fire her?

"Sounding so…so sure of yourself. So confident."

She allowed herself a small laugh. "Well, I *am* confident about this. We shouldn't let this opportunity pass us by."

Another sigh. "Where are you now?"

"Parked at the curb in front of the house."

James fell silent again. This time she could hear a faint tapping through her phone. He must be running figures on his calculator. "We'd have to secure the truck, make sure we have room in the warehouse…I'll need a little time to work out the logistics. Do you think your eager heiress can wait a few minutes?"

Diana felt the tension ebb from her shoulders. Not only wasn't James firing her, but he actually seemed persuaded. Her uncharacteristic confidence had won him over. "A few minutes, sure," she said. "Not a few hours."

"A few minutes. And this house is where? New Hampshire?"

"I'm just south of the state line, in Massachusetts. A few miles north of Brogan's Point," she told her boss.

"Brogan's Point. The antiques capital of the world," he said, his voice tinged with sarcasm. "Who would have thought?"

"I've made some lucky finds, that's all," she said modestly. Just because he wasn't firing her didn't mean she ought to brag that stumbling upon two fantastic deals in as many days had been due to her superior skill rather than a stroke—or two strokes—of luck. Luck was a huge part of it. So was the fact that she was exploring a region Shomback-Sawyer rarely visited. The firm tended to track estate sales closer to the city, and to rely on tips from colleagues and past customers. Diana was checking out collections that would have fallen under Shomback-Sawyer's radar. She was alert and observant, and she trusted her instincts. She was *confident*.

"Next thing I know, you're going to suggest that we open an office up on Cape Ann so you can keep scouring the area for new finds. All right, let me see what I can work out. I'll call you back as soon as I can."

Diana said goodbye and thumbed the icon to end the call. She didn't want to consider how much the idea of opening an office in Brogan's Point appealed to her. She knew James had been joking when he'd suggested it. Brogan Point was barely an hour's drive north of Boston. Shomback-Sawyer didn't need an outpost here.

Besides, she reminded herself, she liked living in the city. She'd grown up in Brookline, the sprawling urban town that shared more than half of its border with Boston. She'd been riding the T all her life, visiting the Museum of Fine Arts by herself from the time she was ten years old, shopping on Newberry Street by the time she was fifteen, and attending Red Sox games at Fenway Park for as long as she could remember. Currently, she rented a lovely flat in the South End. Peter resided in a charming, and much larger, place in Back Bay, but Diana had insisted that they maintain separate residences until they got married. She loved the South End—the restaurants, the boutiques, the humming energy of the city.

Didn't she?

In Boston, she couldn't jog on the beach. In fact, she rarely jogged outdoors in the city because there was too much traffic. Instead, she ran on a treadmill in a fitness center down the block from her apartment, where membership cost her $500 a year.

And at night, even with her windows closed, the city's noise seeped into her bedroom. She never had the pleasure of being blanketed in silence when she slept, because silence didn't exist in a city. There were always car engines, horns, dogs barking, distant sirens, the ranting of some inebriated person staggering down the street at two in the morning.

Nighttime in Boston was nothing like the tranquility of Brogan's Point. Diana slept more deeply in her broad, cozy bed at the Ocean Bluff Inn, where the only sound was the faint whisper of waves rolling onto the shore a few hundred feet from her window, than she ever did in Boston. She woke up better rested, her mind sharper, her nerves absorbing everything around her with a sensitivity usually dulled by the city's clamor and clutter.

God help her, she liked living here.

Visiting here, she silently amended. She was only visiting, not *living.*

Her fondness for Brogan's Point had nothing to do with Nick, she assured herself. She hadn't even seen him today. He hadn't been standing by the retaining wall with his morning coffee when she'd jogged along the beach—she'd been watching for him and she hadn't seen him. Which was a good thing, she reminded herself. If she'd seen him, she might have done something crazy, like fling herself at him and resume kissing him, picking up where they'd left off last night.

Where *she'd* left off. She'd ended the kiss because she had to. She couldn't pursue anything with him until she'd sorted out her feelings about Peter.

She also couldn't pursue anything with Nick because, for all she knew, there was nothing to pursue. He was a sexy dude willing to enjoy a no-strings fling with a tourist. He was a local boy looking for fun. He was...

She didn't know *what* he was. She knew pathetically little about him.

At the moment, she felt as if she knew pathetically little about herself, too. Her emotions were more turbulent than the ocean during a storm, a churn of whitecaps and undertows and whipping winds. She had no idea what she wanted...other than Nick. She knew she wanted him.

Her phone vibrated in her hand, and she acknowledged that she wanted something else, as well: James's approval, so she could negotiate with Lenore for the right to haul away the cornucopia of gems and junk inside her late grandmother's house. Nick might be a fantasy, a dangerously alluring bit of flotsam the stormy sea had tossed at her feet. But the contents of the aging house at the end of the crumbling driveway were real. The profit possibilities were stupefying. The sheer joy of stumbling upon so many precious pieces, so many amusing curiosities, so much intriguing history was immeasurable. And the confidence—the understanding that she was ready to start making deals on her own, that she could assess merchandise accurately and take responsibility for bringing it to the firm—yes, she wanted that.

"Our inventory is low after the holiday shopping sprees," James informed her. "We've got space in the warehouse. If we can move everything in one full-size van, we can schedule a pick-up for Thursday. But if this turns out to be a bomb, and all these fabulous pieces turn out to be junk, it's coming out of your hide."

"Fair enough," she said, then mouthed the word *confidence*. "As long as I get a bonus if all these fabulous pieces turn out to be treasures."

"I hope you're right." Again James paused, as if choosing his words with great care. "You've changed Diana."

"For the better, I hope." The David Bowie song echoed faintly in her mind. "I'm going to give the woman an offer she can't refuse. And I'm going to earn that bonus. Because you know what? I *am* right."

—⚬—

Lenore had been thrilled to accept Diana's offer of ten thousand dollars for everything in her grandmother's house. Diana wrote up an agreement and promised to call as soon as the moving van had been scheduled. Once she and Lenore had shaken hands, she climbed back into the rental car and drove to the inn, humming "Changes."

Had she changed? What, besides confidence, had James heard in her words, in her voice? Could he tell, just from talking to her, that last night she'd experienced the hottest, wildest, most arousing kiss in her life?

No. That was not the sort of thing a person could detect in a voice. She was pretty sure they couldn't, anyway.

She warned herself not to think about Nick, his kiss, and the way she'd felt in his arms. She couldn't think about it while she still had the engagement ring Peter had given her, stashed inside her rolled socks in a dresser drawer at the inn.

Peter. Surely she loved him. She'd agreed to marry him, hadn't she? Just because Nick Fiore had bewitched her with a kiss didn't mean she should throw away everything she and Peter had.

As she thought about it, though, she wasn't quite certain she'd ever really agreed to marry him. That they would get married had always just been a foregone conclusion. Her parents and Peter's had been close friends for years, and when Peter and Diana had been born, their parents had begun planning. Like royalty, they'd plotted the merging of their two families when Diana and Peter had been toddlers splashing each other in the wading pool in the backyard of Peter's parents' grand brick mansion. When Diana and Peter had reached primary school—the stage at which boys and girls generally loathed members of the opposite sex—their parents had blithely ignored their squabbling and bragged about the magnificent grandchildren Diana and Peter would someday produce for them. They'd sent Diana and Peter to the same prep school, where somehow Diana and Peter had drifted from antagonists to cautious friends to a couple. She recalled Peter's invitation to the prom when they'd been seniors: "I guess we're going together, right?"

She'd had a crush on Griffin Stanhope that year. She'd dreamed of Griffin asking her to go to the prom with him. But of course he never did. He couldn't. Everyone knew she belonged to Peter.

Everyone knew it in college, too. It was a given. A law of nature. When Peter had presented her with that gaudy diamond ring, he hadn't asked her to marry him. He'd handed her the box and said, "Moving right along…"

At the time, she'd laughed. But it hadn't been funny. It hadn't been the romantic proposal she'd dreamed of. No rose petals strewn across the floor. No bended knee. Not even an *I love you and I want to spend the rest of my life with you.* Just "Moving right along…"

She'd moved right along. She hadn't questioned any of it. Like the apprentice she'd been at Shomback-Sawyer, she'd listened and observed and done as she was told. It was what everyone expected. Diana Simms was not the sort of person who got on the phone and persuaded people to do what she wanted.

Until now.

Strange fascination, she thought as the song floated through her head. She was turning, and she was facing change.

—⁂—

The message light on her bedside phone at the inn was flashing when she entered the room. For a moment, she worried that the message was from Peter, calling to demand that she stop gallivanting around the North Shore and come back to Boston where she belonged, as he'd said yesterday. But he would have contacted her on her cell phone, not the hotel's phone. So would James, or her parents. Or Claudia's friend Lenore if, God forbid, she'd changed her mind about allowing Shomback-Sawyer to cart away her grandmother's belongings. The business card Diana had left with Lenore had Diana's cell number printed on it.

She tossed her purse on the bed, reached for the phone and pressed the button for messages. "Hi," came a man's voice, deep and soft yet slightly gruff, like pebbles wrapped in velvet.

Her memories of kissing that man came rushing back, swamping her, warming her deep inside.

"I never got your phone number," Nick's message continued, "so I'm trying the OB number instead. I know I—we—well, whatever. I'm refereeing a b-ball game at the community center this evening. Middle school kids, but they're pretty good. I thought you might like to see what I do for a living. At least some of what I do. The game starts at six-thirty—it's a school night, so the kids play an early game. Anyway, I hope I'll see you there. This is Nick, by the way." He recited a phone number, said goodbye, and disconnected.

Diana listened to the queue of instructions following his message, then pressed the button to replay it. This time, she jotted down his number, and laughed when he said, "This is Nick, by the way." As if he'd had to identify himself. She would know his voice anywhere. Even if he'd whispered, if he'd had laryngitis, if his voice had been filtered through one of those identity-disguising machines so he came out sounding distorted, she would have known the caller was Nick.

She sank onto the bed, trying to ignore the fact that the mere sound of his voice could fill her with a warmth intense enough to melt her soul—and her resistance. He'd contacted her despite her having fled from him yesterday. Had she not made herself clear? Or had he seen past her rejection and sensed that behind her words lurked a desperate yearning for him?

She recalled that she hadn't said no to him last night. She'd said, "I have to think." He probably believed a full day of thinking was sufficient and he could approach her again.

She shouldn't go to the game. Honestly, why would anyone who wasn't a parent of one of the players want to sit through a basketball game played by a bunch of thirteen-year-olds? What she should do, she chided herself, was put her damned ring back on her finger, call Peter and tell him she'd be back in Boston tomorrow.

Or return to Boston without putting the damned ring back on. Because whenever she went home, whether it was tomorrow or next week or next year, she was going to have to confront the fact that something was changing. *She* was changing.

She couldn't shake the suspicion that if she tried to put the ring back on, it wouldn't fit.

Eight

He must have been nuts, leaving that message for Diana. If she came to the game, he'd want her, just as much as he wanted her yesterday. If he wanted her, he was going to have to tell her the truth about himself, who he was, where he'd been and what he'd done. If she knew that ugly truth, she sure as hell wouldn't want him.

But Ed Nolan had reminded him of who he *really* was: a fighter. Someone who didn't run scared. Someone who confronted his challenges and dealt with them as best he could, even if his best might get him into a shitload of trouble.

What did he have to lose? If he didn't try for Diana, he'd never have her. If he did try for her and she decided his background was too awful, he'd never have her. But there was a chance, however slim, that she'd decide that his screwed-up background was forgivable, that he had somehow redeemed himself, that an attempted murder conviction notwithstanding, he was worthy of her love.

Oh, and she'd have to dump her fiancé, too. Just one more minor detail.

He watched as the teams lined up, nine in red T-shirts along the bench to his left, ten in green T-shirts along the bench to his right, a mix of girls and boys. At their age—early teens—some of the girls were taller than some of the boys, and he didn't have enough players to create an all-girl league and an all-boy league, so he'd created a single co-ed league. He coached both of these teams, which was why he had to referee the game. He couldn't stand on the sidelines with one team or the other. He had to remain neutral.

These were his kids. He worked with them in an after-school program he'd designed with the middle school. The combination of high-stakes proficiency testing and budget shortfalls had cut into the amount of physical education and recess time the students received each day, and he'd convinced the school board that any after-school program he set up needed to include physical activity for everyone, regardless of their athletic ability. At first, some of the boys balked at having to form teams with girls, and vice versa. But a grudging respect had grown among the players. Some of his girl players were pretty damned talented. Some of his boy players had more ego than athletic prowess. He divvied the teams up carefully so they'd be evenly matched. And they loved playing evening games at the community center. They felt like varsity jocks when they played there.

Volunteer coaches stood with the two teams. Nick pulled a ball from the rack, bounced it twice to make sure it was fully inflated, and then crossed to the center of the court. The two tallest players joined him, and eight other players, four in red and four in green, shaped a circle around them. Nick blew his whistle and tossed the ball. The girl in red jumped higher than the boy in green, and the game got underway.

Nick had to watch the game closely. He had to monitor for traveling, elbows, all manner of fouls. Some of his players were meek and clumsy. Some were almost thuggishly aggressive. His primary objectives were to make sure no one got hurt, everyone had fun, and all the players left the game feeling better about themselves than they'd felt before the tip-off. Achieving those goals demanded his full attention.

But it received only ninety-nine percent of his attention. The last one percent skimmed the stands, searching. Friends, siblings, parents, a few school and community center workers sat scattered along the scuffed wooden bleachers. Not exactly a capacity crowd. If Diana came, he would see her.

He did. Right after the first basket was scored, he spotted her. Not knowing any of the other people in the stands, she sat by herself, dressed in a simple beige sweater and jeans, her hair falling in tawny waves around her face, her dazzling eyes fixed on the players.

A boy—Will Czerny, a brilliant kid with serious anger issues whom Nick had been working with for a year—dribbled toward him, and Diana followed the action until her gaze met Nick's. She smiled hesitantly and fluttered her fingers in a tentative wave.

That one tiny gesture infused Nick with energy. He gave a quick nod, then turned and jogged down the court, watching Will dribble past a guard and make his lay-up. Nice play, and Will hadn't plowed anyone down en route. Nick left his whistle dangling around his neck—no need to blow it—and glanced up at the scoreboard in time to see two more points added to the red team's score.

The game went well. Only one minor flare-up occurred, between two boys Nick happened to know were good friends. He'd assigned them to separate teams because if they'd been teammates they would have combined to terrorize their opponents. On separate teams, they negated each other.

He wished there had been some sort of afterschool sports program when he'd been thirteen, a place where he could have burned off his own anger by running and sweating and shooting a ball into a hoop. A place where he could have talked to an adult who had some familiarity with what was going on in Nick's home, in his life, without telling Nick he was imagining things or warning him that as long as the violence didn't touch him personally, it was none of his business. That was what his parents had told him, and he'd known they were lying. The violence *had* touched him personally, and it *had* been his business.

He wished there had been a safe place where he could have hung out, away from his father's temper and his mother's passivity, a place where he would not have to be a hero—or a criminal.

It was just such a haven he provided to the kids in his afterschool programs. He saw himself in some of them, and if he could keep them from being sucked into the system the way he'd been, he would consider his life well spent.

The game ended with the green team winning by four points. If the game had been played on Friday, he would have packed both teams into a few cars driven by volunteers and taken everyone to the Pizza Pit for a post-game feast. But it was a school night, and the players' parents and guardians swarmed down the rickety bleachers to collect their kids. Nick thanked the coaches and scorekeeper, gave the players a brief speech about how proud he was that they'd played clean and fair, ascertained that everyone had a ride home and reminded them to do their homework. That final remark was greeted by a chorus of good-natured groans. "Wanna tell us to brush our teeth, too?" Will hooted.

"You especially," Nick shot back. "And brush your tongue, too. It looks green." The kids erupted in laughter and stuck their tongues out at one another for inspection. "Yours is blue!" "Yours is black!" "That's 'cause I eat fire!"

He felt Diana's presence even without looking at her. He knew she was standing on the periphery, not wishing to intrude on his pep talk with the kids. Once they headed for the exits, he turned to her.

She wasn't wearing the diamond.

Did that mean she was ready to pick up where they'd left off last night? Had she done the thinking she'd said she needed to do, decided she was done with her Boston fiancé, and come to the community center for the sole purpose of throwing herself at Nick?

Nothing was ever that simple—and nothing in life had ever been handed to him. Ed was right. If he wanted Diana, he would have to fight for her.

Still, the absence of her engagement ring was a good sign.

"That was fun," she said.

Sure it was. Nothing more entertaining than sitting on a hard wooden bleacher and watching a group of unevenly talented tween-ers playing a game of hoops that ended in a score of 43-39.

Yet Diana was smiling. The past hour couldn't have been too painful for her.

"I've got to lock up the equipment and wash up," he said. "Then we can grab a bite to eat, or something to drink."

"Do what you have to do," she said. "I'll wait."

—⋙—

Fifteen minutes later, they were seated across a table from each other at the Pizza Pit, splitting a mushroom pizza. He hadn't wanted to take her to the Faulk Street Tavern, in part because bar food wasn't Gus's strength and Nick was hungry, and in part because he didn't want to risk some other song pouring out of the jukebox and snaring them in its sticky web.

"So I got the go-ahead to buy the entire lot," she was telling him. "It wasn't just that I'd stumbled onto some real treasures in that house, but that my boss trusted me. He trusted my judgment. It was practically like getting a promotion, his letting me buy an entire lot like that. We're going to make a really nice profit on it, even if we wind up tossing or donating half the stuff. The other half is fantastic."

Nick didn't understand much about antiques. Yeah, his Honda Civic had more than a hundred-fifty thousand miles on it, and his house was furnished with pieces purchased at the Goodwill store. But nothing he owned, no matter how old, was worth much.

Her excitement about the estate purchase she'd engineered was infectious, though. He recalled the first time he'd seen her, across the room at the Faulk Street Tavern while David Bowie crooned. Even at that distance and in the dim lighting, he'd noticed that she'd looked drawn. Beautiful but pensive, maybe a little worried.

Not now. Now she glowed.

"When I got your message," she said, "I wanted to see you, to tell you about this."

"About the house full of stuff?"

"About how empowered I feel. I exceeded expectations, Nick. And I love it."

Oh, man. He loved it, too. He loved her for being so excited.

Not that he *loved* her. He just loved how psyched she was, radiant and bubbly. This wasn't about *love*.

Turn and face the strange... The lyric bludgeoned his brain with the force of a lead pipe, nearly flattening him. He covered by reaching for another slice of pizza.

He didn't love her. Of course he didn't. But damn, if this— this *thing* was going anywhere—and who the hell knew where it was going, but if it was—he had to come clean. He had to tell her who he was.

How could he, when she was so happy? *Congratulations on your big score today. By the way, I was convicted of attempted murder when I was fifteen.*

Telling her the truth was the right thing to do. But before he could do that right thing, she started talking again. "I'm so glad you invited me to the game. In all honesty, I wasn't going to come."

"I wouldn't have blamed you," he said, managing a smile. "A group of middle-school kids too short to execute a slam-dunk? Not exactly a thrill."

She smiled. "I wasn't expecting a Celtics game. But...it wasn't that." She sipped from her glass of iced tea, then smiled again, a forced, feeble smile. "I phoned Peter after I got your message. My..."

Her hesitation stretched into a full-fledged silence. "Your fiancé?" he guessed.

She nodded. "I wanted to tell him about my coup this afternoon. I mean, he *is* supposed to be my fiancé. My husband-to-be. I thought, wow, I had this great day at my job. The person I should share this with is the man I'm supposed to marry, right?"

Nick wasn't enjoying the turn the conversation had taken, but he knew he had to listen. What she was saying was important.

"And he just..." Her smile now seemed brave but futile, her eyes glistening with tears. "He said, 'Well, that's very nice, Diana. When are you coming home?' He just dismissed the whole thing. It was like, 'Oh, aren't you a good little girl. Now snap out of it and get back here where you belong.' Like he was patting me on the head and pasting a gold star next to my name."

Having never had a gold star pasted next to his name, Nick could only imagine what that was like. Flattering. Patronizing. Dismissive.

"I was so excited, and he didn't want to share my excitement with me." She was still smiling, but the moisture in her eyes overflowed, a few stray tears trickling down her cheeks. "And I thought, well, I'll see Nick tonight. Maybe he'll get it. Because I just wanted to share with someone. Is that so terrible?"

"No, of course not." He longed to gather her in his arms and hold her tight, to let her rest her head on his shoulder and cry her heart out. Even if she'd be crying over her son-of-a-bitch fiancé.

But she was laboring hard to conceal her distress. When she dabbed at her cheeks with one of the flimsy paper napkins the waiter had delivered with their order, she pretended she was wiping her mouth. She didn't want comforting. She was too proud for that.

"When something cool like that happens," he said, "you want to celebrate. Celebrating alone is the pits."

"Well, I'm celebrating with you."

"I'm honored." He hadn't known he would say that, but it was the truth.

Her tears spilled more heavily now, a trickle turning into a torrent. He handed her his napkin, because hers was sure to be saturated soon. "I'm going to break up with him," she said.

Because of Nick? Because of the fiancé's inability to acknowledge how important her professional accomplishment today was to her?

Because of the song? Because she was changing?

The reason didn't matter. She was breaking up with the bastard. And Nick was thrilled.

Nine

After they'd finished the pizza, he drove her back to the community center, where she'd left her car. She'd made arrangements with the rental company to drop the car off in Boston tomorrow, after which she would pick up her own car and drive it back to Brogan's Point. She wasn't done here, wasn't even close to being done. She wasn't even sure what "being done" might mean. But whatever it meant, she'd rather have her own car while she figured it out.

At least she'd figured one thing out: she had to end her engagement to Peter. It wasn't just his reaction to her big coup today that convinced her. It wasn't his inability to enjoy a beer in a working-class bar without passing judgment on everyone and everything in the place, right down to the glassware. It wasn't his stuffiness, his grumpiness, his arrogance.

It wasn't even Nick Fiore's kiss.

That kiss weighed heavily on her during the brief drive back to the community center. She thought it best that they not kiss again, not only because she hadn't yet officially ended things with Peter but because if Nick kissed her, her brain would go into melt-down mode and she would be unable to think at all. And she had a lot of thinking to do.

The parking lot was nearly empty, and Nick was able to pull into the vacant space next to Diana's car. He turned off the engine and twisted in his seat to face her. "Diana—"

She braced herself. How could she say no if he kissed her? How could she deny them both something she desperately wanted?

But instead of leaning across the gear stick, he simply studied her. Several glaring spotlights hanging from the building's eaves illuminated the lot. The silvery light played over his face, emphasizing its sharp lines and angles and making Diana even more aware of how profoundly dark his eyes were.

"If you're breaking your engagement because of me..." He lapsed into silence for a moment, then continued, "I feel bad about that."

She sensed a subtext in his words, but she couldn't decipher it. Was he saying he felt bad about the possibility that he'd broken her and Peter up? Or was he warning her that even if she ended the engagement, he wasn't about to step in and take Peter's place?

She didn't expect him to. They were still nearly strangers. Close strangers, strangers strongly attracted to each other, but strangers nonetheless. She hadn't grown up with Nick. She hadn't gone to school with him, or beaten him at backgammon, or discussed politics with him. She hadn't seen him at his worst, and he certainly hadn't seen her at hers.

"It's not because of you," she assured him. "It's because..." Because she felt freer and happier and more self-assured without Peter. Because she liked not having to keep taking his emotional temperature, soothing him, making sure he was happy. Because her world seemed more spacious when he wasn't occupying so much of it. Because she was finally listening to herself rather than to him.

She couldn't begin to explain all that to Nick. Instead, she said, "It's because of the song."

"That's crazy."

"I know." She smiled.

He smiled, too, and then leaned forward, as she'd expected him to earlier, and touched his lips to hers. Not a blazing kiss like the one he'd given her on the dock, but a gentle whisper of a kiss, full of promise, full of temptation. It was the sort of kiss that made her want much, much more.

But first she had to sort out her life. She had to do the right thing. "I'm going to Boston tomorrow," she said.

He settled back in his seat, his expression darkening slightly. "So this is goodbye?"

"No. I've got to be back here Thursday to oversee the packing and moving of the estate I bought." That wasn't the only reason she planned to return to Brogan's Point, but to suggest more might be presumptuous. "I'm going down to Boston to meet with my boss and with...with Peter," she said, carefully avoiding the word *fiancé*. She'd stopped wearing the ring, and she had to stop using that word in reference to Peter. "And then I'll come back."

He accepted her statement in silence. Just as she didn't want to make presumptions, he apparently didn't want to, either. She would come back. They'd figure out their next step then. Maybe they'd return to the Faulk Street Tavern and hope for another song to emerge from the jukebox, telling them what to do.

She would come back, and she'd turn to face the strange changes.

A long moment passed between her and Nick. She wished he would kiss her again. She hoped he wouldn't.

He didn't. "Thank you for inviting me to the game," she said. "I'll call you when I get back from Boston."

"Okay." He managed another smile, this one tentative. He seemed as cautious as she felt, as eager and as anxious.

God, she wanted to kiss him again.

"Good night," she murmured, then let herself out of his car.

—⁓—

She made arrangements with the car rental company to drop off her car at one of the company's Boston outlets, then drove south to the city, her suitcase filled with clothes for her laundry hamper and the precious, bubble-wrapped Tiffany lamps wedged into the back seat. As soon as she reached her South End building, she transferred the lamps to her own car, which she kept parked in a neighborhood garage one long block from her building, and then dropped the rental car off and settled the bill. She walked back to her building, wheeling her suitcase behind her. Lugging it up the stairs to her third-floor walk-up, she thought about how nice it had been to have Peter carry it down the stairs for her when they'd departed for Brogan's Point last Saturday.

Not nice enough to justify remaining engaged to him, though. She was strong. She could carry her own suitcase.

She took a moment to appreciate the welcome familiarity of her apartment once she'd unlocked the multiple locks and let herself inside. It was small—a great room with a kitchen, a bedroom and a bathroom—but sun-filled and comfortable. She'd furnished it herself, arranging an assortment of old cast-offs from her parents that had been accumulating dust in their basement, and inexpensive new pieces she'd purchased online. Peter had groused about her having bought chintzy, do-it-yourself junk and he'd refused to help her assemble the occasional tables and breakfast bar stools. Fortunately, the instructions had been pretty straightforward, and a helpful neighbor from across the hall had let her borrow his toolbox. And somehow, by adding an interesting vase here and hanging a framed sepia photograph there, she'd managed to tie the entire room together. Even Peter had grudgingly admitted that her apartment looked good, although he never let her forget how cheap her coffee table was.

She moved through the great room to the bedroom, where she emptied her suitcase into the laundry hamper and repacked the suitcase with clean garments. She paused to water the potted philodendrons along the window sill—hardy plants, they required blessedly little attention—and then left the apartment, bolting all the locks behind her. On her way down the stairs, she sighed, not from the weight of her suitcase but from the realization that Peter might never have occasion to criticize her low-priced furniture again.

She rolled her suitcase down the street to the garage, locked it in the trunk of her Saab, and pointed her car toward Back Bay, where Shomback-Sawyer's main office was located. She was able to find a parking space not too far from the front door. The lamps weighed less than her suitcase, and she didn't have to lug them up or down a flight of stairs. She entered the showroom and headed straight for the elevator.

She had phoned James Sawyer that morning before leaving Brogan's Point, and he was expecting her. His face brightened as she swept into his office with the lamps. "Here, let me help you with that," he said, hastening across his office and easing the carton from her hands.

James was tall and thin, with a narrow face and a hooked nose. Diana thought he resembled a male version of Olive Oyl. He dressed in a prim, prissy style, favoring suspenders and bowties and wing-tipped shoes. Looking at him, and knowing he was one of the founders and named partners of a successful antiques business in an antiques-crazy city, one would never guess that he was known around town for sponsoring auctions to raise money for homeless shelters, soup kitchens and early childhood education programs. He was stern and his personality was as dry as overcooked toast, but within his bony chest he had a generous heart.

He set the box down gently on his desk—a flame mahogany partner's desk dating back to about 1920, a bit fussy for Diana's taste but a beautiful specimen. In fact, James's entire office was filled with beautiful, if slightly fussy, pieces: the leather wing-back chair with its lion's-claw feet, the ornate hunt-board, the burgundy brocade drapes flanking the windows, the elaborately patterned Persian rug. James's office décor was as fussy as he was. Today's bow-tie, Diana noted, appeared to be silk and featured a pattern of birds so closely woven together they might have been an Escher print.

"Genuine Tiffany?" he asked, gingerly removing the bubble-wrap from the lamps and looking for their official stamps and numbers. "Oh, my. Very nice."

"We'll need to have the wiring and switches checked," Diana said. "Given how cheap the price was, I didn't want to take the time to check that at the shop where I bought them. I just wanted to grab them and run."

"Not a problem." He lifted one, admiring it from different angles. "Very, very nice."

"I have the documentation for the purchase," Diana continued, pulling the receipt from her purse.

Usually, James was as fussy about paperwork as about everything else. But he didn't even glance at the slip of paper Diana handed him. He tossed it onto his desk and turned to face her. She realized with a start that his uncharacteristically glowing expression was a reaction not to the lamps but to her. "Look at you!"

She did, glancing down at her jeans—clean but ordinary—and her ribbed sweater and wool jacket. Her hair was probably a bit mussed. She'd been unable to pat it into place when she'd entered the building, because she'd been burdened with the carton containing the lamps. Nor had she taken the time to apply any make-up at her apartment.

It occurred to her that James might disapprove of her casual appearance. But she wasn't planning to spend the day at the office, and he knew that. He was aware that she would be heading back to Brogan's Point today. She needed to be there early tomorrow morning, before the truck arrived to pack up and move the contents of that humble Cape Cod house full of goodies.

She lifted her gaze to James's face and saw he was beaming. "You look so robust, Diana! So invigorated."

"Well, I've had a good couple of days." She was referring to her antiques finds. Everything else about the past few days had been turbulent, to say the least.

"I heard it in your voice on the phone," James said. "And now I'm seeing it. You've changed."

Ch-ch-ch-ch-changes, she thought, suppressing a bemused smile. "In what way?"

"I don't know. I can't put my finger on it. You just seem…more alive, somehow. Whatever it is, it suits you."

"Thank you."

James grinned. "So you'll be up there tomorrow for the big move?"

"Yes. I'd also like to do some more exploring in the area. I feel like there's more to be discovered up on the North Shore. Is that okay with you?"

"If your big purchase yesterday pans out, yes, of course, it's okay with me."

Diana and James exchanged a few more pleasantries before she said goodbye and left his office. In the elevator descending to the ground floor, she allowed herself a moment to savor his approval and his compliments. Did she really look more alive? Did she *feel* more alive? Could a single song have made such a difference in her life?

Apparently, it had.

Yet her smile faded as she reflected the final stop of her trip to Boston. Peter would also notice that she'd changed, but he wouldn't be pleased by the change. The next hour of her life was not going to be anywhere near as much fun as the past hour had been.

The receptionist recognized Diana as she entered the complex of offices that housed the equity firm where Peter worked. The reception area was sleekly designed and modern, with glass walls, streamlined leather seating, and Rothko and Klee paintings on the walls. Not prints—originals. The firm was awash in money.

"Hi, Diana," the receptionist said. She was younger than Diana and model-gorgeous in a snug-fitting knit dress with an asymmetrical neckline, her make-up impeccable, every hair in place. "Is Peter expecting you?"

"No," Diana said, not bothering to add that Peter was certainly not expecting what she'd come here to tell him.

The receptionist's eyes glittered. "You're surprising him! How nice. Let me see if he's in his office." She pressed one perfectly manicured hand to her temple, holding her tiny ear piece in place, and tapped a few buttons on her high-tech console. "Peter?" she murmured. "Guess who's here? Diana!" She probably would have liked to toss a fistful of silver confetti into the air, just to celebrate this wonderful surprise.

The receptionist's joy stoked Diana's sense of dread. This was not going to be a confetti-worthy encounter. It was going to be awful. Maybe she should leave, right now. Maybe she should rethink everything. She and Peter had been a couple forever—or at least, they'd been *destined* to be a couple forever. Everyone wanted it. Everyone believed they were fated to be together.

But that was before Diana had heard the song. Before she had changed.

The receptionist exchanged a few more words with Peter, then released her ear piece and smiled at Diana. "He'll be with you shortly," she reported. "He's on a conference call."

If he were on a conference call, Diana thought, how could he have chatted with the receptionist? Wouldn't his phone line be tied up?

Diana suspected that he wasn't on a conference call at all. He'd asked the receptionist to lie for him. He probably wanted Diana to cool her heels for a while before he granted her an audience with him. He was angry with her, and so be it. He was going to be a lot angrier with her once she ended their engagement.

She returned the receptionist's smile and took a seat on one of the leather sofas. Waiting for Peter to summon her gave her a chance to rethink what she was doing. Was breaking up with him a huge mistake? Was the disappointment her decision would cause her parents and Peter's worth the satisfaction the decision gave her? Was she truly satisfied? What if she floundered on her own? What if she got lonely? What if her days in Brogan's Point were a vacation from reality, and reality—the life she was intended to live—was here, in Boston, at Peter's side?

If ever she needed to talk to her sister, it was now. She and Serena had never been close. Serena had been the rebellious Simms daughter, the one who had never given a damn what their parents wanted. She'd dropped out of college and moved to London, where she worked as a shop clerk by day and hung out with punk rockers at night. She'd cut her hair short and spiky and gotten a tattoo of a rose on her left shoulder. Diana hadn't seen her in a year, but Serena posted photos on her various social media pages. Viewing the pictures of Serena's hairdo and the tat, Diana had been alternately appalled and amused.

Serena had always been wild. To compensate, Diana had always been obedient. Their parents would not have survived two wayward daughters. The more defiant Serena was, the more well-behaved Diana felt she had to be. *Someone* had to be the good girl in the family.

At times, Diana had envied Serena. How liberating it must be not to care! Yet Diana knew there were benefits to remaining in her parents' good graces. They doted on her, praised her, made her feel loved. As a second child, the younger sister of a bold, beautiful drama queen, Diana had always felt kind of insecure and deficient. She lacked Serena's courage and flair. She lacked her certainty. But at least she had her parents' approval.

If she broke up with Peter, she would likely sacrifice their approval. Was she ready for that?

The receptionist had swiveled her chair to her computer and was busily tapping away on her keyboard. No sign of Peter.

Diana pulled out her cell phone. It was evening in London, probably an hour or so past dinner. Who knew if Serena was out clubbing or at home in bed—quite possibly not alone? Diana tapped in a text: *I'm breaking up with Peter.* Then she hit the send button. Somehow, putting it in writing and sending it to Serena helped to solidify her decision.

Another ten minutes passed. Diana checked her emails, relived her meeting with James in her mind, stared at the Rothko painting on the wall facing her and thought about how glad she was to be working with antiques rather than ugly modern art. All those slashes and blotches of black—the painting was truly depressing.

Finally, the receptionist called over to her. "Peter will see you now," she said, rising and beckoning Diana to follow her. Although Diana knew the way to Peter's office, she also knew that no one was allowed to wander unescorted through the maze of offices where staggeringly huge financial transactions took place and rich associates grew richer.

The thick carpet muffled Diana's footsteps. She and the receptionist passed a few glass-enclosed rooms filled with busy-looking people and flickering flat-screen monitors, and finally reached Peter's office. That he had a private office with a window so early in his career reflected his trading and management successes, as well as the simple fact that he was Peter. He got what he wanted. People deferred to him.

His office door was open, and the receptionist gestured that Diana should go in. Peter was seated behind his desk, but he rose as she crossed the threshold. His expression darkened. He clearly wasn't thrilled to see her.

Or maybe his scowl wasn't a response to seeing *her*. It was a response to her attire. "You're wearing jeans," he said.

She took a second to recover. "Yes, I am."

"You look like a slob. Who wears jeans to work? Besides laborers, of course. And slobs."

Oh, for God's sake. "No one at Shomback-Sawyer seemed to mind," she retorted.

"They're probably just happy you're back home, where you belong. As happy as I am," Peter remembered to add. He circled his desk to her side and gave her a polite kiss on the cheek. "You're all done with that Brogan's Point nonsense, I assume. I'd like to put a deposit down on the Newport place—"

"Peter." She eased back a step and took a deep breath. "Brogan's Point is not nonsense. And no, I don't want you to put a deposit down on the Newport Place."

"You really like that inn better? It's pretty, I'll grant you that. But the town, the surrounding environment..."

"Peter." Another deep breath. "We aren't getting married. There or in Newport, or anywhere else."

He frowned, although he looked less angry than incredulous. "Don't be silly."

"I'm not being silly." She dug through her purse until she found the diamond ring, carefully wrapped in a tissue. "I've thought long and hard about this, and I really think we should call off the wedding."

"You haven't thought long or hard about anything. Three days ago, we were discussing menus for the reception."

She conceded silently that three days wasn't very long. But she'd thought hard. More than thought, she'd *felt*. She'd listened to her gut and her heart. She couldn't expect Peter to understand that, and she didn't even try to explain. "I'm sorry, Peter, but…I mean, it's not that I don't love you. We've been friends forever. We've grown up together. But I just don't think we should get married."

"You just don't think at all," he snapped.

A frisson of anger shot up her spine, surprising her. She never got angry. Peter was the angry person in their relationship. She was the peacekeeper, the soother, the calmer of waters.

Not at the moment. "That's a nasty thing to say. I *do* think, and now I'm finally thinking about what's right for me instead of what's right for everyone else. Kind of a first for me, I'll admit."

"Bullshit." The word sounded particularly crude coming from Peter's refined lips. "What's right for you is to marry me, raise a family with me, live a life of ease and grace with me. What's right for you is to fulfill your dreams—"

"*Your* dreams, maybe. My parents' dreams. Not mine. Do you even know what my dreams are?"

"Do *you?*" His voice carried a sneer.

More anger spun through her, fierce and electrifying. She handed him the tissue-wrapped ring and stepped toward the door. "Right now, my dream is to leave this office."

He shocked her by snagging her arm, his fingers closing around her wrist like a manacle. "Don't you dare walk out of this office," he said, his tone now dangerously hushed. "You can't do this to me. To *us.* I love you, Diana. I've always been good to you—and good *for* you. Do *not* walk away from what we have."

His words touched her. Yet whatever affection and need they carried was belied by the painful grip of his hand, and by the fact that he was issuing an edict. She felt less like his equal than like a recalcitrant child about to run into the street, being held back by her father. Peter might be able to convince himself that he was denying her escape in order to save her life. But he couldn't convince her.

"Let go of me," she said, quietly but firmly.

"I don't want you to make the biggest mistake of your life."

"That makes two of us," she said, wriggling her arm until, at last, his fingers relented on her.

She fled through the door, not looking back to see if he was following her. Outside his office, she slowed her pace from a run to a brisk walk so as not to draw attention to herself. She didn't want to humiliate him. He could tell his colleagues that his engagement was off when he was ready to. The last thing either of them needed or wanted was a scene.

She kept walking, sparing a swift nod for the receptionist before she left the office. Not until she'd stepped into the elevator and the door whisked shut did she let out a breath. She was shaking, she realized. Her vision blurred with tears, but through the blur she was able to see the red marks Peter's hand had left on her wrist.

Her purse was shaking, too—or, more accurately, vibrating. She lifted the flap and pulled out her phone. The message light blinked. She tapped the screen and a text from Serena appeared:

Halleluiah!

Through her tears, Diana smiled.

Ten

H e wasn't sure why he decided to head for the beach after work. The day had been warmer than usual, hinting at spring's approach, but by the time he left his cramped office in the community center, the sun had set and the wind blowing off the water was blustery.

He needed that blast of cold. He needed the familiar, sour scent of the ocean filling his lungs. He felt restless, anxious. Like something was about to change.

Not him. He didn't have to change. He was fine.

He parked just off Atlantic Avenue, crossed the street to the retaining wall and stared out at the ocean, nearly black but tipped with lacy whitecaps that remained visible even as the daylight faded away. The salty wind tugged at his hair and filled his lungs. He'd been born into the sound of the surf pounding the shore, and the deep ocean smell. Sometimes he wondered how people who didn't grow up near a coast could stand breathing such bland, odorless inland air.

Maybe that was why he'd driven to the water's edge—for the smell, or for the rhythmic hiss of the waves rolling in to lick the sand, or for the wind. Or for some other reason. *Something* had compelled him to come.

The moment he spotted Diana down on the beach, he knew why he was here.

She sat alone on the sand, wrapped in a coat and scarf, her knees drawn up to her chest and the sea breeze whipping her hair back from her face. He thought about shouting to her, but with the gusts blowing in from the ocean, his voice probably wouldn't reach her. Besides, she seemed absorbed in her own thoughts. If he called to her, he'd startle her.

He should leave her alone. She had said she would call him when she got back from Boston, and she hadn't called. That meant either she wasn't ready to talk to him yet, or she was done with him.

The hell with that second possibility. He wasn't done with her. And if she wasn't ready to talk…he'd just sit quietly beside her, and they wouldn't talk.

He strolled to where the retaining wall ended at the jetty, picked a careful path over the rocks and down to the beach, and walked to her. She was so solitary and still, she might have been a statue. He slowed as he neared her, searching for any indication that she'd sensed his approach. But she was lost in thought, her eyes focused on the dark sky and the darker water.

When he was only a few steps away from her, she turned her head and peered up at him. "Hi," she said. Calmly, quietly, as if she'd been expecting him.

He settled onto the sand next to her. "How was Boston?" he asked.

"Wonderful." She sighed. "Horrible."

Despite the rapidly fading light, he could see that her cheeks were pale and tracked with glistening streaks. She'd been crying. He guessed her trip was more horrible than wonderful. "Are you okay?"

"Yes. I am. Really." She turned back to stare at the water. "I broke up with him."

Her fiancé. Well, that was good for Nick, but maybe not for her.

"I was going to phone you," she said, speaking more to the ocean than to him. "But I didn't want you to see me crying."

He snorted and shook his head. Was she afraid he would think less of her because she was human? Did she think he'd condemn her for having feelings, for mourning the end of something signifi-cant in her life? He looped an arm around her and she rested her head against his shoulder. He could feel more than hear her sobs, faint tremors that rippled through her body.

He had no idea what to say, so he said nothing. He let her weep, let her grieve, let her lean on him.

After a while, the tremors stopped. He wished he was the kind of gentleman who always carried a fresh handkerchief in his pocket so he could hand it to her. He bet her fiancé would have produced a dainty, monogrammed square of linen for her to blow her nose into. "So much for the wonderful part," he joked. "What about the horrible part?"

She managed a choked laugh. "I haven't told my parents yet. They're going to freak out. He'll probably tell them before I have a chance to. He'll probably recruit them to try to change my mind. They adore him."

"That's their problem," Nick said simply.

She flickered a look at him, her eyes clear and wide. "You're right." Then she settled back against his shoulder and sighed again. "He was so angry. I hadn't expected that. I thought he'd be upset, or maybe hurt. But all I saw was anger."

"He was probably trying to cover up the hurt," Nick said, donning his social-worker hat. "Men don't like anyone to see them hurt. It makes them feel vulnerable and weak. So when they're hurt, they sometimes lash out in anger."

She mulled that possibility over, then nodded, her hair sliding against his neck with the motion of her head. "Is that what you do when you're hurt?" she asked.

"I'm never hurt," he said, another joke. "What do you think, I'm one of those weak, vulnerable guys?"

"You're right," she murmured. "About Peter, I mean. He was probably just hurt. I feel so bad. I never wanted to hurt him."

"Only a sociopath wants to hurt others," Nick pointed out. "I don't know how he usually behaves when he's hurt—"

""The situation arises so rarely. People always let him have his own way. I guess I used to let him have his own way, too—until now. I didn't mean to hurt him, though. That wasn't my intention ."

"Of course not."

"He'll get over it," she said, sounding as if she was trying to convince herself. "He's got so much going for him. He's smart, he's handsome, he's rich... Once word gets out that he's available, women will be lining up outside his door."

"You make him sound irresistible." Nick's tone was light, but he felt a twinge of insecurity. What could a guy like him possibly offer a woman like Diana, who'd been engaged to such a smart, handsome, rich man? An occasional lobster dinner? A middle-school b-ball game? Some hot sex? He could certainly offer her that.

"I hope someone does find him irresistible. I want him to be happy."

"How about you? Are you happy?"

"Yes." Again she sounded uncertain. "I'd be happy if I knew he was okay. And if I knew my parents would accept my decision." She shrugged. "Who knows? Maybe they'll be okay with it."

"They don't have much choice," Nick pointed out. "It's your life."

She nestled more deeply into the curve of his arm and returned her focus to the water. The tide was coming in, the moon rising, a bright silver crescent the shape of a smile.

They sat in peaceful silence for a while, listening to the waves, feeling the wind caress them. Eventually, she stirred. "How did you find me? Did you know I'd be here?"

"How could I have known that? I left work and felt like coming down to the beach. I wasn't looking for you." He probably was, subconsciously. He'd been restless, edgy, wondering if he would ever see her again. For all he knew, she could have traveled down to Boston, seen her fiancé, and realized she really did love him, after all. The guy could have gotten appropriately excited about the big purchase she'd pulled off, and he could have swept her into his arms and charmed his way back into her good graces. He could have offered her the use of a monogrammed handkerchief, while he was at it.

A lot could have happened in Boston—wonderful for Diana and horrible, or at least not so wonderful, for Nick. During his turbulent childhood and adolescence, he had always biked to the beach when he needed to decompress. His mode of transportation may have changed since he'd reached adulthood, but the beach was still his destination when he needed to calm down and regain his perspective.

He hadn't realized how much Diana's trip to Boston and her failure to call had agitated him. Thoughts of her had been like a white noise inside his skull all day, barely perceptible but unsettling. So he'd come to the beach—and found her. And the moment he'd spotted her, the white noise had disappeared. More than the beach itself, seeing her had soothed him.

"Well," she said. "Maybe you weren't looking for me, but you found me." She extricated herself from his embrace and turned to face him. "You must be hungry. I think it's my turn to treat you to dinner."

"That's okay."

"No. I mean it. *I'm* hungry. Let's get something to eat. You name the place. I'll pay."

—m—

The place he named was his own house—or, more accurately, a supermarket about a mile away from his place. Diana considered eating in an excellent suggestion. She had stopped at the Ocean Bluff Inn to drop off her suitcase, but she was still dressed in her jeans, which now had grains of sand embedded in the seams despite her having vigorously dusted herself off when they'd left the beach.

She was tired of eating in restaurants, being served, grazing through tasting menus. She hadn't cooked in nearly a week, and while she wasn't the most talented chef in the world, the thought of fixing a simple, home-cooked meal with Nick appealed to her.

Suburban supermarkets were so much more spacious than the neighborhood grocery stores where she did most of her shopping in Boston. She and Nick loaded the cart with chicken, vegetables, a baguette of French bread and, at Nick's insistence, a quart of premium vanilla fudge ice-cream. He assured her he was well stocked with everything else they could possibly need—butter, salad dressing, coffee, spices.

His house was tiny. It contained a small kitchen equipped with twenty-year-old appliances and Formica-topped counters, a slightly larger living room filled with mismatched but comfortable-looking furniture, and a bathroom not much larger than a closet. Despite being ridiculously small, the bathroom was clean. "I've got to buy a new shower curtain," he mumbled when he showed her the room, but she couldn't see anything terribly wrong with the shower curtain hanging from the rod.

He was a bachelor, and she doubted he was earning a six-figure salary as a social worker running programs for Brogan's Point's children. The house might be modest, but it suited him. She couldn't imagine him living in an elegant apartment like Peter's. Nick's eclectic furnishings, the tidy stacks of books and the recently vacuumed carpet covering the living room floor indicated that he took pride in his home. On the living room walls, he'd hung a few seascape paintings. Not masterworks, nothing Diana would have encountered in her art history classes at college, but they were pretty.

"All right," she said once they'd returned to the kitchen and unloaded the groceries. "Go do something. I'll give a holler when dinner is ready."

"Forget that. I'll help."

"If you help, I'm not treating you to dinner."

"If I don't help, you won't know where to find the pots and pans."

She surveyed his kitchen. There weren't too many places to hide pots and pans—some cabinets above the counter, some below. She'd bet the pots and pans were below. She swung open a cabinet door and found exactly what she was looking for—a roasting pan. She pulled it out and gave Nick a triumphant smile.

Still, even if she didn't need his help, she liked having his company in the cozy little kitchen. They worked side by side, seasoning the chicken, scrubbing the carrots and potatoes and broccoli, arranging everything in the roasting pan and shaking assorted spices over the whole thing. Once that was in the oven, she prepared a salad while he disappeared down a flight of stairs to the basement. He returned a minute later holding a bottle of red wine. "I don't have any white, so I hope this will work."

"I like red," she said, and once he'd opened the bottle, she slid the roasting pan out of the oven and added a splash of wine to the chicken.

They didn't talk much while they prepared the meal. Diana was aware of Nick watching her—not in an uncomfortable way, but more to observe what she was doing. "How much garlic powder did you put in there?" he asked. "You didn't measure it."

"I cook by feel," Diana told him. "My parents had a maid when I was growing up. She did a lot of the cooking. I used to help her. She never measured anything, but everything always tasted great."

"I don't measure much when I cook, either," he admitted, "but that's because I don't cook anything that needs to be measured. Spaghetti—you fill a pot with water and toss in a handful of pasta. You open a jar of sauce and pour some on top. No measurements necessary."

Diana made a face. "Homemade sauce is so easy," she told him. "You shouldn't be using stuff from a jar."

"Yeah. My mother—" He abruptly stopped.

"Your mother...?"

"Would say the same thing," he concluded. "Fiore. I'm Italian. I ought to know how to make sauce. Gravy, she calls it."

"Your mother never taught you?"

"I didn't want to learn," he said laconically.

Diana suspected there was more to his story than simply his not wanting to learn. She opted for tact, however, and busied herself wrapping the baguette in foil to heat in the oven.

But as she finished the dinner preparations, as Nick set the small butcher-block table beneath the window with carefully folded paper napkins and mismatched silverware, as she tossed the salad and he pulled two wine glasses from one of the cabinets, a thought tugged at her brain: *you know nothing about this man.*

True, she knew some things. But she didn't know about his mother. More important, she didn't know why his eyes darkened with shadows when he mentioned her, why an emotional shutter seemed to slam shut inside him, barring further inquiry about the woman who'd raised him.

If he were Peter, Diana would respect that locked shutter. She wouldn't press, wouldn't probe. Experience had taught her not to push him into places he didn't want to go. When she did, he became cranky and mean. She had learned that it was wisest to leave certain things unspoken with him, certain questions unasked.

But she was no longer Peter's fiancée. Perhaps one reason she'd left him was that she'd finally come to realize that having to exercise so much caution around him would make for a dreary, exhausting marriage. If she was ever going to get married, it ought to be to someone with whom she could discuss anything, without hesitation or fear.

Nick Fiore and marriage did not belong in the same sentence in her mind. But she was eating dinner at his house. She'd kissed him. She wanted to kiss him again. She wanted to do much more than kiss him. She ought to be able to ask him anything. No holding back. No censoring herself.

She waited until they were seated at the table, they'd sipped their wine, and he'd tasted the chicken and pronounced it delicious. Then she took a deep breath, as if about to dive off a high board into a very small pool, and said, "So, you've got a lousy relationship with your mother?"

His eyes flashed, and then he surprised her by laughing. "You could say that."

"I just did." She laughed, too, relieved that he hadn't blown up at her. "Where does she live?"

"Here."

"Here?" Diana gazed around the kitchen, half expecting to see evidence that Nick's mother resided in this house.

"In Brogan's Point," he clarified.

"So, you grew up right here in town?"

"I did."

"And never left?"

"I went to UMass for college and grad school, but other than that…"

Diana shouldn't have found that fact so amazing. She'd lived her entire life in the greater Boston area, except for a semester of college in Barcelona. She'd traveled to London twice to visit Serena, toured parts of Europe with friends, spent an idyllic week in Cozumel, but as far as actually *living* somewhere, Boston and Brookline were her home.

But Boston was a world-class city, filled with theaters, museums, parks, universities, four-star hotels, boutiques, gourmet shops, and residents speaking dozens of languages. Brogan's Point was a sleepy little Cape Ann hamlet. Could a person actually live his entire life here without growing bored?

Evidently, yes. Nick had lived his life here, and he didn't seem the least bit bored.

"Does your father live in Brogan's Point, too?"

She sensed the shutter slamming shut once more. "No."

Don't hold back, she ordered herself. "Your parents are divorced?"

"He's gone," Nick said tersely.

"Dead? I'm sorry."

"I…" Nick drank some wine as he sorted his thoughts. "I don't know if he's dead. He left town years ago. I don't even know if my parents are legally divorced. I just know he's gone."

"Really?" How could he not know if his parents were still married? How could he not be curious enough to find out?

"It is what it is," Nick said. "My father is out of my life. That's all."

That certainly wasn't all. But Diana decided to do him the kindness of dropping the subject for now. The fact that he'd told her as much as he had—even if it wasn't much—and hadn't lost his temper or accused her of unforgivable nosiness was a victory in itself. She'd touched some sore spots, and he didn't seem to hate her.

That alone made her want to kiss him—and more.

They spent the rest of the meal talking about safe subjects. He told her about coordinating the town's summer programs for teenagers who were too young to get full-time jobs but not too young to get into trouble if they wound up with free time on their hands and nothing productive to fill that time with. She told him about her meeting earlier that day with James Sawyer, and about her task for tomorrow: making sure the estate she'd liquidated was carefully packed and trucked to the warehouse space Shomback-Sawyer had reserved for it.

She and Nick lingered at the table until the wine was gone, then cleaned up together, side by side, occasionally bumping shoulders or elbows and laughing. Nick didn't have a dishwasher, but he had soap, a sponge and a towel, and it didn't take long for them to get the dishes washed and stacked in the rack to dry.

"Some ice-cream?" Nick offered.

Diana patted her tummy. "I'm stuffed."

"There's always room for dessert."

She grinned and shook her head. "You tried to get me to eat too much toast that morning at Riley's, too. I think you're trying to fatten me up."

"No," he said. He was smiling, but his gaze was serious. "You're perfect, just the way you are."

He'd probably intended his words as a simple compliment, nothing more. But they resonated inside her. No one had ever told her she was perfect, with good reason. She was far from perfect. Yet when she tried to recall the last time Peter had told her she looked great, or her parents had told her they were proud of her, she couldn't think of a single instance. She worked so hard to please everyone, yet no one ever seemed quite satisfied with her.

Except James Sawyer.

And Nick.

She was no longer going to knock herself out in the hope that the people who were supposed to love her actually did love her. If they did, they ought to love her for who she was, not for her willingness to please them.

101

She'd heard the song. It had persuaded her to change not just her relationship status but her attitude. Her world view was changing. Her determination. Her...what was James's word? *Confidence.*

"I'm not perfect," she told Nick now. But she said it with a smile, with the self-assurance that he wouldn't try to locate her imperfections and criticize her for them. One advantage of not knowing Nick that well was that, if he *did* decide to harp on her flaws and weaknesses, she could walk away. They had no relationship. She was free. She didn't have to please anyone but herself.

Nick tossed the dish towel onto the counter and placed his hands on her shoulders. "You're close enough," he said. Was he talking about how close she was to perfection? Or how close she was to him? An arm's length away was dangerously close.

Less than an arm's length. He stepped toward her, molded his fingers to the curves of her shoulders, bowed his head, and kissed her.

Close enough, she thought as her mouth softened beneath his, as her body nestled against his, as she sank into the warmth of his kiss. She no longer had to feel guilty kissing him. She had ended things with Peter. She was unbetrothed, unattached, *free.*

Free to return Nick's kiss. Free to part her lips and welcome the invasion of his tongue. Free to wrap her arms around him, to feel the sleek muscles of his back through the fabric of his shirt.

His tongue stroked hers, at first gently and then more hungrily. This kiss tasted better than any ice-cream Diana had ever eaten. Nick Fiore was the most delicious dessert she'd ever had.

He wrapped one arm around her waist as he had the last time they'd kissed. She loved the way that made her feel, petite and possessed. He ran his other hand up her side, under her arm, forward just enough for his thumb to brush the side of her breast. She shuddered.

Maybe she wasn't free. She felt like a captive, imprisoned not by his embrace but by the lush sensations he awakened inside her. She never wanted to escape. She just wanted to keep kissing and kissing and kissing him.

No, not true. She wanted much, much more than his kisses.

"Make love to me," she murmured, surprising herself. She had changed, all right. The old Diana would never have been so bold.

His breath hitched. He pulled back just far enough to peer down into her face. "Are you sure?"

She nodded. She'd said the words once. She wasn't sure she had enough courage to say them again.

Apparently, once was enough. He bowed and brushed her forehead with a light kiss. Then he lifted his hands to her head, digging his fingers deep into her hair on either side of her face and tilting her to receive another, deeper kiss from him. "Okay," he whispered.

Eleven

He led her to his bedroom. It was, like the rest of his house, small but relatively tidy. Most of the room was taken up by his bed, which was flanked by small maple night tables. A tall chest of drawers stood in one corner. Two framed photos of what appeared to be waves crashing against a shoreline of harsh stone formations—Maine or Nova Scotia, Diana would guess—hung on the wall. A pair of sneakers lay near the closet door and a paperback edition of a John Grisham novel sat next to the lamp on one of the night tables, a scrap of paper serving as a bookmark. Diana crossed to the table and lifted the book to read its back cover copy. "Is it any good?"

"I like courtroom dramas," Nick said. "I'm afraid to get an e-reader. If I had one, I'd probably buy every legal thriller ever written."

She smiled. "If you had an e-reader, I wouldn't have known what you were reading." Every little bit of information she gleaned about Nick was precious. His taste in reading. His lack of discipline when it came to buying books. She could relate to that. She had several hundred books downloaded to her e-reader. It was simply too easy to click the buy button.

Tonight neither she nor Nick would be reading. She lowered the book and shifted her gaze to the bed. It was neatly made, if not quite up to the standards of the Ocean Bluff Inn's housekeeping staff. The sheets were a dark red, the color of the wine they'd consumed with dinner. The blanket was tan with red and blue lines crisscrossing it.

She would be lying on that blanket soon, on those pillows, having sex with someone who wasn't Peter for the first time in her life. Was she out of her mind?

If she was, she didn't care.

She turned to Nick, reaching for him as he reached for her. Together they tumbled onto the soft, plush blanket, lying on their sides facing each other, their heads cushioned by the down pillows, their legs intertwined. Nick kissed her again. He kissed her lower lip, the corners of her mouth, the tip of her nose. He nuzzled her throat, nipped her ear. If Peter had been such an effective kisser, maybe Diana wouldn't have left him.

No. Even if his kisses could arouse her the way Nick's did, she would have left him. Even if he touched her the way Nick was touching her, his hands simultaneously gentle and firm, his fingertips grazing her as if he needed to memorize every curve and contour of her body, every rise and hollow, caressing her wrist as if it were as important as her breast, stroking the nape of her neck as if it was as significant as the flare of her hips…She still would have left Peter. She still would have wanted to share this moment, this experience, with no one but Nick.

She touched him as he touched her, gliding her hands along his shoulders, across his ribs, to the buttons of his shirt. Before she could release one button, he was there, flicking the buttons open with impressive speed. He shrugged out of the shirt, tossed it over the side of the bed and then settled back down beside her.

She had expected him to remove her shirt, too, and the rest of her clothing, while he was at it. But he simply continued to caress her through her sweater and her jeans, as if he wanted to give her time to accept where they were heading, and a chance to bring everything to a halt if she chose.

She didn't need time. She'd made her choice. Pushing herself to sit, she gripped the ribbed edge of her sweater and lifted it up, over her head. Her hair fell around her face in disarray, and Nick tenderly brushed it back.

This isn't a relationship, she reminded herself. *Don't fall in love.* But the gentleness of his touch, his thoughtfulness and his sensitivity about any misgivings she might have made it hard for her not to think of love when she thought of Nick. She didn't know him that well, but what she knew…oh, yes. She could love him.

Now that she'd removed her sweater, Nick clearly felt he could remove everything else. He reached behind her to flick the clasp of her bra, then stripped off her slacks and panties in one efficient sweep. His jeans went the way of his shirt, sailing over the edge of the bed, and then they were both naked.

He was all muscle and sinew, all strength and grace. His body was so different from Peter's. Peter kept fit, but his muscles were toned by a personal trainer at an expensive fitness center. Nick looked like someone who had earned his muscles through hard work. He looked like someone who could fight if he had to, and who would win. His biceps, while not bulging, were rock-hard. His chest and abdomen were taut. His legs were a runner's; as a jogger herself, Diana appreciated the definition of the lean muscles in his calves and thighs. She pictured Nick racing up and down a basketball court, shouting encouragement to his kids. She pictured him swimming in the ocean. She pictured him lifting things, building things, fixing things.

She didn't have to picture him easing her onto her back, because that was what he doing. His muscles weren't the only part of him that was rock-hard. He was fully aroused, and when she stroked his erection he groaned, pulled her hand away and kissed her palm. "I'm already there," he murmured, easing down her body so he could kiss her breasts, her belly, the dampness between her legs.

Her body lurched as his tongue slid over her. Peter had never done this to her, and oh…It felt so good. So indescribably good.

She shuddered, too close to coming. "Stop, Nick, stop…"

He lifted his head. "Much better than vanilla fudge," he said, making her laugh, helping her to relax. "You okay?"

"I'm okay."

He reached across the bed, tugged open a night table drawer, and pulled out a condom. "You still okay?" he asked as he tore open the envelope.

"I'm fine."

"Let's see if we can improve on that." He settled between her legs, his knees nudging her thighs apart, and eased into her. Slow and firm, the heat of him melting her, bathing her, permeating her.

Overwhelming her.

She exploded with his first thrust. Her body throbbed, clung, wrung itself out in pulses so sweet they hurt. She heard herself moan, felt her legs tighten around his hips, lost herself in sensation. He continued to thrust, harder and deeper, stroking her until her body convulsed again, even more powerfully. This time he was with her, gasping, groaning, pulsing his heat into her.

Minutes might have passed. Hours, for all she knew. Days. Eons. Time no longer had meaning. All that mattered was now, this bed, this man. All that mattered was the freedom to love Nick Fiore.

It's not love, she told herself. But her heart wasn't listening.

Twelve

H e was still awake at midnight.

Diana slept like the dead. Considering the workout he'd given her, he supposed he shouldn't be surprised. They'd made love twice. They'd taken a shower together. He'd donned a pair of sweat pants and lent her an old T-shirt, and they'd split the container of ice-cream. Then they'd made love again.

Man, he could become addicted to her. Not just because she was beautiful, not just because her body fit so perfectly to his, not because her skin was peach soft, and the curves of her breasts matched the curves of his palms, and she was so hot and wet, and when she came she made a sound deep in her throat, and when he came inside her, he felt as if he was dying and being reborn all at once...but because of her smile, and her velvety voice, and her energy. Because she was one hell of a woman.

She had told him she needed to be awake by seven. She had a big day ahead, that estate deal she'd negotiated and had to oversee. Not a problem; he was usually awake before seven, anyway.

The way things were going, though, he might be awake at seven because he would never fall asleep between now and then. His brain was in overdrive. His brain, his nervous system...His conscience.

The local women he'd had relationships with knew who he was and where he'd been. He'd never had to sit them down and tell them the sordid details of his past. But Diana knew none of that. He should have told her.

How could he? She'd been so open, so eager. So ready to rock and roll. And he'd wanted her the way a thirsty man wants water, the way a drowning man wants air. He'd wanted her from the moment he'd seen her at the Faulk Street Tavern and that song from the jukebox had snared them in its web. Was he supposed to stop everything and say, "Before we get it on, let me tell you about my criminal record."

Yes. That was exactly what he was supposed to do.

And he didn't do it.

He glanced at the clock on his night table. Midnight. He wanted to call Ed Nolan, but if he did, he'd either wake the poor guy up or interrupt whatever he might be doing with Gus. Besides, he already knew what Ed would say: *You should have told her.*

Tomorrow. When they woke up. First thing. He'd come clean.

Which left the rest of tonight. Maybe, if he wrapped himself around her, and embraced her beautiful body, and nuzzled his face into her thick, silky hair, he'd be able to fall sleep.

Fat chance. Just thinking about that caused his dick to perk right up.

Maybe he didn't have to tell her. After all, this wasn't the romance of the century. They were hot for each other—hot like one of those thousand-acre forest fires they were always experiencing out west—but it wasn't as if he and Diana were heading toward 'til-death-do-us-part vows. In a day, or two, or maybe a week, she would return to her life in Boston. She'd stop slumming with a working-class kid from Brogan's Point and go back home to her antiques and her tailored wardrobe and her blue-blood friends. This was a vacation for her. A few days away from it all, spending time in a luxurious inn overlooking the water and enjoying some crazy-hot sex with a local. Nobody was saying anything about a permanent commitment.

He wasn't going to ask her to marry him. He couldn't afford the sort of diamond ring she was used to. He couldn't afford *her.* They would have some fun, they'd screw their heads off, and then they would say goodbye. Why drag the ugly truth into it?

What she didn't know wouldn't hurt her. Why not let her believe Nick was a noble, upstanding citizen with an unblemished past? Why disillusion her?

He settled deeper into the pillow, slung one arm around her narrow waist and drew her back against him. The position didn't do much to ease his aroused state, but somehow, he managed to drift off to sleep.

—⁊⁊⁊—

They went to Riley's for breakfast. Rita spotted them as they entered the place, arched an eyebrow at the sight of Diana pressed close to Nick's side as they waded into the usual breakfast crowd lining up along the counter and swarming near the cashier, and pointed toward the rear of the eatery. With his hand at the small of her back, Nick guided Diana through the throng until he spotted the empty table Rita had indicated.

"It pays to have a friend on the staff," Diana said as she slid onto the banquette facing Nick. "Weren't all those people waiting for tables?

"Some of them," Nick conceded. "Rita looks out for me."

"I think she has a crush on you," Diana said. Her voice had a teasing lilt to it, but her cheeks darkened to a slightly deeper pink.

"Yeah, right." He shook his head. "Not a chance. She knows me too well." Just speaking those words reminded him of what Diana didn't know. *Tell her,* the angel on his left shoulder whispered. *Leave it alone,* the devil on his right argued.

Rita arrived at their table with a decanter of steaming coffee in one hand, two mugs in the other, and two laminated menus wedged between her elbow and her ribs. She set the two mugs down, filled them with coffee without waiting to be asked, and handed Nick and Diana the menus. "The blueberry pancakes look really good today," she said before sauntering away.

"Blueberry pancakes." Diana's eyes widened. "I can't remember the last time I had pancakes."

"Then order them."

"It'll be too much. I'm not used to eating a big breakfast—especially when I didn't jog."

"You can jog later," Nick suggested. He signaled Rita, who hurried back to their table. "Two orders of the blueberry pancakes," he said. "You sold us. Orange juice?" he asked Diana.

"Can I get a small one?"

"Two small OJ's," Nick requested, taking Diana's menu from her and handing it and his own to Rita. As soon as Rita waltzed away, the angel on his left shoulder started nagging him again. *Tell her.*

"The last time I had pancakes was over a year ago, at the bridal shower for one of my friends at the Harvard Club," she said. Her face was bright, her voice bubbly. "They had a buffet, and I made a pig of myself. But, you know, it was a party…" She went on, describing the buffet, describing the décor, describing the gifts her friend had gotten.

The Harvard Club, the devil on his right shoulder whispered. Diana was way out of Nick's league. Why bare his soul to her? She'd be returning to her friends and her Harvard Club parties before long.

So it went over breakfast, as they feasted on what, Diana admitted, were tastier pancakes than the one she'd consumed at the Harvard Club. She told Nick about what the rest of her day would be like—getting to the house ahead of the movers, sorting the goods into valuable stuff and probable junk, overseeing the packing of the valuable stuff, making sure everything wound up on the truck, handing over a check. Tomorrow she would head to the warehouse, where she'd meet an appraiser and start working through the inventory, once again sorting items. The pieces with no value would be donated to appropriate charities. The pieces with modest value would be priced and sold as quickly as possible. The truly valuable pieces would be inspected and sent to restorers, if necessary. Once those pieces were in pristine condition, they would be photographed for Shomback-Sawyer's catalog, posted on the firm's website, and possibly included in an auction.

The process, as she described it sounded interesting. Too interesting for him to interrupt her and launch into a speech about his criminal past.

"I'm talking too much," she admitted sheepishly, then used her fork and knife to lift half a pancake from her plate and deposit it on his, as if they'd been sharing breakfasts for years. "What's on tap for you today?"

"The usual," he said. "I've got to prepare a funding report for the town's budget committee. I have a meeting with one of the nurses at the high school. They've got a couple of pregnant girls enrolled, and we're monitoring things closely to make sure the girls stay in school. The girls don't want to meet with me personally, but I'm coordinating things with the state's Department of Health and Human Services. We want to make sure the girls have every support they need to stay in school."

Diana sighed. "What you do is so important! I feel so petty. Who needs an antique gramophone? Those girls are fighting for their future."

Nick snorted and shook his head. "Yeah, I'm such a saint." *Tell her.*

"After last night, I know you're no saint," she teased, her cheeks flushing with color again. He loved the way she could hit him with a bawdy joke, even if she embarrassed herself way more than him.

They finished their breakfast, Nick polishing off the chunk of pancake Diana had passed along to him, and he handed his travel mug to Rita for a fill-up. Diana took out her credit card, but Nick brushed it away and replaced it with his own. If he wasn't going to come clean with her, the least he could do was pay the bill.

It wasn't enough. He *should* come clean. But being with her, bantering with her, gazing into her sparkling hazel eyes and remembering the lush warmth of her body as he'd made love to her...He wasn't ready to end things yet. And telling her the truth would end things. He knew it would.

He'd let this adventure play out a little longer. He'd keep his mouth shut, and then she'd go home, and she'd never have to know.

—⚏—

The moment Nick Fiore entered the Faulk Street Tavern, Gus could tell that he was a changed man. That song had exerted its magic over him, after all.

She couldn't say he looked better. Or, for that matter, worse. He just looked...*changed.*

At two in the afternoon, Carl Stanton was in his usual seat at one end of the bar, drinking coffee—on the house. Gus refused to sell him any drink with liquor in it, but she wasn't going to make him pay for a drink he didn't really want. He was sad, sulking, angry with her for denying him the whisky he'd ordered, angry with his wife for refusing to let him keep any whisky in the house. At least he was smart enough not to keep a bottle in his car. If Gus ever found out Carl was doing something as stupid as drinking while driving, she'd have Ed all over him before he could beep his horn.

Manny was mopping the dance floor. He put a lot of muscle into it—and he was endowed with a considerable amount of muscle—but the floor would be sticky again by nine that night. Gus wasn't sure why. It wasn't as if people were deliberately splashing their drinks as they walked around.

She was slicing lemons and limes as Nick crossed the room to her. "What can I get you?" she asked as he settled onto a stool.

"A ginger ale, if you've got it."

She smiled, reached into the fridge below the bar and pulled out a can. "What else? You look like you need more than a soda."

"I need Ed," he admitted. "Is he around?"

She shook her head. "There was a fire down on Crawford Road, that old farm stand. Nobody hurt, but it looks like arson. Ed's over there with the fire chief."

Nick's eyebrows flicked upward. "Rossetti's? That place has been empty for years."

"It's been up for sale for years. No takers. I think someone decided to get rid of it the easy way, maybe collect some insurance money."

"Well." Nick sipped his soda. "At least no one got hurt."

"That's an advantage of setting empty structures on fire," Gus noted. She lifted her knife and resumed slicing a lemon, shaping neat, thin wedges. "Anything I can help you with?"

Nick shook his head.

Gus waited patiently. Patience was one of the most important traits a bartender could possess. People came into her establishment to drink, to party, to have a good time—but they also came because they were looking for something. Often what they were looking for was a sympathetic ear. You just had to wait them out.

After a long, thoughtful silence, Nick asked, "Why can't we ever escape our pasts?"

"Why can't we escape our noses? They're a part of us."

"You can get a nose job."

"Hmm. Well, I don't think medical science has come up with some sort of surgery to alter our pasts."

"You can delete data on a computer."

"But it's still there. Ed tells me the forensics guys can dig out all kinds of evidence people thought they deleted. Porn sites. Emails to lovers. All kinds of stuff. You think you've erased it, but it's still there if a person looks for it."

"How about if a person doesn't look for it?"

She added the slices of lemon to a bowl and shrugged. "It's still there."

He nodded and drank some more soda. "I've got to tell Diana, don't I."

Gus recalled the pretty, doe-eyed woman who'd offered to buy the jukebox a couple of days ago—the pretty, doe-eyed woman who'd gotten caught up in "Changes" along with Nick. "I thought she was wearing an engagement ring," Gus said.

"Not anymore. She broke off the engagement."

"She changed, huh."

Nick flashed a dark look at Gus. "All right. Let's assume I wanted to change, too. Why can't I change the part of me from my past that I don't like?"

"You know what, Nick?" Gus set down her knife. "That part from your past isn't so bad. I mean, sure, it's bad, but it happened. It's over. You got screwed, but you overcame it."

"Some people don't think I got screwed."

"I do. Ed does." She reached for a lime. "The folks who don't think you got screwed aren't worth worrying about." She sliced. "Is Diana worth worrying about?"

"Yeah." The word slipped out and Nick winced, as if he hadn't wanted to admit that.

"Tell her," Gus said. "If it scares her away, then she's not worth it. If she's worth it, she won't be scared away."

Nick sighed. He nodded. He drained his glass, stood, and slapped a couple of dollars onto the bar. "You're a goddess, Gus," he said as he stood. "I don't know how Ed ever managed to snag you."

"He got lucky," Gus deadpanned.

Nick laughed a little forlornly, turned and strode across the room to the door. Gus watched him leave. He had it bad, she thought. One song, and he was a goner.

She hoped he would be as lucky as Ed.

Thirteen

By the time Diana headed back to the Ocean Bluff Inn, most of the day was gone, and she was rumpled and covered with dust. Even though the movers did the heavy lifting, her back ached from hand-wrapping so many delicate items and arranging them inside cartons and crates. Her hair looked like a skein of yarn after a litter of kittens had played in it, and her shirt was smudged with dirt.

She couldn't remember ever being this happy.

She'd scored a major professional coup. And she'd be seeing Nick tonight. Life didn't get any better.

Which meant, of course, that life could get worse. She was stripped down to her underwear, ready to climb into the porcelain claw-foot tub in the bathroom attached to her room, when her cell phone rang. She lifted it, read the caller's name on the screen, and grimaced. Taking a deep breath to steel herself, she thumbed the connect icon. "Hello, Mom."

"Diana. Good grief, what is going on?"

"I'm fine, thank you," Diana said as smoothly as she could. "How are you?"

"I'm in shock. Peter contacted us yesterday and told us you gave him back his ring. What is the problem? Did you want a different stone? A different setting?"

Diana shook her head to clear it. What planet was her mother calling from? "Mom. I gave him back the ring because I broke up with him. The engagement is off."

"No!" Her mother sounded so shocked, it occurred to Diana that Peter hadn't told her parents the truth. Apparently, he'd told them she'd returned his ring, but not why. "How can that be?"

It further occurred to Diana that her mother was so fixated on Diana's marriage to Peter—and had been so attached to the idea practically since the day Diana was born—that the notion of this marriage not happening struck her as preposterous, beyond the realm of the believable.

Everyone wanted Diana and Peter to marry. Everyone expected it. How could Diana dare to thwart destiny?

"I'm sorry, Mom. I wanted to give the reality a chance to sink in before I told you and Dad. But...I realized I wasn't happy with Peter. I don't think I could ever be happy with him."

"Of course you can be happy with him. He's a good man, Diana. And from such a good family."

"And he'll make some other woman a good husband," Diana said. "His family is great. This has nothing to do with his family. It has to do with the fact that when I'm with him, I knock myself out trying to please him. I'm always giving in to his wishes, always worrying about whether he's happy—and when he isn't, I'm worrying about what I should do to make him happy."

"That's what marriage is all about," her mother said. "Making each other happy."

"*He* doesn't make *me* happy," Diana countered. "And honestly, I don't know if I make him happy, either. I try so damned hard. I shouldn't have to try that hard."

"A successful marriage takes work," her mother said.

A successful marriage also took balance. It took *both* partners working at it.

And it took great sex, she thought, a flush of heat surging through her body as she remembered the night she'd spent in Nick's bed.

"Mom, you'll just have to trust me on this. I'm doing what's right for myself."

"For yourself," her mother said scornfully. "Apparently, what's right for everyone else is irrelevant to you."

Diana flinched. Did her mother really believe that Diana's happiness wasn't as important as her own? Or Peter's? Or Peter's parents'? "It's my life," Diana said, doing her best to filter her rage out of her tone. And wasn't that typical of her? Once again, she was more worried about upsetting her mother than her mother was about upsetting her. She sighed and said, "I've got to go." If she prolonged the conversation, her words would be like lighter fluid on hot coals. Flames would erupt. The conversation would turn into an conflagration. "I'm about to take a bath. I'll call you tomorrow."

"Good idea," her mother said, and for a hopeful moment, Diana believed her mother was as eager as she was to step back from the flames and let the embers cool. "I'm sure once you sleep on it, you'll realize that you and Peter are perfect for each other. We'll get this marriage back on track."

We? Diana shook her head. *No, Mom. We will not.* Diana's marriage was not a group project. It was not a committee decision. It was *her life.*

"I've changed," she blurted out, realizing as soon as she spoke that her mother would have no idea what Diana was talking about. How could she explain about the jukebox, the song, her newfound confidence, her professional accomplishment? How could she explain about Nick? "I'd better go," she said more quietly. "And I'm sorry, but I'm not marrying Peter."

She was still fuming when she stripped off her bra and panties and sank into the steaming water that filled the tub. Why had she said she was sorry? Why did she have to apologize for making her own decisions and determining her own future?

She'd changed, but she had more changing to do. Each change led to another change. Two days ago, she'd become more self-assured in her work. Yesterday she'd become more assertive about her personal life. Last night...

Last night she'd made love to someone who wasn't Peter. And it had been glorious.

For the first time since she'd heard her mother's voice emerging through her cell phone, she smiled.

—◊—

"So, how did the move go?" Nick asked.

They were seated in an elegant dining room at the inn, its glass walls offering a generous view of the ocean. The sky above it was a spread of colors, pink and purple, a few blue-gray clouds rippling across it like the swirls of fudge in the ice-cream he and Diana had devoured last night.

No eating ice-cream out of a waxed-cardboard tub in this place, he thought. The tables were draped with linen; the silverware was sterling silver and weighed heavily in his hands. He'd traded his jeans for a pair of tailored slacks. His legs were used to denim, but this was where Diana had wanted to eat dinner.

She'd insisted on paying, too. "I'm exorcising a demon," she'd said. When he'd argued that that wasn't much of an explanation, she'd elaborated. "I came here with Peter to see if we wanted to book our wedding here. And I came to realize I didn't want to book a wedding with him, here or anywhere else. I just want to eat here like a normal person, not trying out the caterer's tasting menu and bickering with him over whether the crab puffs are better here or at some other place we also looked at."

"Does that mean we should order the crab puffs or avoid them?" Nick asked.

Diana laughed. "Order whatever you want. We're celebrating."

Cheerful though she was, he sensed an undercurrent of…not quite tension in her, but something. Something gray, something down. "What are we celebrating?" he asked. Personally, he wouldn't mind celebrating the hot sex they'd enjoyed last night—and the promise of more hot sex tonight, if she was willing. But he suspected she had something else in mind.

"The big move today went perfectly," she told him. "Nothing broke. Nothing was lost. Everything fit into the one truck, and it's all in the warehouse now. My first major deal!"

That was worthy of clinking his wine glass to hers. She'd ordered a bottle of some fancy red with a French name, and it tasted great.

He just had to remember to be careful with the delicate glass. Pick it up the wrong way, and the thin stem might snap in two. He was used to handling basketballs, not crystal goblets.

The waiter came to take their orders. Just to be safe, Nick skipped the crab puffs—they sounded too fussy for his tastes, anyway—and ordered a steak. Diana requested something a lot more elaborate, involving shrimp, asparagus and assorted other ingredients that were listed on the menu in elegant gold script.

Once the waiter was gone, Nick gazed at her. A candle enclosed in glass sat at the center of the table, flickering amber light over her face. She'd worn a lacy white blouse and a dark skirt, and one of the several thoughts circulating through his mind was that he'd love to tear both the blouse and the skirt off her and do the naked tango with her, right here, on the plush carpet, with that panoramic view of the ocean beyond the glass wall.

Another thought was that he still sensed a shadow of something in her eyes, an emotion that didn't have anything to do with celebrating. Asking was probably a big mistake, but he asked anyway. "What went wrong?"

She'd lifted her glass to drink—and the graceful goblet seemed to fit her hand a lot better than his. His question made her pause, the glass inches from her lips. She looked perplexed. "What do you mean, what went wrong?"

"Sure, the liquidation went smoothly. Your first big score and all that. But...I don't know. You don't seem as happy as you should be."

The smile that curved her mouth was sweet and sad and almost helpless. "I had a difficult conversation with my mother, that's all."

Nick smiled, too, suspecting his smile was just as helpless. "Mothers," he muttered. "What did she say?"

Diana sipped her wine, lowered her glass and sighed. "She found out that I'd ended things with Peter. I was going to tell her—in person. And really, it should have been up to me to tell her. But Peter told her, instead. She's furious."

He imagined her mother would be even more furious if she knew Diana had broken her engagement because she'd heard a song at the Faulk Street Tavern. And more furious yet if she knew Diana had spent last night in Nick's bed. "Any particular reason she's upset, or just in general?"

"Both, I think." Another sad little smile. "My parents love Peter. Maybe more than they love me."

"I doubt that."

She dismissed his words with a wave of her hand. "They've been dreaming of this wedding since Peter and I were in diapers. Peter's parents are their best friends. Peter and I grew up together. It was all so perfect. He was everything they could hope for in a son-in-law. The right blood lines, the right schools, the right income."

"Maybe they thought he'd make you happy."

"Who knows?" She took another sip of wine, then leaned back as the waiter appeared with their salads. "I don't think my happiness was particularly high on their list of concerns. When I said I wouldn't be happy with Peter, my mother seemed to think that was irrelevant. She acted as if I was selfish for not going through with the marriage. I was letting everyone down."

"That's their problem, not yours," Nick said.

"They'll make it my problem," she muttered, looking disconsolate. "My sister had to move all the way to England to avoid their manipulations. I always tried to compensate for that, to be the best possible daughter. If I married Peter, I'd still qualify for that title. But that's not a good reason to get married."

Nick nodded his agreement.

"I want to be my own person," she said. "For once in my life, I don't want to have to worry about making everyone else happy."

"You won't get any argument from me." Of course, he hoped she'd make him happy later tonight, when he finally got to strip off her blouse and skirt. But he'd make her at least as happy.

"Mothers," she said glumly, echoing his earlier plaint. "If I ever have children, remind me not to meddle in their lives."

As if Nick would be available to issue that reminder when she became a mother. But he played along. "I'll remind you."

"Your mother can't be as bad as mine," she said.

He caught himself before swearing. "She's worse."

"Does she meddle in your life?"

Tell her. The nagging voice of conscience resonated in his head. The little angel on his shoulder. The voice of Gus, dispensing words of wisdom while she stood behind the bar at the Faulk Street Tavern, slicing lemons.

He picked up the steak knife the waiter had brought for him, hefted its wooden handle, set it down. He gazed out at the water. He tried to find the courage to come clean. "I'm not...I'm not the guy you think I am," he finally managed.

Diana peered intently at him. Her eyebrows dipped slightly above the bridge of her nose. "What guy do I think you are?"

He shrugged. "A social worker. A do-gooder. Someone who runs programs for kids."

"And you're not that?"

"I am." Deep breath. *Tell her.* "I did time in the juvenile justice system."

"Okay," she said slowly, and her brows straightened, her frown fading. He watched her watching him. She didn't look pleased, but she didn't look horrified, either. He wondered how many people with criminal records traveled in her circle.

"That's it? *Okay?*"

"If you were a juvenile...well, lots of kids screw up when they're young. Then they grow up and put their past behind them."

Nick had grown up. At times he felt he'd skipped right past grown-up to old. But he doubted he could ever put his past behind him.

Tell her.

"I was convicted of attempted murder," he said.

Fourteen

Diana dropped her fork. It clattered against the edge of her salad plate and fell to the thick carpet with a muted thud. In a matter of seconds, the waiter had scooped the fork off the floor and set a clean replacement to the left of her salad plate.

As if the pretty plate of arugula, endive, grape tomatoes and balsamic vinaigrette could tempt her. Her appetite was gone.

Murder?

Attempted murder, he'd said. Was she supposed to be relieved that his intended victim was fortunate enough to have survived?

Tears clogged her throat, a salty lump that made swallowing next to impossible. What did she know about this man? They'd locked gazes over a song at a bar. She'd left her fiancé for him. Well, for herself, too, but Nick Fiore had been the catalyst—Nick, with his dark eyes, his dark hair, his intensity. His rugged physique. His modesty. His innate goodness.

What goodness? He'd nearly killed someone!

Oh, God. She'd made love with him. She'd lost herself in his arms, several times. She'd never known sex could be so pleasurable, could leave her feeling satisfied on such a soul-deep level. She'd never slept more soundly than she had last night, enveloped in his protective, possessive warmth, lulled by the steady rhythm of his breathing.

"The verdict was wrong," he added.

"Of course it was," she snapped, a strange, frantic energy bubbling along her nerves. Didn't every convict believe the verdict was wrong? Didn't they all believe they'd been cheated, misunderstood, abused by the system?

She'd made love with a would-be murderer!

"I didn't want to tell you," he said. "I was afraid you'd react this way."

"What way?" Her voice sounded brittle to her, like thin ice splintering. "Juvenile justice. Sure. Some kids get busted for smoking a joint. Some get nailed for underage drinking. You got convicted of attempted murder."

"Diana." He reached for her hand and she recoiled. Shoving back her chair, she searched the dining room for their waiter. She couldn't eat. She couldn't remain seated at this table. She needed air. She needed to move. What she really needed was a long jog on the beach, but the sun had set and she was wearing a skirt, and—

"Is everything all right, miss?" the waiter said, whisking across the room to their table.

"Please cancel our dinners," she said. "I'll sign the check to my room."

"Diana," Nick said.

"If you're hungry, you can stay and eat your steak," she said with what she considered extreme generosity. "I've got to go."

Nick stood, dug into his pocket and pulled out his wallet. He handed the waiter a wad of cash. "Here. Keep it."

Diana rose to her feet as well. "I said I'd sign it to my room."

Ignoring her, Nick shook his head at the waiter, who seemed dumbfounded by the amount of money Nick had handed him. Diana didn't wait to watch them settle up. She bolted out of the dining room, through the inn's quaint lobby and out onto the porch.

The night was pleasantly cool, the air thick with the ocean's perfume. The breeze rising up off the water tangled in her hair as she raced to the edge of the porch, her hands fisted around the rail as if that was the only way to keep herself from charging down the bluff to the beach. She gulped in deep breaths and kept her eyes open so they wouldn't fill with tears. A few faint stars pricked the night sky.

She heard footsteps behind her. She didn't have to turn to see Nick. She could feel him, his essence shimmering in the air around her, sparking as if the atmosphere was charged with electricity.

"Can we talk?" he asked.

She refused to look at him. "It's a free country."

"My father used to beat my mother."

Her no-tears strategy wasn't working. She felt her vision swimming. A strange dizziness washed over her, making her legs feel weak.

Maybe she swayed, went pale and appeared about to faint, because Nick gripped her arm, firmly but gently, led her away from the railing to one of the sturdy Adirondack chairs, and lowered her into it. As soon as she was settled, he released her, as if he could sense that she didn't want him touching her.

He sat in the chair next to hers. She continued to stare out at the ocean, afraid of what she would see if she looked at him. A murderer? The son of a wife-beater? The man with whom she'd spent a night making love?

"My father beat my mother," he repeated. "Usually he just smacked her around a little, or hit her in places where it wouldn't show. When I was a child, I couldn't do anything about it. Except watch. Or withdraw. Usually my mother would tell me to go to my room so I wouldn't have to see it. I could hear it, though. The walls were thin."

"I'm sorry," Diana said, meaning it. It must have been traumatic for him. Maybe the trauma of it was what had turned him into a criminal.

"When I got older and stronger, I tried to talk my mother into leaving him. She kept saying he didn't mean to hurt her, he loved her, he just had a temper. She'd tell me it wasn't my problem. She said I should just leave when my father acted that way. But one night, when I was fifteen, I didn't leave."

Diana didn't want to hear this. It was going to be awful. She wished she could press her hands to her ears, but even if she did, she knew she wouldn't be able to block out Nick's low, steady voice.

"My father had been drinking. He came home late, and his dinner was cold. He started smacking my mother around. And I just couldn't stand it anymore. So I pulled him off her and hit him. Pummeled, him, really. I guess I was a little crazed. All I wanted was for him to stop beating her. I wasn't trying to hurt him."

"But you did," she said. Her horror was gone, replaced by a forlorn sense of resignation.

"Maybe I *did* mean to hurt him." Nick sounded resigned, too. "I swung a chair at him. In the court, that chair became a deadly weapon. He was knocked out cold. My mother was screaming that I'd killed him. She called the police and they arrested me." He fell silent, apparently lost in memory for a few seconds. "My father was hospitalized for a while. Broken ribs. A fractured skull." He exhaled. "Yeah. I meant to hurt him. I'd been watching him hurt my mother all those years. Every now and then he'd whack me, too, until I got too big for him to take on. It was his turn to experience pain. I wish I could say I felt guilty, but I don't."

"The justice system found you guilty."

He exhaled again, a long, weary breath. "The public defender assigned to my case thought I'd be charged with assault, but it wound up being attempted murder. He was sure I'd be acquitted, because my mother would testify that my father had been battering her and I'd only been trying to defend her."

He fell silent. All Diana heard was the whisper of the waves lapping the shore. "So how did you wind up convicted?" she finally asked.

"My mother testified that my father hadn't done anything to her. She said he was a good man and she had no idea why I tried to kill him."

Diana gasped—and finally turned to stare at Nick. He stared back at her, his eyes piercing, his chin raised slightly, as if daring her to deny what he was telling her. "Why would she do that?"

"Who the hell knows? Maybe she loved him. She was his wife. So she sacrificed me."

"Oh, Nick." What else could she say? She thought her mother was awful because she was trying to pressure Diana into marrying

Peter. That seemed so trivial compared to what Nick had endured. His mother's choice was so much crueler than anything Diana had ever experienced. "Have you worked it out with her?"

A cold laugh escaped him. "What am I supposed to work out? I was fighting for my life, and she turned her back on me. She refused to tell the truth, and I wound up with a criminal conviction."

Emotions spun like a tornado inside Diana, buffeting her. "You make it sound so straightforward, Nick. I'm sure it was more complicated than that. Battered wives don't think clearly."

"Are you defending her?"

"Of course not. She did a terrible thing to you."

"I spent three years in the system, Diana. Locked up. When I aged out of the juvie system, my criminal record was sealed, but it's there. I've got a conviction. I'll have it for the rest of my life—because my mother couldn't bring herself to tell the truth." Another long silence, and he said, "I'm telling the truth now, Diana. I didn't want to tell you, but you deserve to know."

Her eyes welled with tears, making him appear to waver as she gazed at him. "Thank you for trusting me," she said.

He emitted a bitter grunt. "Yeah. I trusted you, and you walked out on me."

"I was shocked. You can't blame me for that."

He shrugged and looked away. She interpreted that to mean he agreed. He wasn't blaming her.

And she was beyond shocked now. She'd been shocked when he told her about his conviction, but now she was even more shocked that his mother could have betrayed him the way she had. She was shocked that a boy could have been so abused by his mother and the justice system, and yet have matured into the person Nick was, a decent, caring man who watched out for other children and kept them from falling through the cracks the way he had.

Her struggles seemed so petty in comparison to what Nick had lived through. Her mother was upset because she wasn't going to marry the man her mother wanted her to marry. Peter was upset because she'd broken up with him. They were angry with her because she'd changed—but she was convinced that change was for the better. She was stronger and more self-possessed than she'd ever been before. They would simply have to accept it.

They might be annoyed and disappointed. But they had never testified against her. They'd never lied in court, leaving her to suffer for a crime she hadn't committed. The irony of Nick's past—that he'd been convicted of a crime because the woman he'd fought to defend had abandoned him—was a wound she couldn't begin to fathom.

"Has your mother apologized for her part in what you went through?" Diana asked.

He shrugged. "Yeah, she's apologized." His voice was flat. Clearly he didn't think much of his mother's apology.

"She's right here in town," Diana recalled.

"I see her as little as possible."

"Do you talk to her at all?"

"She calls me sometimes." He exhaled, sounding weary. "She'll invite me over for dinner or ask me to do an errand for her. She called a few days ago and told me one of her window shutters fell and she needed it nailed back on."

"Did you fix it?"

"Sure," he said sarcastically. "There's nothing I'd rather do than drop everything and race to her house to fix her freaking shutter." He shot Diana a sharp look. "Yeah, I'd rather spend an evening rehanging her damned shutter than being with you." His tone hinted that perhaps hanging his mother's shutter might be more pleasant for him than this conversation.

Still, his broken relationship with his mother struck Diana as terribly sad. Her mother was angry, yet Diana couldn't imagine their not remaining in touch. In time, she was convinced, her parents would accept her decision not to marry Peter. They'd resent it; they'd pressure her to rethink it. They'd argue with her. She'd argue back. It was what adult children did with their parents.

Nick clearly didn't do that with his parents.

"You told me your father was gone. I assume that means he doesn't live in town?"

"I have no idea where he is," Nick said coldly. "After he recovered from his injuries, he took off. No forwarding address. No money to support my mother. No paperwork." He allowed himself a humorless laugh. "As far as I know, they're still married."

"I think after a certain number of years, your mother can claim she's been abandoned and get a divorce, even if your father isn't around to sign the papers."

"Well, she never did that. She used to say the church wouldn't allow a divorce, but that's not true. You can't get remarried in the church, but you can get a divorce. She never took that step, though." He shrugged. "Who knows? She probably still loves the bastard."

Maybe she did. Battered women sometimes remained attached to their batterers. It was a totally irrational thing, but they did. Maybe Nick's mother's refusal to divorce her husband was just one more reason he was estranged from her.

Yet despite his hostility toward his mother, he seemed to have healed himself. He'd kept going. He'd survived the horror of a criminal conviction, overcome it, triumphed. He was living a good life now, giving back to a world that had forsaken him. "You're an amazing man," she said.

He snorted. "I'm a guy who almost killed my father. There's nothing admirable about that."

"It's admirable if you were trying to save someone else's life."

"Maybe I wasn't." He stared out at the dark ocean, now barely distinguishable from the equally dark sky above it. "Maybe I just hated my father because he'd been beating up on my mother for so many years. He drank and became a bully. Maybe I hurt him because I hated him."

"I don't believe that," Diana said. She honestly didn't. Not because she didn't want to believe a man she loved could be that cold-hearted, but because she knew Nick. She knew him enough to know that he was a good man.

She loved him.

Astonished by the realization, she twisted in her chair to look at him. He must have sensed her gaze on him, because he turned to her. Even in the evening shadows, she could see the turbulence in his expression, the pain and regret and fear. The hope.

"Nick," she murmured, reaching across the arm of her chair to take his hand.

As soon as her fingers touched his, he stood, clasped her hand in his and pulled her to her feet. His arms came around her as hers came around him, and they kissed. At first the kiss was light and forgiving, but soon it grew deep and needy, as dark as the night enveloping them.

She was scarcely aware of them crossing the porch to the door, wandering through the lobby to the stairs, climbing them to her room. She didn't hear her footsteps on the thick rugs, didn't feel the slick surface of the key card as she slid it into the slot and clicked the door open. She didn't notice the pale light from the bedside lamp, the plump pillows, the plush duvet covering the bed. She was conscious of only one thing: Nick. His hand clasping hers. His warmth permeating her. Her love for this strong, brave man.

He kissed her again, and she was lost. This had to be love. It was so much more powerful than anything she'd ever felt for Peter. It left her dazed. Intoxicated. Yearning. Aching. Her hands tugged at his clothing. Her fingers seemed suddenly incapable of the most simple tasks—unfastening a button, untucking a shirt tail. He was much more dexterous. Her blouse slid down her shoulders, her skirt down her hips. She hated the garments because they separated her skin from his touch. She loved them because they were apparently so easy to remove.

Once he'd stripped her naked, he helped her to remove his own clothing. Then they tumbled onto the bed. It was big, the duvet soft, the mattress cushioning and cradling her back. Nick rose above her, his arms propping him, his hips pressing against hers with an urgency that matched her own churning emotions.

She yearned. She ached.

She loved.

His tongue plundered her mouth. His fingers tangled into her hair, traced the curves of her earlobes, stroked the underside of her chin. He slid down to kiss one breast and then the other, sucking hard on her nipples, causing her back to arch and her breath to catch. He kissed her belly. Her hip bones. Her crotch. For a few hedonistic seconds she believed her favorite part of him was his mouth—but then she decided that wasn't true. Her favorite part of him was his soul.

"I don't have anything with me," he whispered.

She knew at once what he was referring to. "It's okay," she assured him. She'd been engaged to Peter a long time. She'd taken care of protecting herself.

"You sure?"

She was sure she wanted Nick, needed him, loved him. She was sure this moment was everything she'd been waiting for, everything she'd ever dreamed of. "I'm sure," she murmured, opening for him, reaching down and guiding him to her.

Their bodies merged, fused, burned together. His thrusts were slow, purposeful. Given how desperately they'd been kissing, she would have expected him to be wilder, but this wasn't just sex. It was a merging of minds and hearts as well as bodies, and Nick seemed to want every instant, every motion, every sensation to matter.

Her muscles flexed. Her nerves tensed. Her breath caught. She closed her eyes, wanting to savor the sensations.

"Open your eyes," he whispered.

She obeyed and found him gazing down at her. His hair was disheveled—her doing, she admitted as she dug her fingers convulsively into the dark, wavy locks. His jaw was tense. His eyes were as soft as she'd ever seen them, a deep, mellow brown, taking her in, absorbing the sight of her.

Oh, God, yes. She loved him. She loved Nick Fiore.

Her body arched in a blissful release. She shuddered, convulsing around him, feeling him climax inside her, hot and hard. They moaned together, a sweet, ragged chorus of bliss. Of love.

Slowly, carefully, he eased off her. He rolled onto his back, nestling his head deep into one of the oversize down pillows, and drew her against him. His shoulder was her pillow. It was much harder than a pillow, but she didn't mind.. She couldn't imagine anywhere she'd rather rest her head.

He stroked his fingers lightly up and down her arm as his breath slowed and his body cooled. She traced an aimless pattern across his chest, smiling when his nipples stiffened, smiling again when his abdominal muscles clenched at her touch.

Love. This had all happened so quickly, it was all so intense, but she couldn't deny what she felt. Nick was the most honorable man she'd ever known. He had triumphed over injustice and betrayal, and now he was giving back, giving of himself to kids who might have been dealt the same bad hand he'd had when he was their age.

What would her life have been like if she hadn't entered the Faulk Street Tavern last Saturday night? She would be acquiescing to Peter right now, saying that if he really preferred that ostentatious mansion in Newport, Rhode Island, they would have their wedding there. She would be yielding to her mother and buying some frou-frou white gown that cost more than the national debt. She would be at Shomback-Sawyer in Boston, pacing two steps behind James, taking notes and nodding at whatever he said. She would be knocking herself out to make everyone happy.

But she *had* entered the tavern. And she'd heard the song. And she'd changed.

Her hand stilled on Nick's chest, her palm feeling the deep thrum of his heartbeat. She'd changed, because of the song.

"Nick," she murmured.

"Hmm?"

"You have to change."

Fifteen

Great. Diana was one of *those* women—the ones who adore you, support you, make you feel like a million bucks, take you into their beds and into their hearts…and then try to change you. Nick tried to laugh off her comment, but honestly, it irritated him.

And he didn't want to be irritated right now. He was unwinding, wallowing happily in post-coital drowsiness. Loving the way her compact body felt against his. Loving the way her knees nudged his leg, and the way her hair splayed across his arm like a net of silk. Loving the way her breath skimmed across his throat and her fingers sketched his skin.

And she wanted to change him?

How? Was she going to tell him he had to eat less red meat? He'd given up cigarettes. He drank with restraint. He worked out. If he wanted to eat a damned slab of steak, he would.

Did she think he should drive more slowly? Listen to opera? Replace his leather jacket with a tailored wool blazer? Was she going to try to turn him into a stiff, proper imitation of her former fiancé? *Sorry, babe—that's not going to happen.*

"The song," she said. "The song said we had to turn and face the strange changes. We had to change. I've changed. You need to change, too."

"I'm not changing," he said. "I'm where I want to be."

"You're perfect, huh." She laughed.

He allowed himself a reluctant smile. No, he wasn't perfect. That didn't mean he wanted to change. Being imperfect was all right with him. "Fine," he said, just to shut down this conversation. "I'll get a haircut."

"Hair grows back." She lifted away from his shoulder and peered down into his face. He remembered what she'd looked like the instant she'd come, the instant before *he'd* come. She'd been the most beautiful woman he'd ever seen, her eyes as bright as diamonds, her mouth so soft and lush, her skin the gentle pink color of a springtime sunset. Her body had been so tight around him, her hips rising off the bed, her hands clenching. No condom. Just skin to skin, soul to soul.

Remembering made him hard enough to agree to change anything she asked for. A new job? A new face? Whatever she desired, he'd do it.

No, he wouldn't. He'd never changed for any other woman. As much as he savored the weight and warmth of Diana's body against his, the glow in her eyes, the hopeful beauty in her smile, he wasn't going to jump through hoops of flame for her. She'd described jumping through those hoops for her former boyfriend. Surely she wouldn't turn around at treat Nick the way she'd been treated in her last relationship.

"You need to reconcile with your mother," she said.

He recoiled, appalled by her suggestion. Was she insane? After what he'd shared with her, after what she knew about his life…she wanted him to make nice with the woman who'd sold him down the river?

"Fix her shutter," Diana murmured.

Christ. Nick did not need to hear this. "Diana—"

"No. Hush." She silenced him with a gentle brush of her fingertips against his lips. That one light caress was enough to turn him on again. He was angry and confused…but damn, he was horny for her. Couldn't they just make love and go to sleep, and not have this awful conversation?

Apparently not. She stroked her index finger across his lower lip, pulling back when he tried to catch it with his teeth. She drew a line over his chin, down his throat to his chest. Her smile could have wrung tears from Satan, it was so sweet.

"The song said we have to change," she reminded him. "I changed. You have to change, too."

"What happens if I don't?" he challenged her.

"I'll stop believing that the jukebox was talking to us. I'll believe it was talking to me alone."

She didn't have to say anything more. He understood what she was getting at. If he didn't change, if he didn't believe in the power of the song to bind him and Diana, she would leave.

She might leave anyway. She lived in Boston—which wasn't that far away in miles, but in culture and style it was light-years from sleepy Brogan's Point. Her life was there, her job, her family. Her ex-fiancé.

Even if she left, he knew she wouldn't go back to the ex. She had changed. She'd listened to the song and let its magic transform her.

If he didn't want to lose her, he would have to do the same.

"All right," he heard himself say. "I'll fix the goddamn shutter."

—␣—

The missing shutter was noticeable as soon as Nick pulled his car to the curb in front of the brown-shingled Cape Cod house Saturday morning. Four windows flanked the front door, two on each side. Each window was framed by a pair of white shutters except for one missing shutter that made the house look lopsided. The front yard was small and early-spring scruffy, tufts of grayish-brown grass poking through the soil, resembling a bad haircut. The shrubs flanking the cement front porch looked pruned, though. Someone had made an effort with them.

Nick stood on the front walk, staring at the house as if it contained a dragon he had to slay. Diana could see a muscle ticking in his clenched jaw. His hands were curled into fists. His posture was rigid.

She rubbed the small of his back, a massage she hoped would soothe him. "It's going to be fine," she assured him, even though she had no way of knowing whether Nick or the dragon would win. "*You're* going to be fine."

His jaw tightened even more, but he squared his shoulders and strode up the slate front walk.

"Is she expecting us?" Diana asked, following him to the porch.

"I phoned and said I was coming."

I, not *we.* Did his mother know Diana would be standing beside Nick when he showed up? Did Mrs. Fiore know that Diana and Nick had been all but inseparable every minute they weren't working?

He'd had a full day yesterday at his office, and Diana had spent the day at the warehouse, sorting the items from Lenore's grandmother's house with James Sawyer and trying not to suffocate beneath all the praise he'd heaped upon her. He'd been bowled over by the estate, even more excited about the price she'd paid once he'd had a chance to see what that price had purchased. "Whatever you're doing," James had said to her, "just keep doing it."

What she was doing was taking chances, being adventurous and daring.

What she was doing was loving Nick.

Today, after he fixed his mother's shutter, she would love him even more. Not just because the repair would be a kind thing to do—she already knew Nick was considerate—but because by fixing his mother's shutter, he would prove that he'd changed. They both had to change, according to the song. Diana was a pragmatic person, not into weird woo-woo superstitions, but she knew this: they both had to turn and face the strange changes if the jukebox's magic was to be trusted.

Nick pressed the doorbell button, and Diana heard its muffled chime through the closed door. The door swung inward and a small, dark-haired woman of late middle age stood before them, smiling so brightly Diana's heart broke a little. Nick's mother looked like him—dark hair, although hers was generously laced with gray, and dark, intense eyes, a firm chin and a smile that could illuminate the world.

She was petite, though, small-boned, several inches shorter than Diana. Nick must have inherited his height from his father. The thought of such a tall man slapping around such a small, fragile-looking woman caused Diana to wince inwardly. Nick's fear that his father might kill his mother all those years ago would have been reasonable.

"Come in!" She beckoned them inside but fell back a step as they crossed the threshold. Diana wondered whether she wanted to hug her son. If so, she opted not to. His face wasn't exactly welcoming.

"This is Diana Simms," he said curtly, gesturing toward her. "Diana, my mother."

"It's a pleasure to meet you, Mrs. Fiore." Diana extended her hand and Nick's mother gathered it in both of hers, clasping tight, as if desperate for human contact.

"You'll both stay for lunch, right? I'm making lasagna. Nicky loves my lasagna." She sent him a smile that broke Diana's heart a little more. It was loving and pleading and tinged with a vague hopelessness.

That hopelessness was well placed. Nick didn't return her smile. At least he didn't say they wouldn't have lunch with her. "Let me get to work. Where's the shutter?"

"In the garage. Everything's in the garage—the ladder, the tools, whatever you need. I'm so grateful you're doing this, Nicky. The house looks—well, you can see how it looks. Like it's falling apart. It isn't. I take good care of it. I always have. But I'm too short to fix that shutter."

Nick touched Diana's shoulder. "I'll be outside if you need me."

With that, he was gone.

"Take off your jacket," Mrs. Fiore said. "Make yourself comfortable. I've got things to do in the kitchen."

Diana slid off her blazer, draped it over the newel post of the stairway and followed Nick's mother through the cozy, obsessively tidy living room into the equally cozy, tidy kitchen. The appliances were old, the sink white porcelain, the floor linoleum tiles. But everything was immaculate. Even the twin cat dishes that sat on a rectangular plastic mat near the back door, one filled with water and one with dry cat food, were clean and neat.

Mrs. Fiore must have noticed Diana's gaze. "You're not allergic, are you? Some people are, I know. But Missy is skittish. She'll hide in the basement until you leave. She's scared of most people."

"No allergies," Diana said, wondering if Missy, like her mistress, had ever been abused. Mrs. Fiore didn't seem at all skittish. Indeed, she seemed starved for company. "Is there anything I can do to help?" Diana asked, nodding toward the simmering saucepan on the stove, the pot of boiling pasta beside it, the Pyrex baking tray and the bowl of ricotta cheese.

"Just sit. Please. You're a guest." Mrs. Fiore pushed up the sleeves of her knit cardigan and gave the sauce a stir.

Diana took a seat at the square table pressed up against the wall, which featured patterned wallpaper in a cheerful yellow shade. The café curtains at the window above the sink were the same sunshine yellow, and the table was covered with a yellow and white checked cloth. "Nick uses tomato sauce out of a jar," she said.

"I've tried to teach him how to make real gravy," his mother said with a laugh. "He doesn't want to learn. But that's okay. I keep thinking, if he wants pasta with real gravy, I'll make it for him. He'll come here to eat." Diana was touched by the poignant undertone of her words. She was obviously eager to lure her son home for visits. "I don't cook like this all the time," she went on. "I work, you know. Customer service at the Wal-Mart down on Route One. It's not much, but I didn't go to college like you young people. And I never worked while Nicky was growing up. I wanted to be here with a snack for him when he got home from school. But now..." She shrugged and overturned the large pot into a colander in the sink, draining the hot water from the wide, ridged strips of pasta. "I've got to earn my keep, right? They're good to me at Wal-Mart. It's a nice job. Nicky said something about you work in antiques?"

So Nick had told his mother about her. Diana was enormously pleased. "That's right."

"This whole house is full of antiques," Mrs. Fiore said. "Not that any of them are worth anything. Just old stuff. When you can't afford new, you call the old 'antiques' and it sounds a lot better."

Diana dutifully chuckled.

Nick's mother was quite pleasant. Of course she would be—she'd raised a wonderful son. Yet this same woman, so friendly and full of chatter, had betrayed that son in the worst possible way. When he'd defended her, when he'd protected her, when he'd stood before a judge, fighting for his future, his mother had forsaken him.

Mrs. Fiore prattled as she layered the lasagna into the pan, and Diana added an appropriate comment whenever the woman paused for a breath. Once the lasagna was constructed, Mrs. Fiore popped it into the oven. Within minutes the small kitchen steamed with mouth-watering aromas of tomato sauce, oregano, and garlic.

By the time Nick joined them in the kitchen, the lasagna was done baking, a salad had been tossed, and Mrs. Fiore had told Diana about a pregnant young associate she worked with at Wal-Mart, the tulip and daffodil bulbs she'd planted—"I was hoping they'd sprout by now, but I guess it's still a little early"—and her recent trip to a casino, where she actually came home fifty dollars ahead. "Those slot machines are rigged to make you lose, you know? But I got lucky. I got lemons, I got cherries. I love fruit, especially when I get three across on the screen."

Nick removed his leather jacket and rolled up his sleeves, and Diana stifled a lustful sigh at the sight of his lean, sinewy forearms as he washed his hands at the sink. He dried them on a paper towel, which he scrunched into a wad and lofted into the trash can near the cat's dishes. His gaze intersected with Diana's, and he arched an eyebrow. She gave him a discreet nod, signaling him that her conversation with his mother had gone well.

"So, sit." Mrs. Fiore pointed to one of the empty chairs at the table. "The lasagna is done. What do you want to drink? I've got a nice red vino, soda, iced-tea..."

"Just water, thank you," Diana said, then informed Nick, "Your mother wouldn't let me help at all. She did all the cooking." She wasn't sure if she was telling him this to improve his opinion of his mother or to justify her own lack of contribution to the meal.

He didn't respond, just pulled two tumblers from a high cabinet and filled them with water.

"Do you like it?" his mother asked, once they were all seated and digging into their food.

"It's delicious." Diana wasn't used to eating such a heavy meal for lunch. But the lasagna was marvelous. She'd eaten lasagna at countless restaurants in the North End, Boston's "Little Italy" neighborhood, and Mrs. Fiore's lasagna could easily hold its own with what those restaurants served.

"Nicky, you like it?"

"It's fine," he said tersely.

"I made the gravy with extra basil. I know how you love basil."

"It's good."

"The pasta, it's not too soft? I know you like it *al dente*—"

"Mom." He lowered his fork and stared at her. "You don't have to knock yourself out for me, okay?"

His tone, quiet but firm, pierced Diana's brain like a laser. Suddenly she understood Mrs. Fiore, her ingratiating personality, her need to talk, to entertain, to please. How many times, Diana wondered, had the woman's lasagna failed to satisfy her husband? How many times had he slapped her or punched her because of that failure?

Mrs. Fiore appeared flustered, as if Nick's quiet reproach was itself evidence that she had failed. Her face went pale and she lowered her eyes. "I'm sorry, Nicky."

"No need to apologize."

"Of course there is. There *always* is."

They were no longer discussing the lasagna. Nick stared at his mother again, and she stared at her plate, her fork resting against the edge, her hands folded in her lap. The tension in the room was thicker than the tangy fragrance of the food.

Diana pushed her chair back, realizing that they had wandered into personal territory, into their wounded past. "Perhaps I should excuse myself," she murmured to Nick.

He pressed his hand to her wrist, holding her in her seat. "No, stay. You want me to change? I'm doing my best, but…I need you by my side for this."

Diana's breath caught in her throat. She knew she loved Nick, although he'd never uttered the word *love*. Yet asking her to remain with him as he wrestled his demons to the ground was as just as significant.

His statement seemed to startle his mother, too. She lifted her gaze to Nick and then Diana. Then Nick again.

"I'm trying to forgive you, Mom." The words emerged in a dark rumble, his voice gruff as he struggled to express himself. "I don't know why you did what you did. I don't know why you sold me out that way. But I've been angry for too long. I don't want to be angry anymore."

Tears filled his mother's eyes. "Nicky. I never meant to sell you out. As God is my witness, that was never what I wanted."

"It's what happened."

"I know it looks that way to you. But Nicky…" His mother emitted a sob, and she wiped her cheeks with her napkin. "He scared me so much, Nicky. He healed, and he got out of the hospital, and he threatened me."

"He was always threatening you."

"This was after, though. You were in that foster home, out on bail, awaiting trial. Your father got out of the hospital and he came here, and he held a knife to my throat and told me that if I told anyone he hit me, he'd come back and kill me. And he would have, Nicky. I was sure of it."

"So you figured your life was more important than mine?"

"I would have died for you if I had to," his mother said, her voice wobbling as more sobs undermined it. "But I knew I wouldn't have to. You would be okay. You were strong. He couldn't hurt you."

"Are you kidding?"

"You stood up to him, Nicky. You beat him. You took him down. He was as scared of you as I was of him. I knew you were safe."

"Safe? I was convicted of a crime!"

141

"But you escaped from this house. You freed yourself from this family. You had that wonderful cop looking after you. Officer Nolan. And me…If I went into court and said your father had beaten me, I'd be dead. If I didn't say anything, he would leave and I wouldn't have to get beaten by him anymore. I didn't want to die, Nicky. I was scared, I was a coward, but I didn't want to die."

She broke down, freely weeping. Diana watched as Nick rose, circled the table and pulled his mother to her feet. He wrapped her in a hug—a tentative, awkward embrace, but a protective one. A forgiving one. "All right," he said.

"I'm a terrible mother," she murmured into his chest. "You had a terrible father. And you turned into such a good man, Nicky. Maybe it was best that we set you free."

A dry laugh escaped him. "I was hardly free. I was in the criminal justice system. In detention."

"Free from us. Free from all the hate and fear in this house. I'm so sorry, Nicky, so sorry."

"All right," he said again. "It's done. It can't be changed. Time to move on."

They held each other for a long while. Diana felt like a trespasser on the scene, witnessing such a private moment—until, over his mother's head, Nick directed his gaze back to her. He looked resigned, and relieved. Younger. His eyes glistened, not with tears but with an inner light she'd never seen before. The light of forgiveness. The light of letting go.

Yes, he had changed.

And she loved him even more.

Sixteen

He felt…*changed.* Liberated and free, as if a two-ton weight had been lifted off his back.

He had always enjoyed his mother's lasagna, but today it had tasted better, the sauce rich and fresh, the pasta *al dente,* just the way he liked it. In the past, his mother's fussing to cook her pasta to his specific taste had irritated him. He'd felt that she was overly anxious to please him the way she'd been with his father. "I'm not your husband," he'd wanted to shout. "I'm not that sonofabitch. Not all men are like that."

Yet he'd come close to killing his father. For years he'd feared he *was* like that. If not for Ed Nolan scraping him off the floor and reshaping him into a functioning human being, a student, a responsible adult who could, if not make things right, at least make things a little less wrong, Nick might have turned into a sonofabitch, too.

That he hadn't was a triumph in itself. That he could forgive his mother—that he *did* forgive her—was more than a triumph. It was a rebirth.

When he and Diana took their leave after lunch, Diana paused halfway down the front walk and turned to inspect his mother's house. "It looks good," she said, pointing to the shutter he'd rehung.

"It was a simple fix."

"Simple if you're six feet tall and know how to use a hammer," she said. "There's no way your mother could have done that. She's so small.

"There's this thing called a ladder," he joked. "Even I needed a ladder to hammer in the nails on top."

"Okay, so you have to know how to use a hammer and a ladder," Diana joked back.

He slung his arm around her shoulders as they admired his simple handiwork. Her body nestled within the curve of his arm as snugly as two puzzle pieces locking together. Had the song compelled him to change? Or Diana?

It didn't matter. He would never love that song. But damn it, he loved her.

"Thank you," he said.

"For what? Acknowledging that you know how to use a hammer and a ladder?"

He smiled and pressed a kiss to the top of her head. Her hair felt like warm silk against his lips. "For making a new man out of me."

She turned to face him. "Are you a new man?"

He closed his other arm around her and took her mouth with his. She tasted spicy from the lasagna, but sweet as well, her own special sweetness. Yes, he loved her. Loved her and wanted her. If they weren't standing on his mother's front walk, in full view of her nosy neighbors, he'd let this kiss progress from R-rated to X-rated.

But there were the nosy neighbors, and not even a wall to lean against, let alone a bed to lie down on. Before he made a fool of himself, he eased back, nuzzled her forehead with a final kiss and said, "Here's an idea. Check out of the OB and move in with me."

She blinked, apparently startled by what he'd said. He was startled, too. He'd known his share of women over the years, but he'd never invited one to move in with him. He'd never met a woman he'd wanted to live with. Not until now.

"Are you serious?"

"Yes." Gazing down into her suddenly solemn face, he realized he'd never been more serious about anything in his life. "I know, you've got your place in Boston, and your job. And I'm here in Brogan's Point."

"And we've known each other only a week."

"Yeah. That, too."

She peered up at him, her eyes shimmering, her brow flexing as she sifted through her thoughts. Finally, she spoke. "I guess you'd better drive me to the inn so I can check out."

He couldn't expect more from her than that. Hell, if he could, he'd go ahead and ask her to marry him. Not that he could give her a monstrously huge diamond, or her parents' blessings, or the life she would have had with her rich ex-fiancé. Not that he could expect her even to want to get married so soon after she'd ended an engagement that had been based on a relationship of many years' standing.

But he wanted it. He wanted *her*. He wanted the woman who had changed him, and in the process healed him.

For now, he would take what she offered. He would help her move out of the Ocean Bluff Inn, bring her back to his house, dive onto his bed, and spend the next several hours there with her. Naked.

He opened the passenger door of his car for her, then climbed in behind the wheel. They didn't talk during the drive through town, along the waterfront and north to the inn's winding driveway. But even without words, he communicated with her, his right hand folded around her left, his fingers imparting their heat to her, his need, his love.

He had barely pulled into a parking space and shut off the engine before she was bounding out of the car. Was she as eager as he was to get her stuff, sign her bill and race to his house for some naked-on-the-bed time? It looked that way. Her eyes were bright, her face slightly flushed. Once again her skin made him think of peaches. Honey hair, peach skin…Damn but she made him hungry.

She met him at the rear bumper and laced her fingers through his. Together they strolled up the walk to the veranda—and froze when a tall, well-groomed man rose from one of the Adirondack chairs and started toward them.

"Peter?" Diana said. "What are you doing here?"

Nick noted that she didn't slip her hand from his. He also noted that Peter, the ex-fiancé, was staring at their clasped hands—staring and scowling. He remained on the veranda as they approached, his posture regal, his expression supercilious, as if he believed it was only right that they should come to him, not the other way, and that he should be standing above them.

Not for long. Refusing to retreat, Nick proceeded up the steps until he was eye-to-eye with the guy.

Peter met Nick's gaze for a long second, then turned to Diana. "I've come to take you home," he said. "Get your things. Let's go."

"What are you talking about?" She sounded a touch exasperated but not terribly concerned.

"This has gone on long enough. I gave you a few days to get your head on straight." He looked pointedly at her hand in Nick's and shook his head. "Evidently, you haven't accomplished that yet. But I'm tired of waiting. You wanted a brief vacation from our engagement, so fine. Your last little...whatever. I won't dignify it by calling it a fling." That bit of nastiness, Nick suspected, was directed at him, not at Diana. "Now it's time to get back to reality."

"Peter." Diana eased her hand from Nick's, and he felt the loss of contact like a small death. But she needed both hands to clasp Peter's upper arms in a reassuring hug. "You're the one who needs to face reality," she said gently. "I broke up with you. I ended our engagement. It's over."

"It's not over. You're just—I don't know, experiencing a brief psychotic episode. We're getting married. Everyone wants this."

"*I* don't want it." She still sounded gentle, like a mother comforting a toddler whose balloon had blown away. "I don't want to marry you, Peter. I don't want to go wherever you have in mind to take me. I don't want you to decide what my home is. I'm in Brogan's Point right now. It's where I want to be."

"With *him?*" Peter shot Nick a lethal look.

"Yes. With him."

"You're going to stay here? In this seedy little nothing town?"

"I don't know where I'm going to stay," she said. "I don't have my whole life mapped out anymore. And I like that. Please...I'm sorry you drove all the way here—"

"What about your apartment in Boston?"

"It's still there. I've got five months left on my lease. I'll figure things out."

"No need to. Everything's already figured out. You're coming with me." And with that, he flung her hands off his arms and snagged one of them in a tight grip. "We're going to go inside, get your things, and drive back to Boston. I'll send someone to pick up your car. It's time for you to quit this craziness."

"Stop it, Peter." She no longer sounded slightly exasperated. She sounded downright furious. "I'm not crazy."

"You dragged me to that sleazy bar, you swooned over that stupid jukebox, and you've been deranged ever since. Who is this guy, some local stud? What the hell has gotten into you, Diana?"

"I've changed," she said. "I've changed." She tugged her arm, unable to free herself. "Let go of me."

"Let go of her," Nick echoed. He didn't like the way the guy was holding Diana, his grip so tight, so possessive.

"You keep out of this," Peter snapped at him. "This is between Diana and me."

Nick felt his temper rising like a fever inside him. That grip, those thick, brutal fingers circling Diana's slender wrist like a manacle…and his size, looming over Diana, trying to bend her to his will with his hands when his words weren't enough…

Memories swamped Nick, fierce, violent memories of his father grabbing his mother's arm, shaking her, threatening her. Terrifying her.

He was no longer a little boy, watching in horror as his father beat his mother into submission. He was a man, a man who loved Diana.

A man with a criminal record. His record was sealed, but that seal could be broken if he did the wrong thing.

Yet standing by while this bastard hurt Diana was the wrong thing, too.

His hands reflexively curled into fists and he started to swing.

"Nick! Don't!"

Her voice sliced through his feverish rage like ice water dousing the fire inside him. Miraculously—because he couldn't remember deliberately lowering his arms—he discovered his hands at his sides. His breath came heavy, his eyes burned, and he felt a hatred almost as deep as what he'd once felt for his father. But he didn't hit Peter.

Hell. He wanted to. He wanted to more than he could fathom.

But he didn't. He would have pounded Peter into an oozing mass of pain for Diana. Instead, he *didn't* pound Peter into an oozing mass of pain...for Diana. Because she'd asked him not to. Because if she'd asked him to let go of her, he would—no matter how much he never, ever wanted to let go of her. And if she asked him to hold her, he would, forever. Because if you loved a woman, you listened to her.

The same strength that had infused her voice when she'd shouted, "Don't!" seemed to fill her body. She wrenched her hand loose and backed away from Peter. "You know what your problem is, Peter?"

"My problem is that my intended seems to be experiencing pre-nuptial jitters, that's all."

"Your problem," Diana corrected him, "is that no one has ever said no to you. You're handsome, you're rich, you're charming, and everyone has always said yes. Whatever you've wanted, you've gotten. *You're* the one who's gone crazy—because for the first time in your life, someone has said no to you. When I saw you in Boston and gave you back your ring, you bruised me." She touched her wrist. Nick couldn't see any bruising on her pale, delicate skin, but the mere possibility that this thug, this asshole, this monster had bruised her made Nick's hands tighten into fists again. It took more self-control than he'd realized he had to keep his arms at his sides. "You never hurt me like that before, Peter. You never had to, because you always got your way. I always did what you wanted."

"Well, now I'm not doing what you want. I'm sorry, but that's life. Sometimes things don't go exactly the way you want them to. Get over it."

Peter seemed incredulous. "I didn't bruise you."

"You did," she said. "And it will never happen again. Now go away and leave me alone." She folded her arms over her chest and glared at him, five-foot-four inches of steely resolve. Peter gaped at her, his frown deepening, growing less hostile and more perplexed, as if she were mutating before his eyes, transforming from a compliant little lady into a fire-breathing dragon.

He looked almost frightened, which suited Nick just fine.

One final gaze, and Peter turned, stormed down the steps to the parking lot, and climbed into a silver Mercedes coupe parked not far from Nick's aged Honda. Peter revved the motor and, in an aggressive maneuver, tore out of the lot, his engine roaring and his tires sending loose gravel flying like shrapnel.

Had Diana actually chosen a rattly Honda Civic over a powerful Mercedes coupe? Or had she just chosen to reject the Mercedes? Was she going to reject Nick, too? He'd almost struck Peter. He would have, if she hadn't stopped him. He would have resorted to violence, just like his old man.

"Are you all right?" she asked him.

He'd been focused on the empty space where the Mercedes had been, on the pebbles and dust settling back to earth in its wake. Her question startled him. He spun back to her and found her watching him, looking uncannily calm. "The hell with me. How are you?"

"Never better." She gave him a tentative smile. "You look a little ragged."

"I wanted to punch his lights out," Nick confessed. "Why didn't you tell me he hurt you when you saw him in Boston?"

"I hurt him, too," she said.

"You didn't leave bruises."

"Maybe I did. On his heart, or at least on his ego."

"His ego could use some roughing up."

Diana laughed.

"Diana." Nick gathered her hands in his. They were so small, so soft and fine-boned. It pained him to think that prick had hurt her, and had been well on his way to hurting her again today. Nick would have done anything to protect her—even if it meant a second criminal charge, a stint in prison, a lifelong stain on his soul. He would have done it—but *she'd* protected *him,* instead. She'd saved him from his own worst impulses.

"I love you." He could think of nothing more to say than those three words.

She rose on tiptoe and touched her lips to his. "I love you, too."

"I know it's been fast, and there's still stuff you don't know about me—"

"I'm looking forward to learning that stuff. And you'll learn stuff about me, too."

"I like heavy metal music."

"My feet turn to ice in the winter."

"I used to smoke, but I quit about five years ago."

"I used to bite my nails."

"I hate doing laundry."

"So do I."

Their eyes met. Her smile was so sweet, he felt it resonating inside him. "This is insane," he said.

"Maybe it's magic."

"I didn't use to believe in magic," he admitted, then bowed to kiss her. "But now, I guess I do."

"That's because you've changed," she murmured, then pulled him to her for a longer, deeper kiss.

Epilogue

"I'm a wreck," Nick said.

Ed Nolan grinned and shook his head. They were seated across from each other in a booth at the Faulk Street Tavern. It was three o'clock on a Saturday afternoon, and they both nursed iced teas, Ed because he was on call that weekend and Nick because he would be leaving for Boston in fifteen minutes.

"You'll be fine," Ed assured him.

"Do I look okay? I thought about getting a haircut, but Diana told me not to."

"I'd say you're better off pleasing her than pleasing her parents," Ed said. "And yes, you look okay."

Nick was wearing a suit. The full deal—jacket, tailored trousers, button-down shirt, tie, lace-up shoes. He'd bought the outfit last week. He'd never owned a suit before, never needed one. But then, he'd never driven to Boston to meet the parents of the woman he planned to marry. The very rich, very proper parents.

"I feel like a freaking stock broker."

"You look like a guy who cleans up pretty well," Ed said, then shouted over his shoulder to Gus, "Tell Nick he looks okay."

"You look gorgeous," Gus shouted back. The bar was just beginning to fill up. Carl Stanton sat on his usual stool, hunched over a whisky. A half-dozen young guys were gathered around another table, laughing and swapping stories, a pitcher of beer and a platter of wings forming a centerpiece. A half-dozen young women sat two tables away, sipping exotic martinis and checking out the guys. Manny Lopez stood behind the bar with Gus, unloading clean glasses onto a shelf. If Gus wanted to shout across the room to Ed and Nick, no one seemed to mind.

Nick knew he didn't look gorgeous. He looked clean-shaven and clean-cut and nothing like who he really was. "What if I blow it?" he asked.

"Listen to me." Ed leaned forward, his beefy hands planted on the table on either side of his glass, his expression stern yet fatherly. He looked the way Nick's father had never looked, and that alone gave Nick courage. "Diana loves you. You love her. You make her happy. You treat her right. If her parents are good people, that's what they care about. If all they care about is that you haven't got a fancy title or an executive office, then they're not good people and you don't have to worry about impressing them."

"In other words, I win either way."

"Exactly."

Nick sighed, checked his watch, and swigged the last of his iced tea. "What if I use the wrong fork?"

"What do you think? They'll point at you, snicker, and call you a moron." Ed snorted. "Use whatever fork you want. As long as you chew with your mouth shut, they won't mind."

"What if they say they want us to get married in some mansion in Newport?"

"Diana'll decide where she wants to get married. She's no pushover, in case you haven't noticed."

"I've noticed," Nick said with a grin. That was just one of the things he loved about her—the thing about her that had changed the most since she'd heard the song.

He glanced over at the jukebox, wondering if there was another song in it for him, something that would give him the fortitude to get through this evening with Diana's parents. He was supposed to meet them, along with Diana and her sister, who was visiting from England, at some fancy French restaurant in downtown Boston—he doubted they'd be wearing plastic bibs with smiling lobsters on them, and dining at a table covered in butcher paper—and by the end of the meal, he hoped they'd accept him as the man their daughter loved. Actually, he hoped for more. He hoped they'd like him. He hoped they'd find him smart and honorable and pleasant, the ideal addition to their family. But he'd settle for acceptable.

Diana had sworn that her sister would love him. She wasn't about to vouch for her parents, but she'd told him to be himself, because Nick himself was the man she loved.

How could he be himself when he was dressed in this tailored gray suit?

"I've got to go," he said, nudging away his empty glass and sliding out of the booth. "Wish me luck."

"You found Diana," Ed reminded him, standing as well. "How much more luck do you want?"

"What I want..." Nick's gaze drifted to the jukebox, standing in splendid isolation against the far wall of the tavern. "What I want is a song that'll give me courage."

Gus swung around from behind the bar and strode to their table to pick up the empty glasses. She patted Nick's shoulder. "You don't need another song," she said. "You already got your magic, Nick. Run with it."

He turned to face her. She was smiling, something she rarely did. Impulsively, he kissed her cheek. "You're right," he said. "I'll run with it. No—I'll *fly*." He gave Ed a nod, then strode to the door and out, off to Boston to be with the woman he loved.

—⁕—

Ed slung an arm around Gus. It pleased him that her height matched his. That seemed to make things easier, somehow.

The door swung shut behind Nick. "He'll be fine," he said, echoing the assurance he'd given the kid.

"He'll wow them," Gus agreed.

"Now you're gonna tell me it's all because of that jukebox?"

Gus shrugged noncommittally. "Believe what you want. And let me believe what I want."

153

He eyed the jukebox and gave her a squeeze. "I've gotta get back to headquarters. I'll be off at six."

"You know where I'll be at six," she said, angling her head toward the bar.

He released her and took a step toward the door, which also brought him a step closer to the jukebox. He eyed it again, then rotated back to Gus. "You got a song in there for me?"

"Pop a quarter in the slot," she said, a teasing undertone in her voice. "Maybe it'll play 'Take Me Home Tonight.'"

Ed grinned. Gus winked, then sauntered to the bar, the empty iced tea glasses in her hand, her slim hips shimmying just the slightest bit.

Nick Fiore wasn't the only guy in love, Ed thought with a sigh.

—ɷ—

True Colors

Book Two

One

"We've got a problem," Monica said.

Emma set down her paintbrush and blinked herself into the here and now. She'd been lost in her work, dabbing shadings into the stone façade of the castle behind Ava Lowery's half-finished face. To Emma's left stood an easel holding a pin board that displayed twenty close-up photographs of Ava, a five-year-old bundle of energy who hadn't wanted to sit still while Emma had snapped the pictures, so some of them were a little blurry. To Emma's right stood another easel holding images of medieval castles, unicorns, jewel-encrusted tiaras and satin gowns. Directly before Emma stood the easel containing the painting she was working on—her very first Dream Portraits commission since her arrival in Brogan's Point four months ago.

A warm wash of sunlight flooded the loft through the glass wall behind her stool. If she turned around, she would be rewarded with a spectacular view of scattered trees and rooftops and outcroppings of granite sloping down toward the heart of town, and beyond it the ocean. But she needed that wonderful natural light behind her, spilling onto her canvas, way more than she needed the distractions of a beautiful view.

Immersed in her painting, she hadn't heard Monica climb the stairs to the loft. The stairs and loft were floored in white wall-to-wall carpeting—what sane person covered the floor with white?—but Emma had spread a patchwork of canvas drop cloths across the floor of the loft to protect the ridiculously impractical carpet from paint spatters. She should have heard Monica's shoes scratching across the canvas. She *would* have, if she hadn't been so intensely focused on the castle she was painting.

Despite that intense focus, she'd heard Monica's voice. In particular, she'd heard the word *problem.* "I've already used up my allotment of problems for this year," she said. She was smiling, but it was true. Things had finally turned around for her— thanks, in huge part, to Monica—and she really wanted to enjoy a few problem-free months before the next onslaught of problems crashed over her.

She'd been sleeping on her ex-boyfriend's cousin's couch in the Dumbo neighborhood of Brooklyn when Monica had phoned last November and said, "Look—you and Claudio are history and you're living out of a suitcase. And I'm living in this fabulous house for dirt-cheap. There's plenty of space here, and a sun-filled loft where you could paint. Three and a half bathrooms. Kiss New York goodbye and come to Brogan's Point."

Emma had come. She'd scrounged up a few local art students. She'd knocked herself out promoting her Dream Portraits business, and she'd finally gotten her first commission. She wanted only good news from now on.

Maybe the problem Monica had mentioned was something simple. A clogged toilet? Emma knew how to use a plunger. A blow-up between Monica and Jimmy? Emma had survived her own blow-up with Claudio. She could nurse Monica through a heartbreak. Jimmy wasn't good enough for Monica, anyway, although Emma was wise enough to keep that opinion to herself.

Monica didn't look heartbroken, however. Emma tore her gaze from the painting she'd been working on and scrutinized her friend's expression. As an artist specializing in portraiture, she knew how to read faces. Monica's face was not sad or dejected. It was concerned and annoyed.

Clogged toilet or the equivalent, Emma thought with relief.

"Our asshole landlord wants to sell this house," Monica said.

That was not the equivalent of a clogged toilet. "What do you mean, sell it?"

"Sell it. Find a buyer and unload it. Stop renting it to us."

That was a problem. In fact, it was a *problem*. Emma had no idea what property values were in this picturesque seaside town an hour north of Boston, but she could guess that any house as spacious and new as the one she and Monica were renting, with a gorgeous ocean view and three and a half bathrooms, had to be worth some serious money. "I don't suppose we can buy it from him," she said.

Monica laughed bitterly. "If someone dies and leaves us a million dollars, maybe. I just got a call from Andrea."

"Andrea?"

"My mother's friend. The realtor who got me this deal. The landlord—Max Something, I can't remember his last name—lives out in California or somewhere, and he'd asked Andrea to rent this house out until he figured out what he wanted to do with it. He didn't want it sitting empty while he did whatever the hell it is he does in California, or wherever the hell he is. I got a year's lease—way below market value, because he thought I was doing a favor for him, occupying the place, turning lights on and off and scaring away potential vandals."

"You're so scary," Emma joked.

"Well, not me in particular. A tenant, any tenant, as long as I was responsible. Which I am," Monica insisted, evidently in response to Emma's smirk. "I got this deal because my mother knew Andrea, and she knew I didn't want to live down the hall from her and my dad at the inn. Anyway, our landlord—Max Whatever—can't evict us until June, because of the lease. But he might want to start showing the house now, which means we have to give Andrea access and keep the place tidy."

"Oh, God," Emma groaned. "Tidy? Anything but that."

"It isn't funny."

"I know." Emma drummed her fingers on one denim-clad knee. Her overalls were speckled with paint. So, she noticed, were her fingers. She would probably have less difficulty keeping the house clean than keeping herself clean, but either way, *tidy* didn't come naturally to her.

Monica was much tidier than Emma. Right now, on a day off from her job, she was wearing stylish skinny jeans, a fitted blouse, and ballerina flats that didn't have a single scuff on them, let alone freckles of paint like Emma's battered canvas sneakers. Monica often worked weekends at the Ocean Bluff Inn and got a couple of weekdays off in exchange, but her schedule varied so much, Emma couldn't keep it straight. Fortunately, she didn't have to. When Monica had a day off, she did her best to stay out of the loft, leaving Emma in solitude to paint, staying out of the way when Emma was working with her art students. Emma sometimes heard Monica downstairs, unpacking groceries, running the vacuum cleaner over the ridiculous white carpet, or chatting on the phone, but Emma had the ability to submerge herself so deeply in her work that she was hardly aware of whatever was going on in other parts of the house.

Creating art in this house, in this loft, was so much easier for her than her situation in Brooklyn had been. There, she'd been forced to paint while sharing space with three other artists in a converted factory broken into floor-through lofts. None of them could afford to rent a studio alone, so they'd pooled their resources and split the rent on a loft in the building. They'd each claimed a quarter of the loft space and did their best to ignore one another while they were working. Not ideal, but the arrangement had worked well enough as long as Emma had been living with Claudio.

But then she'd caught him screwing around with a naked model in his much grander, unshared studio—that would teach Emma to surprise him with a spontaneous visit in the middle of the day. He'd owned the co-op apartment they'd been living in, so she'd been the one to move out. Fortunately, his cousin Marie had insisted she liked Emma better than Claudio—"Can I get custody of you?" she'd asked—and Emma had wound up on her couch for a few months, until Monica had bailed her out by inviting her to move to this house in Brogan's Point.

Which was leased in Monica's name. The story of Emma's life, she thought with a sigh. Maybe someday she'd earn enough money to be able to sign her own name to a lease.

Actually, if their landlord insisted on selling this house out from under them, someday might have to come soon. "If he evicts us, you'll move back to the inn, right?"

Monica nodded grimly. "I'm not moving in with my parents. No way. But they've got an efficiency apartment there I can use." Monica's parents owned the Ocean Bluff Inn, a landmark hotel nestled against the shoreline just north of downtown Brogan's Point, and Monica was apprenticing her way into the management of the inn. She'd been working there since high school, first as a chamber maid, then as a waitress in the inn's assorted dining rooms. During college, when she and Emma had met and become best friends, she'd worked summers as a desk clerk in the lobby. Her parents insisted that she experience every job at the inn so she'd learn the business inside and out.

Emma didn't just adore Monica; she was intrigued by her. Emma was an artist, and she'd grown up in a ramshackle old house in Vermont, where her parent grew their own food, her father did carpentry and her mother snagged part-time jobs when money grew tight. Business people—people who got steady paychecks, people who paid their income taxes on time, people who dressed stylishly even on their days off—were like another species to Emma.

In college, she'd met plenty of members of that species, but she'd mostly hung out with her fellow art majors. Pure chance had assigned Monica as her roommate. However, in spite of their differences, they'd instantly become fast friends. Maybe it was a case of opposites attracting. Or maybe it was simply that Monica was smart and kind and loyal—and as intrigued by Emma as Emma was by her.

"I really don't want to move back to the inn," Monica confessed. "Not into that tiny apartment, anyway. My parents have a gorgeous suite there, six rooms, eighteen hundred square feet. I guess that'll be mine if they retire and I take over management of the place. But that's a long way off. And I can't stay there with them now, not with Jimmy."

Emma considered pointing out that, as a twenty-six year old woman, Monica was certainly entitled to invite her boyfriend into her bed—even if he wasn't good enough for her. But she recognized the awkwardness of doing that in her parents' home. There simply wasn't enough privacy.

At least Monica had access to the efficiency apartment she'd just mentioned. Emma would have to make her own living arrangements if she got evicted from this house. Brogan's Point wasn't exactly overflowing with rental housing, let alone rental housing affordable to an artist just getting started. She could move to another, cheaper town, but then she'd lose her students, the main source of her income.

And she'd need a studio, too.

Shit. This wasn't just a problem. It was a *problem.*

"All right," she said, determined to remain optimistic. "We've got until June. He can't kick us out before then. Maybe something will happen in two months."

"Yeah." Monica was clearly the less sanguine partner in their friendship. "Someone can die and leave us a million dollars. Better yet, Max the landlord can die."

"Or change his mind," Emma said diplomatically. "Maybe he'll find out that the real estate market is really depressed right now, and he'll decide it's not a good time to sell."

"Or he can die," Monica argued. "That would work for me."

Emma laughed. Reluctantly, Monica laughed, too.

"It'll work out," Emma assured her. "Things always do work out the way they're meant to."

"Except when they don't," Monica said darkly. She turned toward the stairs down to the first floor. "Get back to your painting, girl. You're going to need the money."

Two

It looked better than he remembered it.

Staying away for a year had clearly been a good idea. During that year, he'd regained his perspective, his balance, his sanity. He could evaluate the house with detachment. It was no longer the elegant retreat he'd envisioned when he'd bought it for Vanessa, no longer the extravagance he'd lavished upon her. She was gone from his life, and soon this property would be, too.

He hadn't remembered that the front walk was paved with bluestone and the front door was flanked by those round bushes with the dark, leathery leaves and voluptuous pink blossoms. He couldn't remember what they were called; botany was not his area of expertise. Whatever they were, they were in bloom now, vibrant splashes of pink where in his memory he'd visualized only gray clapboard and stark glass. He hadn't remembered the pine trees, so tall and straight he could imagine the seafarers of an earlier era creating towering masts for their schooners from them. He hadn't remembered the isolation of the house, perched as it was on a rise with a breathtaking view of the town and the ocean beyond.

He did remember that the house's architectural style was modern. He liked modern. He liked the sharp angles and broad planes of the house, the simplicity and geometry of it. He remembered that the first time Vanessa had looked at the place, she'd said, "It's kind of cold." Then she'd rethought that opinion and said, "Kind of cool, actually." He'd thought she was cool for loving it. Eventually, he'd realized she was just cold.

But he'd bought it for her. And now she was gone, and he would sell it.

He strode up the walk, trying not to let those gaudy flowering shrubs distract him, and pressed the doorbell. Through the glass sidelight bordering the door, he heard the bell resonate inside the house.

A few seconds later, he saw movement through the glass, first a shadow and then a woman approaching the door. He hadn't expected anyone to be home. He'd rung the bell as a courtesy before letting himself inside, but he'd expected his tenant, Monica Reinhart, to be at work at three-forty in the afternoon. According to Andrea Simonetti, the real estate broker who'd set up the rental, Ms. Reinhart worked at that big inn in town, in some sort of management capacity.

The woman he viewed through the glass did not look like a manager. She was petite, with wild red hair tumbling in curls around her face. She wore a baggy sweater, baggier cargo pants, and canvas sneakers, none of her apparel particularly new or neat. Trailing behind her were two little girls, maybe eight or nine years old, their hair pulled back in ponytails. Both had on oversized men's tailored shirts, the tails of which fell to their knees.

As soon as the red-haired woman spotted him, she fell back a step, then turned and said something to the girls. She didn't open the door.

Fair enough. She didn't recognize him, and she was apparently smart enough not to open the door to a stranger. He tried to signal her through the glass, digging his wallet from the hip pocket of his jeans so he could show her his driver's license, but she took another step backward and then moved the girls and herself out of his line of sight.

He abandoned his wallet and pulled out his cell phone instead. He'd programmed Monica Reinhart's phone number into it, even though he'd never had occasion to call her. Andrea had served as a go-between for them, but he'd wanted his tenant's number, just in case.

He tapped it, listened to her phone ring twice, and then: "Hey, this is Monica. I can't come to the phone right now. Please leave a message."

Oh, come on. She was standing on the other side of the door. Why couldn't she answer her phone?

He tapped on the glass. She and the kids refused to move back into view.

All right. He didn't want to scare the shit out of her, but *he* knew he was harmless, even if she didn't. He slid his phone back into his pocket, removed the front door key, and slid it into the lock. The door swung open.

He found Monica huddling with the two girls, pressed up against the coat closet door, all three of them pale and wide-eyed. Monica had one girl tucked securely under each arm, and she had her damn cell phone in one hand. "Get out," she snapped. "I'm dialing 9-1-1."

"I'm Max Tarloff," he said, spreading his hands palm up to show he wasn't holding any weapons.

She frowned, as if his name meant nothing to her.

"Your landlord."

"Max Something?"

"Max Tarloff."

Her mouth fell open, then slammed shut. He probably shouldn't have noticed her lips. They weren't covered in lipstick, and the light in the entry foyer wasn't exactly bright, but he could see that those lips settled into a natural pucker, a little too full for her face. Her complexion remained pale, and despite her red hair she had no freckles, at least none that he could see. Sharp cheekbones, though, and a wide forehead, and pretty hazel eyes. Her hair was so thick and long and curly, he could imagine losing small objects in it.

His key, for instance. He pocketed it so she wouldn't think he was planning to attack her with it.

"Tarloff," she repeated. "Monica could never...Oh, I mean..." She faltered, then loosened her grip on the girls. "I think it's okay."

"He has his own key," one of the girls said.

"Well, yes. As the landlord, he would." She peered up at him. "I thought you were in California."

"I was. Now I'm here."

"But we—I mean, you're not going to evict us, are you?"

Why was she acting as if he were an ogre, planning to boot her into the street, where she could live in a cardboard box? "I thought Andrea explained to you that I plan to sell the house when the lease is up in June."

"She told Monica, but…I mean, it's not June yet."

That was the second time the woman referred to Monica. Evidently, she was someone else. Someone who was living in his house, if her comment about being evicted was anything to go by.

And perhaps he *should* evict her, because he'd rented this house to Monica Reinhart, not Monica and some other woman, and two little girls. Sure, the house was too big for one person, but he'd rented it only so there would be someone living inside it, making sure the pipes didn't freeze in the winter and the roof didn't leak during the spring rains. He'd set a ridiculously low rent because he'd felt Ms. Reinhart was doing him a favor by living here. An empty house was an invitation to mischief. He didn't want people to think the place was abandoned.

Anyway, he didn't need the money. What he'd needed was a quiet, discreet person turning the lights on and off and announcing to the world that the house was occupied.

"Who are you?" he asked.

"She's our art teacher," one of the girls announced.

"You interrupted our class," the other added.

A class? An *art* class? In his house? What the hell? "Who are you?" he asked in a tight voice, not wanting to erupt and frighten the children—or have the woman phone 911. "That's number one. And number two is, are you running a school in my house?"

"Not a school, no." She loosened her grip on the two little girls. "Why don't you go upstairs and do a little more work on your collages while I talk to Mr.—Tarkoff?" she asked him.

"Tarloff." *Number three, why don't you know the name of your landlord?*

"Mr. Tarloff. Go, go, go!" She sent them toward the stairs with a gentle nudge, then turned back to Max. "I'm Emma Glendon. I'm sharing the house with Monica."

Max watched the girls as they scampered up the free-floating stairs to the loft. He was a nanometer away from losing his temper, but he didn't want to explode in front of her students. "Number one, you are not on the lease. The lease offers no subletting provisions. I did not give permission to Ms. Reinhart to open this house up to additional tenants."

The woman gazed up at him and he tried to ignore how lush her lips were. But when he steered his gaze away from them, it settled on her eyes, which were wide-set and fringed in dense lashes a shade darker than her red hair. Her irises contained a multitude of color—green and gray and amber. The way she peered at him gave him the uneasy sense that she could see more than he'd like.

Not that he had anything to hide. He just felt...unnerved.

"What was number two again?" she asked when his silence extended beyond a minute.

Number two? Right. "Number two, this property isn't licensed for commercial enterprises. It's not insured for you to be hosting classes with children. You need a permit from the zoning board to do that, and I know you don't have one, because as the landlord, I'd be the one to have to request it."

"It's not a commercial enterprise," the woman said. "It's two little third-graders who come here and make collages."

"They called it a class."

"I teach them things. Parents teach their children things, too, but that doesn't make their houses commercial enterprises."

He glanced toward the stairs and scowled. "Are they your children?"

"No."

"Are they paying you to teach them whatever the hell it is you're teaching them?"

She hesitated long enough for him to know the answer.

"That makes it a commercial enterprise," he said. "Most parents don't charge their kids to teach them how to tie their shoes." He scraped a hand through his hair in exasperation. He wasn't sure what he was most upset about: the fact that Monica Reinhart was in breach of her lease, the fact that if something awful had happened—say, a pint-size art student got injured in his house—his insurance wouldn't cover it and he might just find himself afoul of the law...or the fact that Emma Glendon, with her wild, fiery hair and her paint-spattered clothing, oozed sex appeal.

He couldn't figure out why. She was no Vanessa. She was short, unfashionably curvy, and messy. A smear of paint tattooed her left hand. Not his type. Not at all.

"All right," he said, as much to himself as to her. "You're going to have to vacate the premises."

"At the end of the lease. I understand."

"Now," he said. As soon as the word emerged, he felt terrible. Since when had he become such a tyrant? It wasn't as if he was a landlord by profession. If he was in breach of zoning laws, he could hire an army of lawyers to rectify the situation.

But he wanted this house vacated. He wanted it sold. He wanted to put this part of his life to an end. He couldn't move on as long as he still owned the place.

And it was probably going to be more difficult to evict two tenants than it would have been to evict one. Two tenants and a couple of pint-size Picassos in pigtails.

He was angry. He thought he'd overcome all his anger, his bitterness, his resentment. That was what this year had been about: rebalancing his life. Reclaiming it. Healing. And then moving on.

The red-haired art teacher standing in his entry hall only complicated matters, making it harder to rebalance, reclaim, heal, move on. Of course he was angry.

Before he could say anything more, anything that would make him feel even angrier, he yanked open the door and stormed down the bluestone front walk. The fat pink flowers on those shrubs couldn't possibly be mocking him, but it felt as if they were.

Three

"Who was that?" Abbie asked.

The little girl's voice distracted Emma from her inspection of the white carpeting on the steps leading up to the loft. She'd noticed a few faint smudges of dirt, but nothing that looked like paint or glue or ground-in clay, nothing a vacuum cleaner or a little rug shampoo couldn't remove. At least she hoped so.

She wondered if the condition of the floors mattered anymore. The guy was kicking her to the curb, literally—or as literally as possible, given that the road leading to the house didn't have a curb. Whether or not the carpet was in pristine condition seemed irrelevant. He would probably confiscate the security deposit just for the hell of it.

She didn't want to discuss him with Abbie and Tasha, but she wasn't about to lie, either. "He's my landlord," she said as she joined the girls at the work table, which held a chaotic clutter of construction paper, cotton balls, satin ribbon, aluminum foil, toothpicks, fabric, salvaged giftwrap, and magazines, pages of which had been scissored to shreds. Although Abbie and Tasha insisted they were old enough for pointy scissors, Emma had supplied each with snub-nose scissors—they cut just as well as pointy ones, so why tempt fate?—and a jar of rubber cement.

She loved having her young students create collages, which encouraged the children to think abstractly about shape and texture and the juxtaposition of images. Collages were messy. They were fun. And they didn't require fine motor skills. Not everyone could draw or paint. But anyone could make a collage.

The collaging materials with which she'd armed the girls were indeed messy, strewn and scattered across the work table. They were messier than Emma's hair or her clothes, messier than the drop cloths protecting the carpeted floor. She supposed she should be grateful that Max Whatever hadn't come upstairs and seen Emma's class in action.

The hell with gratitude. If he'd climbed the stairs to the loft and viewed the bedlam of two exuberant eight-year-olds creating collages, Emma's fate would have been no worse than it already was.

He was evicting her. *Now,* he'd said.

"What's a landlord?" Tasha asked.

Emma pasted a brave smile on her face. Tasha and Abbie's mothers were each paying her thirty dollars an hour to teach their daughters some basic art skills. They weren't paying her to whine about her imminent homelessness.

"A landlord," she said, bending to pick up a linty cotton ball which had migrated from the table to the floor, "is someone who owns a house."

"My daddy is a landlord," Abbie bragged.

"Well, it's someone who owns a house—or a building—and rents it out to other people to use. That man owns this house, but he rents it to Monica and me so we can live in it." Using a present-tense verb to describe what the man was doing didn't seem quite accurate, but Emma decided a shade of dishonesty was allowed, under the circumstances.

She needed to phone Monica to warn her that Max Whatever was in town—and worse, that Max Whatever was ousting Emma from his home. Possibly Monica, too. He'd seemed mad enough to kick them both to the non-existent curb.

Yes, he was mad. Mad Max.

She suppressed a bitter laugh and reached for her cell phone. Just a few minutes ago, she'd been about to tap in the emergency number, summoning the police to the house to save her and the girls from an intruder. Wouldn't that have been fun. Maybe the cops would have carted Mad Max away before he could give Emma the boot. A mistaken arrest would have pissed him off even more, but the result wouldn't have been any worse for Emma. It couldn't be worse.

She stared at her phone for a moment, then shoved it back into her pocket. She couldn't call Monica while her students were present. Besides, when Monica was working, she usually turned off her cell phone, which meant Emma would have to try to reach her through the inn's switchboard, and that in turn might mean having to leave a message with an assistant. This was not a situation about which Emma wanted to leave a message.

She checked her watch, peeled a blob of dried rubber cement off its face and said, "Class ends in five minutes. Let's finish what you're doing and tidy up the studio." Calling the loft a studio made the entire enterprise seem just a little more professional.

Which would no doubt piss Mad Max off even more.

While the girls scrambled to adorn their collages with a few final items—gummed gold stars in Tasha's case, a heart-shaped patch of paisley fabric in Abbie's—Emma gathered a few more fallen bits and pieces from the floor surrounding the table. While she tossed the detritus into the trash pail, she thought. About her impending homelessness. About how miserable she'd been sleeping on Claudio's cousin's couch before Monica had rescued her by inviting her to move to Brogan's Point.

About Max.

He wasn't what she'd pictured the few times Monica had mentioned their landlord. Max seemed like an old man's name, but Max Whatever couldn't have been much older than thirty. He was tall and thin, clad in jeans, sneakers, a brown wool blazer and a muffler wrapped several times around his neck, the kind of knitted scarf a girlfriend might make for her guy.

Emma tried to imagine Max's girlfriend. Tall. Thin. Bristling with self-righteous indignation, like him.

Beautiful, like him.

Only now, when he was safely out of the house, could she allow herself to contemplate the intriguing lines of his face, the contrast of his straight, narrow nose and his thick, wavy hair, the juxtaposition of that dark hair with his pale blue eyes. His eyelashes had been downright phenomenal.

Not that Emma paid attention to a man's eyelashes, except in a detached, appraising way. She painted portraits. She noticed facial details—professionally. Men's eyelashes did nothing for her personally. As an artist, however, she found them intriguing.

In fact, she had found all of Max's features intriguing. The faint hollows beneath his cheekbones. The sharp angle of his chin. The hint of bronze in his complexion. Even if Monica hadn't mentioned that he lived in California, Emma would have guessed that he hadn't spent the past few cold, snowy months in Massachusetts.

As riveting as his features were, he'd tried hard—with reasonable success—to keep his emotions hidden. His anger hadn't exploded from his face. She'd noticed it in the tension around his mouth, in the flinty chill in his eyes as he'd regarded her. But unlike, say, Claudio, who used to erupt like Vesuvius at the slightest provocation, Max had been restrained, his emotions held in check.

That only made him seem madder to Emma. She was used to people who flung their emotions around like confetti on New Year's Eve. Artists didn't erect many walls between themselves and the world. They needed to be able to see, feel, experience everything around them. You couldn't pick up on the subtle details of a flower or a seascape or a face if you had a thick wall of self-protection separating you from everything out there.

Painting Max's portrait would be a fascinating challenge, she thought. Especially painting it as a Dream Portrait, with his amazing face surrounded by his dreams. Unlike Ava Lowry, who dreamed of being a princess, Max probably dreamed of...what? Being obeyed by his tenants? How would Emma depict that visually on a canvas?

The doorbell rang, and she flinched, panic seizing her at the possibility that Max had returned with a constable in tow, perhaps, or a sheriff. Who was in charge of evicting tenants? Was it something the local police could take care of? Would they point a service revolver at her and force her to pack all her things and remove them from the house while they watched? Fortunately, she didn't own much, other than her art supplies.

Where would she store her easels and paints if she wound up living in a cardboard box on the corner of Atlantic Avenue and South street? Would the teeny-tiny apartment Monica had access to at the Ocean Bluff Inn be big enough? Doubtful. Monica's wardrobe alone was at least three times as big as Emma's, and then Monica had all her make-up and toiletries. She wouldn't have room for Emma's things as well as her own.

Emma realized that the person ringing it was probably Tasha's mother. The girls' mothers carpooled, and Abbie's mother had picked them up after their last lesson.

The girls snatched their collages from the table and raced each other to the stairs. Emma watched them clamber down to the first floor, giggling and elbowing each other. What if one of them fell? Would she be sued, or would Mad Max, the home owner, be held liable? What sort of insurance would he need for her to hold her art classes here? Would he require special insurance if Emma didn't call them art classes? What if she said they were simply occasions when she invited a couple of young friends over to make collages?

Fortunately, Abbie and Tasha were agile. No falls, no injuries. If anyone *had* gotten hurt, it wouldn't do them much good to sue her. She had no money to pay any claims.

Correction: she had sixty dollars, the two checks Tasha's mother handed her before oohing and ahhing over their collages. She thanked Emma and chased the girls down the front walk to her van, parked at the edge of the road. Emma waved them off, then turned away and closed the door.

Her vision took in the entry hall, with its stark white walls and white carpet. The walls needed some paintings hanging on them. Better yet, they needed color. The kitchen had slate-gray tile on the floors, and the living room sofas were a dark gray. The furnishings had come with the house—a good thing, since Monica, having grown up in a hotel, didn't own much in the way of furniture, and Emma owned even less. But as much as she loved living here, sharing the airy rooms and the splendid views with her best friend, Emma didn't much like the décor.

Not only was Mad Max a nasty landlord, but he was also a tasteless one. He'd had the good sense to purchase this fabulous house, but he'd given it a chilly, colorless ambiance. Emma decided she hated him.

She'd still like to paint him, though.

Four

Max entered the Ocean Bluff Inn and zeroed in on the clerk behind the burnished wood counter. She was dressed neatly in a blazer and blouse—the counter blocked his view of her lower half, so he couldn't see whether she was wearing slacks or a skirt, but he felt safe in assuming that whatever she had on was appropriate. Her hair was neat, her lips glistening with a soft pink lipstick.

Monica Reinhart, he guessed. The proper professional he'd rented his house to. The young woman Andrea Simonetti had sworn would make a perfect tenant, taking care of his property until he decided what to do with it.

He took a deep breath and crossed the cozy lobby to the counter. Another man might storm across the room and light into the woman, but Max wasn't given to displays of temper. He was kind of surprised that Emma Glendon had triggered so much anger in him, an anger hot enough that it hadn't burned itself out in the time it took him to drive down the winding, weaving roads back to town and this hotel.

Monica tapped a few keys on her computer and then turned and smiled at him. A middle-aged couple descended the broad, carpeted stairs to the lobby, and Max hesitated, figuring it would be better for Monica to assist them first. Even if he didn't lose his temper with his tenant, he didn't want to discuss her breach of their lease—or possibly *breaches*, plural—in front of hotel guests.

But they strolled past him and out the front door to the veranda, leaving him and Monica alone in the lobby. He approached the counter and asked, "Monica Reinhart?"

Her smile unflinching, she shook her head. "Kim Seaver. Can I help you?"

Okay. *Not* Monica Reinhart. He wondered if Ms. Reinhart would turn up in baggy old pants spattered with paint, like her illegal roommate. "I need to talk to Monica Reinhart."

"She's in a meeting with the tennis court people," Kim informed him. "The court needs to be resurfaced before the season starts. Is there something I can help you with?"

"No. It has to be Ms. Reinhart."

Kim quirked one eyebrow, as if trying to guess what he needed to see her colleague about. If it were her business, he would have told her. He wished she would put her eyebrow back down.

"You're welcome to have a seat and wait. The parlor is quiet." She gestured toward an arched doorway off the lobby. "Or you can have a drink in the lounge. Or the TV room—"

He didn't want a drink. Or a TV. He wanted to discuss his house with Monica, and then he wanted to sell the damned place and get on with his life.

"Oh, wait—here she comes now," Kim said, her attention snared by chattering voices that drifted into the lobby from a back corridor. "You're in luck." The smile she gave him was oddly coquettish, which made him recoil. He didn't trust flirtatious women.

The woman he presumed to be Monica Reinhart soon appeared in the hallway leading into the lobby from somewhere beyond the check-in counter. She was flanked by two burly men in work clothes—rugged jeans, flannel shirts, denim jackets. She, however, was clearly a graduate of the same school of grooming as Kim. She wore a tailored blue blazer over a plain white blouse, a pale gray skirt, nylons and dark shoes with low heels. Her hair was straight and dark, neatly trimmed to chin length, and her face was buffed and polished. She seemed to be everything Emma Glendon was not.

"Monica, this gentleman is here to see you," Kim said cheerfully, then gestured toward Max. Did she actually wink at him?

He didn't want to know. Seizing the moment, he extended his right hand across the counter and introduced himself. "Max Tarloff."

Monica's smile lost a bit of its luster as his name registered on her. Then she brightened again, with some effort. He could see the struggle as the corners of her mouth edged upward. "Yes, of course. Max Tarloff." After shaking his hand, she slid hers free of his grip and turned to the workmen. "So—clay surfaces, new nets, work with the landscape people and leave the fence as is."

"Right," one of the workmen said. "We're on it."

"Thanks." She turned back to Max, then glided around the counter. "I'm sorry—I didn't know you were coming to town."

"Well." He spread his hands as if to say, *here I am.*

"Why don't you come to my office?" She beckoned him around the counter and toward the back hall. Kim gazed after them, her expression calculating.

No, he wanted to shout at Kim. *I'm not here to flirt. I don't have a personal relationship with Monica Reinhart, and I don't want a personal relationship with you. I want to get that wild-haired woman out of my house and I want to put it up for sale. And I want to forget it ever existed.*

Doing his best to ignore Kim, he followed Monica down the hall to an office barely large enough to contain a small teak computer desk and a few chairs. The window behind the desk looked out onto a patio. While she might boast her own office, Monica was too young to roost high on the executive ladder at this resort. He supposed the offices overlooking the ocean were reserved for the head honchos.

He waited until she'd taken her seat behind the desk before he lowered himself into a chair facing her. The chair seemed better suited to someone her height than his; his knees jutted out, nearly banging the desk. Inching the chair back, he bumped the wall behind him. He felt like Alice after she'd eaten the cake that said "Eat Me" and outgrew the house she was trapped inside.

"It's so nice to meet you face to face," Monica said.

He braced himself against the charm offensive she seemed determined to launch. "Ms. Reinhart," he said, choosing to keep things as formal as possible. "I stopped by the house before coming here. Some other person—who wasn't you—was living there."

"Emma," Monica said. "My best friend."

"According to the lease—"

He was interrupted by the ringing of a telephone on the desk. "Excuse me," she murmured before lifting the receiver and tucking it against her cheek. "Monica Reinhart speaking...Hi, Dad. Yes, the tennis court guys were here.... They'll get it done before Memorial Day. Don't worry.... Well, with the weather, they couldn't...It'll get done, Dad. In time for the season.... No, they're leaving the fence. Just like we discussed.... Okay. 'Bye." She lowered the phone and gave Max an apologetic smile. "I'm sorry."

He checked himself before reassuring her he didn't mind. He didn't, really; after all, he'd just barged in on her, interrupting her work day. He hadn't made an appointment, and he ought to be grateful she'd invited him into her office. But he didn't want things to get too friendly between her and himself. He was pissed off, and he wanted to stay pissed off.

What had he been saying before the phone rang? Monica thoughtfully reminded him. "According to the lease...?"

He nodded. "According to the lease, you were supposed to be the only person living in the house. No sublets were allowed."

"Emma isn't subletting. She's just staying with me."

"I rented to you, not to her. I wasn't renting the house to make money—obviously. The rent is way below market value. I just wanted someone—one quiet, responsible adult—to stay in the house and make sure the pipes didn't freeze in the winter."

"They didn't," Monica said sweetly. "I made sure."

"The lease was a simple arrangement. Straightforward. Low rent, one person. But you invited someone else to live with you—and even worse, she's running a school out of the house."

"It's not a school," Monica argued. "She just does art with some kids. I don't suppose it matters though, does it? Andrea told us we're going to have to vacate the premises in June. Unless you'd like to consider renewing the lease." She sent him a hopeful smile.

"That's not going to happen." Damn Monica Reinhart for being so pleasant. She was coming across as civil and polite, and he was coming across as some sort of monster.

But he was *pissed off.* He'd flown into Boston, rented a car and driven up to Brogan's Point, intending to make sure his house was still standing and then stop by at Andrea Simonetti's real estate office to discuss listing the house for sale. Then he'd planned to drive back south to Cambridge, to spend a couple of days visiting his beloved mentor, Professor Stan Weisner, and indulging in a beer or two at one of his favorite college hangouts.

He hadn't expected to find that wild-haired woman in his house—with a pair of kids in tow. And to learn that she was living there, and running a commercial enterprise without his permission, without a zoning clearance, without any of the legal necessities...

He'd been taken advantage of before. He wasn't going to let that happen again, regardless of how civil and polite Monica Reinhart was.

Her phone rang again. "Oh—excuse me," she said before lifting the phone and directing all her civility and politeness toward her caller. "Monica Reinhart speaking...No, that's up to the landscaper. He has to work around the sprinkler heads. Talk to Barry about it, okay?" Another contrite smile as she set the phone back in its cradle. "We've really loved living in the house," she told him. "We've put every effort into taking good care of it. We've shoveled the driveway all winter, even though technically that wasn't our responsibility. We scrubbed all the outdoor furniture on the deck and stored it in the basement. We thought about hanging some pictures—well, Emma did. She's an artist. She loves being surrounded by art. But we didn't want to put any nail holes into your walls, so we left them bare."

"An artist. Right," he muttered, a vision of that short, curvaceous woman with her flamboyant mop of hair flashing through his mind.

"Did she tell you about her Dream Portraits? This is so cool—she paints a portrait of a person and surrounds the portrait with that person's dreams. The one she's working on now is a portrait of a little girl who dreams about being a princess. So she's painting a castle, and a crown…I think she's going to include a unicorn, too. She's so amazingly talented."

Max didn't want to hear how amazingly talented she was. "She's painting this portrait in my house?"

"Oh, she's very careful. She's laid drop-cloths all over the floor."

Wonderful. She was not only running a school in his house, but also painting castles and unicorns. "There are licensing and insurance issues—"

The phone rang again. Monica held her hand up like a traffic cop, halting him, and then answered the phone. "Monica Reinhart speaking…Where's Donna? She should be handling that." Monica listened for a moment, then sighed. "All right. I'll be there in a minute." She hung up the phone and sighed again. "I've got a nervous bride-to-be who wants to change her menu for the fifth time, and our events planner took the day off to get a root canal. I'm sorry. I really have to deal with this." She rose, and Max reluctantly stood, too. "Do you have a place to stay while you're in town?"

"I was planning to stay in Cambridge."

"But you're here, and it's such a beautiful day. Why don't you spend the night at the Ocean Bluff Inn as my guest? It's off season. We've got some vacant rooms. Please. As my guest," she repeated.

She was being too damned nice, which made him suspicious. And he hadn't intended to stay in Brogan's Point during this trip. Brogan's Point had never particularly appealed to him. Sure, the ocean was pretty, but Vanessa had been the one who wanted to live here. He was more of a city person. He'd grown up in New York, he currently lived in San Francisco, and this place was too quiet. Too tranquil.

"Thank you, but—"

"I insist." Monica circled the small room to the door. "Why don't I have Kim set you up in a room, and then you, Emma and I can meet for a drink at the Faulk Street Tavern at—" she glanced at her watch "—six o'clock and we can discuss this whole lease thing. You really can't leave Brogan's Point without having a drink at the Faulk Street Tavern. And you can't leave Brogan's Point without spending a night at the Ocean Bluff Inn. I'll have Kim take care of it."

With that, Monica strode out of the office and down the corridor, her sensible leather shoes carrying her at a brisk clip.

He didn't want to stay here, in this beautiful New England resort. He didn't want to have a drink at the Faulk Street Tavern, wherever that was. He definitely didn't want to get friendly with Monica Reinhart and her illegal roommate.

A castle. A unicorn. If there was one thing Max loathed, it was whimsy.

He should just drive over to Simonetti Realty and let Andrea take care of everything. Get Emma out of his house, inspect the premises, have an appraisal done, get the place listed. He could drive back to Cambridge and enjoy a drink at one of his old haunts instead of some picturesque little seaside tavern. He could get on with his life.

That was what he should do...But another memory of Emma Glendon, her lush hair and her even lusher lips, lodged itself in his brain. And he found himself at the counter in the lobby, allowing Kim to book him into a third-floor room.

Five

Emma had been to the Faulk Street Tavern only a handful of times since moving to Brogan's Point. She knew it was a landmark—although why, she couldn't say. It was kind of scruffy, just this side of drab. The drinks were inexpensive, but given her finances, she couldn't even afford inexpensive. Why go out for drinks when she could buy a cheap six-pack at the supermarket for not much more than a single drink at this bar? The wait staff at the Faulk Street Tavern was soft-spoken and mellow, but most people in Brogan's Point were soft-spoken and mellow, especially compared to the barmaids Emma had encountered in Brooklyn. The décor was pedestrian. The only special thing about the Faulk Street Tavern was the funky antique jukebox standing against one wall.

But when Monica had phoned her, told her to put on some decent—by which she meant not paint-spattered—clothing and haul her ass over to the place at six o'clock, Emma didn't argue. Apparently, Mad Max had tracked Monica down at the Ocean Bluff Inn and conveyed that he was not happy with his tenants. Or, more accurately, his tenant and Emma, whom he regarded not as a tenant but as some sort of toxic intruder.

A cockroach? A bedbug? A lethal dose of radon? Just because she and Monica had stretched the terms of the lease—no, they'd merely *interpreted* it differently from him—didn't mean she posed a threat to his precious house.

To be safe, however, she'd obeyed Monica's edict and dressed in a long brown skirt, a tunic in an interesting weave of brown, tan and moss green, and her most expensive shoes, a pair of tooled leather boots that Claudio had bought for her when things had been going well between them and that, obviously, she couldn't return to him once things had stopped going well. Before dressing, she'd taken a shower and washed her hair, just to make sure there were no flecks of paint or glue in her long, unmanageable mane.

She understood the importance of making a good second impression on Mad Max, even if her first impression had flunked the test. This meeting needed to go well. It was bad enough that he seemed inclined to evict her and Monica because they'd breached— no, *misinterpreted*—the lease. What if he sued them for damages?

She'd have to pawn her boots, for starters.

"We're going to make nice," Monica had explained when she'd phoned. "We're not going to be stubborn or sarcastic. Are we," she added for emphasis.

"Who, me? Stubborn and sarcastic?"

"Like that. Behave, Emma. Keep your mouth shut and let me do the talking. I'm better at this kind of thing than you are."

Anyone in the world had to be better at it than Emma.

But she'd washed her hair and donned her boots. And she'd arrived at the Faulk Street Tavern only five minutes late, even though she'd had to walk all the way down the hill into town from the house, a hike of nearly three miles. She couldn't afford a car. Living in New York City, she hadn't needed one. In Brogan's Point, she'd gotten used to walking.

Fortunately, the boots were extraordinarily comfortable.

Monica and Max were already seated in one of the booths when Emma entered the bar. The place wasn't that crowded; it was a weeknight, and still a bit early for pub crawlers. She strolled past the tables and across the scuffed wood dance floor at the center of the room to the booth her housemate and her nemesis occupied. Max courteously stood as she neared the table.

God, she'd love to paint his portrait. She'd remembered that his eyes were beautiful, but she hadn't remembered exactly *how* beautiful they were. Like precision-cut amethysts, surrounded by those dense black lashes.

She slid into the booth next to Monica, facing Max. "Hi," she said. She assumed she was allowed to say that much.

Max nodded and resumed his seat. Monica beamed a thousand-watt smile his way. "Let's order some drinks," she suggested, beckoning a waitress with a wave. "Max? What would you like?"

He eyed her warily, then slid his gaze to Emma and looked even more wary. "What do you have on tap?" he asked the waitress.

She rattled off a list of beers. He ordered a Sam Adams, and Emma requested one, as well. Monica opted for a dirty martini. "Can you bring a bowl of nuts or something?" she added. "What does Gus have that we can munch on?"

"Want me to get a menu?"

"No." Monica aimed her blinding smile back at Max. "I'm sure you'd like to save your appetite for dinner at the inn. Only one of our dining rooms is open for dinner during the off-season, but the chef is fabulous."

Max pressed his lips together in a grim line. Clearly, he was not buying what Monica was selling.

Emma tried not to fidget. The nape of her neck felt damp; blow-drying her thick hair usually took forever, and she hadn't had forever that evening. She'd hoped her walk down the hill in the brisk spring air would have finished what the blow-dryer had begun, but apparently it hadn't.

Or maybe the chill at the nape of her neck was caused not by her shower but by dread. This time tomorrow, she might be homeless.

"Mr. Tarkoff," she began.

"Tarloff," he corrected her as Monica kicked her under the table.

"I'm sorry. I mean, call me Emma and I'll call you Max. Would that be okay?"

"Emma, let's wait until our drinks get here," Monica said pointedly.

"I'll let you do all the talking," Emma promised, then turned back to Max. "I just want to say that I'm petrified about winding up homeless. I've taken really good care of your house, and I have nowhere else to live, so I'm really up the creek if I get kicked out. That's all. If you two want to debate the terms of the lease, I'll stay out of your way."

Max's gaze narrowed on Emma. Evidently, he hadn't expected her to be so blunt, to express her fear so honestly. She hadn't expected to express it so honestly, either. But she'd hoped that if she gave voice to her panic, she'd win a few points for candor.

"I don't want to make you homeless," Max said. Maybe he had a conscience, after all. Maybe she could guilt him into letting her stay at the house until she found a new residence. And some space to run her classes and Dream Portraits, because she'd need the income to pay for the new residence.

She started to thank him for his compassion, but he cut her off before she could speak. "The thing is, you can't run a business from a private house without getting a zoning variance."

"This is Brogan's Point," Monica reminded him gently. "Everyone knows everyone here in town. We aren't sticklers for those kinds of things."

"What if one of Emma's students tripped and fell in my house? As the owner, I'd be liable."

"There's nothing in the lease that says I can't have guests in the house," Monica pointed out. "Let's say I had a guest and she tripped and fell. You'd still be liable."

"I've got insurance for that. I don't have insurance for a student paying to participate in a commercial venture in my house."

The waitress arrived with their drinks and a heaping bowl of mixed nuts. "Gus said to tell you if you want something more substantial, the wings are good tonight," the waitress informed them.

"Do you want wings?" Monica asked Max.

He shook his head.

Once the waitress departed, Monica took over. "The lease runs through the end of June. If you don't sell the house July 1st, you may as well let us stay there month-to-month until you do sell—or at least until we can make alternate living arrangements. No sense having the house stand empty if you can be earning some money with it."

Emma experienced a surge of gratitude. She knew Monica was saying this on her behalf. Monica already had alternate living arrangements.

"Money isn't the issue," Max argued.

Before he could clarify what the issue was, a man approached their table. He had a blandly handsome face topped by light brown hair, with sideburns that crawled just a little too far down his cheeks. He wore a cheap suit, his tie loosened. Emma suppressed a grimace. Monica did nothing to suppress her grin. "Jimmy! I didn't know you were going to be here."

"Hey, babe!" Jimmy leaned across Emma to kiss Monica's cheek. "Yeah, a few of the guys decided to do a little TGIF action after work." He gestured toward a clot of young men, all dressed much like Jimmy. He was a car salesman. Emma assumed his buddies were, too.

"It's not Friday," Monica pointed out.

"That never stopped us. Hi, Emma," Jimmy said belatedly, and rather coolly. She suspected that his opinion of her matched her opinion of him. He shot Max a quizzical look, then turned back to Monica. "Who's this? Emma's new squeeze?"

Monica sent him a warning glance. "This is Max Tarloff, our landlord."

"Oh." Jimmy held up his hands in mock surrender. "My bad. I keep telling you, Monica, move in with me and you won't have to deal with a landlord."

"She'd have to deal with you," Emma muttered. Someone must have stuffed some money into the jukebox, because it suddenly began blasting an old Rolling Stones song, drowning out Emma's words. Just as well. She didn't need Jimmy joining Mad Max in the Let's-Give-Emma-Shit club.

"Jimmy." Monica's tone grew steely, even though she was still smiling. "Can we talk for a minute?"

Emma slid out of the booth without being asked. Monica followed her out of the booth, apologized to Max, clamped her hand around Jimmy's elbow and hustled him away from the table.

Emma resumed her seat. Max gazed after Monica for a moment, then shook his head. "I tried to talk to her in her office this afternoon, but her phone kept ringing."

"She's a busy lady," Emma said. "Always in demand."

Max regarded Emma in silence for a moment. "That's an old song," he finally said. "Microsoft used it in an ad for one of its operating systems a few years back."

"That jukebox is full of old songs. And nobody knows what they are, according to Monica."

"What do you mean? Aren't they listed on the front of the jukebox?"

"Nope. You put a quarter in—the price is as ancient as the music—and you never know what songs will come out. It's supposed to be haunted, or magical, or something."

A faint smile whispered across Max's lips. "I don't believe in magic."

"I do," Emma said, meeting his gaze.

His smile widened. "Really?"

"I don't believe you can say *abracadabra* and wave a magic wand and make things happen. But I do believe you can take a bunch of paint and spread it across a canvas in such a way that it changes the world. It's just colors and shapes, but those colors and shapes can reveal the artist's soul—and the subject's soul, too—and it can move people to tears. How can that not be magic?"

"Lots of things move people to tears. It isn't magic. It's a matter of brain chemistry, reflexes, psychological issues. If you fall and scrape your knee, you might cry. That's not magic. It's the body's neurological reaction to pain."

Emma hadn't expected to venture into a scientific discussion with him, let alone a philosophical one. She considered pointing out that if he evicted her from his house, she'd probably wind up weeping hysterically, and that wouldn't be because she'd scraped her knee. That would be much more akin to magic. Black magic. Bad magic.

But she was too intrigued by the analytical turn he'd taken. "Are you a scientist?" she asked. "I thought maybe you were a lawyer, given how hung up you are on liability insurance and clauses and all that." She realized she knew nothing about Max, other than that he lived in California and he was her landlord. And that he was a hell of a lot younger than she'd expected. And that if he'd been responsible for the décor of his house, he had no taste.

And that he had beautiful eyes. A beautiful mouth, too. His lips were thin but distinct, anchored by his sharp nose above and his strong chin below.

"I work in the high-tech industry," he said.

"High-tech is science. It's magic, too, if you ask me."

Another smile flickered across his face. His mouth was even more beautiful when he was smiling.

"How did you wind up with a house in Brogan's Point?" she asked. "Especially *that* house. It's so atypical for this area. Most houses around here are very New-England style. Colonials, Cape Cods, saltboxes...and you own this amazing modern house with walls of glass."

His smile vanished. "Why I bought the house is irrelevant," he said dryly. "All that matters is that I plan to sell it, as soon as possible."

"Right. But I think Monica made a good point about letting us stay in the house until you sell it."

He shook his head, then lifted his glass and sipped his beer. "When I was a kid, my family rented an apartment. Ugly little place. One bedroom. I slept on the couch in the living room. There was a big water stain on the kitchen ceiling. But it was in a gentrifying neighborhood, and the landlord decided to take the building co-op. He said we could stay in the apartment until it sold. Every time he brought in a potential buyer, one of my parents or I would be sure to stare up at the kitchen ceiling. The buyer would look up, notice the water stain, and leave. We wound up living in that apartment an extra two years until the landlord finally fixed the leak and repainted the ceiling."

She tried to imagine a pint-size version of Max, all tousled dark curls and attitude, his piercing blue eyes aimed at a water stain. "Your house doesn't have any leaks," she noted. "Your ceilings look fine."

"I'm just saying, it wouldn't be hard for you to delay a potential sale. You're smart. You'd find a way."

She shouldn't have been so pleased that he considered her smart. But she *was* smart—smart enough to change the subject. "So, you're in high tech. What are you, a computer scientist?"

He mulled over his reply. She didn't think she'd asked such a difficult question, but he seemed to feel he had to weigh his answer carefully. Finally, he said, "My work isn't that interesting."

His evasiveness made it interesting. "Let me guess," she said. "You developed some amazing new app and became a billionaire."

Another tenuous smile. "You found me out," he confessed.

At least he had a sense of humor. A begrudging one, but it made him seem a bit more human to her. She visualized the Dream Portrait she'd do of him—his angular features, his dazzling eyes, the thick, dark waves of his hair, and a background of computers, code, tablets, graphics, gadgets and gizmos. If he were a billionaire, he could certainly afford one of her paintings. He could afford millions of them.

She smiled back at him. Hell, she'd offer him a discounted price on his portrait. She would have such a good time painting it.

The Rolling Stones song ended and the jukebox pumped out a new song. An old song, really, but Emma recognized it. It was one of the many songs her mother used to sing when she was gardening or puttering around the house. Emma's mother had an awful voice; if she occasionally hit the right note, it was purely by luck. She also had a habit of mangling the words. Yet those classic rock and pop songs her mother used to torture had embedded themselves in Emma's memory.

I see your true colors, shining through...

When someone with a good voice sang it, it was a beautiful bal-lad. Emma felt a lush warmth fill her as the singer's voice curled around the words, sweet and searing. It vanquished the chill of her damp hair and the fear of homelessness hanging over her. She felt enveloped in the song.

Her gaze met Max's across the table, and she felt even warmer. He stared at her as if suddenly transfixed. By the song? By Emma?

She heard nothing but the music. The din of conversation, the clink of glasses, the rhythm of footsteps and scrapes of chairs against the floor—all the noise faded. Nothing entered her but the song, and the sight of Max Tarloff watching her intently, intensely.

The bar disappeared. The other patrons. The waitress. The tall, square-jawed, tawny-haired bartender. The beers on the table, and the bowl of munchies. The entire universe evaporated, leaving behind only a song.

A song, and the man facing Emma.

When the song ended, silence.

And then Monica's voice, shattering the odd spell the song had spun around Emma. "Hello? Slide over, Emma, so I can sit."

Emma gave her head a sharp shake. She noticed Max doing the same. Embarrassed that she'd zoned out so completely, she shifted on the banquette, moving herself and her beer toward the wall so Monica could join her and Max at the table. "I'm so sorry," Monica said to Max, apparently unaware of whatever had happened in the cozy booth while she'd been away.

What *had* happened? Emma had no idea. She felt as she'd been in the grip of a fever, and now it had broken and she was healthy again, but altered. The song was still inside her, tattooed onto her soul.

"That was a friend of mine," Monica explained to Max, gestur-ing toward Jimmy, who had gathered with his buddies at the bar. "He can be clueless sometimes."

Ordinarily, Emma would have cracked that Monica was correct on the "clueless" part of that claim, but underestimating sorely on the "sometimes" part of it. But she didn't trust herself to speak. Her mouth felt the way it did after dental work, before the Novocain wore off.

Max flexed his lips, and once again Emma wondered if he was recovering from the same weird symptoms that had overtaken her. He took a sip of beer, cleared his throat and said, "That's all right."

"I feel bad about the insurance thing," Monica said. "If you want Emma and me to pay the additional premium so your liability is covered, we can do that."

Emma wanted to slam her foot into Monica's shin—not only because she owed Monica an under-the-table kick but because Emma couldn't afford to pay an additional premium. Monica didn't earn much, but she received a steady salary, paid weekly, and if she had to, she could ask her parents for help. They were big on urging their daughter to be self-reliant, but in a pinch, they'd come through for her.

Emma's parents were big on self-reliance, too. In a pinch, she believed they would want to help her out, too. But like her, they had no money to spare.

"It doesn't seem worth it, since the lease is up in a couple of months. And there's the zoning issue," Max said. His brain-fog must have dissipated more quickly than Emma's, if he could discuss lease dates and zoning laws. He turned to look at her, and she was once again stricken by the color of his eyes. So very blue. *True blue,* she thought, the song shimmering inside her. She saw his true colors— or at least the true blue of his irises.

"How about if I help you find a place outside my house where you can teach your art class?" he said.

Emma gaped, as startled by his offer as by the cool beauty of his eyes. "That would be great," she managed.

"All right." He slugged down the rest of his beer. "Let's see what we can scare up." Abruptly, he scooted out of the booth and stood. "I'll be in touch," he said, then strode across the tavern to the exit and out.

Scowling, Monica turned to Emma. "What the hell just happened?"

Good question. "I—he left," she stammered. "And stuck us with the bill for the drinks."

"I invited him here," Monica assured Emma. "He knew I was treating. Is he serious? Is he going to find you studio space?"

"I don't see how he can. It's not like he knows this town." The last traces of mist floated out of Emma's brain and reality settled onto her, cold and heavy. "Any studio space he finds is going to be too expensive for me, anyway. And I'm still going to wind up home-less—unless he finds a studio that has a bed in it."

"We've got a couple of months," Monica reminded her.

"He could kick us out tomorrow," Emma shot back. "We're in breach of the lease, aren't we?"

Monica gazed toward the door through which he'd vanished, then swiveled back to Emma. "I don't think he's going to," she said. "If he's going to help you find studio space, he's not going to kick us out. He's a good guy."

Emma wouldn't go that far. She wasn't sure what kind of guy he was.

All she knew was that the song had walloped him the way it had walloped her. And he'd been as shaken by it as she was.

—⚇—

Gus watched the tall, dark-haired man bolt out of the tavern. She didn't know who he was, but she knew what had happened to him. Not in the particulars, but she was well aware of the peculiar power of the jukebox over some people.

He'd been nailed by it. He and Monica's red-haired friend.

Gus didn't know the redhead. She was a newcomer to Brogan's Point, and she rarely came into the tavern. But Gus knew Monica Reinhart. Hell, she'd known Monica when the kid was just a bump in her mother's abdomen. Like Gus, the Reinharts were in the hos-pitality business. The Reinharts' brand of hospitality was a bit more upscale than hers, but their inn and her bar were both landmarks in town. Gus knew that the Reinharts often recommended the Faulk

Street Tavern to the Ocean Bluff Inn's guests, even though they had a cocktail lounge at the inn. And Gus was always happy to send travelers up the road to the inn if they needed a place to stay.

She'd watched Monica grow from a scrappy kid into a hard-working teenager, into an even harder-working adult. She'd sometimes found herself wishing Monica had been just a couple of years older, or her own sons a couple of years younger. Gus's younger son and Monica would have made a great pair. Now that they were all old enough that the age difference didn't matter, her boys no longer lived in town. And Monica was still dating Jimmy Creighton, who'd been a good-looking twit as a teenager and hadn't evolved much since then.

Sometimes Gus wished a tune from the jukebox would seize Monica and spin her around, give her a different perspective on life and love. But this evening, it seemed as if Monica's friend had been the one spun around.

Monica's friend and that lanky stranger. Just recalling how quickly he'd fled from the bar caused Gus to smile.

Manny Lopez, Gus's assistant, lumbered the length of the bar, hauling a case of vodka from the storeroom downstairs. Gus was strong, but Manny had been a linebacker in high school, and he was still built like one, big and solid, with muscles as tough as the rubber in the radial tires on Gus's four-by-four. He carried the case of liquor as if it were no heavier than a box of tissues. "Gonna be light tonight," he said, commenting on the sparse crowd.

"It's early yet," she assured him as he set the carton down and began unloading the bottles. "Jimmy Creighton and his friends'll drink enough to keep us in the black."

Manny laughed. Gus smiled, but she wasn't actually joking. Monica could do so much better. All she needed was a little nudge. Or maybe for Will to swing back into town and decide he liked Brogan's Point, after all. Gus's older son had a wife, a baby and a mortgage down in Quincy. He wasn't going anywhere. But Will still rented, and that Boston rent he was paying devoured a huge portion of his paycheck. He could come back to Brogan's Point, find work here, settle down, notice that Monica had blossomed into a lovely lady.

Gus's smile widened. Her sons were every bit as stubborn and headstrong as she was. She'd never fulfilled her mother's dreams, choosing basketball over ballet, marrying a bar owner and joining him in the business, taking it over after cancer had claimed him, and currently enjoying a nice, comfortable, out-of-wedlock affair with Ed Nolan, one of Brogan's Point's finest. Gus's mother frequently made comments about Ed's not buying the cow when he could get the milk for free. Gus ignored her.

She glanced over at the booth where Monica and her friend were seated. With the man gone, Monica had switched benches so she faced Emma. They bowed their heads together over the table, conferring intensely. Gus couldn't see Monica's face, but she could see the redhead's.

Pretty girl. Crazy hair.

And a dazed expression.

The jukebox had gotten to her, for sure.

Six

That song. He didn't even like it. Too schmaltzy. Too whiny. Why the hell couldn't he get it out of his mind?

He liked hip-hop, raw and thumping. Maybe his taste in music—or lack of taste, his parents insisted—had been a reaction to the violin lessons he'd been forced to take as a child. Every week he'd had to trudge down Brighton 7th Street to Mr. Chomsky's apartment, where he'd spend an hour sawing away on his cheap, battered fiddle while Mr. Chomsky would mutter, "So much talent going to waste because you don't practice enough! Apply yourself!" Max had wanted to apply himself to the stickball games going on in the street or to the stretch of beach beckoning him from the southern end of Brighton 7th, not to mastering vibratos and bow positions.

But his parents were old country, old school, old everything. They might have emigrated from Russia and embraced their newly minted American citizenship, but the only music they considered worthwhile was what Tchaikovsky, Prokofiev, Mussorgsky, Stravinksy and Shostakovich had written. They'd hated that their only child listened to that "loud, trashy stuff—I can't even call it music," his father would rail. "Not in my house. I won't allow it."

Other teenagers might have been sneaking smokes and booze beneath the elevated tracks of the B train running through the neighborhood. Max had been sneaking Ludacris, Ja Rule and Eminem.

He sure as hell hadn't been developing a taste for pop ballads like "True Colors." Yet that song had flowed from that antique-looking jukebox straight into his skull and settled in for a nice, long stay.

His accommodations at the Ocean Bluff Inn were spacious and pretty, the walls a muted beige, the bed decadently comfortable, king-sized and piled high with pillows. The room was silent; the windows faced away from the ocean, so he didn't hear the waves breaking against the sand, and the hotel was clearly not filled to capacity, so no voices seeped under his door from the hall. But he couldn't sleep, not with that freaking song playing over and over in his head. *Beautiful, like a rainbow...* So sweet. So cloying.

It wasn't just the song that had taken up residence like a squatter in his gray matter. It was the actual squatter occupying his house: Emma Glendon. Emma with her extravagant hair and her astute eyes. Red hair, hazel eyes. Were those her true colors, or did she make use of Lady Clairol and wear tinted contacts?

Why should he care?

Damn it, he *did* care—enough to volunteer to help her find studio space. As if he could possibly be of any assistance in that. He knew nothing about Brogan's Point. He'd bought a house here only because Vanessa had been from the area—the North Shore, she'd called it—and wanted an East Coast base. They'd been engaged to be married. He'd wanted her happy. She'd picked out the house, and he'd said, "Sure."

He'd been a fool then. And here he was, being a fool again, helping that red-headed creature to find a new base of operations once he'd evicted her.

One big difference between her and Vanessa, of course, was that she hadn't asked him for his help. She'd seemed started by his offer, as startled as he himself was when he'd made it. He'd been under a spell when he'd spoken, bewitched.

He was a man of his word, however. His parents may have failed to instill in him their passion for Tchaikovsky and Rachmaninoff, but they'd taught him to honor his commitments, to follow through on his promises.

So he'd find Emma a place to set up her easel. At least he'd try.

And then he'd remove her from his house, put the damned place up for sale, and get on with his life.

—⟋ⱴⱴ⟍—

"Tell me again about the magic," Emma asked Monica.

Early morning sunlight filtered through the trees and streamed into the kitchen through a wall of glass. The kitchen didn't offer a view of the ocean as the loft where Emma worked did, but it overlooked the forest of towering pines that bordered the house's rear yard. Emma recalled the views from Claudio's apartment: through the bedroom window a dark, narrow alley, and through the front windows the brick and brownstone buildings across the street. If you stood deep in the corner of the main room and peered westward through the window furthest from that corner, you could glimpse the drab steel cables of the Manhattan Bridge. Not the whole bridge itself, just a few of the cables.

Moving to Brogan's Point had taken some getting used to, but the views from her current home were vastly superior. Unfortunately, her enjoyment of the view wasn't going to last. God knew what views her next home would have. The pavement beneath her cardboard box? Maybe a flap, with "This Side Up" and an arrow printed on it?

She and Monica sat side by side on stools, their coffee steaming in mugs on the granite island occupying the center of the room. Monica was working her way through a bowl of oatmeal, but Emma had no appetite. Just sipping her coffee was a struggle.

"What magic?" Monica asked.

They were both dressed for work, Monica in crisp slacks and a tailored blouse, Emma in her paint-spattered overalls. She didn't have any students today, and she intended to make as much progress as possible with her Dream Portrait of Ava Lowery. She didn't hold out much hope that Max would find her a studio any time soon, if ever, and she needed to get Ava's portrait done and a nice, fat check from Ava's parents in her pocket before she ventured out to find a studio on her own.

"That magic jukebox at the Faulk Street Tavern. What's the story with that?"

Monica scooped a dab of oatmeal onto her spoon and consumed it slowly, licking her spoon as if it were a lollipop. "According to legend," she said, her voice taking on the stentorian quality of a documentary film narrator, "sometimes the jukebox will play a song that speaks to only one or two individuals in the bar. No one else will especially react to it, but the people it's aimed at will be changed by it."

"Changed in what way?"

Monica shrugged. "Changed in a way they need to be changed."

As explanations went, that was pathetically vague. "So someone could hear a song and realize she needs a haircut?"

"I think the change is more profound," Monica said. "It's just a myth, though. Don't you dare cut your hair."

"I wasn't planning to," Emma said, then hid behind her mug, taking a long, scalding slurp of coffee. She didn't want Monica to think she'd been changed profoundly by that song yesterday. She wasn't even sure she'd been changed at all. Max, yes, but not her.

Then again, the insomnia she'd endured last night was a change for her. Usually, when she couldn't sleep, it was because she was so energized by a project. She'd been known to stay up half the night working on a canvas, fueled by adrenaline and goaded by her muse. But the previous night's sleeplessness had nothing to do with her art. It had to do with Max Tarloff. She'd lain awake, restless and edgy, picturing the mesmerizing glow in his striking blue eyes as the song had wrapped itself around him and Emma. She'd visualized the delectable shape of his mouth. She'd imagined that mouth on hers, imagined it grazing down her body...

A wave of heat washed through her. She shifted her legs on the stool and took another drink of coffee, praying that Monica wouldn't notice how ridiculously turned on she was. By thoughts of their landlord, of all people! By thoughts of the man who would be kicking them out of the house the instant their lease was up, if not sooner.

"So the song from the jukebox changes the person who paid for it, right?" Whatever bizarre effect "True Colors" had had on her and Max, neither of them had put money into the machine and punched the numbered buttons for that song. Surely its magic had been intended for someone else. They were just collateral damage.

Monica shook her head. "No one can choose what song will come out of the jukebox," she said. "No one even knows what songs are inside the jukebox, except that they're all old. According to Gus, they're all songs that were hits while you could still get records on vinyl. The jukebox can't handle CD's or MP3's."

"And you can't choose which song it will play?" Now it was Emma's turn to shake her head. "People put in money and then they simply have to accept whatever song comes out?"

"Yep."

"That doesn't seem fair."

"Well, no one is forced to put money into the machine. And it's only a quarter for three songs. The price hasn't changed in decades. For twenty-five cents, people are willing to take a chance. It's kind of fun. You put in a quarter and then the jukebox surprises you."

Some surprise. If that song meant Emma would be plagued with insomnia for the rest of her life, she'd be pretty damned pissed. If, on the other hand, that song compelled Max to find her a new studio…well, she couldn't be pissed about that.

"Who's Gus?" she asked.

"The owner of the Faulk Street Tavern. That tall woman with the short hair behind the bar."

"I wonder if any of the songs ever changed her. She's in there listening to the jukebox every day."

"I don't know." Monica glanced at her watch and slid off her stool. "I've got to go. If Max stops by, be nice. He seemed a little less prickly last night."

"That's because you were so sweet," Emma pointed out. "I don't do sweet very well."

"It's time you learned. The sweeter you are, the less likely he is to boot us out of the house before the lease is up."

"All right." Emma stared at the strong black coffee in her mug. Maybe she ought to stir some sugar into it. Sweet coffee might sweeten her mood.

She remained on her stool, staring into the mug while Monica rinsed out her dishes and stacked them in the dishwasher. Would Emma's next residence have a dishwasher? Would it even have a kitchen? Would she have to eat off an aluminum mess-kit, like a soldier in the midst of a battle?

She was in the midst of a battle now, and the thought of eating caused her stomach to clench. She supposed soldiers felt the same way. Not knowing your future could sure suppress your appetite.

At least she wasn't getting shot at.

She refilled her mug and trudged up the stairs to the loft. Sleepy or no, distracted or no, she had to get back to work on Ava's Dream Portrait. Painting could be magical, as she'd told Max yesterday at the bar. Perhaps if she wielded her brushes, if she finished the castle, and added the unicorn and a dazzling, bejeweled crown to the picture, some magic would rub off on her.

The right kind of magic. Magic that would provide her with enough money to live on and a roof over her head—and the ability to get a good night's rest. Was that too much to ask for?

Seven

A ndrea Simonetti seemed perturbed. "Monica had a friend visiting her," she told Max. "There's nothing in her lease banning visitors."

"This is a bit more permanent than a visit," Max told the broker. The real estate company where she worked was located inside a building that looked like an actual house, with shingles and shutters and a cute brick chimney, although the house sat on Main Street and was abutted by a driveway that led to an asphalt parking lot in back. Andrea's office was the size of a small bedroom, but instead of a bed, it contained a broad desk with a computer humming on it, and the walls were adorned with a few framed certificates attesting to Andrea's professional status and several dozen glossy photographs of houses for sale.

"In other words, the friend is living in your house," Andrea surmised.

Max nodded. "Not just living there. She's running a business out of the house."

"A *business?*" Andrea's impeccably tweezed eyebrows arched so high, Max was afraid they'd collide with her hairline.

He laughed. "Not *that* kind of business. She teaches art. And that's the thing. I can't have her running a school in the house, with little kids doing finger-painting and trashing the place."

"Is the place trashed?" Andrea's eyebrows soared again.

"Not that I could see."

"We need to do a walk-through," Andrea said, jotting a note on the small pad on her desk. "Monica is liable for any damage to the place. We've got the security deposit, but—"

"The thing is, this second tenant..." What could he tell Andrea about the second tenant? That her hair was the color of fire and her lips made him think of plums, sweet and tart and juicy? That beneath her baggy apparel he could detect the sort of enticing curves most women went on drastic diets to eliminate and most men dreamed of? That a stupid song had scrambled his usually orderly mind and he was no longer quite sure of who he was?

No. He couldn't say any of that. Just thinking it gave him a headache.

"She needs to work," he said. "I want to help her find someplace else to hold her classes."

"I don't see how that's your responsibility," Andrea said, her tone indignant. "I'm so sorry. I should have checked to make sure Monica was honoring the terms of the lease. I've known the Reinharts for years. Monica is a good girl. I assumed she would entertain friends in the house—and I assumed she would do so in a civilized manner. No blow-outs, no keggers, no inviting half the world over via Twitter."

"Forget parties. Forget trashing the place." Max tried to steer Andrea back to the issue that concerned him. "You know the available properties around here. Is there any reasonably priced space where Emma could hold her classes?"

Andrea shrugged. "I'd have to research it."

"Please do." Max rose from his chair.

Andrea peered up at him. Her lipstick was as impeccable as her eyebrows, the dark pink applied with precision. Max had never understood the allure of lipstick. If you wanted to kiss a woman, you didn't want to kiss some cosmetic product. And if you didn't want to kiss her, lipstick wasn't going to change that.

"What about listing the house?" Andrea asked. "Do you want to go ahead with that?"

"I plan to sell it," he assured her. "But don't list it yet. They have two more months on the lease."

"Selling a house takes time. Especially an unusual house like yours. It's fabulous, but it's not exactly your standard-issue Boston area home. I know we'll get a good price for it, but it might take longer to find a buyer who loves it as much as you did when you bought it."

Max wasn't sure he'd ever loved it. Vanessa had. He'd bought it for her.

But that was none of Andrea's business. "If you want to get started on some preliminary work—have it appraised, photograph it, make sure everything is in order—that would be fine. But don't list it yet. I'll let you know when I'm ready to take the next step."

Leaving Andrea's office, passing two younger brokers at their desks in the front room and stepping outside into the sunny afternoon, Max tried to puzzle out why he was suddenly less than eager to sell the house. Every remotely possible explanation led back to that stupid song. *Like a rainbow?* What the hell did rainbows have to do with anything?

He strolled down the driveway to the lot in the rear, where he'd parked his rental car, and climbed in. Had he been at Logan Airport only yesterday, signing the paperwork in that area of the terminal where all the rental car desks were clustered? Had it been a mere twenty-four hours ago when he'd phoned the Hyatt Regency in Cambridge on his way out to the rental car lot and told them he'd be checking into his room that evening, after a quick trip north to Brogan's Point?

Why was he still here? Why had he spent a night in the Ocean Bluff Inn instead of the Hyatt? Why hadn't he told Andrea to go ahead and list his house for sale?

Why did he want to help Emma find studio space? Yesterday, when he'd seen her huddling inside the front door of his house with those two little girls, her thumb poised on her cell phone so she could dial 911, he'd had no interest in helping her. Quite the opposite—he'd been startled and then enraged to discover her living in the house. He'd wanted her gone.

Now…Now he didn't know what he wanted.

Because of that ridiculous song? Or because of Emma's stubborn chin and her defiant attitude, her lush lips and her amazing hair?

He pulled out of the driveway and cruised slowly down Main Street and then Atlantic Avenue, searching for studio space. As if he knew what such a thing would look like. The businesses lining the street had signs and displays in their windows: hardware store, boutique, gift shop, consignment shop, knitting shop, diner. Nearly all the stores were occupied, and none of them seemed like a suitable venue for an artist to hold classes and paint.

What did Max know about artists, anyway?

He wondered what Emma had done to create a studio in his house. Had she just taken a room and filled it with art supplies? Was the room full of half-finished canvases? Did it reek of turpentine?

Without consciously thinking about it, he steered out of town and up the twisting back road that climbed the hill to his house. Other houses stood along the road, nestled among the pine trees. Some were set back from the street by long driveways, and others loomed close to the roadway. His house sat at the top of the hill on a two-acre plot. An architect had designed the house for himself twenty-five years ago, and sold it only because he'd reached the age when New England winters were more than his arthritic joints could tolerate. Max was only the second person to own the house—and he'd never even hung his jacket in one of its closets. That was actually rather pathetic. An architect's dream come to life, and Max owned it, and he'd spent not one single night under its roof.

He reached his driveway and let the car roll to a stop. The scent of the ocean, so prominent down the hill, along Main Street and Atlantic Avenue, was overtaken here by the fragrance of the surrounding pine forest. Although he couldn't smell the ocean, he could see it. The architect had cleared enough trees to provide a spectacular vista from southeastern-facing side of the house.

Max turned from the ocean view and regarded the house thoughtfully. He could see why Vanessa had fallen in love with it. Too bad she'd never really gotten to enjoy the place. She'd furnished it, decorated it, discussed her plans with him. And then everything had fallen apart.

At one time, that thought would have filled him with bitterness. Standing on the front walk right now, making his way to the porch, pressing the doorbell…The song he'd heard in the bar last night drifted through his head, and to his amazement, he felt no bitterness at all.

As she had yesterday, Emma peeked through the sidelight. Unlike yesterday, however, today she felt safe in opening it when she saw Max on the other side of the glass. Even though he had a key and could have let himself in, he remained standing on the front porch as she opened the door, gazed up at him, and said, "Hi."

As if she'd expected him.

"May I come in?"

"Sure." She stepped back and he entered the house.

He wanted to focus on the house itself, to view it the way Vanessa had the first time Andrea had shown them the place. He wanted to see it not as a burden to be shed but as a home, a place where Emma and Monica lived.

White carpeting, was his first thought. *Not very practical.*

Emma smiled hesitantly. "I'm working right now, so…"

"I didn't mean to interrupt you," he urged her. "I just wanted…" *To see you,* he almost blurted out. "To see your work space. You need a new studio. What is that going to entail?"

She turned and strolled ahead of him down the hall. His gaze journeyed from the tumbling waves of her hair down her compact body, clad today in baggy denim overalls. Her hips shimmied gently with each step. Her feet were small, her sneakers spattered with paint. Fortunately, all the sneakers left on that impractical white carpet were tread marks. The paint must have dried long ago.

As they entered the great room and neared what Andrea had called a floating staircase—one that rose from the center of the room, not bordered by walls—he heard what sounded like a low chuckle coming from Emma. "What?" he asked.

"Did anyone ever tell you you talk funny?" she asked, then hurriedly added, "I don't mean that as an insult. It's just—I mean, *what is that going to entail?* No one says *entail* in casual speech."

Max hesitated, his foot on the first riser as she proceeded up the stairs. "They don't?"

"No one I know does."

"You know me." He followed her up the stairs to the loft. Few people noticed that he spoke—well, *funny* wasn't the word he'd use to describe his speech. He loved language and all the words it provided for him. He used them whenever he needed them. *Entail* was a perfectly good word. "English isn't my first language," he told her. He wasn't sure why he'd revealed that about himself. But then, he wasn't sure why he'd driven up the hill to the house in the first place. He wasn't sure why he was doing a lot of things.

Emma had already reached the loft. She spun around and stared at him. "Really? I never would have guessed. You speak beautifully. You just use unusual words sometimes. What's your first language?"

He didn't answer right away. He was too distracted by the sight of the loft, which she'd converted into a splendid work space. The floor was covered with thick, stained drop cloths. Canvases stood stacked against a wall, draped in plastic wrap to prevent them from marring the wall itself. Sturdy shelving along another wall held supplies. A large table stood at the center of the loft, old and scarred and covered with paints, brushes, and a jar of murky solvent. Three easels stood near the table, the center one holding a rectangular canvas, maybe two feet by three feet, that featured a painting of an adorable little girl, her eyes bright, her cheeks a soft, tawny peach hue, her rippling blond hair topped by a bejeweled crown. Behind her face, a half-painted castle loomed, and what appeared to be a unicorn stood on the stretch of green lawn beside the castle. The easels flanking the painting held photographs and sketches of the girl, the castle, and the mythical horned creature.

Max was mystified. "A unicorn?"

"It's what I call a Dream Portrait," Emma explained. "I paint the person and surround her with her dreams. Ava Lowery dreams of being a princess. What's your first language?"

"Russian," Max said, his gaze riveted to the painting. He picked a path carefully over the drop cloths for a closer look at the canvas on the easel. The afternoon's natural light flooded through the glass wall of the great room, bathing the painting in a warm, golden glow.

"Russian?" Emma said. "Really?"

"I was a toddler when my family came to America," he told her. "A year and a half old. For the first few years we were in the United States, my parents spoke only Russian, so that was what I learned first. I picked up English pretty quickly, though."

"Wow. Russia! Why'd they come here?"

He shrugged. "A better life. More freedom."

"So where did you grow up? Where did you learn English?"

He finally tore his gaze from the painting to look at Emma. Her face glowed even more beautifully than that of the little girl on the canvas. He didn't think his life story was particularly interesting, but her eager curiosity touched him. "Brighton Beach. It's a neighborhood in Brooklyn where many Russian immigrants live. Little Odessa, it's called."

"Sure, I've heard of Little Odessa. Before I moved here, I was living in Dumbo." He frowned, picturing the cartoon elephant with the big ears. "Down Under the Manhattan Bridge Overpass," she explained. "It's on the western edge of Brooklyn. Lots of artists live there. Lots of lofts converted into studios. It's getting gentrified, so the artists will probably be forced out soon by high rents."

He'd known his way around Brooklyn pretty well while growing up, but he had never heard of that neighborhood. "Dumbo," he said, then shook his head. "I gather Brooklyn has become somewhat more upscale since I left."

"You live in California now, right?"

"San Francisco." He ambled around the loft, careful not to trip over the wrinkles and bumps in the cloth covering the floor. The view of the ocean through the glass wall was spectacular. "I like living near the ocean."

"This house qualifies," Emma said, glancing toward the glass wall for a moment and then gravitating back to the easel. "You should keep it."

"It's a little far from San Francisco. I would have a difficult commute to work."

"Big deal. The U.S. has two oceans. You might as well have homes near both of them."

The idea was tempting. But this had been Vanessa's house, not his, not theirs. She was gone, and he wanted her house gone, too. Perhaps that sentiment was irrational, but he was rational ninety-nine percent of the time. He could allow himself one tiny percent of irrationality.

"I guess that would be pretty expensive," Emma conceded. "Two houses. Sheesh. I can't imagine owning even one house. But if I were you, I'd dump the San Francisco place and keep this one." She studied her painting thoughtfully, then lifted a paintbrush and dabbed a touch of shading to the castle's main turret.

"As I said, I work in San Francisco," he said, not adding that he could work on the east coast as easily as the west. Computers, phones and airplanes could keep him connected. And overseeing his foundation and his investments wasn't exactly the most demanding job in the world. He had Janet running the office in San Francisco. She was alarmingly competent. And he was a call or a text away if she needed to contact him.

He could work here as easily as there. He could convert the magnificent loft into an office and manage the foundation while gazing out at the ocean. His office in San Francisco was on Market Street, which he supposed offered a pretty enough view for an urban vista. But it wasn't as stunning as the view through the glass walls of his house.

Vanessa's house, he reminded himself.

Emma took a step back from her easel and scrutinized her painting. She had the easel positioned facing the wall of glass so the daylight streaming through the panes would illuminate it. He studied her profile. Her nose had a slight bump in it, not visible when viewed straight on. Her chin was surprisingly strong. Or maybe not so surprisingly, he thought. She was clearly a tough woman, determined and stubborn. Did the shape of a woman's chin correlate to her personality?

She startled him by turning suddenly, so she was facing him. "I'd like to paint you," she said.

Her words surprised him even more than her abrupt movement. His own words surprised him even more. "I'd like to kiss you."

Eight

*H*oly *crap.*

Staring at him, Emma had been thinking about the stark lines of his face, the hollows of his cheeks, the vivid blue of his eyes. She'd been thinking about how she would position him on the canvas—three-quarter view would probably be best, with him looking past the left shoulder of whoever stood in front of the canvas, because his left side was just a tiny bit more interesting than his right—and how she would capture the twining texture of his thick, dark hair.

But now she was thinking only of his mouth, wondering how it would feel pressed to hers, wondering how it would taste.

Like a rainbow...

Of course not. Mouths did not taste like rainbows. Kisses did not convey color. And she absolutely couldn't let him kiss her, because he was her landlord, and he wanted her out of his house, and if they started something romantic, or just plain sexual, the landlord-tenant power dynamic between them would inevitably be a part of it. If she slept with him, would he reduce the rent? If she didn't kiss him, would he have the local constable nail an eviction notice to the front door?

The possibilities tumbled and jumbled inside her mind, making her queasy. "I don't think..."

"No," he said more to himself than to her. "No, I—I'm sorry. I don't know what I was thinking." He spun away and stared at the panoramic view beyond the glass wall.

He seemed oddly vulnerable, his broad shoulders slumping, his hands buried in his pockets as if to prevent himself from touching anything.

Touching her.

God, she wanted that. She wanted him to touch her. She wanted to paint his hands as well as his face. She wanted to paint his dreams, just as she was painting Ava's little-girl dreams of a castle and a unicorn.

"I should go," he said.

She agreed. He should go. The air around them was thick with unspoken thoughts, unexpressed desires. Yet she didn't want him to leave. "It's your house," she said.

He snorted a laugh. But he remained where he was, making no move toward the stairs.

The silence stretched for a minute, and she said, "So, can I paint you?"

At that, he turned. "What would painting me entail?"

There he went, using the word *entail* again. She smiled. "Well, I could do it the way I'm doing Ava's. I'd snap a bunch of photos of you and then paint from the photos. Or you could pose for me, but that would take a lot more of your time."

He nodded slightly, mulling over the options.

"And then I'd have to ask you a few questions—about your dreams." It occurred to her that asking him about his dreams might be terribly intimate, more intimate even than kissing him. It wasn't as if he were a little girl who loved playing make-believe. He was her *landlord*, for God's sake.

Yet he'd said he wanted to kiss her. If he could cross boundaries with that comment, surely she could cross boundaries by interrogating him about his dreams.

Or maybe not. A discrepancy existed between them. He had the power to kick her out of the house. She had no power at all.

None of this was right. She'd been a fool to mention painting him. Typical of her—reckless, barreling ahead without first considering the ramifications. She should have thought about what painting him—what pursuing anything beyond a landlord-tenant relationship—would *entail* before she suggested it.

She started to tell him to forget the whole idea, but before she could speak, he said, "Okay. Paint me. When can we start?"

She blinked, stunned. The afternoon sunlight glazed his face, bringing every angle and hollow into stark relief. His eyes…She would have to mix cerulean blue with a bit of zinc white and maybe a hint of cypress green to capture their unique color. His skin tone? Amber, yellow ocher, a touch of gold. His hair? A dense mix of burnt umber and perylene black. Colors danced inside her head.

Max's colors.

Another blink snapped her back to reality, or at least to more pragmatic concerns. She had to finish Ava's portrait first. It was near completion; another day or two, and it would be ready for framing. Emma needed to warm the castle up a bit—she'd modeled it after some photos of medieval European castles, which tended to be cold and dank and kind of foreboding, not the stuff of a young girl's fantasies. A bit more gold in the stones would fix that. And she wasn't satisfied with Ava's hair; it needed a touch more gold, too. Ava's face was as close to perfect as Emma could hope for, her dress looked lovely, and the scepter in Ava's hand looked like a little like a magic wand, which Emma thought Ava would love.

Tomorrow morning she had an art class with the doctor twins, Willy and Wally Stenholm. One of them was a retired optometrist, the other a retired podiatrist—Emma could never remember which was which—and their wives had insisted that they take an art class with Emma because they had no hobbies to keep them occupied in retirement, and they were getting on their wives' nerves. Their parents had run a millinery shop, back when such things existed, and the two septuagenarians loved painting hats. Whatever. They paid Emma well, and each week she created a still life arrangement with a hat for them to reproduce on their canvases. She'd picked up some interesting hats at the Goodwill store, and Monica had introduced Emma to a friend of hers who worked at the local high school and allowed Emma to borrow a few hats from the theater club's costume stash. Last week the doctor twins had painted a police hat from the school's production of *Guys and Dolls*. Tomorrow they would be painting an arrangement of old-fashioned headwear from the local community theater. It wasn't high art, but she charged the doctor twins twice as much as she charged Abbie's and Tasha's parents, and they happily paid.

"We could start on Friday," she suggested, then held her breath, waiting for Max to come to his senses and back out.

"Friday. Good." He nodded briskly, then strode to the stairs and down, as if he wanted to leave before he did that come-to-his-senses thing and returned to the subject of leases and clauses and eviction.

Emma watched him as he reached the bottom step and headed for the front hall in long, loping strides. She heard the faint squeak of hinges as he opened the front door, the solid click as he shut it.

This was definitely weird. Arguably crazy. Would he still insist on her moving her operations out of his house if she was painting him? Would he still demand that she pack up and go? Would he render the artist he'd just hired to paint his portrait homeless?

He hadn't exactly hired her. They hadn't discussed her fee. She hadn't printed out a contract for him to sign. Maybe he expected her to paint him for free in exchange for remaining in the house. Which might not be a bad deal.

Except...She shook her head as she once again contemplated what a mismatch they were. He might be at the mercy of her paintbrush, her vision and creativity, but she was at the mercy of his property ownership. Painting him didn't change the fact that he could still force her out of his house.

—◊◊◊—

Friday.

That gave him a full day to recover from bizarre spell he was under. One entire day to take care of business, drive down to Cambridge, visit with his mentor from MIT, and remember who he was: Max Tarloff. Computer geek. Rich guy. San Francisco resident. Property owner eager to sell the ocean-view house he'd bought on Boston's north shore two years ago, when his brain had been outvoted by his heart.

Surely that wasn't what was happening now. His heart had nothing to do with Emma Glendon and her fanciful painting. He was just...bewitched. Or bored. Or *something.*

He hadn't felt so muddled when he'd first met her. He'd considered her attractive, certainly, but he encountered plenty of attractive women. He'd also considered her a problem, which she was. He'd been annoyed with her. Angry. Exasperated.

What had happened to change his perspective?

It couldn't have been merely that he'd viewed the painting she'd been working on, fascinating though it was. He'd had no idea what her paintings were like when he'd offered to help her find some studio space elsewhere in town. That offer had been utterly irrational. His consenting to let her paint him was equally irrational. Both decisions only dragged him further from his goal of selling the house and getting on with his life.

True Colors.

The possibility that the song was what had turned him around, paralyzed certain thought centers in his brain, and made him lose track of his plans and goals, was as crazy as everything else. Yet what else could have caused his mental meltdown?

He consoled himself with the thought that Emma seemed to have been transformed, as well. At their first meeting, she'd distrusted him. She'd resented him. She'd contemplated calling the police on him. And now...

She wanted to paint him.

And he wanted to kiss her.

Don't think about that, he cautioned himself. *Think about the painting.*

When had he ever been interested in fine art, of all things? His parents had coerced him into those violin lessons, but he'd hated them. His passion had been for stickball, the beach, hip-hop, computers, and eventually girls. By the time he was twelve, he'd mastered C++ and Java programming. He and his Linux operating system had made sweet music together, far sweeter than any sound he'd ever coaxed out of his violin. In high school, he and Laurie

Peretzky in high school had made much sweeter music. In college, he and Jenna Parsons. And for a couple of glorious years, he and Vanessa.

Much sweeter music than that cloying "True Colors."

The drive from Brogan's Point to Cambridge took less than an hour, which meant he could easily return to the Ocean Bluff Inn tonight if he chose. He still had a room waiting for him at the Hyatt Regency in town, however. He'd left his clothes and toiletries at the inn, but he could purchase a few necessities in the city if he decided to stay there. For some reason, he thought it might be best to keep his distance from Brogan's Point for a while—or, more specifically, to keep his distance from Emma, at least until his brain resumed its normal functioning.

He was able to park in one of MIT's visitor lots. Pocketing the claim ticket the lot attendant handed him, he strolled the familiar streets of the campus, basking in the gentle nostalgia characteristic of a returning alumnus. MIT wasn't a beautiful campus. It lacked the ivy-covered colonial buildings of Harvard, just a mile up Mass Avenue. The buildings here were designed for science and engineering, and they looked it—gray and utilitarian, labeled with numbers rather than names. Even Building 10, with its symmetrical pillars and the Great Dome rounding its roof, looked austere in an ancient Greco-Roman sort of way.

He checked his watch. Ten-thirty. Too early to call Janet; it was only seven-thirty on the west coast. Besides, he'd spoken to her last night and didn't have to check in with her today. According to her, the foundation was operating quite smoothly in his absence. A few financial reports had come in, but nothing he needed to review immediately. She would scan them and email them to him if he wished, but really, nothing at the office demanded his urgent attention, and she hoped he was enjoying his trip back east.

He might be the chairman of the New World Foundation, but Janet could run the place well enough without him. Possibly even better, since he wasn't in her way, meddling, questioning, analyzing.

He strolled through campus to the Strata Center, assuming he would find Stan Weisner in that building—one of the few oddly shaped structures on campus, but certainly nothing reminiscent of picture-postcard ivy-covered college campuses. The Strata Center housed much of the computer science department. When Max had been Stan Weisner's student, he'd called Stan Professor Weisner, but in the past ten years, they'd become first-name-basis friends. He and Stan bounced ideas off each other. Stan had been an early investor in Max's start-up when it had been little more than the manifestation of Max's honors thesis, and as a result, Stan was now significantly wealthier than he'd been back in the days when Max had called him Professor Weisner.

A schedule on Stan's office door indicated that he was currently teaching a class. Max noted the classroom number and strode down the hall. As an undergraduate, he had loved Stan's lectures. No harm in catching the final few minutes of his mentor in action before they settled somewhere to drink coffee and talk shop.

The classroom was full—and why wouldn't it be, since it was a computer science class at one of the world's preeminent science and technology universities? Max discreetly slipped into the room through a door at the rear and lowered his lanky body into the only empty seat he saw. At the other end of the room, Stan, his round pink face framed above with wild silver curls and below with a matching silver beard, chattered enthusiastically while scribbling code onto a whiteboard in his indecipherable scrawl. His students leaned forward, some squinting at the squiggly figures on the white-board, some tapping the keyboards of their laptops and tablets, some merely shaking their heads in confusion.

If anything, Stan's hair and beard looked shrubbier than ever, almost as if his face were at the center of a flower. Max wondered if Emma would want to paint Stan. Surely his radiant face, surrounded by all those chaotic curls, was more worthy of her talents than Max's was.

His smile faded. He'd traveled to Cambridge, at least in part, because he didn't want to think about Emma. But there she was, lodged in his brain. *Like a rainbow.*

No. Not like a rainbow. Not like that stupid song.

Stan finished jotting something on the whiteboard and spun around, words spewing from his mouth and his hands flapping like a chicken's wings. In mid-sentence, he spotted Max and let out a hoot. "Maxim!" he hollered, pronouncing Max's name as the way Russian parents did: *Mahk-SEEM.*

Every student in the room swiveled around to stare at Max. He sank as low as he could in the chair, but that did nothing to discourage their gawking.

Even if it had, Stan wasn't about to let him remain anonymous. "Max, come on up here!" the professor bellowed, gesturing with a wide sweep of his arm. "Do you know who this is?" he addressed his students, who continued to stare at Max until, with reluctance, he hauled himself out of the chair and trudged to the front of the room. "This is Max Tarloff," Stan continued. "One of the most brilliant CS majors ever to walk the halls of this esteemed institution. Probably the most brilliant student I ever had who didn't go on for a Ph.D."

Max rolled his eyes. He remembered Stan's efforts to persuade him to apply to graduate school, and his own unwillingness to be persuaded. He'd had a business plan embedded in his honors thesis, and he'd wanted to pursue it. That had turned out to be the right choice for him.

"Okay, so you haven't heard of Max Tarloff," Stan said, obviously noticing the blank stares of his students. "Maybe you've heard of NWES? New World Encryption Strategies?"

The students stopped looking confused. "That's you?" a young man in the front row asked.

Someone further back in the room murmured, "Holy shit!"

"That's Max," Stan boasted.

Max rolled his eyes again. He wished he was still seated in that chair in the back row. Or maybe hiding under the chair. He didn't like the spotlight, and he definitely didn't like being viewed as a ridiculously successful titan of the computer industry, even if that was what he was.

"While he was an undergraduate, Max developed a system for encrypting information from credit cards and other scanned material to protect it from hackers and pirates. Brilliant stuff, boys and girls."

"I had a good professor," Max said, trying to deflect some of the attention to Stan.

"You bet he did," Stan said, happy to toot his own horn as well as Max's. "He graduated from MIT, moved to San Francisco, raised some capital and started a company. Some of you may have heard about its acquisition by Google three years ago."

Awe shimmered in the gazes of the students as they regarded Max. Uncomfortable as the object of such reverence, he shifted his weight from one foot to the other and focused his gaze on the ceiling tiles. He would have preferred that the universe hadn't heard about the acquisition, but the sum Google had paid Max for his company had been staggering—just over a billion dollars. Google would have paid even more, but Max had insisted on retaining some patents and licensing agreements, guaranteeing him a steady income from his innovations.

As if he needed a steady income. Even after distributing much of the windfall to his investors and employees, he'd been absurdly wealthy. He'd bought his parents a house and convinced his mother to retire from her job as a cafeteria lady at P.S. 209; his father had insisted on continuing to drive his cab, but he'd reduced his hours and volunteered for fewer night shifts. Max had invested some of his money in new start-ups, a few of which were prospering and earning him more income. He'd donated generously to MIT's scholarship fund. And he'd set up the foundation—the best thing he'd ever done, even if it had cost him Vanessa. Maybe *because* it had cost him Vanessa.

Hands shot into the air throughout the classroom. Stan's students had questions for Max. Dozens of questions.

"Why did you call your company New World?"

"Because technology is a new world," Max said. "Also, because my family immigrated from the Old World to America, which we considered the New World."

"What advice do you have for people like us who want to develop new apps?"

"Forget the apps," Max answered. "How many apps do we need on our phones to find the nearest seafood restaurant? How many apps do we need to play time-wasting games?"

"But that's where the money is," someone called out.

"It's not going to change the world," Max argued. "Do something useful. Develop software that will help doctors pinpoint the kind of tumor a cancer patient has. Develop software that will make automobiles safer. Develop software that will protect consumers who scan their credit cards, so no one can steal their data and empty their bank accounts."

"You've already taken care of that," Stan reminded Max.

"How rich are you?" a girl near the back of the room asked, a question that prompted a good deal of laughter.

"You want me to flunk her?" Stan joked.

"No, I'll answer her," Max said solemnly. "I kept enough money to live comfortably and used the rest to establish the New World Foundation. We fund educational programs. Scholarship money for college kids, and also programs at younger levels. Pre-K programs in poor communities. Tutoring programs. Classes for immigrants who need language help. We've teamed up with several organizations that fund educational programs in Africa."

Some of the students looked marginally less impressed with him. Evidently, they thought he ought to be spending his wealth on private jets and ocean-worthy yachts. Or maybe on modern, glass-walled houses with stunning water views.

Other students looked more impressed. But Max hadn't set up his foundation in order to impress anyone. To him, it had simply been a matter of his having greater wealth than he could make use of. He could live the rest of his life without ever wanting for anything. Beyond that, why sit on his money when he could instead use it for something worthwhile?

Besides, money sometimes attracted the wrong people—people who wanted that money. People who pretended to like you because you could do things for them. People whose values skewed in directions Max didn't exactly admire.

People who wanted to use you. People who could hurt you.

Fortunately, the students' questions veered from a tabloid-worthy interest in his wealth to the technology he'd developed. His scribbles joined Stan's on the whiteboard, and he reveled in the sheer joy of just doing science, exploring, experimenting, thinking hard. Of all the ups and downs in his life, the years he'd spent at MIT, surrounded by computer geeks like himself, had been among the best.

He needed this kind of exchange, this kind of mental exercise. Running the foundation was interesting enough, and spiritually rewarding. Monitoring his investments had its own satisfactions. Meeting with colleagues on the boards to which he'd been named was pleasant. Consulting with government officials searching for new encryption strategies allowed him to demonstrate his gratitude toward the country that had taken his family in. Interrogating fresh-faced young techies about the projects they wanted him to invest in stimulated him, even though he often found that their science instincts weren't as strong as their hunger for the kind of wealth he'd achieved.

But talking with like-minded souls about pure research...That was joy.

He wondered if Emma felt a similar bliss when she discussed art with other artists, if she experienced the same rush of giddy satisfaction when one of her students drew a line just so or captured just the right hue in a painting.

And he wondered why, when he was in his milieu, in the heart of MIT's computer science building, he still couldn't stop thinking about Emma.

Nine

Emma had misgivings about meeting Monica at the Faulk Street Tavern Thursday evening. But she had to hike down the hill, anyway, and Monica had sounded excited when she'd phoned Emma an hour ago. "I've got an idea," she'd said.

Great. Emma needed an idea. Or two. Or three.

She needed a lot more than ideas. She needed money, and she needed her head examined, not necessarily in that order.

The day had started out well enough. Last night she'd declared Ava Lowery's Dream Portrait finished. If she held onto it any longer, she'd wind up tweaking this and that, making the emerald lawn surrounding the castle a slightly deeper hue, adding a bit more sparkle to Ava's crown, or maybe to Ava's eyes. As an artist, she knew that no creative work was ever really done; there was always one more thing you could improve on. At some point, you simply had to be brave and say, "Enough."

Because Ava's painting was her first paid project in Brogan's Point, Emma had included framing in her price. She was hoping Ava's Dream Portrait would be her calling card. If Ava's parents liked it enough, they would show it to their friends and recommend Emma. A frame would make the portrait look just a bit better, like wrapping an elegant satin ribbon around a gift-wrapped box and tying it into a gorgeous pompom-shaped bow. A frame made the painting look complete.

She'd started the day with her art class with the twin doctors, during which they'd happily painted the hats she'd arranged for them—a vintage blue 1940's cloche, complete with a gaudy plume and a fascinator, juxtaposed with a man's gray fedora. She'd borrowed the hats from the wardrobe room of the Point Players, a community theater troupe for whom she'd helped create the set when they'd staged *The Real Inspector Hound* in February. She'd placed the two hats atop a buff-colored cloth on the table in the loft, creating a noir-ish kind of still life. Willy and Wally had loved it.

Once they'd left with their newest hat paintings, Emma had packed up the hats, pulled on her tooled leather boots, and marched down the hill.

She'd left Ava's portrait in the loft, afraid it might get damaged if she carried it to town. If she owned a car, she could have laid it flat in the trunk and brought it with her, so she could hold it up beside various picture frames to assess which frame complemented the painting most effectively. But without a car, she would have had to hand-carry the painting down the hill, which would not only have been unwieldy but would have put the painting at risk. A car might splash mud from a puddle onto it. A low tree branch might snag it. A bird might poop on it. It was definitely much safer in the loft. Emma could pick out a frame without the presence of the painting.

She already had a pretty good idea of what style of frame would work best with Ava's Dream Portrait, and she had the painting's measurements written down and tucked into her purse. Monica had promised to drive Emma south on Route 1 to a big-box craft store after work. Emma would have plenty of frames to choose from there.

Since Monica was doing this favor for her, Emma couldn't very well refuse to meet her at the Faulk Street Tavern. "We'll have a drink and discuss my idea," Monica had said, "and then we can drive down to Peabody and buy a frame."

Emma had nothing against bars in general, especially bars like the Faulk Street Tavern, which was unpretentious and boasted prices about half of what she'd had to pay for drinks in Brooklyn. In fact, she'd liked the Faulk Street Tavern just fine, until the day she'd sat across the table from Max and "True Colors" had poured through the speakers flanking the stained-glass peacocks on that funky old jukebox. Ever since then…

She'd felt weird. As if she couldn't quite perceive things as they were, or as they ought to be, or as she expected them. As if the colors of the world surrounding her were slightly off, the blue of the sky carrying an undertone of green, the ocean glittering with dark red highlights, the asphalt of the roads more purple than gray.

She didn't know where Max was. He'd said he would meet with her Friday so she could start work on his portrait, and the thought filled her with a disconcerting combination of excitement and dread. She'd printed out her boilerplate contract for him, but she hadn't filled in any of the blanks: deposit, final cost, delivery date. She had no idea how much to charge him. On the one hand, he was a businessman of some sort who owned a spectacular, undoubtedly valuable, house, so he could probably afford a high price. On the other, he was Emma's landlord. He controlled her future—at least, her housing future. If she overcharged him, he might be offended enough to evict her.

On yet another hand—she exceeded her allotment of hands, but her relationship with Max, if that was the right word, was too ambiguous for only two hands—he'd said he wanted to kiss her. And on one more other hand, she hadn't let him kiss her.

She'd wanted him to. She'd wanted his hands—only two, but they were large and strong-looking, and no gold band circled his left ring finger—to gather her to himself, and she wanted him to press his mouth to hers, and she wanted...

Things she shouldn't want.

He's your freaking landlord, she reminded herself.

Monica hadn't yet arrived at the Faulk Street Tavern when Emma entered. Five o'clock on a Thursday evening, the joint wasn't exactly hopping. A man sat alone at the bar, hunched so deeply over his glass that his nose nearly rested on the rim. A few younger guys who smelled of the ocean sat in a booth, a pitcher of golden beer and a platter of wings occupying the center of their table. They wore denim and flannel, not fisherman's gear, but Emma had learned that it took more than a shower and a change of clothes for a crew member of a trawler or lobster boat to lose that lingering ocean scent.

Not that she minded. Growing up in Vermont, she'd rarely visited the ocean—she recalled her parents taking her brother and
her to the beach in Maine once, but the water had been too cold to
swim in. Still, Emma had fallen in love with the rich, sour fragrance
of the sea. Living in Brogan's Point, even if only for a few months,
had reminded her of just how much she loved that smell.

Behind the bar, the tall, square-jawed woman with hair the color
of dead pine needles hovered at the register, counting and sorting
cash into its drawer. She glanced up at Emma's entrance, shot her a
fleeting half-smile, and then turned her attention back to the stack
of bills in her hand. Next to her, a beefy young man with black hair
and tawny skin unloaded glistening glasses from a tray.

Unsure whether to take a seat at one of the many empty
tables or wait for Monica's arrival, Emma circled the room with
her gaze. The jukebox stood across from the bar, beautiful in
a flamboyant way, with its glossy, veined wood and its colorful
peacocks. A faint shudder rippled down Emma's spine and she
spun away. What if another song spilled out of the jukebox while
she was there? What if that song dazed and haunted her the way
"True Colors" had?

She crossed to one of the empty booths and sat with her back to
the jukebox, as if that would keep her from hearing it if someone
popped a coin in and it started to play.

She didn't have to sit alone for long. Just minutes after her
arrival, Monica swept in. She got a much warmer smile from the
woman behind the bar. No doubt that woman—what was her name
again? Something masculine, Emma recalled—had known Monica
her whole life. Brogan's Point wasn't that small a town, but all
the people who owned long-time business establishments in town
seemed well acquainted with one another.

"Hey, Gus," Monica called to the woman as she strolled across
the room to Emma's booth.

Gus. Emma lodged the name in her memory.

"I'm getting a glass of wine. What would you like?" Monica asked
Emma in a quieter voice.

Evidently, it was too early in the evening for the wait staff to be working. Emma squinted at the bar, trying to recall what beers were on tap. "A Sam Adams, I guess," she said, digging into her purse for her wallet.

"I've got it," Monica said, waving Emma's money away and sauntering over to the bar to get their drinks. She returned to the table in less than a minute, carrying a goblet of white wine, a glass of Boston lager and two square cocktail napkins. She settled onto the banquette facing Emma, passed her the beer and then tapped her goblet against it before taking a sip. "So, did you finish the painting?"

Emma nodded. "It came out pretty good."

"It's better than *pretty good.* I've seen it."

Emma shrugged off her friend's praise. She was edgy, anxious about what Monica's grand idea might be. "I still have to photograph it for my portfolio," she said. And then I'll frame it. I appreciate your giving me a lift to the frame store."

Another wave of dismissal from Monica. Then she leaned forward, her dark eyes glowing with excitement. "So, I've been thinking," she said. "We've got this housing situation—"

"*I* have this housing situation. You're all set."

Monica shook her head. "You're all set, too. You can live in the studio apartment at the inn."

Emma frowned. "You said it was really tiny. I don't see how we can—"

"Share it? Nope. You can have it all to yourself. I'll move in with Jimmy."

"No," Emma blurted out before she could stop herself.

"Why not? I think it's a great idea. I don't want to live that close to my parents. But they're not your parents. Their proximity shouldn't matter to you."

Emma took a deep breath. She'd said no awfully quickly, and bluntly. If this was Monica's brilliant idea, it sucked. But Emma didn't want to risk offending her best friend by pointing out that the apartment at the inn belonged to the Reinhart family and, more important, that Jimmy was an ass. "That's a big step, moving in with a guy," she said instead.

"You should know. You lived with Claudio," Monica reminded her.

"And look what happened. He cheated on me and I wound up sleeping on his cousin's couch."

"And then I rescued you," Monica said with a smile, clearly pleased with herself.

"You can't keep rescuing me," Emma argued. "Especially not this way."

"It'll work out," Monica assured her. "I've known Jimmy since high school."

"And you two have spent more time broken up than together. You broke up freshman year of college." Emma remembered that period all too vividly. Monica had been alternately mopey and furious, and Emma had served as sounding board, shrink, and buddy, dragging Monica to parties and gatherings to keep her from wallowing in misery in their dorm room. "You broke up at least three times during college."

"Four times," Monica said with a blithe shrug.

"And a few times since we graduated."

"So I think I know what I'm getting into," Monica said. "Is Jimmy perfect? No. Do I want to spend the rest of my life with him? The jury's still out. Do I love him? Yes."

"Can he be a jerk sometimes?" Emma couldn't resist saying. "Yes."

Monica only laughed. "Like I said, I know him. He's got a two-bedroom place at Colonial Heights," she told Emma, naming a complex of red brick garden apartments just south of town. "So if he's getting on my nerves, I can move into the other bedroom."

"I bet he'd really like that," Emma said with a snort. "'Jimmy, you left the toilet seat up again, so I'm not sleeping with you tonight. But thanks for letting me live here.'"

Monica laughed again. "Yeah, right. I'm going to go all Lysistrada on him because he's left the toilet seat up. If women did that every time their partners left the toilet seat up, the human race would die out."

Emma shared her laughter. Just as she'd dragged Monica to parties during her numerous break-ups with Jimmy in college, Monica had dragged Emma to a performance of the ancient Greek comedy when one of the campus theater groups had staged it. In the play, the heroine, Lysistrada, organized the women of her city to deny their soldier-husbands sex until they ended the war. The play made a wonderful statement about women using their sexual power over men to bring about peace.

It would be nice if women could use that same sexual power to train their men to lower the toilet seat when they were done peeing. But Jimmy required a lot more training than merely his bathroom manners. He was shallow. He was egotistical. He took Monica for granted.

"I appreciate the offer," Emma said, "but no. I'm going to solve my housing problem on my own. I'll find someone with a room they want to rent in their finished basement, or over the garage."

"You won't get enough natural light in a basement," Monica pointed out. "How will you paint?"

"How will I paint at your family's hotel? You said that studio apartment is tiny."

Monica conceded the point with a sigh.

"I'll find a place to rent. And I'll find some studio space to paint." *Or Max will find it for me.*

No. Just as she didn't want Monica to rescue her, she didn't want Max to rescue her. She'd been independent her whole life. Even as a child, living with her parents, she'd learned how to take care of herself. As loving as her parents were, they were awfully flaky. Lacking money to buy a lot of picture books, Emma's father used to read a road atlas to her and her brother. He'd had Emma climbing on the roof of the house with him when she was a toddler, helping him repair loose shingles. Emma's mother would have sent her to school in shorts and flip-flops in the middle of January. By the time Emma had been in kindergarten, she'd learned how to make sense of New England's harsh weather and dress appropriately.

She'd figured out how to apply to college on her own. She'd figured out how to compile a portfolio and how to fill out the financial aid forms which won her the scholarship aid she'd needed. She'd figured out which laptop computer would work best for her, and she'd bought it. Surely she could figure out how to find an apartment within her admittedly meager price range.

Besides, she'd rather live in a tent on the beach than see Monica moving in with Jimmy. Monica was smart. She was pretty. She was generous. She was far more stylish than Emma. Sooner or later, she was going to figure out that Jimmy wasn't worthy of her. Emma was hoping for sooner.

"What if you can't find a place?" Monica asked, her eyes shadowed with concern. "I'm afraid you're going to move away from Brogan's Point. And I like having you here."

"I like being here," Emma agreed. "I like living with my BFF. I've got students here, and I want to build my Dream Portrait business. At least for now, I need to stay put. But not if it means you have to move in with Jimmy."

Monica let out a long breath. "He doesn't like you much, either," she admitted.

Emma laughed.

The tavern's door creaked as it opened and shut, admitting more patrons. A trio of young women came in together, then another couple of ocean-smelling guys wearing thick-soled boots and shrubby beards. Boats must be docking and businesses closing for the day, freeing their employees until tomorrow. The room vibrated with the energy of people ready to decompress or to socialize, people chatting, people thirsty for whatever Gus might pour into their glasses.

"Jimmy's like comfort food," Monica explained. "I know what to expect with him. There's no anxiety, no worries. No big let-downs."

"Wow," Emma muttered. "It sounds so romantic."

"He's good in bed," Monica added.

Well, that was something.

The door creaked again and a couple of men entered. The younger one wore leather and denim, and his hair was a windblown mess of dark waves. The older man had a bluff, square face and striking silver hair. He wore a police uniform. "Is the place getting raided?" Emma asked, shooting a wary glance toward the cop. "I'm over twenty-one. How about you?"

Monica grinned and shook her head. "That's Ed Nolan," she murmured, although Emma doubted anyone outside their booth could hear her. "He's Gus's boyfriend."

"Whoa. She's quite a cougar."

Monica's grin widened. "The older guy."

Emma followed the two men with her gaze as they crossed the room to the bar. A few more patrons trickled in behind them, and the tables began to fill up. "Who's the younger guy?" she asked.

"Nick Fiore. He was a couple of years ahead of me in school."

His leather jacket carried a hint of danger. So did his unkempt hair, his snug jeans, and his swaggering gait. "How could you choose Jimmy over him?" Emma asked.

"I doubt he ever noticed me," Monica said, then pressed her lips together and shook her head. "Besides, he was a mess back then."

"He doesn't look like a mess."

Monica pursed her lips. "He got arrested," she said, then paused. "For trying to kill his father."

Emma felt her eyebrows shoot up.

"It was very ugly," Monica said. "Thank God he got his shit together eventually."

"I guess he must have, if his drinking buddy is a cop."

"He runs a bunch of programs for at-risk kids through the community center. I mean, he's a good guy, but…In high school, he was definitely troubled. I kept my distance. And like I said, he probably didn't even know I existed."

Emma watched the two men for a minute. They stood at the bar, chatting amiably with Gus. At one point, the cop slung his arm around the younger man's shoulders and they laughed.

The community center. Emma had passed it often on her strolls down the hill. It was one of those utilitarian municipal buildings constructed of textured tan bricks and steel-framed windows. She'd entered only once, when she'd gotten caught in a sudden downpour without an umbrella. The place had seemed pleasant in a bland, civic sort of way, with a gym, a swimming pool, assorted offices and multi-purpose rooms.

She wondered if the center had an art room, a studio where she could teach her classes. If she remained in Brogan's Point, she'd be part of the community, wouldn't she? And that would entitle her to use the community center. If she wound up renting a room in someone's basement or over a garage, as seemed likelier than her finding another modern mansion with ocean views and excellent natural lighting renting for dirt-cheap, she could continue to earn a modest living teaching at the community center.

"What's his name again?" she asked Monica.

"Ed Nolan or Nick Fiore?"

"The one who isn't the cop. Nick Fiore?"

Monica tilted her head, assessing Emma. "Are *you* going after him?"

He was attractive, no doubt about it. But he wasn't Max Tarloff.

Which was the stupidest thought Emma had had all day.

"I'm going after the community center," Emma said, sliding out of the booth.

Monica opened her mouth, but Emma didn't wait to hear her question. She had to approach Nick Fiore now, before she lost her nerve or contemplated the logistics enough to conclude that using a room at the community center for her art classes was a stupid idea.

Someone must have stuck a coin in the jukebox, because as Emma strolled across the dance floor to the bar, the room filled with the sultry baritone of Elvis Presley singing "Jailhouse Rock." Well, *that* had to be a sign, she thought with a smile. She still wasn't sure what the jukebox had been trying to tell her when she and Max had been enveloped in Cyndi Lauper's plaintive voice crooning about true colors, but if Elvis could sound so downright cheery about incarceration, the jukebox must be telling her that Nick Fiore was fully rehabilitated and not too messed up any more.

"So I said to this bozo, 'Telling a cop to eff himself is usually not a good way to avoid getting arrested,'" the officer was saying as Emma approached him and Nick Fiore, "and he says, 'Gee, you're right, officer. I should have told you to eff your mother.' Needless to say, I arrested him."

"My tax dollars at work," Nick muttered.

Behind the bar, Gus said, "I know the F-word, Ed. I raised two boys. Nothing shocks me."

"But I didn't want to shock this lovely young lady," the policeman said, turning his bright smile on Emma. Nick traced the policeman's gaze to Emma and smiled as well.

"You girls ready for another round?" Gus asked.

"No, we're fine," Emma told her. "I wanted to talk to… Nick Fiore, right?" She extended her right hand. "I'm Emma Glendon."

"I hate to tell you, honey, but he's already taken," the policeman warned her.

Emma grinned as Nick shook her hand. "I want to discuss business. Or art. Or both."

"That sounds ominous," Gus said. "You sure you don't want another drink?" Although her voice was as dry as chalk, Emma suspected she was joking and obliged her with a laugh and a shake of her head.

Nick lifted his beer and angled his head toward an empty booth. "Sure, we can talk. But I've got to warn you, I don't know much about art. Or business, for that matter."

She followed him to the booth, settled across from him and took a deep breath. "I'm a friend of Monica Reinhart's," she began, then pointed toward Monica, who had twisted in her seat to observe Emma and Nick. Realizing that they were both staring at her, she smiled feebly and fluttered her fingers in a wave. "You went to school with her, but she said she didn't think you knew who she was."

"Her folks own the Ocean Bluff Inn, don't they?"

So he *did* know who Monica was. Too bad he was already taken. Emma had exchanged less than a dozen words with him, but that was enough to convince her he was a much finer specimen of manhood than Jimmy. "Right. Anyway, she and I are close friends, and we're about to lose the lease on the house we're renting. The thing is, I'm an artist and an art teacher, using a loft in the house as my studio. Once we lose our lease, I'll lose that space to teach my art classes. Monica said you worked at the Brogan's Point Community Center, and I thought, maybe there's a room there I could use for my classes."

Nick didn't say no. He didn't scowl or guffaw or shove her off the banquette. He drank some beer and ruminated. "You want to rent a room, or access a room for free?"

"Well, I'd prefer free," Emma said. "It's not like I make tons of money teaching art to children and retired doctors."

"That's who you work with? Kids and retirees?"

"I'll teach anyone willing to pay me. I'm an artist." She hoped he understood what that meant: she was chronically broke.

"Okay. So you want to charge money for your classes, but you don't want to pay rent on your studio space."

When he put it that way, it sounded cheap and chintzy. "I'll pay rent if I have to, and if I can afford it. Or maybe I could earn the use of the studio by doing other work at the center. Like, maybe I could teach a free class for kids who can't afford to pay, and then I could charge the retired doctors—who, believe me, can afford to pay. Maybe we could arrange something like that." She hesitated, then added, "Or I can scrub sinks and mop floors."

"The community center's janitorial staff is unionized," he informed her. "So forget about that." He ruminated, sipping a little more beer. "I run some after-school programs at the center," he said. "Sports activities, mostly. Maybe we could incorporate some art activities, too. I don't know if I've got the budget for that, or if we've got a room you could use. I'd have to discuss it with the center's director."

"Jailhouse Rock" stopped booming from the jukebox. He still hadn't said no. "I'd be very grateful if you would," she said. "Or if you could tell me who the director is, and I could meet with him myself."

"Her. The director is a she." Nick regarded her thoughtfully. "Let me talk to her first, and poke around my budget to see if I've got any spare change I could put towards art in the after-school program. Or my summer program. Give me your number, and I'll call you after I've made some inquiries. How does that sound?"

"Fantastic," Emma said, doing her best not to jump onto the table and indulge in a victory dance. She didn't have a victory to dance about, yet. All she had was the promise of a possibility.

He pulled out his cell phone and she recited her number for him to program into it. They shook hands again and slid out of the booth. She watched him stride back to his friend at the bar, then spun around and allowed herself a few prancing, celebratory steps, her boots tapping gently against the dance floor as she started back to the booth where Monica awaited her.

Then she froze as another song emerged from the jukebox, slow and sweet and haunting—and crazily familiar. *True Colors.*

She turned to stare at the jukebox, and then at the door, where Max Tarloff stood, staring back at her.

Ten

He'd had the hotel room in Cambridge lined up. He'd had a plan for dinner with Stan Weisner and an invitation for drinks with MIT's president, who generally treated Max as visiting royalty whenever he visited his alma mater. Max had written some very large checks to the school. The president went out of his way to make him feel welcome.

Ordinarily, he would have accepted the president's invitation and enjoyed dinner with Stan. But he'd wound up taking a rain check on both engagements. He'd told himself he wanted to return to Brogan's Point because he'd left his toothbrush at the Ocean Bluff Inn.

Yeah, right.

Arriving back in town, he'd driven directly to his house at the top of the hill and found it empty. Not sure where Emma might be, he'd steered back down the hill in the direction of the inn. Slowed at an intersection by Brogan Point's modest rush-hour traffic, he'd spotted the Faulk Street Tavern on a side street off Atlantic Avenue—a stolid, unpretentious building, no neon sign calling attention to it, no velvet-rope crowd lining up to get in. What the hell, he'd thought. Instead of having a drink with MIT's president, he could have a drink with some of the locals. Until he sold his house, they were technically his neighbors.

He didn't want to acknowledge his hope that Emma might be inside. It was too silly, too crazy. He'd driven to Cambridge to put some distance between her and himself, yet he'd spent most of the day thinking about her. About her fiery hair and her flinty personality, about how he'd wanted to kiss her. About how he'd agreed to let her paint his portrait. He was a rational man, a computer whiz, a business mogul—and she was like an insidious virus, invading his software and making him behave in ways that made no sense.

He parked, entered the pub—and yes, Emma was there. Seated at a booth with a man, leaning toward him, engrossed in an intimate conversation with him. The man appeared to be about Emma's age. He was dark, scruffy, a bit dangerous-looking in a black leather jacket.

Max immediately felt like an idiot. He'd been fantasizing about Emma, agreeing against all reason to let her paint his portrait when he ought to be furious with her for living in his house without his permission, and running a damned school there, too. And meanwhile, she was involved with some other guy. *Shit.*

But then she stood, walked from the table, and saw Max. And that stupid jukebox song began to play again. *True Colors.*

She walked directly toward him. She looked fearless, and beautiful. Her baggy jeans failed to conceal the sweet curves of her hips and the length of her legs. Her eyes were wide, her tantalizing lips shaping a half-smile that made him want to kiss her even more.

She reached him and her smile grew fractionally larger. "They're playing our song," she said.

"Is that really our song?"

She shrugged. Her smile was tentative yet inviting, warm yet slightly apprehensive.

"Can you—" he angled his head toward the door "—step outside for a minute?"

She glanced over her shoulder to another table—not the table she'd shared with the guy, who, Max noticed, had also abandoned the table and was now standing with a police officer at the bar, but another booth where Monica Reinhart sat nursing a glass of wine. Emma held up a finger, signaling Monica that she'd join her in a minute, and then let Max hold the door open for her.

The evening air was pleasantly cool, briny from the ocean breezes drifting up from the beach beyond Atlantic Avenue. Two couples strolled up the block, talking and laughing, and edged past Max and Emma to reach the bar's door. Max waited until they were inside and he and Emma were once again alone on the shadowed side street. He waited because he wasn't sure what he was going to do. He waited because the dusk light had an orange glow that made Emma's hair shimmer like curls and swirls of flame.

Then he stopped waiting. He cupped his hands over her shoulders, pulled her into his arms, and kissed her.

Her mouth tasted even more delectable than it looked, sweet and soft, like the flesh of a nectarine. Her lips parted and her hands skimmed his sides and circled around to his back, holding him close. She kissed him as eagerly as he kissed her.

This was why he'd declined the MIT president's invitation, and told Stan he couldn't remain in town for dinner. This was why he'd skipped checking into the Hyatt Regency in Cambridge. It had nothing to do with buying a damned toothbrush. It had been *this*. This obsessive, encompassing, mind-boggling need to kiss Emma.

He wasn't sure how long the kiss lasted. Minutes. Hours. An eternity. Less than an instant. What he *was* sure of was that when they finally came up for air, he believed he wasn't the same person he'd been before.

"Max." Her voice was softer that a breath, so soft he couldn't tell if she was angry or upset or turned on, or all of the above.

"Should I apologize?"

"No." She lowered her eyes and shook her head. The lush waves of her hair captivated him. He couldn't stop himself from lifting a hand to the top of her head and stroking his fingers through the thick, fiery locks.

She sighed, angling her head slightly, allowing him to caress the skin behind her ear. "I couldn't stop thinking about you all day," he confessed. "It's crazy. I hardly know you, and what I know, I'm not sure I like."

That got a laugh out of her. "Well, I hardly know you, either. But one thing I do know about you is, you're honest."

Not as honest as she believed, but he didn't argue the point. Instead, he pressed a kiss to her hair, which was cool and silky against his lips, and then to her forehead, which was warm and smooth and made him want to kiss every square centimeter of skin on her body. "All right," he murmured, then touched a kiss to the outer corner of her left eye. "I've got a king-size bed at the Ocean Bluff Inn." A kiss to the outer corner of her right eye. "I also happen to own a house here in town, and I know it's got a few beds in it."

Her sigh sounded almost like a purr, a deep vibration in her throat. She tilted her face so his mouth could find hers again. "No," she said just before locking her lips to his.

He kissed her for a long, luxurious moment, then pulled back. "No, what?"

"No, I can't go to bed with you."

"Can't, or won't?" He grazed her chin with a kiss.

"Won't." She brushed her lips against the hollow of his neck. "You're not my type, Max." Her fingers flexed at the small of his back, sending an electrifying jolt of arousal through him. "I'm an artist. You're a landlord."

"I'm a hell of a lot more than that." He tightened his arms around her, pressing his hips to hers, letting her know what she was doing to him.

She made that purring noise again. "You're a businessman. You're someone who cares about insurance and liability and stuff like that."

"And you're someone who obviously doesn't." He smiled in spite of himself.

"I mean, it's not like we've got some grand relationship going." Her hands slipped an inch lower on his back, and his dick grew an inch harder. "It's just—"

"Chemistry," he said.

"I was going to say animal attraction."

"I think chemistry, you think biology." He used his thumbs against the delicate bones of her jaw to raise her lips to his once more.

They kissed deeply, hungrily. Drawing back, she said, "Let's call the whole thing off." He must have looked appalled, because she grinned. "It's an old song. 'You say *po-tah-to*, I say *po-tay-to.*' You think chemistry, I think biology." She sang, "Let's call the whole thing off," in a lilting melody.

"I like 'True Colors' better," he told her—an admission that surprised him as much as her. He hadn't thought he liked that song at all. Yet it had brought her across the tavern to him, hadn't it? It had delivered her into his arms. For that alone, he loved it.

"I do, too," she admitted, edging back a step. She jerked her hands from him, as if they'd been glued to him and she'd had to exert herself to break the adhesive. Another step back, and he could see, even in the waning light, that she was flushed, her lips glistening, her eyes not quite focused. "I really have to go," she said. "Monica is waiting for me."

That was a lame excuse, but he didn't challenge Emma. If she didn't walk away from him, she would wind up in his bed—either at the inn or at the house. And she wasn't ready for that. Physically, maybe, but not emotionally.

He wasn't ready for her emotionally, either, but he didn't care. He wanted her, anyway.

He would have to wait. Maybe while he did, he would come to his senses and realize that pursuing anything with Emma, physical or emotional, was a stupid idea. In a matter of days, he would have the house listed. He would be back in California, living his life. An interlude of hot sex would be terrific, but he didn't need it to survive, and he wouldn't chase Emma if she didn't want to be caught.

She reached for the door to the bar, but when her fingers curled around the handle, she turned back to him. "About tomorrow, I have to go to the community center in the afternoon. They may have a room I could use as a studio. So come early."

Come early? Oh. Right. She meant *come to the house.* Because she was going to paint his portrait.

And he was going to…what? Pose while she gazed at him and analyzed him and moved his hand this way and his leg that? He was going to sit as motionless as a vase or a bowl of fruit while she objectified him on a canvas?

Of course he was—because he'd said he would. Because posing would mean spending more time with her, getting to know her better, maybe finding out that they were more than a conflict between chemistry and biology.

Because while she was gazing at him, he could be gazing at her, imagining her naked, imagining her lying beneath him.

Imagining her seeing rainbows when she came.

Eleven

The next morning, Emma was still freaking out.

She hadn't slept well. More accurately, she hadn't slept at all. Infused with a nasty mixture of adrenaline, bewilderment, and sweat-inducing arousal, she'd lain in bed, trying to figure out what the hell had happened between her and Max outside the Faulk Street Tavern.

Inside the Faulk Street Tavern, too. The whole thing had started when that damned song had started playing.

That blessed song.

She was in love. No, she wasn't.

She was in lust. No, it was more than that.

She was in trouble. That much was certain.

Good God. Who would have guessed that Max Tarloff could kiss like Casanova on steroids? She couldn't recall ever being so turned on by a few kisses. She couldn't recall every being so turned on at all.

And he was her flipping landlord. And she was supposed to paint him. Definitely, she was in trouble.

She hadn't told Monica about the encounter outside the pub. When Emma had rejoined her friend at their booth, Monica had immediately started pumping her for information about her conversation with Nick Fiore. Emma had welcomed the distraction, happily discussing the possibility of scoring some studio space at the community center. "If you can work at the center, you'll probably attract a lot more students," Monica had pointed out. "You can post class schedules on the bulletin boards there, and in the center's newsletters. This could work out fabulously, Emma! Not only would you have space to teach, but you'd generate a lot more income. People would go to the center, swim a few laps, and then spend an hour painting—and paying you."

"*If*," Emma had emphasized. "First I have to see if there's a room at the center I can use." Even if there was, Emma's housing problem would not be solved. But if the community center worked out, she could live in someone's basement or above someone's garage and not have to worry about breaking zoning laws by conducting her art classes in a non-commercial venue.

For all his fussing about those stupid zoning laws, Max seemed to have no objection to her beginning work on his portrait in his not-zoned-for-commercial-use house. Of course, all she would be doing today would be photographing him and interviewing him a bit, so she could get a sense of what his dreams were for the background imagery.

The thought of interviewing him made her queasy. The thought of being alone in the house with him made her giddy. She was tempted to beg Monica to take the day off and stay home, but then she would have to explain why. What would she say? "Max and I need a chaperone so we won't jump each other's bones the minute he gets here."

She couldn't talk about her steamy interlude outside the Faulk Street Tavern with Max, not even with her best friend. Not until she'd made sense of it—which seemed pretty freaking impossible.

Tired of lying in bed, battling insomnia while her brain tied itself in macramé knots, she'd arisen at five and gotten to work framing Ava Lowery's painting. The frame she'd purchased after she and Monica left the pub yesterday evening complemented the painting beautifully. Ava's parents would be pleased. Ava—the little princess—would be ecstatic.

Emma waited until after Monica had left for the Ocean Bluff Inn and she had the house to herself before showering, attempting futilely to tame her hair with a round brush and her blow-drier, and fretting far longer than necessary about what to wear.

Her baggy, paint-speckled jeans and overalls made her look like
an artist, but they weren't exactly flattering. Her few skirts *were*
flattering, but they would set too formal a tone for her morning
session with Max. She tried on three different tops before settling
on a cotton sweater in a bright turquoise shade and a pair of khaki
slacks that had seen better days—but then, all of her clothing had
seen better days. Once she and Claudio had broken up and she'd
had to fend for herself, her budget hadn't allowed for splurges at
New York City's boutiques and department stores. Even the consignment shops in her Dumbo neighborhood had been too pricy
for her.

She fussed some more with hair before giving up and letting it
curl any which way it wanted. She checked her watch four times.
She tested her digital camera to make sure it didn't need new bat-
teries. She choked down a cup of coffee, then brushed her teeth.
Not that she and Max were going to kiss again. She just didn't want
to have coffee breath.

At a few minutes past nine, the doorbell rang. She gave herself
a mental slap on the cheek and a stern reminder that she was a
painter and this was a professional engagement, that if Max decided
to go forward with the project, she would charge him for her time
and talent, that—for God's sake—he was her landlord. That his
willingness to consider having her paint his dream portrait and his
offer to help her find studio space had meant nothing more than
that he'd fallen under a weird spell cast by a Cyndi Lauper song in
an antiquated jukebox with peacocks on it.

The song's weird spell was why they'd kissed, she reminded
herself. Yesterday's spasm of lust wouldn't have occurred if "True
Colors" hadn't suddenly escaped the jukebox and filled the air
when he'd stepped inside the bar.

You are an artist, she lectured herself as she descended the stairs.
Glimpsing Max on the front porch through the narrow sidelight
framing the door, she added, *you are a tenant.*

One more deep breath, and she opened the door. "Hi," she said
brightly.

His smile was hesitant. Did he want to back out? Did he want to run for cover? She wouldn't blame him if he did.

But she hoped he wouldn't, because he was so…damn, so gorgeous. The sky was overcast, but enough morning light seeped through the filmy white clouds to illuminate the striking geometry of his face. Such piercing eyes, such a strong, sharp chin. All that thick, dark hair, as disheveled as her own. Had he blow-dried his hair, too? Had it fought all attempts to tame it, the way hers had?

"Come in," she said, doing an admirable job of behaving as if nothing R-rated had occurred between them yesterday.

He followed her down the entry hall, his footsteps slow but steady. If he wasn't racing up the stairs to the loft in an eager rush to pose for her, he wasn't bolting in retreat, either. He'd dressed in jeans and a ribbed gray sweater that teetered on the narrow line between geeky and stylish but that made her unfortunately aware of his lean, beautifully proportioned physique.

At the top of the stairs, he gazed around. She'd tidied up the loft, although with her art supplies stacked on open shelves and the rumpled drop cloths blanketing the floor, the open space was never going to look neat—not until Max kicked her out and reclaimed the house for himself.

She'd set a stool out for him to sit on, far enough from the work table and easels so she could circle it easily and close enough to the wall of glass for the milky morning light to illuminate his face. His gaze circled the loft, then settled on the stool. "Am I supposed to sit there?" he asked. He sounded kind of apprehensive.

"The seat of honor," she said, flourishing her hand as if it was a royal throne and he was a king.

"I'm supposed to sit on this stool while you paint me?" He lowered himself onto it and frowned. "It's not very comfortable."

"I'm not going to paint you while you sit there," she explained, crossing to the table for her camera. "That would be a waste of your time. What I'll do is take a bunch of photos of you and paint from them."

He eyed her camera warily. "I've never done anything like this before," he said.

He almost made the words sound sexual. Or else maybe she was just imagining an innuendo where none existed. Yet she appreciated his willingness to let her see his discomfort. Maybe she should stop trying to act as if this was just a typical job for her.

"Okay," she said, then forced a smile. "Here's how it works. I take a bunch of photos of you, and I ask you a bunch of questions about your dreams."

"My dreams?"

"Not your bedtime dreams." She felt a blush warm her cheeks when she uttered the word "bedtime."

He didn't seem terribly rattled by her reference to bedtime, though, so she soldiered on. "I paint what I call Dream Portraits. That's a portrait of you surrounded by the things you dream about. Like Ava Lowery's portrait." She pulled Ava's painting away from the wall, where she'd propped it after framing it, and displayed it for him. "She dreams of being a princess, so I painted her surrounded by princess things."

"I don't dream of being a princess," Max said.

Emma laughed. "That's a relief."

He lapsed into thought for a moment. "I'm not sure…I mean, to talk about my dreams? I don't know. That's personal."

The way we kissed was personal, too, she almost pointed out. Opting for discretion, she said, "Painting you is personal," as she returned Ava's painting to its resting place against the wall.

"Yes, but…my dreams?"

"Don't worry. We'll just talk."

He opened his mouth to say something, then closed it, apparently at a loss.

"If you don't want to do this, we don't have to."

"*You* want to, though. You told me you wanted to paint me."

"I do," she admitted.

"Emma." He stared at her, his eyes so intense, so focused, his gaze felt like a physical touch. "About last night—"

"No," she said quickly. "No, no, no. Today is about painting. Not about…*that.*"

"Everything is about that," he said, sounding unnervingly wise.

"All right. Look. I can paint your portrait. You can pay me for the painting. Or not," she hastily added when she saw his brow dip in a frown. "Because I owe you for holding art classes in your house. Right?" She was ad-libbing, trying to read his mind, trying to figure out how to make the situation feel less awkward and less…Damn it. *Sexual.* Maybe she wanted to paint Max's portrait only because painting him was safer than screwing him would be. Both were intimate acts, though. Both involved the dropping of defensive layers, the casting aside of self-protective shields.

He smiled wryly. "How much were you planning to charge me?"

"That depends on how detailed the painting is," she said. "Why don't I take some photos, and we'll discuss your dreams, and then I'll be able to assess what the painting will entail." *Entail.* His word. Now he had her saying it.

She turned her camera on, listened to its motor hum to life, and scrutinized him in the pale morning light. His features would be thrown into stronger relief if she adjusted his head slightly, but she was afraid to touch him. "Could you just turn a little to the right?" she asked.

He shifted on the stool. His expression was pained.

"This isn't going to hurt," she assured him.

"I feel self-conscious."

"No kidding." That coaxed a smile out of him, and she smiled, too.

"I really don't like being in the spotlight."

"Once I have this painting done, you can hide in the shadows. People can admire your portrait and ignore you."

He chuckled.

She started snapping pictures. Usually she was full of patter and jokes, eager to put her subjects at ease. But Max wasn't just any subject, and although she'd managed to tickle a laugh out of him, she felt as self-conscious as he apparently did. Trying to come up with clever chatter would tire her out, so she decided to skip the light stuff and go straight to the heavy. "Tell me about your dreams."

"I dream of not being in the spotlight," he said.

She smiled tolerantly and continued photographing him. "Besides that dream."

He shrugged, then cringed , as if afraid he'd ruined something by moving.

"That's okay," she said. "You can move if you want. I'm going to take a ton of photos, so if some of them come out blurry, no big deal."

"I can move, but I can't move out of the spotlight," he muttered, although his eyes were bright with amusement. "I don't know. I don't dream about big things. Most of my dreams have already come true," he said, his smile gone.

He looked so somber, she snorted. "You sure seem thrilled about that."

He shot her a look. The motion caused the morning light to shift across his face. She could gently nudge his head back to where she wanted it, but she still felt nervous about touching him, even in a professional way. Instead, she decided to snap a few photos of him with shadows angling across his features. "Sometimes," he said, "when your dreams come true, things don't turn out quite the way you expected when you first dreamed them."

"Do you want me to paint some disappointments into your portrait? I guess I can do that. The Dream Portraits I do are usually upbeat and inspiring. And fun. Like Ava's princess portrait. Back in Brooklyn, when I was developing the concept, I painted a ballet dancer I knew, surrounded by all the roles she dreamed about dancing. But I suppose I could do a depressing painting, if that's what you want."

"Of course it's not what I want," he retorted. "All right, then. Upbeat and inspiring dreams. Let me think." His expression changed again, growing pensive as he ruminated. He gazed out the window for a long, silent minute, then said, "I've always dreamed of having a home with an ocean view."

"Then this must be your dream house," she said, trying to capture with her camera the reflective cast of his eyes, the tilt of his head.

To her surprise, he laughed again. After a bit more thought, he said, "The two apartments where I lived in Brooklyn were both a few blocks from the beach. But all I could see from our windows was the street and the air shaft between our building and the next one. Where I live in San Francisco—Pacific Heights—I can see the bay. Not the ocean, though."

"But you can see the ocean from this house. Why do you want to sell it?"

"Because I don't live or work in Massachusetts?" he suggested, turning the statement into a question as if he expected her to grade him right or wrong.

"Tell me about your work," she said. "Do you have a dream job?"

"Yes."

That caught her by surprise. She wasn't exactly sure what he did for a living. If the ridiculously below-market rent he was charging her and Monica indicated anything, he wasn't the sharpest businessman she'd ever encountered.

"I run a foundation," he told her.

"Cool!" That sounded grand, both altruistic and powerful. "What kind of foundation?"

"We focus mostly on education for impoverished children and immigrants. My parents had good educations in Russia, even though when they moved here they wound up with jobs that didn't put their education to use. But they knew it was important for me to learn English and study hard. With a lot of immigrant children, their parents are so overwhelmed that the children don't get the kind of encouragement I got. They need extra support. Their parents need language skills. California is full of immigrants from Latin and South America and Asia, and my foundation funnels grants into programs for them. But we work with programs all over the country. Some programs in Africa, too."

"Wow. That is so cool. No—it's *noble*."

"Feel free to worship me."

"I'll paint your portrait, like the Renaissance painters used to paint their royal patrons." She moved behind him and snapped some photos of his back. He had strong, solid shoulders. Shoulders she wanted to wrap her arms around, the way she had last night. She gave her head a brisk jerk, as if she could shake off the thought like a dog shaking water off its fur after a swim in a pond.

The fact was, she had bigger problems than merely the distraction of Max's appearance, which was as appealing from the back as from the front. How on earth could she depict his dreams of educating immigrants in a painting? What was the visual peg on which she could hang this portrait? If she was going to create a Dream Portrait of him, she needed more to go on than educating immigrant children.

"Have you been to Africa?"

"I've visited Malawi," he told her. "We contribute to a program there, run by Unicef. But I was there for only a couple of days, just to make sure the funds were being used properly. We didn't want our money to wind up in some corrupt politician's pocket."

She sighed. As noble as his work sounded, Africa seemed like a non-starter for her painting. "Do you have any hobbies?" she asked hopefully.

He thought for a minute. "I shoot hoops with friends a couple of nights a week. I go hiking—not too often, but I enjoy it."

Wonderful, she thought sarcastically. She could paint a knapsack.

"I play chess."

"Of course. You're from Russia," she teased.

"Not all Russians play chess," he argued. "I just like the mental challenge. I'm no champion, but I enjoy it. Sometimes I play against my computer. I usually win."

"Do you read? Play a musical instrument?"

He winced. "I studied violin for six years and hated every minute of it."

"Six years? You must have been pretty good."

"I wasn't good at all. And I hated it."

Maybe she could paint a violin with an ax smashing through it. Great. A broken violin and a knapsack. She could call this one a

Nightmare Portrait instead of a Dream Portrait. A chess board had possibilities, though.

"Do you have any pets?" she asked.

"No."

She thought of him, living all by himself in his apartment with its San Francisco Bay view. Then she thought of him not living by himself. "Do you have a wife?" she asked.

He flinched, then spun around on the stool to face her. "Do you think I would have kissed you if I did?"

"Some men would," she said, trying not to shrink from the intensity of his stare.

"I'm not one of them."

"Well. Good." She smiled, trying to lighten the moment.

He didn't return her smile. Instead, he reached out and snagged her wrist, nearly making her drop her camera. He pulled her toward him, then rose from the stool. "If I had a wife," he murmured, "I wouldn't be making love to you."

She opened her mouth to point out that he wasn't making love to her. And then she understood what his fierce, hungry gaze was telling her. Standing so close to him, feeling his fingers circling her wrist, warm and firm but not forcing, she knew that hunger. She felt it just as fiercely.

In his eyes, she saw his true colors. He was a stern, solemn property owner, someone who did good works and obeyed zoning laws. But he was also a man burning with desire. A man who would make love to her.

She knew it. She wanted it.

With his free hand, he pried the camera from her grip and set it on the stool. Then he slid his arm around her waist and pulled her closer to himself, much closer. So close her breasts pressed into his chest when she inhaled. She needed that breath, though, because once he took her mouth with his, breathing was impossible.

They kissed. And kissed. They kissed like last night—no, not like last night. This kiss was deeper, wilder, needier. This kiss wedded not just their lips and tongues but their souls. Her hands fisted on his shoulders, those broad, strong shoulders she'd been admiring just minutes ago as she'd snapped photos of his back, and he cupped one hand over the curve of her bottom, drawing her against him, letting her feel his arousal. His other hand made its way to her head, where he tangled his fingers into her hair, the stubborn waves and curls that had refused to relax beneath her blow drier earlier that morning. That her hair was a mess didn't seem to bother him in the least.

After an endless minute, he tore his mouth from hers, but only to graze her cheeks, her brow, the soft, vulnerable skin of her throat. She felt her legs sway beneath her, and he tightened his grip on her butt, guiding her against the bulge beneath his fly. He unraveled his other hand from her hair only to tug at her shirt, skimming it up so he could slide his hand across the skin of her back. Her skin was warm, but his hand was hot. Everywhere he touched, she felt a burning deep inside.

She brought her hands forward and down, resisting the urge to forge a direct path to his fly and instead shoving his sweater upward. He leaned back far enough for her to pull it over his head, along with the gray T-shirt he had on underneath. He released her to free his arms from the sleeves and tossed the garments aside. His gaze strayed past her and he muttered, "The window."

"Don't worry about it," she said, staring at his chest. It was perfect—not too bulked up, not too lean. Streamlined muscle, a scant growth of hair along his sternum, a flat, hard stomach punctuated by a narrow navel framed in another smattering of dark hair. She wanted to paint him shirtless. She wanted to paint him naked. The hell with painting—she just wanted him naked.

"It's all glass, Emma," he said, his voice cracking slightly as she stroked her hand lightly across his pecs.

"We're too high for anyone to see us," she assured him, thinking, *I'm high on you. I'm high on this.* The loft was on the second floor, and the nearest neighbor lived several acres away, with enough trees between the two properties to obscure that house. If she couldn't see it, she assumed that no one in that house could see her and

Max. And even if they could, she didn't care. The thought of stopping what they were doing for the time it took to walk to her bedroom was unbearable.

Max apparently needed little persuasion. He yanked her shirt off and groaned as he gazed at her chest, her breasts straining against the stretchy cups of her bra. She'd never been one for lacy, flimsy underthings, and her bra was strictly utilitarian. Maybe that was why Max wasted little time in flicking open the clasp and slipping it down her arms and away. A rumble of sound, want and pleasure and anguish, rose from his throat. "You're so beautiful."

"I was thinking the same thing about you," she whispered, lowering her mouth to kiss one flat, tan nipple.

He gasped, twined both hands into her hair and pulled her head away, only to lock his lips to hers once more. Their tongues dueled, their breaths merged. Their hands moved simultaneously down to their slacks, Emma fumbling with the fly of his jeans, Max deftly locating the fly of her khakis. He got hers undone first, and she felt the fabric shimmy down her legs. He slipped his hands under the elastic of her panties and shoved them away, then wedged one hand between her thighs, pressing, sliding deep, spreading her dampness with his fingertips.

She couldn't breathe. Couldn't think. Couldn't get his damned jeans off him. She was shaking, much too close to coming.

She heard a faint laugh from him as he nudged her scrabbling fingers away with his free hand and popped the button of his waistband. The zipper made a hissing noise and then he sprang free of the denim, large and hard and...God, yes. Beautiful.

Reflexively, she arched one leg around his. He laughed again. "Not standing up," he whispered. "We'll kill ourselves."

If they did, she die happy. But she pulled back from him long enough to survey the loft. The table had too many art supplies on it. The stool wasn't stable. The canvas drop cloth was thick and stiff and spattered with paint.

He grabbed her hand and started toward the stairs. All right, so they'd abandon the loft, her favorite place in the whole house, a room open to the magnificence of the surrounding landscape, the ocean view. They'd walk down the stairs and around to her bedroom. They'd be reasonable and civilized, and...

No. The stairs were covered in soft carpeting. That would do.

At the top stair, she pushed him down. With a startled gasp, he sat, and before he could question her she straddled him, settling onto his lap, her thighs sandwiching his hips and his erection rising between their bodies. She bowed to kiss his mouth.

Another sexy sound growled up from his throat, his chest. If he'd had any thoughts of speaking, let alone wandering through the house to her bed, he abandoned them. Instead, he kissed her back, flexed beneath her, gathered her breasts in his hands and kneaded them, stroking her nipples with his thumbs. He broke the kiss and lifted her higher so he could replace his hands with his lips, nuzzling, licking, gorging himself on her breasts. She reached down between them, lifted her hips, guided him into her.

They moaned in harmony. They rocked in synchronicity. He arched against her as she pumped against him. Her body tensed, trembled, teetered on the edge of bliss...and then exploded in a cascade of deep, aching pulses. She collapsed against him and he held her, panting, sighing, gradually growing still beneath her.

For the first time since moving into this house last autumn, Emma decided that she liked the carpeting, after all.

Twelve

He'd come here hoping for everything and expecting nothing. Well, in truth, he hadn't hoped to make love on the stairs leading to the loft—and he hadn't expected that, either. But he'd known Emma would be magnificent. He'd known she would be all sweet curves and fiery hair and devouring kisses. He'd had a taste of her yesterday evening, and once he'd had that taste, he'd wanted the full banquet.

She felt surprisingly light in his lap, her head resting against his shoulder, her hair spilling over his skin and tickling the underside of his jaw. She fit perfectly in his arms. The step he sat on was even more uncomfortable than the stool, but he didn't want to move. He wanted to sit exactly where he was. With her. Like this. Forever.

That was a crazy thought. This whole situation was crazy. He knew hardly anything about her, other than that she was an artist and she was broke. If he were looking for a woman—which he wasn't—two items that wouldn't be on his list were "artist" and "broke."

"Mind-blowing sex" *would* be on his list, however. Pretty high up on the list. And what he'd just experienced with Emma...

Mind-blowing was an understatement. *Defense-shattering* came closer. *Universe-destroying.* He felt stripped naked—not just his body but his heart, his soul, totally vulnerable, unprotected.

Unprotected. Shit.

"Emma." His voice was muffled by her hair.

She heard him, though. "Hmm," she said drowsily, her breath whispering across the skin of his neck.

"Emma, I didn't use anything."

"It's okay." She leaned back slightly so she could speak. "I'm protected. And I'm healthy."

"I'm healthy, too," he said. She gave him a drowsy smile and settled back against him.

He closed his arms around her again and sighed. He was healthy, but he didn't feel protected. He felt altered in ways he wasn't sure he liked. Life was safer when he thought about protection—not only condoms but emotional protection. He'd had bad experiences. He'd been used. He'd been hurt. He'd been taken advantage of. He had to be careful.

With Emma, he hadn't been even remotely careful, either now or yesterday, when he'd kissed her. Or pretty much every minute since he'd sat across a table from her in that bar and heard "True Colors" pour from the jukebox.

He was a smart guy. He'd developed a unique computer encryption system and started a company. He'd earned a fortune. He'd created a foundation and he was its executive director. If someone held a gun to his head, he could probably still play the *Theme From Schindler's List* on his violin. Badly, perhaps, but he could play it.

Yet with Emma Glendon, he was someone else. Someone he hardly recognized. Someone wild, someone utterly reckless.

"What do we do now?" he asked. It wasn't a rhetorical question. He really had no idea where to go from here.

"Well…" She traced her index finger down his sternum, swirling it through the hair growing there. "We could make love again, if we were sure it wouldn't kill us. Or we could put or clothes on and resume the interview."

Not the interview. He'd felt profoundly awkward discussing his dreams with her. As far as making love again, that would be wonderful, but it wouldn't solve his problem. It wouldn't transform him back into the man he'd been before he'd met Emma. And she was right—another round of sex would probably kill him. At the very least, he'd need to consume a few energy bars first, and maybe a fistful of megavitamins.

"I still don't know about your dreams," she said.

"One of them just came true." His statement obviously touched her. She leaned back and gave him such a sweet smile, he felt his blood shimmer in his veins.

His claim surprised him as much as they flattered her. Who the hell was this sentimental creature, this romantic lover who knew just the right thing to say to a woman? Not Max Tarloff.

"Another option…" she traced her finger down his chest again, sparking stirrings of renewed lust in his groin "…would be to get something to eat. I didn't have any breakfast this morning. I'm starving."

Energy bars, he thought—enough fuel to power him through some more epic lovemaking. "All right," he said. "Let's get something to eat."

Slowly, cautiously, she extricated herself from his embrace without tumbling down the stairs. Like her aimless finger trailing across his skin, her radiant smile caused his dick to twitch back to life. But when he stood, he knew he'd need more than her smile to get him going once more. His thighs ached and his back was sore. He prided himself on staying in shape. Apparently he wasn't in the sort of shape conducive to screwing on stairways.

Uninhibited in her nakedness, Emma strolled across the loft to where their clothing lay in a disheveled heap. She slipped her shirt over her head and tugged on her jeans. Then she carried his clothing to where he stood, gob-smacked not just by her glorious beauty but by the realization that she hadn't bothered to put on her underwear. More twitching in his groin. He ignored it as he donned his own clothes. "Why didn't you eat breakfast?" he asked, recalling the concoction—a parfait glass dish filled with layers of yogurt, fresh berries, and granola—with which he'd started his morning at the Ocean Bluff Inn.

She smiled again, another blindingly lovely smile. "I was a nervous wreck about your coming here. I was afraid something like this would happen." She tossed back her head and laughed. "And it turns out I was right. Maybe I can earn some spare cash telling fortunes and predicting the future. I could scrounge up a crystal ball and a deck of Tarot cards and set up shop on Atlantic Avenue."

He remained silent, unsure of whether he should give voice to what he was thinking: that she hadn't needed any skill at prognostication to know this would happen. There had been an inevitability to it. As forceful as the song that brought them together, their attraction simply had to travel to its final measure—which had turned out to be hot sex on the stairs.

She pranced down to the first floor, light on her bare feet, and he plodded down behind her, wishing he felt as breezy as she looked. She also looked rumpled, her lips rosy from his greedy, devouring kisses and her hair a lush tangle of curls. On her, "rumpled" was gorgeous.

Like her, he was exhilarated. He was exhausted in the best possible way. But a vague foreboding gnawed at him. She was his tenant. She needed spare cash. This was all wrong.

And yet he wanted her. Possibly even more than before.

He'd spent even less time in the kitchen of his house than in the loft. Of course, he'd spent little time inside the house at all—touring it with Andrea Simonetti and Vanessa before he'd purchased it, wandering through it and listening to Vanessa gush about the space, the views, the airiness of the rooms. She'd talked as much to Andrea as to him, describing what she'd want to do with this room, how she'd decorate that one, the updates she was planning for the master bath: "A jetted tub, of course. And one of those towel warmers."

"Whatever you want," he'd said, not really caring about the temperature of his towels as long as she was happy.

She'd been excited about the kitchen, and as he followed Emma into the room he could see why. It had been updated just prior to when he'd purchased the house, and it presented a sleek, clean arrangement of granite counters, stainless-steel appliances, white cabinetry and bright lighting, including a row of three cone-shaped metal lamps hanging from a bar above the center island. Vanessa had eaten sparingly and worried incessantly about gaining weight, but she'd liked things new and shiny, and this kitchen certainly fit that profile, even after Monica and Emma had been using it for a year.

Emma glided around the room as if she actually knew what she was doing. She pulled a carton of eggs from the refrigerator, set a pan on the stove, and got to work breaking eggs into a bowl. "Are omelets okay with you?" she asked as she pulled a whisk from a drawer.

"If it's not too much trouble."

"I love cooking," she said. "When I was growing up, we cooked everything from scratch. We had chickens. There's nothing like fresh eggs from your own chickens—who haven't been fed antibiotics and commercial feed. The yolks are such an intense yellow. Like the heart of a daisy."

He settled on one of the stools at the center island; it had a molded seat and a backrest and was much more comfortable than the stool in the loft. Emma's movements as she whisked the eggs mesmerized him—yolk and white liquefying and blending into yellow. Not the heart of a daisy, unfortunately. A paler yellow, almost lemony.

"Did you grow up on a farm?" he asked.

"Not a commercial farm." She turned from him to swing open the refrigerator again, this time to remove cheese, mushrooms and chives. The refrigerator's shelves weren't as barren as his usually were—he was a huge fan of take-out, and he stocked only the essentials in his fridge: milk, beer, a couple of apples, a bag of bagels that lacked the chewiness and sour undertone of the bagels he'd grown up eating in Brooklyn. And leftover take-out containers. Always a varied collection of those.

She pulled a knife from its slot in a wooden block and began to chop the chives. "My parents are back-to-the-earth hippies. They were middle-class suburban kids who met in college and decided to buy a few acres in Vermont and make a go of it. We had a big vegetable garden and the chickens. We had a cow for a while when I was really little, but raising dairy cows is a lot more complicated than just carrying a pail out to the barn and milking the animal. So my parents wound up selling the cow to a neighbor who ran a commercial dairy farm, and we'd get our milk there. It was all very rustic."

She turned from him once again, this time to retrieve a loaf of bread and a tub of butter. She clicked a dial on the stove, igniting one of the burners, slapped the pan onto it, scooped a blob of butter into the pan, and got busy grating the cheese.

"Brooklyn must have been quite an adjustment for you," he said. He knew full well that there was nothing rustic about that congested New York City borough.

She grinned. "I went to Boston University. After four years in Boston, I was used to traffic and noise and crowds. And eggs that weren't quite so yellow."

"Growing up on your parents'—well, whatever it was. Not a farm."

"Just a piece of land in the middle of nowhere," she said.

He nodded. "So when you grew up there, was your dream to live in a city?"

Her gaze met his across the center island. If she could ask him about his dreams, he could ask her about hers, couldn't he? Even if he wasn't going to paint her, even if he was going to sell this house and return to San Francisco, he could still ask her about her dreams.

She didn't seem as uncomfortable as he'd felt when she'd questioned him. "I can be happy anywhere," she said. "City life, rural life, it's all good." She poured the beaten eggs into the pan, creating an appetizing sizzle. "My dream is to have a roof over my head and some studio space with good lighting."

And by selling the house, Max was going to deny her that simple dream.

But he'd promised to help her find new studio space. Maybe he could find her housing, too.

Maybe he could bring her back to California with him.

He stifled a sardonic laugh. That wasn't going to happen. She might have given herself to him this morning, but last night outside the tavern, she'd warned him she wouldn't make love with him because he was a businessman. And a landlord. She'd said that as if landlords were evil.

Perhaps, when they were evicting tenants, they were.

But she *had* made love with him. So maybe he had a chance of... Of what? No, he couldn't bring her back to California with him. *Get real, Max.*

She deftly flipped the omelet in the pan, then layered in the cheese and mushrooms and folded the egg around it. "Can you check the toast?" she asked.

A few minutes later, they were seated side by side at the center island, each with a plate full of steaming omelet and golden toast, and a mug filled with coffee she'd reheated from earlier that day—she apologized about that, but it tasted fine to him. "This is delicious," he said after taking a bite of his omelet. "Obviously, your talents extend beyond painting."

"They extend beyond cooking, too," she reminded him, twirling her fork to break a stretchy thread of melted cheese.

Her wicked smile made him grin. "Indeed they do," he said, thinking he'd sure as hell like to see how those talents of hers manifested themselves on a surface more comfortable than the stairs. Taking a bite of toast, he pondered various strategies to get her into bed, or at least onto the sleek modern couch in the great room. Then he reproached himself. He owed her something more than a satisfying orgasm. He could make her dream come true, couldn't he? "So," he said, "we'll make sure you have a well-lighted studio and a roof over your head."

She seemed momentarily taken aback by his having changed the subject. Then she shrugged. "I have that now," she reminded him. "Right here."

"No," he said swiftly, then shook his head and belatedly tried to soften his words with a smile. "I can't let you stay here. I have to sell this house. I'm sorry, Emma."

"Is it a financial problem? You need the money?"

The last thing he needed was money. "No. It's...a personal matter."

"This house means something to you," she guessed. "Something bad?"

He really didn't want to discuss it with her. But he couldn't lie to her, not when she was so sweet and open with him. "I bought this house for my fiancée," he told her.

"Oh." Something went cold in her face, her eyes no longer radiant, her lips tightening. "You should have told me you were engaged."

"I'm not. Not anymore."

She thawed slightly. "You got rid of the fiancée, and now you want to get rid of the house."

"Something like that," he agreed. "Except that I didn't get rid of the fiancée. She got rid of me."

The light in Emma's eyes changed again, warm with sparks of emerald and gold. "Did she break your heart? The bitch!"

He was amused and touched by her rush to his defense. "My heart healed," he assured her.

"Not completely." Before he could argue, Emma explained, "If it had, you wouldn't be attaching emotions to this house. It's just a building, right? A beautiful building with fantastic natural light— but you wouldn't be so anxious to sell it. If you were completely over the bitch fiancée, you'd double the rent and make some money on this place. I shouldn't have said that," she added with a self-deprecating smile. "If you doubled the rent, I'd have to move out anyway. I couldn't afford it. Monica might be able to, though. Now she's stuck trying to decide whether to relocate to a teeny-tiny apartment at the inn or to move in with her boyfriend, who—just for the record—is an asshole."

Max wanted to refute her claim. Of course he was over Vanessa. The only reason he wanted to sell the house was that he saw no reason *not* to sell it. His life wasn't in Massachusetts. He had no use for the house. It was just more thing to own, one more responsibility, one more liability. Emma was correct in pointing out that he could increase the rent and turn the house into a source of income, but he didn't need any more income.

He couldn't say any of those things, though, because he was too intent on trying to suppress his laughter. He loved the matter-of-fact way she referred to Vanessa as "the bitch fiancée," and her succinct assessment of Monica's boyfriend. And then the urge to laugh faded as he acknowledged the truth in her words. The house was just a building. An asset. If he were truly over Vanessa, he wouldn't care about the house's fate, one way or another.

Yet it *wasn't* just a building. It was Emma's home. She was the one acutely aware of the building's beauty, its natural light. Selling it meant subjecting her to upheaval, both personal and professional.

"Let's not talk about the house," he said. He didn't want his mind crammed with Emma's words, her wit, her sharp observations. He didn't want to reflect on that upheaval his actions were likely to cause her. He ate another forkful of omelet—damn, it was tasty—and turned the conversation back to her. "Let's talk about your ex-boyfriends."

"Ex-*boyfriends*? Plural?" She grinned.

"I have no doubt you've broken dozens of hearts."

"Dozens! Yeah, sure. I started dating when I was three."

"Up there in the wilds of Vermont?"

"Hmm, you're right. The only other kid I saw when I was three was my brother. Who I didn't date."

"I'm glad to hear it."

"My high school was pretty small, too."

"You went to Boston University. That wasn't small."

She conceded with a shrug. "You're right. There were at least a dozen guys there. I tried my best to break their hearts, but I'm not sure I succeeded." She noticed his plate was empty and slid off her stool to clear the dishes.

He stood, gathered their mugs and carried them to the sink. "Surely you broke at least one heart," he teased.

"Maybe. If I did, it wasn't deliberate."

They worked together smoothly, rinsing the dishes, stacking them on the dishwasher racks. "I find it odd that you're unattached," he justified his curiosity. "You're beautiful, you're talented…You're very sexy."

Her cheeks grew rosy. She was even more beautiful when she blushed. He recalled the blush of her naked breasts, the intensity of her well-kissed lips when their bodies had been joined. *Beautiful* seemed a woefully inadequate word to describe her.

"I was with a guy in Brooklyn," she told him. "Claudio. He was a painter, too. Abstract expressionist. He liked dark colors painted with big, strong swipes of the brush. All his paintings looked like anger to me. But then he developed an unexpected yearning to paint portraits—of one particular woman."

"I take it that woman wasn't you?"

"No. She was an artist's model. I guess she knew some good poses." Emma shrugged, not seeming terribly upset. "In retrospect, I think the worst part was that when Claudio and I broke up, I had to move out of the apartment, because it was his. I really hate being homeless." She sighed, shook the excess water off her hands and dried them on a towel. When she turned to him, she was smiling. "It's not your problem," she said. "You want to sell this house. That's your right. I'll find somewhere else to live. But now—"she put down the towel and checked her watch "—I've got to find somewhere else to paint. I told Nick Fiore I'd drop by the community center today to see if he could scare up a studio for me."

Max didn't know who Nick Fiore was. He *did* know he ought to phone Janet. He had a foundation to run—even if she could manage the office well enough in his absence. He ought to phone Stan Weisner, too, to see if they could arrange a dinner down in Cambridge. He ought to check in with Andrea to get the house listed for sale. He ought to carry Emma off to bed and make love to her properly, on soft sheets, on a plush mattress. Languorously. Indulgently. Wickedly.

But she wanted to go to the community center. "Can I come with you?" he asked.

Thirteen

An hour passed before Emma and Max left for the Brogan's Point Community Center. They decided to shower first. And even though the house had three and a half well-appointed bathrooms, they wound up showering in the same bathroom, at the same time, which slowed things down considerably.

Max's body was an esthetic masterpiece. Emma was not just a woman who had experienced several mind-boggling orgasms, thanks to that body; she was also an artist. She couldn't keep herself from admiring the supple, graceful contours of his physique, the ridges and indentations of his bone structure, the sleek undulations of his musculature. The sprinkle of hair across his chest, tapering down to the taut, slightly rippling surface of his abdomen, transformed from gentle curls to dark streaks as the shower soaked his skin. His eyes were simultaneously dark with passion and bright with amusement as he skimmed her body with soap and watched her twist and writhe come beneath the steaming spray of water.

She wanted to paint all of him. Not just his face, not just his dreams but every part of him, from his neatly angled toes to his knobby knees, to his narrow hips, his navel, his pecs, his broad, sturdy shoulders, his amazingly beautiful face. And his groin. She'd like to paint that thick, hard erection, maybe gild it in gold, frame it in filigree and hang it over her bed to admire every time she lay there.

She did lie there, after they'd finished showering and found themselves panting and wet in places the shower hadn't dampened, and so they'd raced to her room to make love again.

It was early afternoon by the time they headed down the hill to the community center to see Nick Fiore. Fortunately, Emma hadn't arranged a specific time for her meeting with him. Equally fortunately, she was able to travel down into town in Max's car, which saved her the several-mile hike she'd gotten used to since moving into his house.

Max might own real estate in Brogan's Point, but Emma felt like a genuine town resident when she introduced the two men. Nick's office was so small, all three of them barely fit into it, but Nick was gracious and friendly, and—thank God—he remembered his discussion with Emma from yesterday evening at the Faulk Street Tavern. "We've got a room here that might work out for you," he told Emma. "I think I can arrange for you to use it rent-free if you're willing to donate some of your time and expertise to the town's programs. It would be great if we could include art in the after-school program I run for teenagers here. I sure as hell can't offer that on my own. Basketball, yeah. Art? Forget it."

"If I could use the room for free for my own classes? Of course I can put together an art program for your after-school kids." Emma was giddy at the thought of securing free studio space. If she could do that, she could devote more of her sparse income to paying the rent on whatever residence she was able to scare up for herself. She couldn't live in Monica's studio apartment at the inn, and now that Max had, however vaguely, explained why he wanted to unload his house—the ex-fiancée, the broken heart—Emma couldn't resent him for wanting to be rid of the place, even if that choice would render her homeless.

"Come on," Nick said, leading the way out of his tiny office. "I'll show you the room."

They paraded down a hall, Emma following Nick and Max bringing up the rear. A few offices lined one side, the doors labeled "Director of Senior Services" and "Parks Department." She caught a whiff of chlorine as they strolled past the entrance to the town's indoor pool. They continued past the locker rooms, around a bend in the corridor, past the gym where, she assumed, Nick ran his basketball program, and through a door.

The room was bigger than Nick's office, which wasn't saying much. It had no window, which was a serious drawback. The only light source came from glaring fluorescent ceiling fixtures—*ugh*. Not good light for art.

But it had enough square footage for a work table and some shelves. She could squeeze a supply cabinet into the corner. If the town would provide the room, perhaps it would also provide some basic furniture. Emma would supply the art equipment. She was doing that already with her classes in Max's house.

She paced through the room while Max and Nick watched from the doorway. Pale green cinderblock walls—*ugh* again. If she wanted to display her students' work, she'd have to tape it to the walls, which might ruin the paintings and collages, or else buy or build some free-standing pin boards. She could bring in directional goose-neck lamps to create direct illumination. She recalled passing a bathroom just a few doors down the hall; she could take care of clean-ups there.

With a little effort, she could make this room work.

It was free. Of course she could make it work.

"It's perfect," she told Nick.

His smile transformed his face, erasing its brooding shadows. She wouldn't mind painting his portrait, either. He wasn't Max. He didn't make her heart race. But she could admire him with her artist's eye. Definitely an appealing subject.

"Great. Once the school year ends, my after-school program ends, too. But I run summer programs. We could really use an art counselor, or teacher, or something along those lines. My budget sucks, but if you're willing to work for shit wages—"

"If I can use the room for my own classes, as well, I'll work for shit wages for you. Artists are used to shit wages. We're supposed to starve. It's part of the package."

Nick laughed and nodded. Max only studied her, his eyes dark and intense.

As they strolled back down the hall to Nick's office, Nick discussed all the bureaucratic steps necessary to grant Emma the use of the room and add her to his summer staff. Meetings with his board. Paper work. Budget issues. If she was going to run an art program, he'd need her to fill out an application, supply a résumé, provide references. His voice washed over her in a meaningless babble. This information was important, and she'd pay attention once she had to. She'd sign the papers, present her portfolio, dance pirouettes for his board, jump through hoops of fire, whatever was required to gain her access to the free room. She didn't want some irate town guardian to banish her because she lacked the proper licensing, the way Max had reacted to her classes the first time he'd met her, when she'd been running her class with Abbie and Tasha in his house.

After another series of hand-shakes, Emma and Max left the community center. The late afternoon air was warm, the sky paling as day gave way to evening. A hint of salty, musky perfume lifted off the ocean and flavored the air. "This is wonderful," Emma said, twirling in a happy dance in the parking lot outside the community center. "I've got a studio!" Indeed, the day was as close to perfect as she could imagine. She had a studio. She had dozens of photos of Max, and the opportunity to paint him. She had great sex.

Of course her life wasn't perfect. She still needed to find a new home. And she wasn't sure with what dreams she could surround Max in his portrait.

And he would be leaving. She'd opened her body to him, and she'd never been able to open her body without also opening her heart and her soul. He mattered to her. He was important. She wanted him in her life. She wanted to know his dreams, his hopes, his goals. She wanted much, much more than he was in a position to give her.

She'd known that before she'd kissed him. She'd known it when they'd gazed at each other and Cyndi Lauper had serenaded them from the jukebox at the tavern.

Looking at Max, she saw his true colors shining through. They were vivid, shimmering, brilliant. But what did they reveal? Who was he, really?

—⁂—

Gus finished counting the last of the tens in her cash drawer and nudged it shut. Even now, in the twenty-first century, a lot of her patrons still preferred to pay their tabs in cash. Some of them didn't want their husbands or wives to find charges from a bar on their credit card bills. A few of the old-timers didn't trust credit cards at all. A lot of the young ones—the deck hands on fishing boats, the laborers, the clerks in touristy shops where business fell into a comatose state during the winter months—didn't earn enough income to trust themselves with a rectangle of plastic from Visa.

So Gus relied on cash, which saved her money, since she didn't have to pay credit card fees on cash transactions. All she had to do was maintain an adequate stash of legal tender in the register. She felt perfectly safe carrying her daily profits—often thousands of dollars in cash—from the tavern to the bank every day. Everyone in town knew she was Ed Nolan's partner. No one was going to mess with a police detective's girlfriend, especially when she was six feet tall, and her assistant, Manny Lopez, was built like a linebacker for the Patriots, and she ran the most popular bar in town.

She glanced toward the front door, which remained stubbornly shut. Ed had told her he would come to the bar this afternoon, and he hadn't. Nothing to worry about, she assured herself, but she couldn't keep from glancing obsessively at the front door every few minutes.

Ed was working on a drug case. A high school kid in a neighboring town had overdosed on heroin. Fortunately, he'd survived, and he'd told police he'd gotten the heroin from a crew member on one of the boats that trawled for cod out of Brogan's Point. Ed had been waiting for that boat to come in today. He had backup. He was going to arrest the guy, run him in, and then come to the Faulk Street Tavern to let Gus know all had gone as planned.

She hadn't told him she was anxious about his safety, and he hadn't acknowledged that she might be anxious. They never discussed stuff like that.

But…She was anxious.

She eyed the front door for the thirtieth time in as many minutes, then steered her attention to a table of women drinking exotic martinis. She glanced at the bowls of barbecue-flavored peanuts lined up on the counter near the door to the kitchen. She checked out the table of older guys drinking whisky and arguing over the latest Red Sox losing streak. Then the front door again, praying for Ed to swing it open and stroll inside.

No sign of him.

She reminded herself that her worries were groundless. Ed was tough. He had backup. No captain would allow a twenty-something crew member onto his cod boat armed with anything more dangerous than a utility knife.

A utility knife could do a lot of damage.

Ed had faced worse, she reminded herself. He'd be fine.

Manny emerged from the kitchen, lugging glistening racks of glasses straight from the dishwasher. He shot Gus a quick smile before setting the racks onto the back counter and sorting the glasses onto shelves—stemware here, tumblers there, highball glasses in their allotted place. Could he tell she was concerned? Would he think she was weak for counting the minutes and wishing she could will the front door to open?

It did, and she felt her breath slide out of her on a sigh of relief, which was replaced by a pang of disappointment when she saw two people, neither of them Ed, enter the bar. That pretty red-haired girl, Monica Reinhart's friend, stepped inside first, followed by the tall, lanky, dark-haired fellow Gus had seen at the bar with Monica and the red-head. She ought to know their names. Anyone who came into the Faulk Street Tavern more than once qualified as a regular. And the girl had introduced herself yesterday, when she'd wanted to talk to Nick Fiore. What the heck was her name? Emily?

"Want me to take that?" Manny asked, motioning with his head toward the booth where the couple seated themselves. It was too early for the waitresses to start their shifts, and none had arrived at the bar yet. Gus could serve the couple, though. Manny was busy with the glasses, and damn it, she wasn't worried. She could take an order, fill it and deliver it without his help.

She waved him off, then sidled over to the newly occupied table, laid two square cocktail napkins on its scarred wood surface, and asked, "What can I get you?"

The man eyed the woman courteously, allowing her to order first. "Do you have any champagne? I feel like celebrating." She smiled at the man. "Is that all right?"

"Order whatever you'd like," he said, although he didn't seem to be sharing her high spirits. Her face radiated a blend of happy emotion—exuberance, satisfaction, serenity. His darker features were matched by a darker mood.

She grinned at Gus. "A glass of champagne," she said.

"We've got Moët, Mumm, and Tattinger." Champagne wasn't a big seller at the tavern, and Gus didn't stock much. Too often, someone ordered a glass or two and the rest of the bottle lost its effervescence and had to be disposed. Still, she had to include a few bottles of bubbly in her inventory. She hadn't kept the bar in business for thirty-plus years by denying her customers what they wanted. Sometimes those customers wanted champagne.

"Whichever one is cheapest," the redhead said with a shrug. "I wouldn't know the difference, anyway."

Gus nodded and turned to the man. "A Sam Adams lager."

"Tap or bottle?"

He asked for a bottle. Gus nodded again and left the table, casting a quick look toward the front door en route back to the bar. No sign of Ed.

He's tough. He has backup. He'll be fine.

As she worked the mushroom-shaped cork on a bottle of champagne, she forced her attention from the door back to the couple. She was pretty sure they'd been targeted by the jukebox's magic a couple of days ago. She tried to remember what song had been playing when they'd been in that afternoon, seated at the very same booth, staring at each other. Had the song brought them together? Right now, she'd guess it had torn them apart. They really seemed to be moving to two different tunes, the girl's upbeat and dance-able, the guy's dirge-like, something in a minor key.

When it came to the jukebox's alleged powers, Gus was immune. No song had ever cast its spell on her, or on Ed. She wouldn't mind having "Staying' Alive" boom through the speakers when Ed was seated on a stool across the bar from her. That was a song a cop needed to hear.

She caught a motion near the entry with her peripheral vision. *Don't look,* she cautioned herself. *You're acting like a fool.* But she looked anyway—and in walked Ed, looking calm and confident, like someone who'd accomplished exactly what he'd intended and hadn't shed a drop of sweat in the process. He met her gaze, smiled, and sauntered toward the bar, his expression just this side of smug.

Gus felt all the tension drain from her spine, her muscles, her nerves. The champagne cork came free with a festive pop. *He's tough,* she thought. *He's fine.*

—∿—

Emma seemed to think she'd won the lottery. Her smile, always a thing of beauty, now looked laser-bright, and her eyes glittered like Fourth-of-July sparklers. All because that guy at the community center, Nick Whatever, was allowing her to use a storage room as her studio.

She wouldn't yearn for that horrible little windowless room—and she wouldn't have to machete her way through acres of red tape and bureaucratic paperwork—if Max allowed her to remain in the house. He could do that so easily. He didn't need the money selling the house would bring him. And she did need the house. The loft offered so much space, so much light. If he were painting her dream portrait, it would feature her face, so open, so lovely, her angular cheeks and narrow chin shaping a valentine, and her resplendent hair, and her wide green eyes—glowing not like sparklers but like fireworks bright enough to illuminate the sky. And the dream surrounding her would be the loft in his house, filled with her easels and paints, her energy and creativity.

She was excited about the room at the community center because it was her only option. Max had given her no other choice, and she was the sort of woman who could view no choice as the greatest opportunity in the world.

He hated himself.

One word, one minor change of plans, and the house could be hers. He didn't need it. She did.

Except that he'd bought that house for another woman. A woman who, he'd learned too late, had loved him only because he could buy her things. He'd been so crazy in love with Vanessa, he hadn't been able to refuse her anything. She wanted a house on a hill overlooking the Atlantic Ocean? No problem. It was hers.

Emma hadn't asked for the house. She wouldn't. Unlike Vanessa, Emma had no idea how easy it would be for Max to give her that house, and three more just like it, if she wanted them. Even though much of his money was now controlled by his foundation, he still had more than he could ever hope to spend in his lifetime. If Vanessa had stuck around, she might have been pleasantly surprised to discover that, despite establishing the foundation, he was still absurdly wealthy.

He ought to tell Emma the truth. He ought to let her see his true colors, just as the song urged. But if he did…It would change everything. She'd stop viewing him as a Russian immigrant who grew up in a Brooklyn tenement and felt uncomfortable discussing his dreams. Of course he felt uncomfortable discussing them, especially with a woman he desired as much as he desired Emma. What was he supposed to say to her? "My dream is to be loved for myself, not for my wealth." That made him sound so pathetic.

And how the hell was Emma supposed to paint that dream, anyway?

"This is just so cool," she yammered, her words tumbling over one another in her excitement. "Not only do I have a place to work, but I've got another job! Or I will, if I pass muster with Nick's board. I don't have a teaching credential, but I've got plenty of experience working with kids. In high school and college, I spent my summers as an art counselor at a camp. And I've taught art to individuals—in gross defiance of zoning laws. Shame on me!" she added gleefully. "I should get letters of recommendation from Abbie's and Tasha's parents. I really hope this committee isn't hung up on stuff like art education credentials. Nick implied the job pays crap, so they can't expect me to be some sort of art professor, right?"

She paused when the bartender appeared with a bottle of beer and a slender fluted glass of champagne. The bubbles streaming upward through the pale liquid reminded him of Emma's personality: round and fizzy, rising as high as they could go.

He felt like shit.

"Of course, I still need to find a place to live," Emma said after taking a sip of her drink. "But as long as I have a place to work, I'm good. I can always buy a tent."

"You don't have to buy a tent," he said curtly.

"Just joking." She reached across the table and gave his hand a gentle squeeze. "But at least now I don't have to worry about finding a place to live where I can also work."

He drank some beer straight from the bottle, relishing its sour flavor. Closing his eyes, he pictured that small, windowless room in the community center, its linoleum floor, its cinderblock walls, its sheer ugliness. She was thrilled because she thought it was her only option. But it wasn't.

"Look, Emma—if you want, I'll take my house off the market. I don't have to get rid of it. If you want to continue to live there…"

She'd raised her champagne flute to her lips, but his words clearly startled her enough to make her lower the glass and gape at him. "But you came to Brogan's Point to sell the house."

"It can wait."

"And I can't keep teaching there. You said so yourself. There are those nasty zoning laws. And insurance issues, and liability. All that legal stuff." She pressed her lips together, effectively smothering her radiant smile. "Taking the room at the community center means I'll be able to teach there this summer in Nick's program. So I'll earn a little more money and maybe make contact with more people who might want to commission Dream Portraits." She shook her head. "I can make it work."

"You could make it work in my house, too. Stay. Stay as long as you want. We're not a landlord and tenant anymore. We've gone beyond that, haven't we?"

She stared at him, suddenly wary. "What do you mean?"

He wasn't sure what was troubling her. "Emma. We've made love. Several times." Several spectacular times, he wanted to add. "You can stay on in the house. Forget about the rent. That's the least I owe you."

Her expression went from wary to deflated, from deflated to suspicious. Her voice was cool, barely an inch from icy. "You don't owe me anything, Max—unless you want to pay me for your portrait. I can't calculate the cost until I figure out what the painting will... *entail.*" She seemed to trip over that last word, for some reason. "But as far as the house...I don't need you to do that."

"Do what? Take it off sale? It isn't even *on* sale yet."

"You don't have to let me stay on in the house because we had sex. I didn't make love with you because I wanted something in return. You don't *owe* me anything." She sighed again. The fireworks vanished from her eyes, extinguished by a layer of tears. Extinguished by Max. "What happened this morning was special. It was freely given, at least on my side. And now you're offering to pay me for it. I put out, so you'll let me live on your property rent-free. Just so generous of you, Max." Her voice cracked and she averted her gaze.

"Emma." He kept his voice low, as unthreatening as possible. He wasn't sure what he was dealing with right now, other than an irrational woman. Math he could understand. Computers. Code. But women? He was totally at a loss. "I'm just trying to make things easier for you," he said.

"Did I ask you to do that? Do you think I need you to make my life easier? I made love to you because I wanted to, because you turn me on, because...because that stupid song convinced me I saw your true colors. But I think I'm seeing them now. I slept with the

landlord, and now the landlord *owes* me a favor. The hell with that."
She slid out of the booth and stormed toward the door.

Max raced after her, shooting the bartender a look he hoped
she would read as a promise to return and pay his tab. Yes, he was
diligent about paying what he owed—a trait Emma seemed to
believe was highly objectionable.

He caught up to her just outside the tavern's front door—the
place where he'd first kissed her, where he'd first realized how
much he wanted her. "Emma." He grabbed her forearm, closed his
fingers around the slender limb. "Stop."

She turned to face him. She wasn't crying, but he saw a few
glistening rivulets streaking her cheeks where tears had skittered
down to her chin. "It's okay, Max," she said. "I was wrong. I thought
I knew you better than I did. The song…" She lowered her eyes
and shook her head again, just as she had inside the tavern. "I'm
an artist. I see colors. I think they're true, but maybe sometimes
they aren't. Artists tend to see things the way we think they are, not
always the way they really are. We see dreams."

"You're not seeing *me*," he argued. "I care about you, Emma. I
want you to work in a big, open space with lots of light. I'm offering
to let you continue to do that in my house."

"No, thanks," she said, easing her arm from his grip. "I'm going
to take a walk, Max. I need to clear my head." She spun away and
stalked down the street.

He watched until she turned the corner and vanished from
sight. What was her problem? He was trying to make things easier
for her, and she was acting as if he were a creep.

Let her take her damned walk, he though as he yanked the door
open and headed back inside. Let her walk until her feet ache. He
didn't care.

He shook his head at his own self-deception. The fact was, he
cared too much. He cared so much, he wanted to tell her the truth
about himself—that he was richer than she could imagine, that
he was practically richer than *he* could imagine. That making her
life easier would create no hardship for him. That he could be her

patron as well as her lover. That he could arrange things so she would never have to worry about where she would live and where she would work.

And either she would embrace him—because she wanted his money to make her life easier—or she would hate him for trying to buy her. Either way, he would lose .

Fourteen

The long walk up the hill was exactly what Emma needed. The air was humid enough that anyone who saw her hiking back to the house would assume she was sweating, not crying. And by the time she reached the house, she wasn't crying anymore, anyway.

How could a day that had started so wonderfully turn rotten so abruptly?

The day wasn't completely rotten, she reminded herself as she unlocked the house and let herself in. She'd lined up a new work space—nowhere near as nice as the loft; Max was right about that. But the room at the community center would do. And she had a new potential source of income. Thanks to the community center, she'd be able to paint. She'd be able to teach. She'd be able to take care of herself.

Emma had a remarkably well-developed gene for responsibility. Growing up, she'd eaten food her family had grown on their own land or bartered for with their neighbors. She'd learned from her father how to repair a leaky roof, and from her mother how to sew a shirt. She wasn't averse to accepting gifts—she liked getting gifts, actually—but only gifts freely given. Like the boots Claudio had given her, simply because she'd seen them in a boutique window and said, "Aren't those gorgeous?"

Sex was a gift, too. You gave it to someone you liked, someone you loved, someone to whom you were irresistibly drawn. Someone who fit you in all the right ways, like the interlocking shapes of an Escher drawing.

She'd shared something powerful with Max. She had reveled in every moment of it, every sweet, sharp sensation. It had been something pure, something generous and open. No conditions. No strings. Something as true as the colors in a rainbow.

And then he'd transformed it so it was about a landlord and a tenant and him *owing* her something.

She cursed.

"Wow, you're in a good mood," Monica said, emerging from the kitchen and joining Emma in the entry hall as she turned the bolt on the front door. Monica must have driven her car into the garage; Emma hadn't seen it parked on the road in front of the house. Monica had changed from the conservative work apparel she'd had on that morning into a droop-shouldered sweater and a pair of stylish jeans. A glass of white wine in her hand, she eyed Emma up and down. "You should have let me know you were hiking the hill," she said. "I would have driven down and picked you up. What's wrong?"

"Nothing," Emma muttered, then sighed. "Everything. Is there more wine?"

"I just opened a bottle." Monica beckoned her toward the kitchen. "Come and tell me what happened."

Emma settled on one of the stools at the center island while Monica moved directly to the refrigerator to fetch the wine. She had begun dinner preparations—a package of chicken sat defrosting on the counter, and an onion, some carrots and a flowery crown of broccoli lay beside the sink. Ignoring the food, Monica filled a second wine goblet with chilled Chardonnay and handed it to Emma. It wasn't champagne, for which Emma was very grateful.

"Max and I..." Just saying those words ignited a pain in her chest, round and hard. There was no *Max and I*. Emma had thought there could be, but there wasn't.

"Our landlord?" Monica asked.

Emma nodded dolefully. "I'm an idiot. I know."

"You're not an idiot. What happened?"

"I thought..." She heaved a sigh. "I thought something was going on between us."

"Something romantic?"

Emma nodded.

"You slept with him?"

Another nod. Emma wasn't sure she wanted to reveal, even to her best friend, what an impulsive, reckless, poor judge of character she was. "And he turned it into a tit-for-tat thing. He made me feel…" She sipped some wine. Icy and dry, it soothed her throat, and her soul. "I mean, I thought I was falling in love with him. I felt so close to him. Like we understood each other. Like we knew each other on a really deep level. And he…" She swallowed the quiver in her voice. "He told me I could stay here in this house."

Monica scrutinized her across the center island. Evidently, Emma wouldn't have to explain further. Monica got what Emma was implying. "In other words, he'd let you live here like a kept woman?"

"I don't think he meant it quite that way, but that was how his offer felt to me. Maybe I'm too sensitive, I don't know…" She drifted off, once again sinking into a bitter self-evaluation. Impulsive. Reckless. Poor judge of character.

"So—wait a minute. He was willing to continue to rent the house to us?"

"He said he wouldn't sell it. I could live here."

"Because you slept with him?"

One more sad, pitiful nod.

"Emma." Monica sounded not judgmental but confused. "I know he's a good-looking guy. Very good-looking. But…shit, Emma. Why on earth would you have sex with the landlord."

Emma stifled her sigh by sipping some wine. "It was just—like this spontaneous thing. Magic."

"Did he break your heart?" Monica's voice bristled with righteous anger.

"No," Emma assured her, although for some reason she wasn't quite convinced of that. How could Max have broken her heart? They hardly knew each other. Surely what she'd felt for him couldn't be love.

Yet the pain increased inside her, swelling like a tender bruise in the center of her soul. *Something* was broken, that much was certain.

"So it was just one of those things," Monica summarized. "And then he botched the aftermath."

"Maybe we both botched it," Emma conceded. "Maybe he didn't mean his offer the way I took it. Maybe I overreacted. I don't know." She felt her tears returning, and in the stark white light of the kitchen, she couldn't pass them off as perspiration.

"Then there's a chance we can fix this," Monica said briskly, setting down her glass and digging in her hip pocket. She pulled out her cell phone and started tapping the buttons.

"Don't call him!"

"I'm not calling him," Monica said. "I'm calling Andrea Simonetti to see if Max listed the house for sale. If you're right about him, he might do something out of spite. If you're wrong about him, it's possible he was serious about letting you stay on in the house. And honestly, if he does, I want to stay here, too. That efficiency apartment at the inn is so tiny—and much too close to my parents. It would be practically like moving back in with them. Ugh." She shuddered.

"What about living with Jimmy?"

Another shudder. "The more I thought about that, the less I liked the idea. You know him—if I moved in, he'd say, 'Oh, you're running a load of laundry? You can wash these clothes of mine while you're at it.' I don't want to do his laundry. I don't want to clean up his messes. He's a great guy, he's fun, he makes me laugh, he's good in bed, but I don't want to have to pull his hair out of the shower drain." As she spoke, she tapped her phone, then held it to her ear and listened. After a minute, she said, "Hey, Andrea. It's Monica Reinhart. I'm glad I caught you..." After a couple of minutes of chit-chat, she said goodbye and disconnected the call. "He hasn't listed the house," she informed Emma with a smile. "Andrea hasn't heard from him in a couple of days."

"I don't know if I can live here," Emma said dolefully. "Not after..."

"Not after you and he had one of those things? That's no reason to give up on the house. We both want to continue living here. Before he showed up on our front doorstep, we were figuring on renewing our lease, right? You can work this out with him. Don't be a wimp." She tapped her phone again, her thumbs flying over the screen. She stared at it, squinted, enlarged it, scrolled. Her smile faded. "Damn."

"What?"

"I just accessed the inn's registration files. He's checked out."

"He has?"

"Fifteen minutes ago."

"So…he's gone, but he didn't put the house up for sale." Emma wasn't sure what that meant. She wasn't sure of anything, except that at the rate she was sipping her wine, she was going to need a refill soon.

"Our lease doesn't expire until the end of June. He's still got a few weeks to kick us out. He might go back to California and have Andrea take care of everything for him."

A few more tears leaked out of Emma's eyes. She didn't want Max in California. She wanted him here. She wanted him to come to the house and tell her he hadn't meant his offer the way it had come out. She wanted him to say he was thrilled that she'd found a new work space, and he hoped she'd find an affordable new place to live, and he couldn't wait to see her Dream Portrait of him. She wanted him to take her in his arms and kiss her, and murmur that one of the things he loved about her was her independence, her self-sufficiency, her ability to survive even though she was an artist living in a society that didn't value artists terribly highly.

But now he was gone. Back to his job, directing a foundation? Back to his view of San Francisco Bay? Back to a life that had never really had a place for her in it?

San Francisco Bay. The Atlantic Ocean.

Suddenly she knew the dream she would paint in his portrait. Because damn it, he might have vanished, but she was going to paint his Dream Portrait, anyway.

—∞—

Stan Weisner seemed delighted to see Max hovering in the open doorway to his office. "Finally, you're going to take me out to dinner," Max's old professor said, his mane of curls shimmering like polished silver springs in the glare of the fluorescent fixture in the ceiling—a fixture that reminded Max of the equally harsh lighting in that room Emma was so thrilled about turning into a studio.

Max had found Stan at his desk, finishing up some work before he left campus for the evening. After apologizing for having passed on dinner the other night, Max had insisted on taking Stan out tonight. Stan had phoned his wife to inform her of his dinner plans, and he was beaming when he hung up the phone. "She's thrilled," he said. "If I went home for dinner, she'd have to prepare a real meal. Instead, she'll just open a can of something and read a book while she eats. Should I let *El Presidente* know you're back in town? We could stop at his house for a drink if you'd like."

Max didn't want to socialize with the university's president. He didn't want to be fawned over and thanked for his generosity. What he really wanted to do was hole up in his room at the Hyatt Regency, just a few blocks up Memorial Drive from the campus, and lose himself in a bottle of vodka. Russian psychotherapy, his father used to call it.

But he owed Stan a better visit than the one they'd had a few days ago, when Max had wound up taking over Stan's comp-sci class and then had raced back to Brogan's Point to see Emma. And he owed himself the opportunity to think about something—*someone*—other than her.

She'd been right to blow up at him, even if she'd blown up at him for the wrong reason. She didn't know the right reason. She didn't know that he hadn't come clean with her, that he hadn't told her who he truly was, that he hadn't revealed to her how insignificant the house and her meager rental payments were to him. He hadn't trusted her enough to tell her. He owned that mistake.

She'd made it clear, when she'd stormed out of the Faulk Street Tavern, that she was in no mood to repair their barely begun, terribly fragile relationship. Perhaps he should have chased after her, imposed himself on her, forced her to listen...to what? His confession about having more money than any human being could ever possibly spend in a lifetime? His explanation that he'd shifted most of that money to his foundation—and still had more than he needed to live in luxury for the next hundred years? His revelation that the last woman he'd loved had left him when he told her he'd used most of his fortune to set up a foundation instead of spending it on her?

Emma didn't lust after his money. She didn't even *know* about his money. He'd learned not to discuss his wealth, certainly not with anyone he knew as little as he knew Emma.

Yet when he looked at her, when he touched her, when he kissed her...he felt a deeper knowing. Like that enchanting song, he felt that he saw her true colors. Those true colors implied that Emma was the sort of person who would like him not more but less, once she knew how rich he was.

That didn't compute. People loved money. They loved wealth, and luxury, and not having to scrimp and scrape to get by. They loved not having to worry about finding an affordable place to live and work. Why should Max believe Emma was different?

It was the song he didn't trust—not Emma but the song, which had given him the absurd belief that he could see something in Emma that probably wasn't there.

If he didn't trust her, he didn't trust himself even more. He'd misread Vanessa so utterly, why should he assume he'd suddenly developed the ability to comprehend women's minds and souls?

He and Stan strolled up Mass Avenue, chatting about Stan's students, his final stretch of classes before the exam period began, his usual gripes concerning the challenges of securing grants to fund his research. They paused at each restaurant they encountered, scrutinizing the posted menus and peering inside. Eateries Max remembered from his student days, when he'd had no money to dine out, looked less tempting today than they had when they'd been beyond his reach. Now, no restaurant in the entire country was beyond his reach.

Eventually, he and Stan found a menu that appealed to them. Fortunately, the restaurant was able to seat them without a reservation.

"Enough about me," Stan declared, once the beers they'd ordered had been delivered to their table. "What's going on with you? Still enjoying being the richest man on the planet?"

"No," Max said, not having to think. He wasn't the richest man on the planet, not by a long shot. And since he'd divested himself of so much of his wealth when he'd established the foundation, he technically wasn't as rich as most people assumed he was. But he *was* rich. And at the moment, he didn't enjoy it.

Stan chuckled. "Fund my research," he joked. "Let me lighten your load."

"Submit something to Janet," Max suggested. "As a rule, we don't fund university research, but for you I could make an exception."

"Nah, that's all right." Stan waved his hand as if erasing Max's words from the air between them. "I'll get my funding on my own. We don't want people accusing you of playing favorites with your foundation. And here we are, talking about me instead of you again." Stan drank some more beer and leaned back in his chair. "Tell me why a guy who should be on top of the world looks like he's on his way home from a funeral."

Max managed a chuckle. "Do I look that bad?"

"On a ten-point glum scale, I'd score you at least a nine. I thought this was supposed to be an easy trip for you. Divest yourself of some real estate, visit your old stomping grounds, let MIT throw rose petals at your feet, and humor your old honors advisor." He leaned forward, suddenly frowning. "You didn't come back east for a funeral, did you?"

"No. No, I'm fine." The waitress returned to their table, and Max gave the menu a perfunctory glance before ordering a steak. He had no appetite, but he had to eat.

Once the waitress had gathered their menus and departed, Stan studied Max more closely in the muted lighting of the restaurant. "So, what's the problem? Anything I can help you with?"

"I doubt it," Max said, realizing as soon as he'd spoken that his words implied there *was* a problem. Not a major disclosure; Stan had already figured out as much.

A weighted silence stretched between them, lasting until the waitress returned with their salads. Max knew he had to say something. Stan was his friend. During the four years Max had been at MIT, Stan had been practically a father figure. Max had confided in him about his money woes—back then, he'd been juggling a scholarship, a loan and two jobs, both tutoring fellow students and washing dishes in one of the campus refectories. When one of his roommates started self-medicating his depression with copious amounts of pot and booze, Max had asked Stan for guidance. When Max's mother had been diagnosed with early-stage breast cancer, Stan had offered him reassurances, steered him to useful medical websites, and given him enough money to buy a bus ticket to New York so he could see her after her surgery.

He hadn't confided in Stan about girlfriend woes, because he hadn't had many girlfriends as an undergraduate. MIT's computer science department hadn't been overflowing with female students when he'd been there. He'd dated a Wellesley student for a while, and he'd been quite infatuated with a Smith girl who'd decided, after a few months, that her two-hour drives to Cambridge to visit him were wearing her out. But while he'd been passionate about his research, he'd never actually been in love with a woman. Not until Vanessa.

He wasn't in love with Emma, either. The very idea was preposterous.

"Here's the thing," he said, unsure of what he was going to say until the words flowed past his lips and into the air. "There's a jukebox in Brogan's Point."

"A jukebox." Stan accepted Max's statement with a curious nod. "I haven't seen one of those in ages."

"This one looks like an antique, something you'd see in a black-and-white movie from decades ago. It plays old songs." Max shook his head, aware of how strange he must sound to Stan. "I think it put a spell on me."

Stan erupted in laughter. "Like Voodoo? Come on, Max. You're a rational guy."

"Some things defy rationality." Max shrugged. "The jukebox played this song, and the next thing I knew, this woman and I... Well. It's stupid. I don't want to go into it."

"What song?" Stan grinned mischievously. "Maybe it'll work on my wife."

"No. Really. It's silly."

"What was that really hot disco song? 'Love to Love You, Baby.' Oh, man." Stan's smile softened, growing nostalgic. "Very erotic. Or 'When a Man Loves a Woman.' The original version. Percy Sledge."

"'True Colors,'" Max told him.

"What? Wasn't that song used in a commercial? I sort of remember—cameras, or film, something like that."

"It must have been a long time ago," Max said. "Do cameras still use film?"

"So, tell me about this spell."

"I'm embarrassed," Max admitted. "I'm a scientist. I believe in facts, data. Things I can see."

"And yet," Stan argued, "music *can* put a spell on people. I don't know about a camera commercial, but some music...a Bach fugue, for instance. It's mathematical, but also emotional. Or Debussy. You listen to *Clair de Lune* and you can actually see the reflection of a full moon in a pond. Or Percy Sledge singing, 'When a Man Loves a Woman.' My wife used to throw herself at me when she heard that song. I ought to dig out the CD and see if it still has that effect on her." He paused to butter a hunk of bread and take a bite. "'True Colors.' Okay. What did this spell make you do with the woman?"

Fall for her. Fall and fall and fall, like Alice tumbling down the rabbit hole. A whimsical fantasy story to go with the whimsical fantasy that hearing a pretty pop tune in the presence of Emma Glendon could turn his soul inside out and upside down.

"She's an artist," he said. "A painter. We have nothing in common."

Stan dismissed this with a snort.

"I offered to help her out a little, financially. She was insulted. She acted as if she thought I was trying to buy her."

"She sounds like she's got integrity. See? You and she have that much in common."

"I have no integrity," Max muttered. He'd treated her like a recalcitrant tenant, and then like a hot mama. He'd had sex with her for no better reason than that he'd wanted to and she'd made herself available. He'd refused to tell her the truth about himself.

"Don't get all Russian on me," Stan chided. "I know pessimism and depression are part of your ethnic make-up, but you've been in the U.S. since you were old enough to stop sucking your thumb. Russian gloom doesn't suit you."

Max sighed. "Maybe she's just too good for me."

"That I can believe," Stan teased, then turned as the waitress approached with their entrees. "Ah, steak. If that doesn't dispel your mood, *Mahk-SEEM*, then I'm shipping you back to St. Petersburg."

The steak, along with a second beer, did cheer Max a bit. Or maybe it was simply Stan's jovial personality. When they parted ways at the Kendall Square T stop, Stan to head for home, Max contemplated returning to Brogan's Point. By now, the Hyatt ought to be used to his making reservations and then not keeping them.

But as he strolled to the hotel overlooking the Charles River, he thought better of returning to Brogan's Point tonight. Stan had nearly convinced him that there was nothing crazy about being bewitched by a song—even a song used as the soundtrack for a TV commercial about photographic film—and that a healthy, red-blooded man couldn't be blamed for jumping the bones of a gorgeous, red-haired painter.

Not jumping her bones. Making love to her.

That was the catch, the thing that brought his spirits back down. He and Emma had made love. Kissing her, filling her, coming inside her—it had meant something.

He should have told her the truth about himself. Instead, he'd more or less thrown money at her.

He couldn't go back to Brogan's Point, not until he was ready to come clean with her. Maybe she would love him because he was rich and she would appreciate access to his money. Maybe she would hate him because he could buy and sell her a million times over.

Lose-lose.

It would probably be best just to fly back to San Francisco, forget about the house, forget about Emma. Forget about a shimmering song that claimed to be about seeing the truth but had in fact lured him down a blind alley.

Fifteen

Emma didn't need to look at the photos she'd taken of Max, let alone print them and pin them to a board beside her easel for reference. His image was imbedded on the insides of her eyelids, emblazoned on her soul. She could see his vivid blue eyes, fringed with dark lashes. She could see the angle of his chin, the slight hollows beneath his cheekbones, the sharp line of his nose, the dark, silky waves of his hair, which always seemed just a bit windblown. She could see his strong shoulders, his leanly muscled chest. She could feel the heat of his skin against her palms as she touched him...

She gave her head a resolute shake. The temperature of his skin had nothing to do with her painting of him.

She'd never before painted a portrait from memory. But Max... She had him memorized.

"I don't see his true colors," she said aloud, her voice barely a whisper in the quiet house. Monica had headed off to spend the night with Jimmy. She might not want to do his laundry or clean up after him, but as she'd told Emma, he was good in bed.

Monica's departure had suited Emma fine. Tonight she was restless, revved up, and she didn't want to explain her midnight spasm of creativity to her friend. She just wanted to paint and paint and paint. Being alone in the house meant not having to justify herself.

"I don't see his true colors," she said again, her voice hovering like a tendril of smoke in the airy loft. "But I've got his dream nailed down."

Adrenaline pumped through her veins. She'd thought about brewing a pot of coffee, but she didn't need caffeine to keep her awake. Instead, she'd brought the open bottle of Chardonnay and her wine glass upstairs to the loft, and she fortified herself with occasional sips of the cold, crisp beverage.

Wasn't wine supposed to make you drowsy? If so, this wine had failed in its mission. Emma simmered with energy, hummed with it, trembled with it. Her nerves were strung tight, sensitive to the spread of light on her canvas, the play of colors as she dabbed nurdles of paint onto one of the old ceramic dishes she used as a palette and blended the nurdles to get the precise degree of darkness for his hair, the right mix of pink and tawny brown for his complexion. His eyes...Damn, it was hard to recreate that crystalline blue. A dab of cerulean, a dab of cobalt, a generous blob of zinc white, a hint of silver. She mixed the paint studied it, mixed it some more, and added a little more cobalt and a little more zinc white. *There.* The true color of Max Tarloff's eyes.

How could she see him so clearly? How could it feel as if he were in the loft with her, posing for her, watching her, wanting her as much as she wanted him?

What if she'd completely misunderstood him? Judged him unfairly? He'd offered to let her stay on this house because he'd wanted to help her. Had that been such a bad thing?

It had forced her to acknowledge the inequality between them. It had reminded her that he was her landlord and that her housing situation depended solely on his whims. It had made her feel dependent on him, indebted to him. Maybe he hadn't meant to emphasize the difference in their status—she the impoverished renter, he the generous landlord—but that was how she'd felt. If he hadn't realized she would take his gesture that way, well, he hadn't seen her true colors, either.

Dumb-ass song.

She continued painting, her brush strokes precise and controlled, and Max slowly revealed himself on the canvas. When it came to painting, at least, she knew his true colors. The face and upper torso taking shape on her easel resembled not the man who had sat awkwardly on a stool while she'd snapped photos of him, and who'd been so reluctant to discuss his dreams, but rather the man she'd kissed, the man she'd caressed, the man against whose warm skin she'd traced teasing patterns with her fingertips.

As for his dream, the one dream he'd shared with her...She might be completely wrong about it. He might have just told her to distract her, to prevent her from digging deeper into his psyche. He'd put so much effort into concealing his true colors. But she had the one dream he'd confessed to, and as the painting materialized beneath the bristles of her brushes, that one dream seemed right. In fact, it made her wonder whether he'd offered to let her stay in the house not because he'd had sex with her but because he wasn't yet ready to let go of his dream.

What would she do with the painting, once it was done? She couldn't sell it to him. She doubted she could keep it. Yet there it was, the swirls of his hair defined by glints of light, his face in semi-profile, his eyes gazing off to the left, toward the view he dreamed of. Something in her rendering of him made him appeared both wistful and satisfied, anchored in this place even though he didn't live here. Was he from Russia? Brooklyn? San Francisco? No matter. In Emma's portrait, he looked like someone who had been searching for a home and had found it at last.

He'd probably hate the painting. She supposed she could keep it for herself, a memento of a man she'd given her heart to, even though he'd kept his heart locked away from her, refusing to let her artist's eyes *really* see him.

Stupid, stupid song. She hated it. She hated that it had bewitched her and made her fall in love with a man who had deliberately kept his true colors hidden from her.

Yet she found herself humming it as she worked.

—w—

No one answered when he rang the bell.

He checked his watch again. Nine-fifteen. Not terribly early, even for a Saturday morning. He rang the bell again, then shielded his eyes with his hand and peeked through the glass sidelight into the entry hall. No sign of life.

Emma and Monica couldn't have moved out yet. Emma didn't even have a place to move to. Certainly she couldn't camp out in that stuffy little room at the community center. That was a public building—offices, a swimming pool, a gym, a hub of Brogan's Point activity. Not a homeless shelter. And her situation there hadn't been finalized yet.

She'd joked about living in a tent—although, given her back-to-the-earth childhood, maybe she hadn't been joking. He couldn't believe she would have evacuated the house that quickly, though.

However, she could have gone out that morning, or last night. She could have returned to the Faulk Street Tavern, heard some other song spilling from the jukebox—"When a Man Loves a Woman," perhaps; hadn't Stan said that song had an aphrodisiac effect on his wife?—and gazed into some other man's eyes. She could have gone home with that other man, gone to bed with him. Moved on, even if she hadn't yet moved out.

Max rang the bell one last time, then pulled his key from the pocket of his jeans. It was his house, after all. He was allowed to enter it.

Silence greeted him as he closed the door behind him. "Hello?" he called out, not wanting to startle Emma if, God forbid, she'd brought that other man back here for the night. Bracing himself for that possibility, he ventured down the hall toward the great room, moving cautiously, doing his best to clomp his feet so she'd hear his approach. The plush white carpet absorbed his footsteps, though. And if she and the other man Max had conjured in his imagination had spent the night together, they'd probably be sound asleep now.

Why had Vanessa chosen to floor the house in white carpet? It was pretty, but so impractical. Had she planned to make visitors remove their shoes at the front door, and pad around in their bare feet? Would she have provided slippers for her guests?

He didn't exactly mind the white carpet, but it would have to go. He knew nothing about interior decorating, and even less about color. Would brown carpeting be boring? Would green make the house look like a golf course? Would red be too garish? Once he had the place recarpeted, should he ask the installers to save a scrap of the carpet from the stairs to the loft as a souvenir of the hottest sex he'd ever experienced?

In the kitchen, he found an empty wine glass on the counter by the sink. It looked clean, but when he lifted it to his nose, he could smell a residue of wine in it. A bowl containing a banana, a couple of apples, and a twig of green grapes sat on the center island. Surely if Emma and Monica had moved out, they wouldn't have left their fruit behind. Or a dirty glass. The last time he'd been in this kitchen, when Emma had made him a delicious omelet for breakfast, he'd been impressed with how tidy the place was.

Of course she and Monica hadn't moved out. They had another month and a half on their lease. Monica was probably with her boyfriend, and Emma was with…

He didn't want to think about it.

He felt a little like a trespasser as he moved through the airy, sunlit rooms on the first floor. *You own this house,* he reminded himself. *It's yours.* Yet it felt like Emma's more than his. More, even, than Vanessa's. Emma had lived there for only a few months, but in those few months she'd made the place her own.

He circled back to the great room and started up the stairs to the loft. At the top, he froze.

Emma lay sprawled out on the floor, her hair a tangle of fiery red around her face, her baggy cotton sweater and jeans spattered with paint, her feet clad in her familiar, paint-stained canvas sneakers. A smear of paint marked her chin like a blue scab. Her chest rose and fell in a steady rhythm. She was sleeping.

Beside her, on an easel, was a painting of Max, staring out at a panoramic view of the ocean. In the painting, he might be seated on that ghastly, uncomfortable stool, which stood exactly where it had been when he'd posed on it just twenty-four hours ago. He might be gazing through the wall of glass at the Atlantic Ocean at the bottom of the long, panoramic hill on which his house stood.

His house. Emma's home.

He scrutinized the loft. The table at the center of the room held tubes of paint, a jar filled with several paintbrushes in various sizes, and a plate smudged with blends of paint—some blue, some yellow merging into a rich, dark green, the color of the sea in the painting. Dollops of black and brown swirled together like veins in marble, just as his hair in the painting was black with veins of brown. Two intense blues lightened with pale paint to create the color of his eyes.

The table also contained another empty wine glass, and an empty green wine bottle. The glass in the kitchen assured Max that Emma hadn't drunk the entire bottle herself. Someone—Monica, he hoped—had drunk at least a glass of it. And Emma didn't look drunk. Her breathing was relaxed and steady, her complexion a healthy peach hue.

Besides, if she'd gotten drunk, she couldn't possibly have produced such an amazing painting. Max knew all the myths about tortured artists drinking or ingesting or shooting up assorted intoxicants and then, under the influence, allegedly creating masterpieces. He didn't believe those myths. Great artists might be substance abusers, but the artwork they accomplished while drunk or stoned was never as beautiful or moving as what they might accomplish while sober.

Max was a scientist. He indulged in alcoholic beverages when the occasion called for them. And he'd never come up with as good a solution to a programming challenge after drinking a few beers or a vodka as he'd come up with after consuming a mug of strong black coffee or a glass of steaming Russian tea.

Emma wasn't drunk. Just asleep. Since this painting hadn't existed yesterday, she must have painted it overnight. No wonder she was exhausted.

She couldn't possibly be comfortable, sleeping on the rumpled, stained drop cloths spread across the floor of the loft. To pick her up and carry her to her bedroom would be awfully presumptuous. But to leave her on the floor seemed heartless.

Before he could decide what to do with her, she stirred. A soft sound—half a purr and half a sigh—slipped past her parted lips. They looked rosier than he'd remembered, in contrast with her smooth, pale skin and that blot of blue paint staining her chin. Then her eyes fluttered open. She peered up at him, looking sweetly befuddled. At least his presence didn't alarm her. Finding him in her loft didn't cause her to scream or recoil in horror.

"Max?" Her voice was thick with drowsiness.

"You didn't answer the doorbell, so I let myself in. I'm sorry."

"No, that's all right." She rubbed her eyes with one hand and pushed herself up to sit. "It's your house."

He almost retorted that it was hers more than his, but he wasn't sure if that was true. He also wasn't sure if his apology was for having entered the house or for having said the wrong thing yesterday—or for having failed to say the right thing.

"I thought you'd gone back to California. Monica said you checked out of the Ocean Bluff Inn."

"I just went down to Boston," he said. "Actually, Cambridge. I wanted to see an old professor of mine."

"Oh, you're a Harvard man?"

"M.I.T."

She shoved a heavy tangle of hair back from her face and sighed again.

"Either way, I guess you're a genius, right?" She remained seated on the floor, apparently not quite fully conscious. She yawned, rubbed her eyes, rolled her shoulders, yawned again.

He needed to move down to her level, rather than towering above her. He considered sitting on the stool—no, too uncomfortable. Or on the stairs—no, too erotic a memory attached to that place. Instead, he dropped onto the floor facing her, but not too close, not crowding her. He crossed his legs, rested his elbows on his knees, folded his hands, and watched her.

"To be able to paint something like that—" he gestured toward the painting "—is genius. It's amazing."

"It still needs work," she said. "I've got to extend the seascape and the sky. The ocean needs more turbulence, I think. And I didn't get your sweater right. I have to do some more shading, give it some more dimension. It's funny—I had no trouble picturing your face, but your sweater caused me problems."

He shot the painting another awed look. "You did all that last night?"

"Last night into this morning, until I finally had to take a nap." She yawned yet again, reminding him of a cat. A beautiful, sexy cat stirring awake after dozing in a patch of sunlight.

"It's extraordinary." He peered up at the painting from his position on the floor. "Different from the painting you did of the little princess girl."

"That painting was much more representational," she agreed. "This one is more impressionistic. Rougher lines, less blending of color. I don't know. If I'd done it during the day, when I was fully rested, and I'd relied on the photos I took of you...But I didn't want to. I wanted to *feel* the painting, not copy the photos."

"Well." He continued to study it, then shook his head, trying to wrap his head around the idea that she'd created the painting without photos, without him posing for her. By *feel*. "It's amazing," he repeated, wishing he had the vocabulary to capture the painting's effect on him. Did she *feel* the wistfulness with which she'd imbued the painting? Did she *feel* the loneliness he saw in the her rendering of his eyes, the stubbornness in her rendering of his mouth? Did she *feel* how troubled he was, how desperate to make things right and how worried that his attempt would only make things worse?

"Feel free to name a price," she said, then gave a half-hearted laugh that made him wonder if she seriously wanted to sell the painting to him. "We never discussed what I charge for my work, let alone signed a contract. But I sure as hell could use the money."

Okay. She'd raised the issue, however unwittingly, before he'd had to. He drew in a breath and said, "We have to talk."

"If it's about the house—"

"It's about the house and a lot more," he said. Her eyebrows lifted slightly. She looked intrigued.

He didn't want to intrigue her. He wanted to make her understand who he was, and to love him not because of it but in spite of it.

He wanted her to love him.

So much was at stake. But if he wasn't honest with her, nothing else would matter. He took a deep breath for courage and said, "I'm very rich."

Emma snorted. "Compared to me, everyone is very rich. Even Monica."

"No, Emma. I'm talking *rich*. Top one-percent rich. Top one-tenth-of-one-percent rich."

She angled her head slightly, as if appraising him in this new light. "Well, I assumed you weren't poor. This house isn't exactly a shack, and you were renting it to us for peanuts. I figured either you were stupid or you were nuts. Or you were so rich, you didn't need to charge us a high enough rent to cover your mortgage and taxes on the place."

"There is no mortgage. I paid cash for it." Did he sound arrogant? Snotty? "Emma...I'm one of those gazillionaires you read about in the business pages—assuming you read the business pages, which you probably don't," he added when he saw the faint smirk curving her lips. "I'm a computer scientist. A software engineer. I developed an encryption program that protects credit card transactions, among other things. I got some venture capital funding, hired a small staff, and developed the software until it was ready to market. A major player in the industry offered me a ton of money for the company. So I sold it."

"And now you have a ton of money," Emma concluded.

"Yes and no." He considered his words and reminded himself to be honest. "Yes. I have a ton of money. But a smaller ton of money than I might have had. I've got a seat on the board of directors of the company that bought mine, which pays a ridiculous amount to each of us whenever the board meets. I've made some smart investments in other start-ups. But even without that income…After the sale, I distributed shares of the profit to my staff and investors. But I had an obscene amount of money. More than I knew what to do with. More than was right, frankly."

"Right?" She looked intrigued again. "Is there a right amount?"

"No one should have as much money as I did, not when there are so many people in the world who have so much less. I set up a foundation—the New World Foundation—and put most of my money into that. It funds educational programs, both here and abroad. One of our focuses is education for immigrants, helping them to assimilate and get up to speed. I was lucky I was young when I came to America—I learned English quickly and started school with my peers. My parents spoke some English, which helped. But we have so many immigrants in this country who have so much to contribute, and they come here unprepared for our schools, or with language issues. New World funds a lot of educational programs devoted to helping them."

"That's nice," Emma said. She looked mildly perplexed, as if unsure why he was telling her all this.

So far, he'd told her only the good parts. He pushed onward. "When I sold my company, there was a party to celebrate the acquisition. I met a woman at the party. Vanessa."

He'd half expected Emma to react in some way. Most women didn't like to hear about other women, at least not in the context of romantic entanglements. But Emma didn't seem the least bit jealous or annoyed. She sat unflinching, her eyes now fully in focus, her expression curious. "Your fiancée?" she asked.

"My ex. Yes." He ruminated for a moment. "She was…how can I put this? I was a computer geek from M.I.T. She was the sort of woman you expect to see on the cover of the *Sports Illustrated* swimsuit issue. There was more to her than her beauty, of course. She was intelligent. She was fun. We started seeing each other. We got engaged."

Emma said nothing. She simply watched him, waiting.

"And then, we broke up." Not true, and he corrected himself. "Vanessa left me. But not before I'd bought her this house."

Emma's brow dipped in a frown. "You're still not over her, are you."

"I'm very much over her," Max assured her. "But I bought this house only because she wanted it." He fidgeted for a moment with his watchband, stalling. He hated to admit what an idiot he'd been. But he had to be honest with Emma, and being honest required him to acknowledge his foolishness. "She'd grown up in New England, and she said she'd always wanted an ocean-view house. We looked at a few places in Maine, but the winter weather is so brutal there. Then we found this house. She said she wanted it, so I bought it. I told her to decorate it any way she wanted. It was hers."

"So she's responsible for all the white," Emma said. "The walls, the carpet—it's kind of sterile, if you ask me."

"Not my true colors," he joked, his gaze flicking toward the painting on the easel. The colors Emma had used to depict him and the ocean were so rich, so lush, so vibrant. He should have figured she wouldn't be a huge fan of Vanessa's austere decorating choices.

"Meanwhile, I set up my foundation. I funneled more than half my wealth into it. Vanessa was appalled."

"You should have consulted her," Emma said, surprising him by taking Vanessa's side. "A big financial decision like that? The couple ought to make it together."

"She didn't want to make financial decisions," he explained. "That wasn't why she was upset. She was upset because my personal worth had been cut by close to two-thirds."

"But...you said you still have a lot of money."

"I do. But I had a lot less than I had when she'd accepted my proposal. She wanted to marry a billionaire. A mere millionaire wasn't good enough for her."

Emma scowled. "It's not like you blew the money on something stupid. I mean, a foundation—that's pretty noble."

He made a face. "I didn't do it to be noble. I did it because it seemed like the right thing to do. I wanted to see the money put to good use, helping people the way my family could have been helped when we first arrived in America. And helping kids in poorly funded school districts. Helping kids become more math- and science-literate. Helping kids in developing countries, where the need is so great. The foundation was a way to spread my wealth around and let it accomplish some good in the world. I couldn't have spent all that money if I lived to be a thousand years old." He sighed. "Apparently, Vanessa *could* have spent all that money. She was furious with me for not granting her the opportunity."

Emma absorbed this. "So she broke up with you, and you were stuck with this house."

"I never really considered it my house. I didn't even want to think about it. I was grieving. And feeling like a schmuck. I thought she'd loved me. *Me*, an egghead from M.I.T."

"A very sexy egghead," Emma said, tickling a faint smile out of him.

"I found Andrea Simonetti running a real estate office in town and asked her to rent the house. I didn't want it sitting empty, but I couldn't sell it until I'd looked at it one more time. And for a year, I couldn't bring myself to look at it, because seeing it and remembering how stupid I'd been to buy it for Vanessa would make me bitter. But this spring, I finally decided I was ready to sell it. I never gave any thought to the tenants. Until I met you."

"And discovered I was running an illegal art school on the premises."

"I was angry about that."

"I know." She smiled.

She wasn't responding the way he'd expected. She seemed rather placid about everything he'd told her. She'd known about Vanessa—he'd told her that before—but she hadn't known about his wealth. Perhaps she just didn't care about him enough to be angry that he'd concealed the truth about himself for so long. Or perhaps she was an extremely clever actress, behaving blasé so she could get her hands on his money, the way Vanessa had wanted to.

He simply couldn't believe that of Emma, though. The one time he'd tried to give her something—the continued use of this house—she had rejected the offer, and she'd rejected him.

"I would never try to buy you," he said. "I hope you know that."

She averted her eyes and toyed with one of her shoelaces, twisting it around her finger and then releasing it. "I never thought you were trying to *buy* me," she said slowly. "But yes, I'm poor. I'm your stereotypical starving artist. I'm okay with that. I didn't become a painter to get rich. I became a painter because painting is what I do. It's how I process the world."

He could more or less understand that. He processed the world through mathematics, through logic, through computer code. Different medium, but essentially the same idea.

"I don't mind being poor. I grew up poor. I'm used to not having much. It's no big deal to me. As long as I have a roof over my head, some food in the fridge, an occasional glass of wine, and my art supplies, I'm fine. I don't need more than that."

"That sounds more noble than my foundation," he joked.

Her eyes flashed with emotion. She didn't smile. "I don't mind being poor, but I'll be damned if I'm going to be someone's charity. That's how you made me feel, Max. Just when I'd figured out a way to make everything work—a place to teach my art, a way to earn a little extra income—you stepped in and acted as if I *couldn't* make everything work. You offered to fix everything for me. I didn't know how rich you were. I didn't know that my staying on in this house wouldn't make any difference to you, money-wise. What I knew was that we'd slept together, and then you offered me the house because you *owed* me. You made me feel like a whore."

His heart broke a little. "God, Emma. I never meant that." He wanted to reach for her, gather her to himself, hug her until he could convince her that he'd had only the best of intentions. He'd wanted her to have everything she wanted: a roof over her head, food to eat, wine to drink, a place to create her art. That was all.

She wanted so little. He had so much.

"I thought you'd be angry with me for not telling you who I was. I feel I've been dishonest with you. But I've learned to be very discreet about my wealth."

"You were afraid that if I knew how rich you were, I'd turn out to be another Vanessa, huh."

He shrugged.

"In case you haven't noticed, I do not look like a *Sports Illustrated* swimsuit model."

"I'd have to see you in a swimsuit to know for sure," he said.

There. A hint of a smile.

"I don't want your money, Max."

"What do you want?" he asked. "If you were going to paint your own dream portrait, what would you paint?"

Her smile widened. She gazed past him, through the glass wall at the morning beyond, the wide blue sky and the wide green ocean below it. "Paint," she said. "I'd paint paint, and canvases. I'd paint time. I don't know how to paint that, but that's what I want. More time. I'd paint a bottle of wine, or maybe champagne." She turned back to him. "I'd paint an ocean view, just like yours."

"I didn't realize the ocean view was my dream until you got me to acknowledge it," he admitted.

"It's a good dream. There's something elemental about the ocean. It's where we all came from. Where we started."

"All things being equal," he said, "would you let me make that dream come true for you? Would you let me give you an ocean view?"

"If you're talking about this house—"

"I'm talking about *you*, Emma. I'm talking about *us*. You took this house and made it a place of creativity, of beauty. But it needs more. It needs color."

She eyed him quizzically. "You want me to redecorate the house?"

He couldn't abide the distance between them any longer. He reached out, snagged her hand, and drew her to him. Once he had his arms closed around her, he felt totally at peace, the same way he felt when he gazed out at the ocean. "Just by living here, you made this house yours," he said. "It's your home."

"What about Monica? She lives here, too."

"She lives here," he agreed, "but you inhabit the place. You make it a place of learning, of sharing, of creating. If you want to pay me rent, pay me rent. I don't care. I just want you to stay here. No," he contradicted himself. "I want *us* to stay here. I want this to be *our* place."

"Our little love nest?" she asked skeptically, even as she snuggled closer to him.

"Our home. You can make it into a home."

"You live in San Francisco."

"My foundation is there. I can fly back and forth. I don't have to be there every day. I've got a phone. I've got a computer. I've got enough money to buy a private jet if I need one." He brushed his lips against her brow. "I'm not giving you anything, Emma. I'm asking *you* to give something to *me*."

"What can I give you? Other than the painting?"

"Love. Trust." He used his thumbs on her chin to tip her face up, and he pressed a kiss to her mouth. "Color. Fill my world with color, Emma."

They kissed again, slower, deeper, a kiss that shimmered with light and shadow and shape, a prismic array of colors. A kiss that convinced Max that Emma was the source of all things beautiful in his world, that with her talent and creativity she could turn anything he might imagine into a reality. A kiss that assured him that he could share her vision, that if he saw the world through her paintings—through her eyes—their love would shine like a rainbow.

A kiss that proved his dream didn't exist merely on canvas. It existed here, in this room overlooking the ocean. It existed in this kiss.

Sixteen

Saturday was always a busy night at the tavern, and thank God for that. Gus earned half the week's take on that one night alone.

Tonight was no exception. The day had been warm, and even though the summer season hadn't officially begun, the town beach had been swarming with visitors that afternoon. According to her two waitresses, who'd spent the day at the beach themselves before checking in for work, only a few brave souls had waded into the icy water, but plenty of people had taken to the sand, reading and building castles, playing volleyball and tossing Frisbees.

A fair share of those beach-goers had chosen to end their day with some liquid refreshment at the Faulk Street Tavern. The place was packed, the noise level high, the liquor flowing and the cash register humming.

Even so, she kept an eye out for Ed. He'd said he would stop by later that night, which meant he'd help her close up and then accompany her back to her apartment for the night. She doubted he'd be in before ten, but she watched for him, anyway. She didn't like worrying about him, and tonight she wasn't worried. He wasn't on a high-risk case. He wasn't chasing down a drug dealer on a trawler. She didn't need him to come to the tavern to reassure her that he was safe.

Tonight was about want, not fear. She wanted to see him. She liked looking at him—and sleeping with him. Nothing wrong with that.

Many of the booths and tables were occupied by Faulk Street Tavern regulars. More regulars lined up along the bar. A group of lobstermen at one table celebrated a particularly profitable haul with a couple of bottles of pricy single-malt scotch. A crowd of young couples had pushed several tables together into a long row; the women ordered festive mixed drinks but the men were mostly sticking with beer. Manny raced back and forth from the kitchen, delivering steaming platters of wings, onion blossoms, and mini-pizzas.

Gus wondered if she should improve the food offerings. People came to the tavern mostly to drink, not to eat, but if they ate, they stayed longer and drank more. Manny was skilled enough at food preparation to serve up the basics, but it might be time to consider hiring a chef for weekend nights.

Someone must have slipped a quarter into the jukebox. An old Frankie Valli song began to play: "Can't Take My Eyes Off You." Schmaltzy, but no one ever said there was anything wrong with a love song being schmaltzy. The dance floor quickly became clogged with couples, arms wrapped around each other, bodies slowly swaying to the romantic song.

She finished filling a couple of pitchers of beer, set them on a tray, and noticed the door opening. She recognized the couple who entered. Impossible not to remember that red hair. Her own hair had been like that once—well, maybe not quite as intense a shade, and certainly not as long and wild. Now her hair was tempered with gray, and she kept it short so she wouldn't have to pin it back while she worked.

On Monica's friend, the long, curly tresses looked good.

The man with her looked good, too.

Champagne yesterday, she recalled. Champagne and a beer. And then the woman had stormed out of the place.

Tonight, she didn't look as if she had any intention of storming anywhere. She held hands with the man, smiled up at him, then led him through the crowds in search of a table. *Good luck with that,* Gus thought.

Eventually, they gave up on snagging a table and worked their way over to the bar. They waited while a couple of guys wearing

Hurley Plumbing Supplies shirts ordered Mojito's, then took their turn at the bar. "Champagne? Gus asked.

"No. Champagne didn't work out so well," the red-haired woman said with a smile. *Emma,* Gus recalled, the woman's name suddenly popping into her brain. She recalled the woman introducing herself when she'd approached Nick Fiore a few days back, when he'd been standing at the bar. *Emma.* "I'm sticking with beer tonight."

"You still get your bubbles that way," Gus joked, then eyed the man.

"Two Sam Adams lagers," he ordered. "I guess we'll go with bottles."

Gus nodded, pulled two beers from the refrigerator under the counter, snapped off the tops and reached for a couple of chilled glasses. When she turned back to the couple, Emma said, "We're in love."

"That's definitely worth some bubbles," Gus said.

"It's because of the song," Emma told her. "From the jukebox."

"I'm not sure I believe that," the man said.

Well, Gus thought, this isn't their first argument. They'd been at odds yesterday. And they'd obviously survived yesterday's argument, if they were announcing their love today.

"He's a scientist," Emma explained. "He'd like to pretend he doesn't believe in magic. But deep in his heart, he does."

"Deep in his heart is all that matters," Gus murmured.

"The song was 'True Colors,' by Cyndi Lauper."

Gus nodded. So many people came and went, but when a song from the jukebox exerted its magic, she had a way of remembering.

"Can we play it again?" Emma asked, waving toward the jukebox at the far end of the room.

Gus shook her head. "You can put in a quarter, but the jukebox will play whatever it wants to play. You can't control it."

"That's crazy," the man said.

"No, it's not. It's magic." Emma rose on tiptoe and kissed his cheek.

The man asked Gus to start a tab for them, which meant they planned to stay a while. Maybe they'd get lucky, and "True Colors" would pour out of the jukebox for them. Even if it didn't, they were already lucky. They'd found each other.

So some other song would play. And some other couple would be touched by it, enchanted by it. Maybe tonight.

—⁜—

Wild Thing

Book Three

One

Monica had no idea how many straws a camel could carry on its back. She only knew that if she was a camel, she'd reached her limit.

And really, it was not a big thing in and of itself. Just one last straw. Just Jimmy being Jimmy.

But enough. Her back had broken. She was done, done, done.

She sat at a table at the Faulk Street Tavern, nursing a glass of wine. Maybe she should have ordered something stronger, but she wanted to remain clear-headed while she contemplated that single, final straw and waited for her best friend to join her. Emma was teaching an art class at the Brogan's Point Community Center, but she'd promised to come to the pub as soon as her final student departed. Monica calculated that Emma's trip from the community center to the bar would take about ten minutes. Emma didn't own a car, although her gajillionaire boyfriend could buy her a fleet of Lamborghinis if she asked him to. Of course, one reason he was so crazy about her was that she would never ask. His wealth meant nothing to her.

She *had* acquired a bicycle, however—used but in excellent shape—which enabled her to scoot around town a little more rapidly than traveling by foot. Monica glanced at her watch and hoped Emma would arrive soon. If she finished her glass of wine before Emma showed up, she might order another, and that would be the end of her clear-headedness.

Jimmy. The asshole.

Last night was the tenth anniversary of their first date: the junior prom in high school. Monica hadn't even been aware that

Jimmy Creighton knew who she was back then. They'd traveled in different circles. She'd been an A student, diligent and disciplined, working at her parents' inn when she wasn't doing homework or pursuing other moderately egg-headed activities. Jimmy had been a cut-up, a funny, handsome guy who took nothing too seriously. Yet for some reason—maybe on a dare—he'd invited her to be his date for the prom. And for some reason—maybe because he was the cutest guy who had ever asked her out—she'd said yes.

They'd had their ups and downs over the past ten years, but Monica had thought they were mostly on an up right now. They both had jobs, he selling cars and she moving up into management at the inn. The sex was good. They hadn't had a fight in more than a month.

"For our anniversary," she'd told him, "I want to make a special dinner for you. Okay?"

"Sure, of course," he'd said. "I love when you cook for me. If it wasn't for you, I'd be living on buffalo wings and beer."

She'd scheduled a day off for herself yesterday, although she'd shown up at the inn before dawn that morning so she could accompany one of the chefs from the inn to the docks to pick up lobsters fresh off a boat. From there, she'd journeyed to the green-grocer for organic vegetables, and from there to the butcher, and from there to the wine store for a thirty-eight dollar bottle of Bordeaux. Then she'd let herself into Jimmy's apartment, donned an apron, and gotten to work. She'd made lobster bisque. She'd made Veal Oscar, garnishing the veal with lobster meat and asparagus spears and topping it with a *béarnaise* sauce. She'd warmed a loaf of bread. She'd prepared a tossed salad and scalloped potatoes. She'd spread a white linen cloth over the café table that stood in one corner of his living room, and lit a tapered white candle. And waited for him to show up.

The Ford dealership where he worked closed at six. Even allowing for traffic, he should have reached his apartment before seven. At eight-thirty, she phoned his cell. "Oh, hey," he'd said cheerfully. "I'm over at Dave's place. A group of us decided to pop some beers and catch the Sox game on TV. I'll be home by midnight, okay?"

Not okay. Final straw. Monica had blown out the candle, tucked the wine bottle under her arm, and walked out of his apartment, leaving behind her key to the place.

That was yesterday. Today she'd gotten through the day, keeping her grumpiness in check until she realized she wasn't terribly grumpy, after all. After previous break-ups with Jimmy, she'd felt angry or depressed, lost or confused. This time, not really. This time she was ready to shed all those straws Jimmy had been heaping onto her back for the past ten years. She was ready to move on. A little mournful, a little anxious, but ready.

The Faulk Street Tavern was rarely crowded on a weekday afternoon, and today was no exception. Gus Naukonen, who had owned the place since before Monica was born, occupied her usual station behind the bar, wiping surfaces, filling bowls with munchies, arranging bottles. None of the wait staff had arrived yet, but anyone who wanted a drink could walk up to the bar and ask for one, which was what Monica had done. Presumably, so had the young guys in polo shirts and khakis seated around one of the big tables with a couple of pitchers of beer and heaping bowls of popcorn. They were too clean-cut and rich-looking to be a fishing crew. Monica guessed they were college kids, their spring term over and their wealthy families settling into the rambling summer homes that dotted the northern end of town, where the upper-class folks owned what they euphemistically called "cottages" but which Monica called mansions.

She wasn't much older than those boys, but she felt older. No—she felt *mature*. Jimmy was a baby. She'd outgrown him.

A few other tables were occupied, and a man the far side of middle age sat at the bar, slumped over an empty glass. From where Monica sat, she could see Gus shooting occasional glances at the man, as if to make sure he didn't lean too far in any direction and topple off his stool.

Behind Monica stood the jukebox. She had her back to it, but she knew it was there, a magnificent antique rumored to possess magical properties. With its arched wood frame and its stained-glass inset of two peacocks nestling together, it was beautiful enough to belong in a museum. Its contents were a mystery: old songs that had been recorded back when vinyl records were the only available technology. No one knew what songs were in the jukebox, though. They weren't listed on the machine. You couldn't choose a particular song. According to legend, the songs would choose you.

Monica had grown up hearing the myth of the jukebox's reputed magic. She knew that if you put a quarter into the machine, three songs would play, and no one knew what those songs might be, other than that they'd be oldies, dating to her parents' era or even longer ago than that. Sometimes a particular song would strike someone in the room a particular way, bewitching that person, or transforming her, or...*something*. Monica hadn't really bought into the legend until her friend Emma and Max, the gajillionaire, had both fallen under the jukebox's spell and found true love in each other's arms.

Monica supposed that when it came to the jukebox, she was currently an agnostic. She didn't quite believe it was magic, but she didn't quite *not* believe it, either.

The bar's door opened, and Monica glanced over the back of the banquette. At the sight of Emma's wild red hair, she smiled. She was not going to cry on Emma's shoulder. She was not going to fall apart, bemoan the death of her decade-long relationship with Jimmy, turn the afternoon into a pity party. Instead, they were going to hoist their glasses high and drink a toast to Monica's liberation.

"Hey," Emma said, ambling over to Monica's table and sliding onto the banquette facing her. "I hope you didn't have to wait long."

Monica burst into tears.

—⟋⟍—

Some marinas had a rule stipulating that sailboats had to approach their slips on their motors. Ty Cronin preferred the marinas that didn't have that rule. To him, maneuvering a boat into a slip on wind power alone was a welcome challenge. Gauging the coastal breezes, riding in on the jib, tweaking the rudder an inch one way

or the other until you eased alongside a mooring or into a berth…
Sweet. What was the point of sailing if you had to rely on the motor?

The North Cove Marina at Brogan's Point didn't have a motor-only rule, so Ty brought the Freedom into its slip on wind power and technique. He'd had a good run up the coast from Key Biscayne. Some nasty weather off the Carolina coast, but nothing he couldn't handle. The Freedom was a gorgeous vessel: tiny but well-equipped galley, comfortable upholstered sleeping benches, an inboard shower and state-of-the-art commode in the head, and big sails that swelled and curved and maximized the wind's power. He hadn't even bothered with the spinnaker. The boat moved fast enough without it, and this trip wasn't a race.

It was a job. Wayne MacArthur had offered him a nice chunk of change to transport the boat from his winter home in the Florida Keys to his summer home in this seaside town north of Boston. Ordinarily, Wayne had explained, he would sail the Freedom up the coast himself, but he had some business issues detaining him in Florida, and he wanted the boat moored in Brogan's Point before Memorial Day. Ty was cool with that. The list of adventures he'd prefer over spending a week doing a solo ocean run was pretty short. Getting paid for the privilege was a bonus.

He'd never been to Brogan's Point before—or, for that matter, any part of New England. So what the hell. He'd sail up, spend a few days, and fly back to Florida. He had nothing going on there that couldn't wait for a couple of weeks.

He navigated the Freedom into its assigned slip and glided the boat into position with barely a tap against the old tires cushioning the side of the dock. He leaped off the boat and onto the smooth pine planks of the dock, lashed the boat fore and aft, and stood for a moment, his feet planted on the dock's solid surface, his legs adjusting to the lack of roll and pitch.

The May afternoon was mild, warm but nowhere near as humid as the heavy air smothering southern Florida at this time of year. A refreshing breeze lifted off the water, flinging a lock of Ty's hair across his nose. He'd washed his hair that morning when he'd showered, but after a day that had started off the coast of Rhode Island, carried him through the Cape Cod Canal, and blown him into his destination on brisk, strong gusts, he could use some freshening up.

Back on the boat, he spent a few minutes lowering the jib and wrapping it. He cleated the ropes, secured the rudder, and shut down the onboard navigating equipment. Then he ducked into the cabin, yanked off his shirt, and wedged his six-foot-two-inch frame into the closet-size bathroom. Tepid water, a bit of soap, more water and a few swipes with a towel invigorated him. He squinted at his reflection in the small slab of mirror above the sink. A raspy stubble of beard had sprouted since he'd shaved yesterday morning, somewhere around New Jersey, but he didn't feel like shaving again. He felt like getting rich and celebrating.

He donned a fresh shirt, stashed his duffel and laptop inside a storage bin beneath one of the upholstered benches, and secured the bin with a padlock. No saying who might be hanging around this marina. No point taking chances.

His wallet and cell phone stuffed into the pockets of his jeans, he emerged from the cabin and sprang back onto the dock. He snapped a couple of photos with his phone. The boat in its berth. The supply shack at the end of the dock, a massive wooden crate overflowing with bright orange life vests beside the open door. The much larger building on shore, situated midway between this dock and the next one, with a phony-looking anchor painted on its side, and above it the words "North Cove Marina" in nautical blue and gold lettering. Ty texted the photos to Wayne, along with a brief message: "Made it safe and sound." Then he waited.

In less than a minute, his phone vibrated. "Check's in the mail," Wayne had texted back. Ty tapped the phone to open his PayPal account. Twenty thousand dollars had just been added to it.

He grinned, transferred the money to his bank account with a few clicks, and strode up the deck to dry land. The door to the large building was open, and he stepped inside.

The front room was ugly in a familiar way. The pale green walls were decorated with a few nautical-themed prints, framed maps, oversized ropes and doughnut-shaped lifesavers. More boxes of bright orange life vests stood on the floor. A counter extended the length of the room, manned by a skinny kid who looked barely out of high school. He wore a polo shirt with the cute-cartoon anchor insignia stitched above the pocket, and salmon-red slacks.

"Hi," Ty greeted him. "I just sailed Wayne MacArthur's boat in."

The kid opened a loose-leaf notebook. The fancier the yacht club, Ty had noticed over the years, the more old-fashioned. He'd worked at some marinas that operated out of shacks no bigger than an outhouse but managed their slips and monitored conditions with up-to-date computer software. An upscale place like this, where the staff wore shirts with anchors above the pockets, used notebooks.

"What slip did you park in?"

Ty recited the number of the slip Wayne had instructed him to use. The kid flipped through the pages of his notebook, found what he was looking for, then glanced out a window behind the counter and eyeballed the boat. "Nice ship," he said.

"She sailed beautifully."

"Is Mr. MacArthur still on board?"

"No. I brought her up myself. He's flying up."

"Okay." The kid turned the notebook around so it faced Ty, handed him a pen, and asked him to sign his name.

Ty considered asking where the nearest bar was, but then realized the kid was probably too young to drink. Not that that would have stopped Ty when he'd been that age. He'd been filching the occasional beer by the time he was fifteen, not to get drunk but to piss off his grandparents. Still, this was a ritzy yacht club in a ritzy town. He smiled, gave the kid a nod and headed back outside.

Strolling through the parking lot, he tapped his phone, searching for bars in the area. Without wheels, he needed to find a bar close by.

The Faulk Street Tavern. It sounded quaint and New England-y. He called up a map of Brogan's Point and located the place, less than half a mile away. Since he'd have to return to the boat after he'd drunk himself a toast or two, he didn't want to travel too far for his refreshment.

Brogan's Point didn't have much of a downtown. It boasted a nice-looking beach, though, stretching along the ocean below a stone and concrete sea wall. A few shops lined the street bordering the sea wall, and more shops filled the streets intersecting it, two- and three-story buildings constructed of clapboard, brick, and stone. Eateries, hardware stores, ice-cream parlors. A real estate office. A women's clothing boutique. A Starbucks, of course. Turning from the stores, he gazed along the ocean's edge. Not far south of where he stood, several commercial docks lined with trawlers stretched eastward into the ocean. Ty could just make out the silhouettes of some warehouses near the trawlers. Fish markets, he figured.

If a Hollywood director wanted to film a movie in a stereotypical New England seaside town, he could do worse than Brogan's Point. It had everything Ty expected such a place to have, short of a guy in a yellow rain slicker, dropping his R's and eating a bowl of chowder. Or *chow-dah*, he supposed.

He strolled up the street, enjoying the solidity of the asphalt beneath the soles of his sneakers, enjoying the blunt breezes that rose up off the ocean to slap against the side of his head. Yeah, he could see spending a few days here before buying a plane ticket back to Florida. He could sleep on the boat, use up his food supply, and spend some time on the beach, even if the water here wouldn't be warm like what he was used to down in Florida or what he'd grown up with in California. Ocean was ocean. Sand was sand. Ty's parents used to joke that he was actually the son of a mermaid, given his affinity for the sea.

Up ahead he spotted the corner where Faulk Street intersected with Atlantic Avenue. He turned onto the side street and entered the bar.

To his great relief, it wasn't quaint. It appeared to be a working-class establishment, a little dim, a little scruffy, not too crowded but already redolent with the stinging scent of hard booze, beer, and oily, salty edibles. He stood just inside the doorway, surveying the place and considering where he ought to plant himself. The tables all looked too big for one person. A few of the bar stools were occupied, but more were empty. That seemed like the better bet.

He strode across the room, the center of which was clear of furniture. A dance floor? If it were his choice, he would have filled that space with a pool table. But he wasn't really up for a game right now. He'd done a week of hard sailing. He needed to decompress.

The woman behind the bar stood nearly as tall as Ty, with square shoulders, short hair fading from ginger to gray, and a pleasantly weathered face. She had the sort of no-bullshit look of a sports coach, or maybe a shrink. He supposed either of those character types would make good bartenders. "What can I get you?" she asked.

"A shot of bourbon and a glass of whatever you've got on tap," Ty said.

She named a few beers. No connoisseur, he asked for the first one she'd listed, then settled onto a stool and gazed around the room. A group of frat boys sat at one table, cheerfully arguing about the relative merits of Porsches and Ferraris. Three portly older men in faded Red Sox caps nursed their drinks at a table near the door. Two attractive women sat facing each other in a booth to his left, one with long, curly red hair and the other with black hair that ended in a ruler-straight line at her shoulders. They each had a glass of wine, and they bowed their heads together across the table that separated them, engaged in intense conversation. A couple of stools down from Ty, a guy three sheets to the wind slumped over an untouched mug of coffee.

Against the wall opposite the bar stood a jukebox. It looked like something you might find in a catalog, or in one of those stores that specialized in selling new stuff designed to look old. A dome-shaped arch, buttons, fabric-covered speakers flanking a colorful façade of what appeared to be stained glass peacocks, of all things.

He heard the thump of glasses on the bar behind and swiveled around on his stool to discover that the bartender had served his drinks. He tossed back the bourbon in one gulp, savoring its burn down his throat, then followed it with a sip of cold beer.

He had money. He had time. He had liquid refreshment. Life was good.

The din of voices rose slightly as more people trickled into the bar. Ty glanced at his watch: five fifteen. Rotating back around to view the room, he nursed his beer and watched the bar's clientele drift in, most of them just off work from the look of it. Some wore the uniforms of their jobs: garage coveralls, medical scrubs, tailored outfits that included button-down shirts adorned with loosened neckties or colorful scarves, depending on gender.

An energetic woman in tight black pants, her hair pulled into a pony tail, bounced over to the bar. "Sorry I'm late, Gus," she shouted to the bartender as she laced an apron around her waist. "The traffic on Route 1 was a bitch."

"Surprise, surprise," the bartender muttered sarcastically. Ty wondered whether Route 1 here in Massachusetts was the same road as Route 1 in Florida. He was pretty sure it was. Like I-95, Route 1 spanned the length of the country from Maine's Canadian border to Key West. Pretty cool to think you could drive from the nation's northern border to its southern tip on one single road. Maybe some-day he'd hop on his bike and ride the distance, just for the adventure.

The waitress grabbed a tray, shot him a quick smile and headed back into the room, circulating from table to table, checking on the patrons. Ty watched her for a while, then shifted his attention to the two young women conferring in the booth. The one with the black hair was dabbing her eyes with a cocktail napkin. The redhead leaned toward her, giving the dark-haired one's free hand a squeeze. Dykes? Ty wondered. He'd hate to think that two good-looking women like them were unavailable to the male half of the population, but a hot little fantasy flared in his mind at the thought of them going at it. An even hotter fantasy placed him between the two of them, the meat in the center of the sandwich. He laughed at his crassness, told his balls to stop thinking for him, and took another sip of beer.

"Share the joke?" The woman who'd addressed him had stepped up to the bar, blocking his view of the drunk guy with the coffee. She was probably within shouting distance of forty, nice looking and dressed for cruising in a short skirt and a low-cut blouse which displayed cleavage deep enough to swallow small items.

"Just thinking about what an ass I am," he said pleasantly.

"I don't believe that," the woman said. Catching the bartender's eye, she said, "Can I have a Cosmo, Gus?" Then she turned back to Ty. "You're not from around here, are you."

"Is this one of those places where everybody knows everybody?"

"Kind of. I guess you and I should get to know each other, so you don't feel left out."

She deserved an A for effort, but Ty wasn't interested. He smiled politely, drank a little more beer, and said, "I'm just passing through. Running an errand."

"If only all errands ended with a drink," she said, accepting the cocktail glass the bartender handed her.

He rotated in his seat to gaze out at the room again. Business was definitely picking up, more and more tables filling. Another waitress pranced into the pub, her apron already tied around her waist. Two of the frat boys wandered over to the jukebox.

"Brace yourself," the Cosmo drinker said.

"Why?"

"That jukebox is crazy."

How could a jukebox be crazy? He braced himself, anyway, then let out a long breath when the jukebox began pumping music into the room. An old Beach Boys tune—"Fun, Fun, Fun." Ty recognized it because his grandfather on his dad's side was a huge Beach Boys fan. The old man owned the band's albums, cassettes, even sheet music of their songs. He was a crappy guitar player, but he fantasized about becoming the next Brian Wilson. "If you live in California, this is your music," he'd lecture Ty, who would nod solemnly. As a kid, he'd worshipped his father's father.

Throughout the room, people laughed. Some sang along, their voices screeching as they reached for the falsetto notes. A small cluster of revelers moved to the center of the room and started dancing, although it looked more like they were just jumping up and down. Pretty rowdy for a weeknight.

The song ended. "Like I said," the Cosmo drinker repeated, "that jukebox is crazy."

"What's crazy about it?"

"It only plays old songs. Really old songs."

"I guess that makes sense. It looks like an antique."

The woman shrugged. "I don't know why Gus keeps the thing there. I mean, if you're going to have music, it should be music people listen to."

Ty could have argued that people still listened to the Beach Boys. But he didn't want to get into an argument with his chatty new friend.

Another song came on, another oldie. Ty didn't recognize this one, but he thought his musically untalented grandfather could have mastered it. It had had only a few smashing cords, and the singer sounded as if he'd gargled with battery acid before laying down the track. The simple lyrics emerged in a harsh growl: "Wild thing…you make my heart sing…" The singer went on to growl that some woman made everything groovy.

Groovy? Ty started to laugh—and then he stopped. The woman in the booth, the one with the black hair and the teary eyes and the solicitous friend, was staring at him. Staring hard.

And damn, if he couldn't keep from staring right back at her.

Two

Who was he?

Monica knew pretty much everyone who was anyone in Brogan's Point. She might have attended a big-city university, lived in Boston, learned how to navigate Beantown's mass transit system, and mastered the art of marching down a busy street looking straight ahead, avoiding eye contact, aloof to the hubbub around her. But in her chest beat the heart of a small-town girl. A girl who, until yesterday evening, had dated the guy who'd been her escort to the high school junior prom. A girl who was being groomed to take over the family business—a landmark inn in town. A girl who behaved herself, who did what was expected of her, who was respected and admired. Who was predictable.

A girl who could not, by any stretch of the imagination, be described as a wild thing.

The man staring at her from his perch on a bar stool across the pub definitely looked like a wild thing. He was tall, his knit Henley shirt snug enough to hint at his broad shoulders and muscular torso. His hair was a long, windblown mess of dark blond streaked with the sort of glittering platinum highlights only the sun could create. His stubble of beard was a shade darker than his hair. His blue jeans were faded nearly to white and were torn across one knee. His eyes were almost as pale as his jeans.

He was the sexiest man she had ever seen.

One minute she was whimpering and sniffling over Jimmy, and the next she was thinking she wanted to jump a total stranger's bones. Which was completely not like her.

But for some reason, as she gazed at that tall, blond stranger at the bar, the drone of voices and clink of glasses and shuffle of footsteps faded to nothing. Emma could have been a million miles away. Everything in the room blurred into shadow except for the man at the bar and the song blaring from the jukebox. "You mooooove me…" the singer howled.

Monica felt wild.

She flinched, trying to shake off the song the way a dog might shake water off its fur. She didn't really believe that nonsense about the jukebox's magic. She knew about it, she laughed about it, she humored Emma, who swore the jukebox had brought her and Max together and made them fall in love. But Monica didn't actually think an old Wurlitzer could cast a spell on people. Certainly not with an insipid song like this one.

Monica was sensible. Not susceptible to magic spells.

Just to be safe, though, she slid out of the booth and bolted for the door.

She'd barely caught her breath when Emma joined her on the sidewalk outside the tavern. "Monica, what's wrong?"

"Nothing." Monica was too embarrassed to admit that a silly old rock song had spooked her.

"We can't just leave. We didn't pay for our wine."

"That's all right. Gus knows me. She knows I'm good for it."

"No—I mean, I can pay for the drinks," Emma assured Monica. "But I don't want to go back inside without you. You're freaking me out."

"I'm fine," Monica lied. "Just…you know. The whole Jimmy thing. I'm a little weirded out."

"Five minutes ago, you were sobbing about that son of a bitch," Emma reminded her. "I don't want to leave you alone."

"No. It's okay. I'm okay." Monica let out a long, steadying breath. The song had probably finished playing; she could go back inside. Except that if she did, she would see that guy at the bar again, tall and ripped, with his mesmerizing eyes and his bemused smile. He'd stared at her. He'd witnessed her becoming transfixed by the song.

Maybe he'd even read in her expression the uncharacteristic surge of lust she'd experienced while looking at him. She couldn't possibly go back into the pub.

"Look. Here's some money." She pulled her wallet from her purse and unsnapped it. "I'm sorry, but I've got to go."

Emma waved the money away. "I've got the drinks. But what about you? Where are you going?"

"Home. I think...I had a funny reaction to the wine, that's all," she said. The explanation made sense to her, more sense than the possibility that a song from the jukebox had briefly taken possession of her. "I just need to go home and lie down for a while. I'll be fine."

Emma didn't look convinced, but she knew Monica well enough not to argue further. "Keep your phone handy," she said. "I'm going to call you in fifteen minutes to make sure you're all right."

"Okay. Call me." Monica gave Emma a swift hug, then hurried away, heading toward the Ocean Bluff Inn as if she were running a race.

She sprinted up the entry drive to the inn, then slowed to a walk in the parking lot, its gravel and crushed shells crunching against the soles of her shoes. The main building loomed before her, a sprawling Victorian with white clapboard siding, black shutters, a steeply peaked roof and a broad veranda stretching the width of the building in front and wrapping around the sides. The azaleas beneath the porch railing were dotted with scarlet buds, the rhododendrons blooming with splotches of pink, and dark green yews filled in the spaces between the blossoming shrubs. A staff of groundskeepers maintained the twenty-five acre property, but Monica's father often regaled her with memories of his own childhood at the inn, when it had comprised just this one main building and he'd been responsible for weeding the beds in the summer. Now, with several smaller residential buildings and cottages, the Olympic-size pool, hot tub and pool house, the gazebo at the edge of the bluff, overlooking the inn's private beach, and the industrial buildings housing the laundry, maintenance equipment, lawn tractors, snow plows, and massive recycling bins, the inn was practically a village unto itself.

It was also her home. She'd grown up there, as her father had before her. She'd lived in the six-room owner's suite with her parents and spent her childhood believing the pool, the beach, the modular jungle gym, the tennis courts, the patios and hallways and dining rooms all belonged to her. In a sense, they did—or at least, they belonged to the Reinhart family. With ownership, her parents had taught her, came responsibility. She could play in the pool or climb on the jungle gym, but she also had to treat the folks who paid to stay at the inn as her own personal guests. In her teens, she had to help out wherever she was needed, folding the pool towels, gathering abandoned dishware, and when she was old enough, making beds and scrubbing sinks with the rest of the housekeeping staff. After college, she'd been moved through a variety of administrative positions. Her parents wanted her to learn the hospitality business inside and out. Someday, she would be running the Ocean Bluff Inn. It still belonged to her, and would as long as she wished—and as long as she took responsibility for it.

She loved the place. Running the inn had always been her dream. Simply standing before the three steps leading up to the veranda, basking in the bright, lantern-shaped lights flanking the front door and the amber glow spilling from the windows, soothed her.

She was home. She was safe. That ridiculous song hadn't done anything to her.

—⁂—

He continued staring at the empty table where she'd been sitting, unable to shift his focus until the next song boomed from the jukebox, that U2 song about Martin Luther King. From his grandfather's favorite rock band to his father's, Beach Boys to U2, with that odd little song tucked in between.

Wild thing, I think I love you.

Where had she gone? Why had she raced out of the bar so abruptly, leaving the redhead to chase after her?

"Oh, God, I hate this song," the woman next to him muttered, her expansive bosom barely an inch from his elbow. "There's politics and there's music, you know? Keep the politics out of the music, that's what I say."

Ty courteously refrained from telling her she was an idiot. He had a lot more respect for a song about a martyred hero than for one about a wild thing. He discreetly moved his arm away from her chest and drained the beer from his glass. He ought to get something to eat, but he wasn't hungry. Not for food.

He was hungry for the dark-haired woman. He wanted her. He wanted blazing hot sex with her. He wanted her under him, on top of him, naked and wet.

But she was gone, and her friend was gone with her, and he was probably a bigger idiot than the woman beside him at the bar. For all he knew, the woman whose gaze had locked with his while "Wild Thing" played was someone's girlfriend, someone's wife. Hell, the redhead's lover.

And he was a horny bastard who'd spent the past week all by himself on a boat. That might explain why his mind had filled with all sorts of X-rated ideas when he'd spotted the dark-haired woman. That, and the hit of bourbon. He hadn't drunk anything harder than ginger ale while he'd been sailing Wayne MacArthur's boat up to Massachusetts.

Still, the dark-haired woman had looked at him—practically looked *through* him. Her eyes were as dark as espresso, and every bit as intense. Who could blame him for entertaining the thought that, at least for a couple of seconds there, she'd been as hungry for him as he'd been for her? He wondered if she'd spent the last week all by herself on a boat, too.

Yeah, sure. If he wanted to get his rocks off, the woman by his side seemed like a better prospect. But he wasn't a sex-starved kid, willing to get it on with anyone who happened along. He didn't want sex. He wanted sex with that dark-haired, dark-eyed, wild-thing woman.

A total stranger who might be a bitch or a prude or a million other things that would make her a lousy bed partner. *Forget it,* he ordered himself. *Forget her.*

"Gotta go," he told the woman on the adjacent stool as he stood, pulled out his wallet and slid out a ten and a five. He had no idea what his drinks cost, and he didn't care. He just had to leave, fill his lungs and his brain with some fresh night air, and regain his sanity. "Nice talking to you."

The woman looked pissed, but she managed a faint smile. The pub was continuing to fill with patrons. Surely she'd find someone more receptive than he'd been, if she put some effort into it.

Outside, he took a few deep, bracing breaths. The bar was close to the shoreline; he could smell the ocean's briny perfume. In the deepening gloom of dusk, the temperature had dropped a few degrees. He hoped the evening air would work on him like a cold shower, jarring him back to rationality.

He still wasn't hungry, but he knew he had to get some food into him. He'd last eaten hours ago as he'd sailed past Long Island's north fork, a quick peanut-butter sandwich and a bottle of water. He ought to be ravenous.

Heading back down Atlantic Avenue, he recalled having noticed some dining establishments on his walk over to the Faulk Street Tavern. As he neared the retail area, he gazed down a street and spotted a place called Riley's. It looked like a diner, but since he didn't have much appetite, he saw no point in spending a lot of money on a gourmet feast. All he needed was something more substantial than a peanut-butter sandwich.

The place wasn't too crowded. He ordered a lobster roll—he figured he might as well try the local cuisine. While he ate, he searched his smart phone for car rental places in Brogan's Point. If he was going to stay a few days before flying back to Florida, he ought to explore the area a little. He wondered if any of the places listed on his phone's screen rented bikes. One place seemed to have some Harleys available, but he didn't want anything that big. Something like his Honda Rebel back home, compact and fast, would be perfect.

He made a note of a couple of the rental places, paid his bill, and headed back outside. The lobster roll had filled his body, but the only thing that filled his mind was the image of that woman in the tavern. Her hair was so straight, so dark, like a silk scarf's fringe. She'd had a slight build—not the sort of cleavage he'd enjoyed an up-close view of at the bar—and a delicate face. Narrow nose, thin lips, eyes that were almost too big for the rest of her. It wasn't that she was so beautiful. It was just...

Something weird. Something about the way they'd found each other during that song. Almost as if her gaze had been dancing with his. Almost as if their hearts had been synchronized, beating in time with the music.

A submarine roll overflowing with lobster salad hadn't been enough to cure him of his fixation.

Maybe the woman was a witch, a sorceress, like one of the Haitian immigrants down in the Keys who practiced Voodoo or Santeria or some other mystical cult religion. Or maybe the bartender was the sorceress. Maybe she'd spiked his drink with a crazy-making drug. Wasn't he near Salem, Massachusetts, the witch capital of North America?

He laughed. He'd never had the world's greatest imagination, but after a long solo sail, who knew where these ideas were coming from? He ought to go back to the boat and get some sleep. Tomorrow he'd wake up normal, and he'd go and rent a bike.

He strolled back to Atlantic Avenue, figuring he was least likely to miss the turn-off to the marina if he stuck close to the ocean. The tide was low, the water calm. Hardly a breeze. He was lucky he'd sailed into port earlier, when a low but steady wind could power him in to the slip. The sky above the ocean was a deep blue, with thin purple clouds rippling through it like veins in marble.

Yeah, he definitely needed a bike, or a car. His legs were feeling sluggish. The ground was too unyielding beneath them. His feet would hit the pavement and stop, no give beneath them, no play. His knees weren't used to the lack of motion. If he couldn't spend the night in the arms of the wild-thing woman, he needed to spend it cushioned by the ocean. The limbo of sailing—a world where the earth kept shifting, the wind ruled, and he had only himself for company—seemed a lot more reliable than the world of bars and booze and old jukeboxes.

After a long half-hour, he spotted the turn-off to the North Cove Marina. A narrow asphalt lane sloped down to the east, spreading into the parking lot, which was mostly empty at this time of night. At the base of the parking lot was the building with the anchor painted onto it, beyond that a grid of docks extending out into the water. Just knowing he was only minutes away from the Freedom made him pick up speed. If he got to the boat, he could rid himself of visions of the woman and memories of the song. He could be himself again.

He almost didn't notice the pale gray lettering painted onto the darker gray sides of two large sedans parked nearest the dock where the Freedom was moored: Brogan's Point Police.

He slowed his pace slightly, wondering what was up. Coast Guard vehicles at a marina were rarely a good sign, but police cars?

He ventured past the main building and started down the ridged ramp to the Freedom's dock. And halted.

Wayne MacArthur's boat was where he'd left it, but it was surrounded by yellow police tape. Three men stood on the slip, which rocked gently beneath them. Even in silhouette, Ty could tell that two of them were uniformed officers and the third was in street clothes. In the stillness of the evening, their voices drifted across the water in an indecipherable murmur, accented by the metallic clanging of ropes and clamps against masts.

Why were the police at Wayne's boat? Why was the boat surrounded by "Do Not Cross" tape? What the fuck?

Ty had two choices: continue down to the slip and find out what was going on, or make a U-turn head back to town.

If he were a moral, upstanding grade-A citizen, he'd go down to the slip.

But he was Ty Cronin. A carpenter. A marina rat. A guy who had thwarted death. A guy who didn't trust authority figures. A guy who preferred motorcycles to cars, and sailboats to cruise ships. A guy who'd just gotten a cash influx of twenty thousand bucks into his bank account. A guy who trusted his instincts.

His instincts told him to U-turn and walk away. Actually, they told him to *run* away, but that would draw unwanted attention. So he U-turned and walked.

Three

A t the edge of the parking lot, he paused and gazed back at the dock. They were still there, two cops and the third man who, despite his lack of a uniform, looked even more formidable. And that bright yellow tape, marking the boat, cordoning it off.

Ty had a really bad feeling about this.

His stuff was on the boat: clothing, laptop, toothbrush. *Fuck.*

He'd worry about his gear later. Right now, he needed a place to sleep. Exhaustion tugged at him like a riptide, threatening to drag him under. This day had been too long. Sailing. Docking. Drinking. The bar, the song, the woman. And now the police. Thoughts of voodoo and Salem witches pinballed inside his skull.

All right. He'd get some sleep. In the morning, maybe things would make sense. Even better, he might wake up and discover that the world was once again the familiar place he knew, and he'd only just dreamed all this strange shit.

He continued through the parking lot to the road, tapping his phone, searching for hotels and motels. A couple of places were located within a five-mile radius of Brogan's Point, but they were all down on Route 1, where, according to the waitress at the bar, traffic was a bitch. And Route 1 was too damned far to walk.

The only hotel less than a mile away was a place called the Ocean Bluff Inn. It was just up Atlantic Avenue a ways. Probably cost an arm and a leg, but he could afford it. His bank account had just increased by twenty thousand dollars.

He hoped he could buy a toothbrush at the Ocean Bluff Inn.

Following the map on his phone, he hiked in the direction of inn and tried to ignore the noise in his head. Cops. *Wild Thing*. The stacked woman trying to pick him up. The slender woman who'd fled from him—no, not from him. From the bar. From her friend. From the song.

The Freedom gift-wrapped in a police-tape ribbon. Had someone boarded the boat while he was gone, and gotten injured? Or tried to steal something? They were welcome to his clothes, but his laptop...He'd locked it beneath the bench in the cabin. He hoped it was safe.

Damn it, damn it, damn it.

The entrance to the inn loomed ahead, screaming *expensive*. A picturesque gravel driveway bordered in white stones curved up from the road. Granite pillars stood on either side of it, illuminated with decorative lamps. Well groomed plantings flourished at the bases of the pillars. An elegant white sign read, "Ocean Bluff Inn."

More than expensive, the place looked like a destination, not a motel you'd stay at for a night while passing through town but a resort where you'd book a room for a week. He hoped the place wasn't full. If it was, hell. He'd go make a bed for himself next to the ocean on the sand. And probably wind up arrested by those cops. Brogan's Point seemed like the sort of town that would have ordinances against sleeping on the beach.

He trudged up the driveway, hoping this inn had an available room that wouldn't cost a major chunk of the money Wayne MacArthur had wired to Ty's PayPal account. After about fifty yards of pretty drive and prettier landscaping, he reached a parking area surfaced in loose gravel and crushed shells. No more than a dozen cars were parked there. He might get lucky.

His gaze journeyed from the lot to the building beside it—a grand four-story structure of white siding, an angular roof, and wide windows framed in black shutters. The building extended a good seventy feet from side to side and then spread back beyond the parking area. A broad porch with a white railing abutted the entire front of the building. Wooden Adirondack chairs and rockers lined the porch. One was occupied.

By the slender woman with the dark hair and the darker eyes. The woman who'd gazed at him across the tavern and then run away.

Wild Thing.

She'd changed her clothes since he last saw her. Seated in an oversized Adirondack chair, she wore jeans, some sort of skimpy top and a hoodie over it, zipped partway up. Her bare feet were propped on the edge of the seat, her chin resting on her knees, her arms wrapped around her shins. Even in the dim amber light from the fixtures on either side of the double-width front door, he could tell that her toenails were painted red.

He felt a stirring in his groin. Totally inappropriate. Lots of women painted their toenails, and he'd wager a substantial proportion of them chose red polish.

But this woman…There was some sort of weird vibe between him and her. He had no idea what it was. But given how strange the evening had become, he figured there was no point in questioning it.

"You staying here?" he asked.

"I live here." Her voice was smooth and darkly sweet, like the bourbon he'd drunk earlier.

He was so busy contemplating its kick, her words almost didn't register on him. "You *live* here?"

She nodded, not an easy maneuver with her chin resting on her knees.

He had no idea what that meant, so he plowed ahead. "I need a room for the night. Do they have any vacancies?"

She regarded him silently. A breeze rustled through the bushes surrounding the porch and ruffled her hair. "I know where you can stay," she finally said. "Follow me."

Thoughts of the boat, the cops, every footstep and nautical mile, every drink and word and song that had carried him to this place, this moment, this woman…It all evaporated from his brain. She'd told him to follow her.

So that was what he did.

—⚬∞⚬—

She was crazy. Absolutely. Certifiably.

Or maybe she was just…*wild.*

She'd thought leaving the Faulk Street Tavern might have been enough to shake off the spell that song had cast upon her, but it hadn't. She'd returned to her tiny apartment at the back of the inn's main building, changed from her work apparel into comfortable clothing that was as unsexy as possible, and tried to think about what she should eat despite having no appetite whatsoever. She wasn't in the mood to cook anything, but if she moseyed over to the inn's dining room, Jerry and the rest of the kitchen staff would either take offense or summon a doctor if she didn't consume a proper meal.

She'd opened a can of tomato soup, heated it in the microwave in her apartment's closet-size kitchen, and forced it down, thinking about how much more delicious Jerry's lobster bisque would taste— and how that sweet, subtle flavor would have been wasted on her if she'd gone to the dining room and asked for a bowl of it.

She'd tried watching television. Had TV shows always been this stupid? Surely the news was worth watching…. No, it wasn't. If watching meant she'd have to sit still, staring at the screen while a babble of voices and images of violence and people behaving badly assaulted her senses, she would not watch the news. Or anything else.

Nor would she review the inn's maintenance budget. Once Memorial Day arrived, the place would be full—bookings had been strong this year. For the past few weeks, the maintenance crew had been working from dawn to dusk, getting the place spruced up before the summer season began. Painting. Landscaping. Grooming the parking lots and the tennis court. Cleaning and filling the swimming pool. Moving all the pool patio furniture outdoors. Clearing the path down to the beach. The expenditures were high; most of the crew had put in overtime nearly every day. She needed to review the numbers.

But when she turned on her laptop and opened the spread sheets, all she saw was a jumble. The data awaited her attention, but the Excel pages couldn't pierce the fog that swaddled her brain. Random, meaningless numbers filled the monitor.

Slamming her laptop shut, she'd tried to conjure Jimmy's image in her mind. But she couldn't. She'd been with him, on and off, for ten years, yet she couldn't even picture him. Or remember how he sounded when he talked, when he laughed. Or how he smelled, how he felt. He was gone, deleted from her memory.

All she could think of was the man on the bar stool, with his streaky blond hair and his scruffy day-old beard and his torn jeans, and his mesmerizing blue eyes. All she could think of was how absurdly attractive he'd been, like a black hole sucking her in.

Too restless to remain cooped up in her apartment, she'd gone outside onto the porch. The inn was about half full—decent business for the third week in May—but the evening was cool enough that no one was relaxing on the veranda. She had it all to herself, the freshly scrubbed and painted chairs, the light from the lobby and front parlor spilling through the polished windows, the brighter light glowing through the beveled glass of the lamps that adorned the front entry. Curling up in one of the chairs, she gazed out at the parking lot, the shrubs beyond it, the marsh grass sloping down to the inn's small private beach. The sky was dark and almost cloud-less, sliced by a narrow curve of moon. The cool wind rolling up from the beach smelled rich and salty, the perfume of mermaids.

And then he appeared, as if by magic, ambling up the driveway and across the lot, planting himself directly in front of her. How had he found her?

What did it matter? He *had* found her. Fate had brought him here. Karma. The song from the jukebox at the Faulk Street Tavern.

If she thought about it, she'd acknowledge that bringing him back to her apartment was an insane idea, possibly dangerous. She didn't know who he was or what he could do. All she knew was the song, and the night, and the dazzling power of his eyes. Logic was beyond her.

They walked the length of the veranda, around to the side of the main building and through the back door, which led to offices and a service elevator to the owners' suite on the top floor, where her parents lived and she'd grown up. She and the man passed several platforms designed for truck deliveries and continued down the back hallway, beyond a few rooms where extra furniture was stored, beyond the room that contained the housekeeping carts and supplies, beyond the room stocked with toilet paper, soap, and miniature bottles of shampoo and moisturizing lotion, to her tiny apartment at the end of the hall.

She unlocked the door, opened it, and stepped inside. He was right behind her.

He didn't speak. Evidently, he saw nothing odd in her having brought him to her cozy efficiency apartment rather than to the front desk, where she could have checked him into one of the empty guest rooms. He almost looked as if he'd expected her to bring him to her own room. His gaze swiftly circled the diminutive living area, which was separated from the sleeping area by a freestanding hinged screen of carved wood. She'd always been tidy; she'd folded her laptop shut once she'd given up on the spread sheets, and left it on the small writing table in one corner. Her soup bowl sat drying in the dish rack beside the sink. The floor lamp next to the love seat—the living area didn't have enough space for a full-size couch—offered the only light, soft and golden.

She turned to him, wondering what to say. Should she offer him a drink? Food? An explanation? She could provide the first two items on that list, but not the third.

He didn't give her a chance to speak. One long stride brought him close enough to gather her in his arms, and his mouth came down on hers, firm but not hard. Fierce but not forcing.

In that strange, magical moment, kissing him made far more sense than talking would have. His mouth fit hers so perfectly, his lips persuasive, his tongue stroking deep, taking everything she was willing to give. His hands were large and warm, gliding over her shoulders to her back, pulling her against him.

She knew this was wrong. Yet her intellect had disconnected, and her heart, her soul, the portion of her brain still functioning told her it was right. For this instant, she would have this man, this virile stranger who had been delivered to her by some inexplicable, mysterious force. Tomorrow she could be sane again, proper and tame. Tonight she would be a wild thing.

She kissed him back. Kissed him hungrily. Kissed him *wildly*. Her hands slid across his chest, testing the sturdy muscles beneath the cotton knit of his shirt. She let him slide her hoodie down her arms and off, then wedge his hands under her camisole, exploring the curve of her back, the ridge of her spine, her shoulder blades. His touch made her hips grow heavy and her thighs clench. Oh, God, she wanted him, wanted him *wildly*.

She pulled at his shirt. He freed his hands from beneath her camisole to yank the shirt over his head and off. She had barely a minute to admire his rugged shoulders and sleekly contoured chest before he had his hands back on her, lifting her camisole over her head and tossing it aside.

They kissed again, this time touching skin as they did so. He cupped her breasts, caressed them, stroked his thumbs over her nipples until they burned with sensation. She wanted to climb onto him, rub against him, make him relieve the deep, delicious ache he'd ignited inside her. She wanted everything, now.

She broke from him, caressing the length of his warm, sun-bronzed arm until she reached his hand, then slid her fingers through his and ushered him around the screen to her bed. Before she could drop onto it, he caught her by the waistband of her pants and eased them down over her bottom, drawing her panties down with them. She attacked the fly of his jeans, and as soon as he had her pants removed, he dispensed with his own.

They tumbled onto the soft, down-filled duvet covering her bed. Her head sank into the pillows as he rose above her, his warmth blanketing her. He kissed her cheeks, her chin, her throat. He wedged one leg between hers and pressed his thigh against her crotch. He stroked her waist, her belly, her breasts. He was so big, his skin sun-darkened, his hair sun-bleached. A thin trail of tawny hair tapered from his belly downward, expanding into a nest of curls that framed his erection, displaying it as if it were a gift. She ran her index finger from its base to its tip and he groaned.

Bowing, he nuzzled the skin between her breasts, then kissed each one, licked, sucked, made her sigh as the tension inside her increased. Even though she'd been with Jimmy forever, she'd always kept a stash of condoms in her night table for those occasions when they'd broken up. She'd never used them, but she'd left them in the bedside drawer, just in case someone came along to take Jimmy's place.

This man hadn't taken Jimmy's place. He claimed his own place. What she was experiencing right now had nothing to do with breaking up with Jimmy. It was an encounter all its own, detached from Monica's past and her future, a suspended reality, a moment out of time.

She rolled away from him and rummaged in the drawer until she found the box of condoms. Her trembling fingers struggled to tear off the cellophane, and he took the box from her, deftly opened it, and pulled out a rubber. In an instant, he was suited up. He eased onto his back, pulled her on top of him, and whispered, "Ride me."

The only two words they'd spoken since they'd entered her apartment. Demanding words. *Wild* words.

She straddled him, his hands cupping her hips, his thumbs reaching to rub her. She was wet, needy, hurting. Shifting forward, she poised herself above him. He guided himself inside.

She came almost at once, her body throbbing as he arched into her. She moaned, shocked by how quickly she'd succumbed and how immeasurably good she felt. He moved his hands back to her hips, giving her his rhythm, helping her to keep moving when all she wanted was to collapse against him. She dared to open his eyes and viewed him beneath her, looking both helpless and profoundly powerful, pumping hard, breathing hard. Somehow his thumbs found her again, and she felt herself building to a higher peak.

They reached it together. Her body shook; his wrenched. His breath stopped, then started again, broken, carrying a quiet moan.

Wild, she thought. *Wild sex.* Like nothing she'd ever experienced before.

She settled on top of him, her respiration shallow, her heart pounding frenetically. His skin was warm, his body surprisingly comfortable. He softened, unrolled the sheath and dropped it onto the foil wrapper on her night table. Then he stroked his fingers aimlessly through her hair. Her eyes came into focus, and she saw the small tattoo on his shoulder, four neat, indigo block letters: LIVE.

She traced the letters with her finger. "Live?" she asked, pronouncing it as an adjective, with a long *I*.

"Live," he corrected her, pronouncing it as a verb.

"What does it mean?"

He hesitated, then said, "There was a time when I should have died, but I lived."

He should have died? How? Why? Who was he? That last question seemed at once the easiest and the most complicated, so she asked it. "Who are you?"

"Ty." He must have seen her puzzled expression, because he elaborated. "Tyler Cronin. People call me Ty."

"Ty." She tried out the simple nickname and decided it suited him. His name didn't tell her who he was, but it was something. Something that made this encounter marginally less anonymous. "I'm Monica Reinhart," she said.

"Monica." He curved his arm around her, cuddled her to himself, and closed his eyes. After a moment, his breathing grew deep and steady. He had fallen asleep.

She couldn't imagine sleeping. She had just made love with a man whose name she hadn't even known until a minute ago. He was still a stranger to her. Just a name, a tattoo, a tall, strong body, a beautiful face. A golden stubble that had left beard burns on her skin. A man who might disappear in the morning, who might vanish from her life without ever really having been in it.

She felt wicked. Wanton. A little bit worried. And very wild.

Four

She must have fallen asleep at some point, because in the middle of the night he woke her and they made love again, soft, sleepy love. He loved her first with his mouth and then with his body, and she climaxed so many times she wondered if her legs would function when she tried to stand. But he hadn't crippled her. After that second go-round, they'd hauled themselves out of bed in order to wash and to turn off the lamp in the sitting area, and then they'd slid back beneath the covers, curled up against each other, and drifted to sleep. In her dreams she saw his tattoo, four crisp letters, dark yet resonant with hope, with survival, with life.

She arose, as she usually did, at seven. Opening her eyes, she found him beside her and felt a pang of uneasiness. Last night was last night. This morning was…reality. The reality of a strange man taking up most of her bed. He had kicked off the blanket overnight, and she pushed herself to sit, stared at his rangy, beautiful body, and felt a queasy sensation roil her stomach. She couldn't blame it on too much wine last night, because she hadn't even consumed a whole glass. Less than one glass of wine couldn't have made her drunk enough to explain last night's little sexual escapade, either.

It wasn't a little sexual escapade, she thought anxiously. It was a very big sexual escapade. The best sex she'd ever had.

What did that say about her? Was this her first step down a tawdry path of encounters with strangers? Was this the start of a nasty new habit of picking up unknown men in bars and bringing them back to her apartment?

Good lord. Her parents lived in the suite just three floors above her.

She reminded herself that she was an adult. She no longer lived with them. She didn't have to obey them. She didn't have to check in with them, or justify her choices to them.

This hadn't exactly been a choice, though, had it? He'd shown up at the inn, and the night had proceeded with a certain inevitability. He'd found her and they'd made love. Last night couldn't have happened any other way.

That was bullshit, she told herself, swinging out of bed and stalking to the bathroom. She adjusted the shower to a scalding temperature, stepped under the spray, and did her best to scrub her mind as her washcloth scrubbed her body. There had been no inevitability to her inviting Ty into her bed. She'd made love to him for no good reason, nothing she could wrap her rational brain around. She was a slut. Cheap. Foolish. The one thing she'd never been: irresponsible.

Well, it couldn't be undone. She could wash all traces of him from her skin, but not from her soul.

Sighing, she stepped out of the shower and dried herself. The rough texture of the towel reminded her of his hard, callused hands and his scruffy facial hair. The blast of air from her hair dryer made her hot. Tears burned her eyes. She'd cried yesterday evening at the bar before she'd seen him, and here she was again, crying. Tears could be the bookends of this reckless, crazy night.

She stepped out of the bathroom—and there he was, standing by the door, waiting for her. Naked.

Looking at him only made her want to cry even more.

He gathered her into his arms, and her towel dropped to the floor. There was nothing sexual in his embrace, even though they were both naked, their bodies pressed together, the heat of his flesh warming her. She batted her eyes, hating that her tears might be dampening his chest. "Hey," he murmured.

"I'm sorry—"

"No."

"I mean—crying like this—"

"It's okay."

"It's just that—I mean—I've never done anything like this."

He didn't respond right away. She supposed he *had* done things like this—one-night stands, sex with a stranger. But he stroked his hand soothingly through her hair and brushed a kiss against the crown of her head. "Last night was amazing," he said. "I don't know what it means or why it happened, but it was incredible."

True enough. A smile teased her lips in spite of her tears.

"I've got some stuff to take care of today," he said. "I'll be free this evening. Maybe we could do something normal, like have dinner together."

Her smile expanded to a laugh. All right, this was not going to be a lifelong romance. He was not going to occupy the next ten years of her life the way Jimmy had occupied the last ten. But dinner tonight offered a glimpse of a future for them, however brief. "Okay," she said.

"We could meet at that bar with the jukebox. Six o'clock?"

"Okay."

He loosened his hold on her, dipped his head to kiss her lips, and said, "Have you got a towel I can use?"

While he showered, she fixed breakfast. Usually she ate a bowl of oatmeal or corn flakes, but she doubted that would satisfy a big man like him, so she prepared a batch of French toast, sweet and eggy, and sliced up some oranges. By the time he was dressed, she had her table set and the coffee brewed.

"Last night you told me you worked here at this inn," he recalled.

She nodded, inordinately pleased that he remembered that detail about her.

"What do you do?"

"I help to manage the place," she said. "I do a little of everything. My family owns it. If all goes well, I'll be running it once my parents retire. I'm learning the business, one area at a time. Right now, I'm in charge of maintenance."

"You should be in charge of the dining room," he said, devouring a chunk of French toast. "This is delicious."

"I'm not that good a cook. French toast is easy."

He shook his head. "I've been living on sandwiches and freeze-dried food for a week. This is really good."

She extended the platter toward him. "Take as much as you want. I can always make more." Once he'd forked another slice of French toast onto his plate, she asked, "Have you been camping?"

"Sailing up the coast," he told her. "Transporting a boat for a friend."

That sounded ridiculously sexy. "For a whole week? Where did you start?"

"Key Biscayne, outside Miami."

"Do you do that professionally? Transport boats?" She bit her lip as soon as the question was out. *Professionally?* She sounded so stuffy.

He didn't seem to mind. "I'm a carpenter," he told her, "I work mostly in buildings, but I also do restoration work on boats. I love to sail. This guy who docks in the winter at a marina where I do a lot of work asked me to bring his boat to Brogan's Point for him, so I did."

"A nice little vacation for you," she said.

"A paid vacation," he added, then grinned.

"So...I guess you live in Florida." She gave herself another mental kick. Asking him about his profession, then grilling him about where he lived...She must sound like a pushy, needy girlfriend, trying to pin her footloose lover down.

He didn't seem to mind. "At the moment," he said. "I move around."

Great. If he lived in Florida, he would be gone from Brogan's Point and her life sooner or later—probably sooner. If he moved around...he would also be gone from her life. Apparently, her future with him wouldn't extend much beyond dinner tonight.

She would accept that. She would be wild now, while he was here, and once he was gone she could reclaim her old, tame existence.

Hopefully, after he departed, she would be left with happy memories and no ugly scars.

—⁂—

She spirited him from her apartment, down the hall at the back of the inn and out the back door without encountering anyone. He wasn't offended by the notion that she might be embarrassed about his presence in her room overnight. She was dressed for work in clean, stylish business clothes, while he was wearing the torn jeans he'd had on yesterday, and his beard was a day longer and thicker. Of course she didn't want anyone to see them together.

He had to get onto the boat. He needed his toiletries, his clothing, his laptop. He hoped to God that damned police tape was gone and he could board.

He ought to be focusing on the trouble he'd viewed at the Freedom's slip last night. But as he sauntered down the driveway, away from the inn, he could think only of Monica, her soft hair and her soft body, the way she'd peaked and peaked and peaked in his arms. She was astonishing. Beautiful, gentle, smart, sensitive...and hot enough to leave third-degree burns on his psyche.

Today, he'd get his gear, hopefully resolve whatever had merited a visit to the boat from the cops last night, and then find a motorcycle to rent. He'd tool around the area, check out some back roads, fill the day until he could meet up with Monica and fill the night with her. Maybe he'd hang around Brogan's Point a little longer than he'd planned. Maybe she could get a day off from her job at her parents' inn and they could ride up the coast to Maine, or travel down to Boston and be tourists. Or they could spend the whole day in bed, screwing themselves silly. He wouldn't object to that particular plan.

Nearing the yacht club, he saw more cars in the parking lot than before. Two of those cars were gray sedans with "Brogan's Point Police" spelled out along their sides and bars of lights stretched across their roofs. Their lights weren't flashing, but it didn't matter.

The police were still present, and the boat was still cordoned off in police tape.

Shit.

Once again, he wanted to U-turn and run away. But he couldn't. He had to get his stuff.

He reminded himself that he hadn't broken any laws or done anything wrong. He had no reason to fear the police. Whatever had happened to the boat—vandalism, a robbery, someone trespassing and injuring himself—wasn't his fault.

Steeling himself, he continued past the main building, down the sloping gangplank to the slip where the Freedom was moored. A uniformed officer stood near the boat, guarding it. He measured Ty with his gaze, then said, "Are you Tyler Cronin?"

How did the cop know who Ty was? Ty recalled that he'd signed the marina's log when he'd arrived. "Yeah," he said, tamping down his apprehension. "What's going on? Is something wrong?"

Behind the cop, he saw the sailboat rocking gently on its rippling cushion of water. A man dressed in civilian clothes emerged from the cabin. He was tall, with a square face and hair the color of tempered steel. "Tyler Cronin is here," the uniformed cop told him.

The other guy stepped off the boat onto the dock. "Detective Ed Nolan," he introduced himself, then handed Tyler some papers. "We have a warrant to search the boat."

Tyler unfolded the document Nolan had given him. A bunch of legalese; he had no idea what it said, but he'd take the man's word for it that it was a search warrant. "Why?"

"Maybe you should come down to police headquarters with me," the detective said. "We can talk there."

"I've got some stuff on the boat I'd like to get," Ty said, hoping he sounded innocent. He *was* innocent, but the way these two officers were staring at him made him feel guilty as hell. "My clothes, my laptop—"

"Your possessions are all in police custody right now," the detective said. "Let's go down to headquarters and see if we can straighten this out."

Straightening things out sounded good to Ty. But he wasn't naïve. He was in deep shit, and he had no idea why.

Refusing to accompany the detective to the police station was not going to get him out of that deep shit. "Fine," he said. "Let's go."

Five

Rose Cottage had a problem. A water stain had mysteriously appeared on the wall of the first-floor parlor.

Monica should have been upset, stressed, just this side of frantic. The cottages—four small, self-contained buildings nestled into the woods on the western side of the pool patio—were among the inn's most popular accommodations. They were often booked in their entirety by reuning families, wedding parties, corporate executives on a retreat, or any other group that wanted access to the amenities of the resort but also a private enclave for its own intimate circle. The cottages weren't in high demand during the winter months, but as soon as the summer season started, they got reserved very quickly.

Rose Cottage was no exception. It was booked for every weekend from the Memorial Day weekend through Labor Day, and more than a few of those bookings were for an entire week. A couple whose wedding would be held at the inn over the Memorial Day weekend had reserved the cottage for their bridal party and out-of-town friends.

But if there was a water stain on the parlor wall, there was a leak somewhere behind that wall. When Frank from the maintenance crew phoned Monica's office, he warned her that locating the leak might require the plumber to cut through the wall.

"We've got the Kolenko party arriving in a week and a half," she reminded Frank.

"Then I guess we'll have to find the leak, fix it, and repair the wall quickly," he shot back.

"I'll contact Parnelli's," she said, naming the plumbing service the inn used. "I'll tell them it's an emergency." It might not be the sort of emergency that required every available staff member to grab a bucket and bail out a flooded cottage, but with the Memorial Day weekend only ten days away, Monica considered it critical to find and fix this leak ASAP.

Yet she was smiling when she called the friendly dispatcher at Parnelli's and explained the situation. She was still smiling after she left her office and strolled around the pool to Rose Cottage to view the water stain. Still smiling as she studied the oval darkening the parlor's cream-colored wall.

Tomorrow, or the next day, or Memorial Day, or some time in an undefined future, she might start crying again. But today she was a woman who had spent a night having splendiferous sex with a hunky guy with whom she was going to have dinner in just a few hours. She was going to sit across a table from him and feast her eyes on his gorgeous face while her mouth feasted on whatever food filled her plate. Maybe he'd shave and she'd have an unobstructed view of his chin. Maybe she'd reach across the table and trace his cheeks with her fingertips.

Maybe she would learn more about him. Maybe not too much more. That he was a mystery to her added to his sex appeal. If she found out that he bickered with his parents and complained about the barking of his neighbor's dog, that he was a slob and that salad dressing made him flatulent, his sex appeal would plummet. The impetuousness of last night had heightened the experience for her. The understanding that modest, well-behaved Monica could behave wildly with a man she didn't know was the main reason she couldn't stop smiling, even as she touched the water stain and discovered that the wall was wet enough to feel almost pasty.

"What do you think is causing the leak?" she asked Frank.

"We'll find out once we open the wall," he told her. "There's a pipe running behind this wall from a second-floor bathroom. "I'm guessing there's a leak somewhere in that pipe."

His use of the word *somewhere* should have tempered her smile, at least a little bit. What would the plumber have to do if the source of the leak wasn't immediately evident?

Two hours and a gaping hole in the wall later, Monica's mood had down-shifted significantly. Despite cutting the hole as neatly as possible, in an even rectangle of drywall that, ideally, could be fitted back into place like a piece of a puzzle, Frank and the plumber had left the parlor looking as if it had been blizzarded with nuclear ash. White dust and slivers of pasteboard spread across the hardwood floor and Turkish rug in the parlor. Fortunately, the furniture had been moved to the other side of the room first.

The second-floor bathroom above the parlor was in equally bad shape. The plumber had dislodged the sink's vanity, which now sat in the adjacent bedroom, looking alarmingly out of place. The burgundy bath mat looked as if it had been left outside during a snow storm.

And they still hadn't pinpointed the source of the leak.

Monica wound up spending the entire afternoon at Rose Cottage, overseeing the mess Frank and the plumber were creating as if there was a damned thing she could do to minimize it. Every clank and clang and thump made her cringe. The flickering beam of the plumber's flashlight as he ducked his head through the hole and surveyed the pipes made her flinch.

But the leak had to be found and stopped. The walls had to be reconstructed and painted. Vacuuming up the white plaster dust was the least of it.

Her cell phone rang frequently. She did her best to manage other maintenance issues from Rose Cottage. She supposed she could return to her office in the main building—hovering over Frank and the plumber and wincing at each new indignity they inflicted on the walls of the cottage didn't help the situation. But she couldn't leave. She felt like a triage doctor assessing the damage so she'd know just what rehabilitation the patient would require.

A lot of rehabilitation, she thought as the plumber punched his way through the fluffy pink insulation inside the wall, enlarging the space so he could fit his head through and get a better look at the pipe.

"I can see it dripping," he shouted from inside the wall. "Can't see where it's dripping from, though."

Monica sighed. Just because her day had begun magnificently didn't mean it had to end magnificently. Yet it *would* end magnificently. She would have dinner with Ty. They'd talk. They'd touch. They'd do wild things. They'd *be* wild things.

Her cell phone rang again. She stepped away from the plumber's butt and legs, protruding from the hole in the wall, and pressed the button to connect the call. It was nothing major, just an inventory check from the head of housekeeping, listing all the supplies she would be ordering tomorrow. Monica okayed the list, clicked to end the call, and noticed the time on her phone's screen. Five-fifty.

Damn. Had she been in Rose Cottage that long?

"I've got to go," she told Frank. Leak or no leak, she was not going to blow Ty off, or even show up late for their date. After the frustrating day she'd had, she was ready to get back to magnificent.

Not bothering to return to her office, she bolted from Rose Cottage, jogged across the pool patio and headed down the driveway. The Faulk Street Tavern was only a few blocks down Atlantic Street from the inn. Searching for a parking space near the pub's entrance if she drove would take longer than walking there.

She did not want to take longer. She wanted to be wild with Ty *now.*

She entered the tavern exactly at six. It occurred to her that she might have taken a moment to brush her hair and freshen her lipstick. It also occurred to her that had she done so, she would have arrived a few minutes late and not looked quite so eager to see him. Yet she didn't want to play games with him, deliberately arriving late so he would have to wait for her. She'd played games with Jimmy for ten years, and what had that gotten her? Ten years with a guy who'd rather watch a game on TV with his buddies than celebrate an anniversary with her.

She stepped inside the bar, circled the room with her gaze, and realized that she would be the one doing the waiting. Ty wasn't there.

Not because he was playing a game with her. She knew in her heart that he wouldn't bide his time somewhere for ten minutes, forcing her to cool her heels and crank up her humility level. She had no basis for that belief, but she *knew*. He would be leaving her in a matter of days to return to Florida, or wherever his next stop was. They didn't have time for silly courtship rituals. If Ty was running late, he had a good reason for it.

She crossed to the bar, smiled at Gus, and settled on a stool. Gus had been slicing limes, but as soon as she saw Monica, she lowered her knife, dried her hands, and moseyed over. "You look frazzled," she said, placing a cocktail napkin in front of Monica on the bar's polished mahogany surface. "Rough day?"

"There's a leak in Rose Cottage," Monica told her. "They've torn down a wall searching for it. Do I have plaster dust in my hair?"

"No." Gus gave her a reassuring smile.

Monica shrugged. The leak had occupied her for too many hours. Now it was time to delete that mess from her thoughts and focus only on the pleasures that lay ahead. "It'll get fixed," she said, wishing she felt as certain as she sounded. "It's just that with the holiday weekend coming up, the cottage is booked. We need everything back to normal there before the summer surge begins."

"As you said, it'll get fixed." Gus plucked a wine glass from the rack above her head. "Chardonnay?"

"I'm meeting someone," Monica told her, then grinned. "But I guess I can have a glass of wine while I'm waiting."

Gus filled the glass with pale, fragrant wine and set it on the napkin. She said nothing, but Monica sensed a question trapped inside her, one she was too discreet to ask.

Monica answered it anyway. "I'm not waiting for Jimmy. We broke up."

Gus nodded. Only because Monica knew the woman her whole life did she detect the corners of Gus's mouth twitching upward into a faint grin.

"So I'm on the market," Monica continued. "Meeting new people. Exercising new muscles." She allowed herself a private smile as she contemplated all the muscles she'd exercised with Ty last night.

"Will's still single," Gus said, naming her younger son. "Just saying."

"I'll keep it in mind." Gus's sons were a couple of years older than Monica, but Brogan's Point was a small town. She'd always thought the Naukonen boys were cute. But they lived in Boston, and she was a hometown girl.

She sipped her wine, spinning on her stool to gaze out at the room while Gus wandered down the bar to fill an order for a waitress. On the far side of the dance floor, the jukebox sat in silence, regal and elegant, holding its secrets close. Why had it played that clamorous old rock-and-roll song yesterday? Why had it played that song just for Monica and Ty?

Where was Ty, anyway?

She sipped her wine, letting it slide cool and dry down her throat. Closing her eyes, she pictured the chaotic scene she'd left at Rose Cottage, the wall cut away like a skin, exposing the skeleton of insulation, pipes, and wiring it usually hid. What a disaster.

But soon Ty would enter the bar and sweep her away. He'd make her forget all about the leak, at least for tonight.

Any minute, she told herself. Any second now, he'd step inside, tall and buff and radiating sex appeal, and Rose Cottage would no longer exist. Her entire world would consist of her and Ty.

Any minute.

—w—

Some men just didn't deserve to live.

Gus liked men. She'd married one and raised two. She was currently involved with a fine man—Ed Nolan, a public servant, a cop, someone who kept the peace while simultaneously keeping his sense of humor.

But Monica's luck with men wasn't so good. She'd been with that schmuck Jimmy for so long, maybe she just thought that being disregarded and disrespected was acceptable.

Not to Gus, it wasn't.

Whoever Monica's new schmuck was, he hadn't shown up by the time she'd emptied her wine glass. She'd waltzed into the tavern a half hour ago, as bright as a full moon on a clear night, and now that glow was gone, muted like the night sky when a dense ocean fog rolled in. With a sigh, she'd paid Gus for the wine, slid off her stool, and strode resolutely out of the pub.

In her line of work, Gus witnessed a lot of heartbreak. It came with the territory. You poured a drink, and in return, patrons poured out their hearts. The best bartenders were good listeners, and Gus was the best bartender in Brogan's Point, if not all of the North Shore.

What Monica had experienced tonight wasn't heartbreak. Just disappointment. Just pissy, nasty annoyance. Just the recognition—as if she'd needed to learn this lesson again—that some men were jerks.

—⚭—

Monica hadn't expected Ty to be the love of her life, although last night he'd certainly proven himself to be the lover of her life, at least so far. She'd liked him. She'd been drawn to him like iron to a magnet. She'd wanted to spend more time with him. She'd wanted to make love with him again, and again. She'd wanted to go wild with him.

But he was gone. Probably halfway back to Florida by now, or wherever he was headed in his moving-around life.

She was tough. She would survive. One glass of wine had fortified her, and she had a few bottles in her apartment.

She let herself in, flicked on the lamp, and moved directly to the refrigerator, where a bottle of Pinot Noir sat on the door shelf. Her computer desk, holding her lap top and a telephone, stood near the corner of her apartment that passed for a kitchen, and she hesitated. She hadn't stopped back at her office after the Rose Cottage debacle earlier that evening. She'd hiked directly to the Faulk Street Tavern, far too eager to see Ty. She really ought to check her messages before she got hammered.

After tossing her purse onto the sofa, she lifted the handset and punched in the number to access her voice mail. There was a message from Claudia, who'd had front-desk duty that day. A guest had complained about the no-skid mat in his shower. It was too bumpy. Did they have any smoother no-skid pads?

Monica laughed wryly. A smoother pad would defeat the purpose, she thought—too smooth, and your feet would skid on it.

Housekeeping left a message about one of the driers being on the fritz. Someone in the kitchen called to let her know a water pressure problem had resolved itself. The pool service phoned to set up a maintenance schedule for the summer. And then a final message: "Hello, Monica? It's Ty. I didn't have your phone number, so I called the hotel to reach you. I hope that's okay. I'm not going to make it tonight. I'm kind of…well, things are screwed up." A pause, and he continued: "I need a lawyer, Monica. A criminal lawyer. If you can find one for me, I'd be grateful. I'm at the police station now. Thanks. I'm sorry. Everything's really fucked up."

He needed a criminal lawyer? *Everything's really fucked up?*

No kidding.

Her heart thudded against her ribs. Her skull seemed to tighten around her brain, making her head throb. So much for going wild, she thought. So much for making crazy love with a total stranger. He was at the police station. He needed a criminal lawyer.

Who the hell was he? What had she gotten herself into?

Six

As a courtesy, Nolan, the tall, steely-haired cop who'd brought Ty to the Brogan's Point police station, allowed him to remain in an interview room rather than locking him in a cell.

Some courtesy. Ty wanted to change into clean clothes and check his email. Then he wanted rent a two-stroke engine on two wheels, cruise around town, and fill his lungs with fresh New England air. After that, he wanted to meet up with Monica, take her somewhere nice, and feed her. And then screw her silly. He didn't want to sit on a hard plastic chair in a bare, square room, knowing a police detective was spying on him through the one-way mirror attached to the wall. He didn't want to stare at that mirror and see his disheveled, unshaven face, his hands folded on the Formica-topped table next to the remains of the ham sandwich and the empty water bottle Nolan had brought him a while ago, a poor substitute for the dinner he would have shared with Monica. His shirt was wrinkled and his vision was bleary, shadowed by anger and worry.

He and Nolan had chatted for several hours. According to Nolan, drugs were stashed somewhere on the Freedom. Nolan didn't specify what drugs, or how much, or whose they were, although he insinuated that they were dangerous and illegal, that they were in large enough quantity to make a nice profit when sold, and that they belonged to Ty.

"I don't know what you're talking about," Ty insisted repeatedly. "A guy in Key Biscayne hired me to sail his boat up to Brogan's Point for him. He didn't hire me to transport drugs."

"We got a tip that a shipment would be coming up from Florida," Nolan said, his voice low and even. "A reliable enough tip to convince a judge to issue a search warrant."

"But you didn't find any drugs on the boat." Ty couldn't believe their search would unearth anything illicit. He'd lived on that boat for a week, and he hadn't encountered any drugs on it, other than the bottle of over-the-counter ibuprofen he'd tucked into his toiletries bag.

"Not yet," Nolan said. "We're still looking."

It was during the search that Nolan had found Ty's laptop and duffel bag. The cops must have used a bolt cutter on the lock Ty had used to protect his belongings when he'd stashed them yesterday. Nolan had assured Ty that his belongings were safe. Was that a courtesy, too?

Ty didn't just want his stuff safe. He wanted his stuff within reach, or at least within his line of sight. But it remained in the possession of the police department for now. Perhaps some CSI analyst was right that very minute pawing through his clothes, searching for traces of weed in the depths of his pockets, or scouring his emails for hints that he was planning to make millions of dollars selling oxy to school children in a quiet seaside town north of Boston.

"Tell me more about the guy who hired you to sail the boat," Nolan said.

Ty eyed the digital recorder Nolan had set up on one end of the table. He was glad for it. If the cop took a swing at him, he wanted that recorded. He didn't want his words mangled, either. He'd done nothing wrong, and he wanted the digital-cam to record that. "His name is Wayne MacArthur. He's a businessman in Key Biscayne, as far as I know. He owns the Freedom. He keeps it docked at a marina in Biscayne where I do a lot of work on boats. He told me he's got a summer place somewhere around here, and this year he couldn't sail the boat up the coast to his summer place, so he hired me to do it."

"What kind of work do you do on boats?"

"Carpentry. These are pricy vessels. Ocean-going. They often have a lot of woodwork in their living quarters. Sometimes I'll be hired to spruce up a houseboat someone's living on. I work on buildings, too. Residential, mostly." He shrugged. "I guess MacArthur had seen me around at the marina, or maybe he asked the Jeff about me—that's the guy who manages the marina down there—or...I don't know. MacArthur approached me and asked if I'd do this. It sounded good to me."

"And he paid you?"

"Yes."

"How much?"

Ty recalled the lump of money Wayne MacArthur had wired into his PayPal account barely twenty-four hours ago. Twenty grand. A generous sum for a week's work, but given that the gig had been 24/7 and had entailed risk, the payment hadn't seemed outrageously high. If Ty had been hired to run drugs, he would have demanded a hell of a lot more money than twenty thou.

Not that he would have ever agreed to do something like that, for any amount of money. Drugs sucked. Drugs had killed his parents and nearly killed him.

"Twenty thousand dollars," he told Nolan. No point in lying. He had nothing to hide.

Nolan seemed to think that amount was significant. Even though he was recording the interview, he jotted a note on his pad. "So, this gentleman—Wayne MacArthur—paid you twenty thousand dollars to cart drugs up to Brogan's Point?"

"No." Ty tried to keep his exasperation out of his voice. "He paid me twenty thousand dollars to sail his boat up to Brogan's Point."

"Mr. Cronin, things will go a lot easier here if you cooperate with us."

"I *am* cooperating. I'm telling you the truth. What more do you want?"

"Tell me where the drugs are."

"I have no idea."

It went that way for hours. Nolan's circular questioning, Ty's honest answers. Hours, and they'd gotten nowhere. The first time Ty asked to make a phone call, Nolan told him he wasn't under arrest and therefore didn't have the right to make a phone call. It made no sense to Ty that being arrested would afford him more rights than merely being brought in for questioning, but he'd been doing his damnedest to cooperate.

As the minutes ticked by, however, he realized there was a good chance he wouldn't be able to meet Monica at the Faulk Street Tavern as planned. He also realized that even though he didn't know a freaking thing about the drugs the police seemed to believe were on the Freedom, he probably needed an attorney.

At four-thirty, Nolan finally relented and allowed Ty to phone Monica. He didn't have her personal number, so he used his phone to Google the Ocean Bluff Inn and called her through its switchboard, hoping that receiving a message from him on her office phone wouldn't cause her too many problems.

Two hours later, she hadn't called him back, let alone sent a lawyer for him.

He'd probably scared her off. She was a good girl, after all, neat and quiet, professionally oriented, employed in the family business. Not the sort of woman who'd want anything to do with a guy getting worked over by the local constabulary, thanks to a rumor some scum informant had started that the Freedom contained a drug shipment.

Allowed another phone call, he supposed he could call Jeff down in Key Biscayne. The marina manager was the person who'd introduced Ty to Wayne MacArthur. But what could Jeff do for him? He was fifteen hundred miles away. Ty could also tell the police he wanted a lawyer, but like the phone call, he might not be legally entitled to one since he hadn't been charged with anything. And if they provided him with a lawyer, it would likely be some underpaid, overworked public defender. If Ty was under suspicion for bringing drugs into Brogan's Point, he'd need someone good.

He could afford someone good. His bank account was twenty thousand dollars richer than it was a day ago. And he could tap into the trust fund if he had to.

But as the day trickled away like grains of sand in an hour glass, Ty didn't make any more phone calls. Either he'd get charged—in which case, he'd accept a public defender long enough to get arraigned and bailed out, and then he'd find his own good lawyer—or he wouldn't get charged, in which case, he'd walk out of this frickin' room in this frickin' police station and buy a plane ticket back to Florida. He no longer had any urge to explore New England on a motorbike.

He *did* have an urge to see Monica again, to kiss her one more time, touch her, watch her eyes mist over with passion, and hear her quiet moans as he made her come. But that wasn't going to happen. She clearly wanted nothing to do with someone who'd somehow, inexplicably, gotten himself into the kind of trouble Ty was in right now.

Nolan swung open the interrogation room door. Ty didn't read triumph in his expression. Apparently, the cops crawling around the Freedom with their search warrant still hadn't found the drugs Ty had supposedly stashed on the boat. With a sigh, Nolan said, "Your lawyer has arrived."

His lawyer? He hadn't requested a public defender.

That meant Monica must have gotten his message. She'd sent a lawyer. Maybe he *would* see her again. He had to see her, if only to thank her.

The man following Nolan had a lawyer look about him, even if his dark gray suit jacket was rumpled and he'd lost his necktie somewhere along the way. The lawyer's hair was long and floppy, his nose and chin sharp. Ty hoped his legal skills resembled his nose and chin. He needed someone sharp fighting for him.

"Caleb Solomon," the lawyer said, extending his right hand for Ty to shake. His left hand gripped a battered leather briefcase. "Monica Reinhart sent me."

Hearing her name eased Ty's tension. So did the lawyer's handshake, which was firm and confident.

Solomon shot a look at Nolan. "A few minutes alone with my client, please," he said. Nolan nodded and left the interrogation room, closing the door behind him.

Solomon brushed aside the napkin and wrapper from Ty's sandwich, checked to make sure the video recorder was turned off, dropped his briefcase onto the table, and took a seat across the table from Ty. As he unbuckled his briefcase, he said, "Fill me in. What are we dealing with?" His brusqueness was tempered by a smile.

Ty decided he liked the guy. Not that he had much choice in the matter. "How did Monica happen to know a criminal lawyer?" he asked.

Solomon laughed. "She didn't. She called the attorney who handles the inn's legal affairs. He recommended me." He pulled a legal pad and pen from the briefcase, clicked the pen open, and said, "Okay. Tyler Cronin, right?" Without waiting for Ty to confirm this, he wrote Ty's name down. "Tell me your story."

That he didn't first ask for payment made Ty like Solomon even more. Methodically, with as much calmness as he could muster, he told the lawyer about MacArthur's having hired him to sail the Freedom up the coast, about how he'd docked it at the North Cove Marina as instructed, how the police had gotten a search warrant and boarded the vessel while he was away, and informed him they believed a shipment of drugs was hidden on the boat. Ty knew nothing about any drugs. All he'd done was what he'd been hired to do: deliver the boat to its slip in the marina.

Solomon took notes, occasionally nodding, occasionally pinning Ty with a hard, clear-eyed stare. "Have you ever been in trouble with the law?" he asked. "I haven't had time to do any research on you. The police have, though, so I need to know everything they know."

"There's nothing to know," Ty told him. "I mean, yeah, the local cops once caught me and a couple of other kids drinking 3.2 beer when we were seventeen, but they just sent us home."

Another nod. "Are you acquainted with any drug dealers? Anyone who might have set you up?"

"Not that I know of. If Wayne MacArthur is using his boat to run drugs up the coast, he hasn't mentioned that to me."

Solomon wrote "Wayne MacArthur" on his pad. "I'll see what I can find out about him. Is it possible he stashed heroin on the boat without your knowing it?"

"Heroin?"

"According to our friend, Detective Nolan, that's what the cops are looking for."

Ty ruminated. "I guess it's possible there could be something hidden on the boat. There could be some secret compartment I don't know about. It's not like I pried off the paneling to see if anything was behind it." He closed his eyes for a moment, recalling various stretches during the trip—the storm off the Carolina coast, the difficulty catching wind in a stretch of calms east of Delaware, the smooth final leg of the journey. Nothing unusual about any of it. "I didn't notice any imbalance or unusual weight in the boat."

"Let's say there was twenty pounds of heroin on the boat. Would you notice an extra twenty pounds?"

Ty shook his head. "Especially not on the ocean. A few hundred pounds I might notice. Twenty or thirty, no."

"Okay. As I understand it, the police haven't found anything yet, and they haven't filed charges against you. So the first thing we're going to do is have them release you."

"They've got my clothes and laptop," Ty said.

"We'll get them to release those items, too." Solomon stood and offered Ty another smile. Ty wasn't naïve enough to think his troubles were over, but that smile boosted his mood.

Solomon ushered Ty from the interrogation room. Just like that, as if Ty had always been free to leave the dreary cubicle. Perhaps he had, but he'd been trying to cooperate, hoping to win Nolan over. Getting up and walking out would have only made him look guilty, or so he'd figured.

But walking out with his lawyer was apparently allowed. They stopped at a desk in the front room, where Solomon talked with Nolan for a few minutes. A clerk quickly produced Ty's duffel and laptop bag, and Ty listened as Nolan explained that he should remain in town, that he was a person of interest and that the investigation was ongoing. Nolan asked for Ty's cell phone number, but Solomon interrupted and told Nolan that all communications with Ty would pass through Solomon.

Paperwork. Bureaucracy. Affable chit-chat. Ty didn't doubt that it was all essential, but he was desperate to leave the building, to breathe some fresh air, to learn how much Caleb Solomon's representation was going to set him back. To find Monica and thank her for not erasing the phone message he'd left her that afternoon and acting as if their paths had never crossed.

He didn't have to look far to find her. As soon as he and the lawyer exited the police station into the starlit evening, he spotted her sitting on the hood of a car in the parking lot. She wore jeans and the zippered sweatshirt she'd had on last night. The breeze gusting in from the ocean fluttered through her straight, dark hair.

She didn't appear happy to see him. He couldn't recall ever feeling as happy as he felt to see her.

Exercising more willpower than he knew he possessed, he resisted the urge to race across the parking lot and sweep her into his arms. Instead, he remained at Solomon's side, the woven strap of his duffel digging into his shoulder, his hand fisted around the handle of his laptop bag, and simply stared at her. She stared back, her eyes chilly, her expression grim.

"So here's what happens next," Solomon explained. "You come into my office first thing tomorrow morning—" he handed Ty a business card "—and we work out a strategy. In the meantime, I'll research this Wayne MacArthur and review the police files. It sounds like all they've got is some informer telling them there's a shipment of a heroin on that boat. They won't even tell me the name of the informer, although we'll get that in discovery if it comes to that. Which, I assume, it won't, because as far as I can see, Nolan's got nothing on you other than the fact that you were hired to sail a boat. Last I heard, that's not a crime."

"Okay." Ty took a deep breath. "How much do I owe you?"

"I'll send you a bill." Solomon's smile was better than a shot of bourbon. It warmed, it soothed. "Ms. Reinhart said you could afford me."

"I can," Ty assured him. "But my money is tied up in a trust fund. I can't just write a check."

"Not a problem. Let's get this mess straightened out, and then you can raid your trust fund." He patted Ty's shoulder and turned toward a sleek black Beemer parked a few spots down from the car Monica was perched on. "I'll be in my office early tomorrow. Don't sleep late. I expect to see you there by nine-thirty."

Ty watched him stride across the lot to the Beemer, climb in, and rev the engine. Only after he'd driven out of the small lot did Ty turn back to Monica.

She hadn't moved. She remained planted on the hood of the sturdy Subaru like a gorgeous hood ornament, her feet propped on the bumper, her chin resting in her hands as she watched him. He started across the lot and she remained where she was. She wasn't running toward him with arms outstretched, but she wasn't fleeing in the opposite direction, either.

A few feet from her car, he halted. He didn't want to impose on her any more than he already had. "Thank you," he said.

She gave her head a slight shake, more in bewilderment than rejection. "I don't know what I'm doing here. I don't know who you are. I don't know what you've done. I'm not like this, Ty. I don't take risks—with people or anything else."

He wanted to tell her he posed no risk to her. But he knew damned well he did. "I haven't done anything," he told her. "Except be in the wrong place at the wrong time, I guess. Or on the wrong boat in the wrong marina. I don't know why the cops suspect me. I'm not even sure what they suspect me of. All I know is, they're wrong."

"Ed Nolan is a good man," she said.

"Even good men make mistakes."

Her gaze narrowed on him. Did she think he was speaking about himself, as well? Hell, he'd made his share of mistakes over the years—and he wasn't so sure he was a good man. But he hadn't made *this* mistake—whatever mistake Nolan suspected him of.

"Well," she finally said. "Whatever happened, it hasn't killed you. You're still alive."

There was that. He allowed himself a smile. She smiled as well, tentatively, more a glimmer in her large, dark eyes than a curve of her mouth. "I know it's late, but I'm hungry," he said. "How about that dinner I promised you?"

Seven

Fifteen minutes later, they were seated at a table at the Lobster Shack, a dock-side eatery with the best seafood in town. The dining rooms at the Ocean Bluff Inn won on ambience, but, disloyal though it was, Monica preferred the clam chowder at the Lobster Shack.

Tonight wasn't a night for linen tablecloths, elegant china, and crystal stemware, anyway. It was a night for rough-hewn wooden tables topped in brown butcher paper, creased paper napkins in a chrome dispenser on the table, warm buttermilk rolls heaped into a basket made of plastic strips woven to look like wicker, and the thickest, creamiest, clammiest chowder on the North Shore.

The message Ty had left on her voice mail had stolen what little appetite she'd had left after he'd stood her up at the tavern. But the chowder tasted too good, hot and rich, with just the slightest bite of black pepper transforming the soup from comfort food to something special. She spooned some into her mouth, savored the contrast of soft, bland cubes of potato and chewy, sweet clams, and eyed Ty across the table.

He'd insisted on heading straight for the rest room when they'd arrived. He'd left his laptop bag at the table the waiter had led them to, but brought his canvas duffel with him. When he'd rejoined her after a few minutes, he had on a fresh button-front shirt and his beard was gone. Shaving in the restaurant's bathroom wasn't exactly proper behavior, but obviously, he'd wanted to tidy himself up.

Without the beard, he was even more handsome. His cheeks were lean and tan, his jawline angular. The more of his face she could see, the happier she was.

Except that she wasn't happy at all. This man—this stranger—this *lover*—had gotten himself tangled up with the law. On the drive to the Lobster Shack, he'd told her he was under suspicion for bringing heroin into Brogan's Point on the boat he'd sailed up from Florida. He'd told her he was innocent, the police hadn't even found the heroin they claimed was on the boat, and they'd refused to divulge the name of the asshole who'd informed them of this alleged heroin shipment. He told her this was either a huge misunderstanding or someone had set him up for some reason. He told her that he didn't give a shit how good a man Nolan was; the detective was wrong about Ty.

She desperately wanted to believe everything Ty told her. But how could she? She didn't know him. They might have made love, but he was still a stranger.

The chowder helped her to think, though. So did the glass of cold, crisp Chardonnay she'd ordered. One more sip of each, and she said, "Tell me about yourself, Ty. Tell me who you are."

He lowered his spoon, took a drink from the tall, sweating glass of beer beside his bowl, and studied her. "What do you want to know?"

"Everything."

He mulled that over and nodded. Evidently, he agreed she had a right to ask for everything. "I grew up in the Los Angeles suburbs," he said. "My dad was a carpenter. He did construction on movie sets, which was cool. He taught me how to build things, how to make them look right. My mom was from Kansas. She went to L.A. as a graduation present when she finished high school, and she met my father on a beach, and she never went back to Kansas. Love at first sight and all that."

That he referred to his parents in the past tense sent a ripple of anxiety through her. "What happened to them?"

"They were killed in an auto accident when I was thirteen," he told her. "Some crazy kid buzzed out on meth rammed head-on into our car." He ate a spoonful of chowder and added, "I was in the back seat."

She visualized the tattoo on his shoulder: *LIVE*. When she'd asked him about it, he'd said there had been a time when he should have died, but he hadn't. "Oh, Ty," she murmured. "That's horrible."

He shrugged.

"Were you badly injured?"

"Among other things, the accident broke my back. There was some concern about whether I'd ever walk again. A body cast and a year in rehab, and I was walking."

"But you lost your parents."

Another shrug. His words remained measured and stoical, but his eyes flashed with pain and regret. "My dad's dad lived in Los Angeles, but he was in no position to take on a teenage kid in need of intensive physical therapy. So everyone decided the best thing would be for me to move in with my grandparents in Kansas." A wry laugh escaped him. "It wasn't the best thing. They meant well, but we had different world views. They were very conservative, very religious. I could understand why my mom ran off to California and never went back. My grandparents and I fought all the time. They made rules, and I broke them."

Wild Thing, Monica thought. The opening chords of the old rock-and-roll song crashed through her head.

"And there was no ocean in Kansas," he continued. "I needed the ocean. Land-locked doesn't work for me."

Monica could relate to that. She'd never lived anywhere farther than a short drive from the shore. Brogan's Point and her four years of college in Boston, with its beautiful harbor—like Ty, she was happiest when in close proximity to a vast expanse of water and the salty fragrance of sea breezes flavoring the air.

"As soon as I finished school, I did what my mother did and went back to California. I lived with my grandfather there for a while, but he's kind of a crazy dude. An old surfer. He lives in a tiny house that's held together with spit and duct tape, and he sells surfing gear in a shop in Venice. He taught me how to surf, how to wind-surf. Then I headed up the coast to Whidbey Island, near Seattle, where my father's mother lived. Her husband taught me how to sail. I moved to Vancouver and learned how to ski. I moved to New Orleans and learned how to drink bourbon. I moved to Charleston, South Carolina and learned how to restore mansions. I moved to Chicago. No ocean, but Lake Michigan is almost big enough to qualify. I moved to Miami." Another shrug.

He'd told her he moved around a lot. He hadn't been kidding. "Don't you ever want to settle down somewhere and plant roots?" she asked, hoping she didn't sound too conventional—although if she did, she did. She was a conventional woman, after all. Except for those four years of college, she'd never lived anywhere other than Brogan's Point, and never wanted to do anything other than help her parents run their resort.

He tilted his bowl to capture the last of the chowder with his spoon. "I guess if I found a place that made me want to settle down, I'd settle down."

And he hadn't found that place, at least not yet. Surely Brogan's Point wasn't the place. Not that Monica expected him to settle down here. Not that she could possibly have any hold on him. Not that she was even sure she *wanted* to have a hold on him. What he'd told her about himself was both tragic and intriguing, and yet…She still wasn't sure she knew who he was.

"How do you support yourself, moving around the way you do?" Another conventional question, she acknowledged. If he decided that she was square and boring like his Kansas grandparents, so be it.

He smiled crookedly. "I do carpentry. Restorations on buildings and boats. My father taught me a lot. I learned more on my own. There's always work at marinas for someone who knows what he's doing." Another eloquent shrug. "The father of the kid who killed my parents was a wealthy power player in Hollywood. He was able to pull a lot of strings to keep his son out of jail. But he knew that if I sued his kid, the publicity would suck. Or—I don't know, maybe he just felt guilty that his kid had destroyed my family. Anyway, he set up a trust fund for me. Hush money or whatever. I tap into it whenever I have to." He sighed. "Like when I need to hire an expensive lawyer. This Solomon dude is expensive, isn't he."

It wasn't a question, but Monica replied anyway. "I'm sure he isn't cheap. But the attorney who handles the inn's business affairs said he was the best criminal attorney on the North Shore. One of the top in the Boston area. You'll get your money's worth."

"I hope so." Ty set down his spoon, then surprised her by reaching across the table and capturing her hand in his. "I didn't do it," he said, his tone low and earnest. "Whatever that good man Nolan thinks I did, I didn't do it."

Monica nodded uncertainly.

"You don't believe me."

"I...don't know."

He sighed again, and released her hand. Her fingers felt icy and forlorn when he did. Whether or not she believed him, she wanted him. There was no getting around that. For as long as Ty was with her, until he wandered off to some other seaside town or landed in prison, she wanted him.

She shouldn't. But she did.

—⁂—

She looked concerned.

No, she didn't. She looked stricken and shocked, like she was fighting the urge to cry. He almost wished he hadn't told her his story. He didn't usually discuss it. He didn't dwell on the past. He'd lived it, he'd survived it, and now he embraced every day the way anyone grateful to be alive would. He wasn't hideously scarred. He didn't limp. He missed his parents and the happy childhood that had been stolen from him, but there wasn't much he could do about that. You had to adjust your sails to capture the wind, whatever direction it was blowing.

But Monica had asked him to share his story with her, and he owed her that much. The truth was, he owed her a hell of a lot more. She'd found him a lawyer. More importantly, she'd answered his desperate plea for help.

He gazed across the table at her. Her fingers, wrapped around the stem of her wine glass, were pale and slender, her nails painted a muted coral shade that reminded him of the color clouds sometimes turned during a vivid sunset. He watched her sip her wine. Her eyes glistened with unshed tears.

"I've made you uncomfortable," he apologized.

"No. It's okay. I'm just so sorry you had to live through such a horrible tragedy."

"I lived through it," he reminded her. "I'm okay. Sometimes—" and this was something he definitely didn't share with people "—I feel immortal. If I could survive that wreck—" and if he could survive that ghastly year in rehab, and the stifling, smothering years with his grandparents in Kansas, who had never forgiven their daughter for running off to California, marrying Ty's father, and not living the life they'd wished for her, and who had tried to force Ty into their proper, stultifying life "—I can survive anything."

Monica gave him a watery smile.

"I've bungee-jumped. I've sky-dived. I've climbed sheer rock cliffs. I've scuba-dived. I've tried hang-gliding. I ride motorcycles. I've sailed from San Diego to Honolulu—and from Key Biscayne to New England, but you already knew that. What's the point of being scared? If your number is up, it's up. May as well go all out, right?"

"May as well *live*," she murmured. At his questioning look, she nodded toward his shoulder. "Your tattoo."

"Yeah." He'd gotten his tat as soon as he'd returned to California. It had been a celebration of all he'd survived, all the odds he'd beaten. He'd escaped physical death in the crash and spiritual death in his grandparents' custody. He'd survived losing his parents.

"So I guess sailing a boat all by yourself from Florida to Massachusetts is the sort of thing a person does when he's fearless."

"It's not that dangerous if you know what you're doing. I hugged the coastline the whole way. I was never in international waters. The Coast Guard could have found me."

"It's still dangerous," she argued quietly.

He conceded with a shrug.

"More dangerous if you're carrying a cargo of illegal drugs."

All right. She still didn't believe him, didn't trust him. He couldn't really blame her. Who was he, after all, but a footloose stranger who'd literally sailed into town and bedded her on an impulse.

No, he hadn't bedded her. He'd made love to her. It had been more than sex. And it hadn't been on an impulse. It had been because of that song he'd heard in the bar. The jukebox had been playing, and he'd been enjoying his drink and the come-ons of that stacked woman on the bar stool next to him, and suddenly that song had started playing. *Wild Thing.* His eyes had met Monica's, and he'd felt as if their minds had met, too. Their hearts. Their souls.

He'd done crazier things in his life than make love to a beautiful woman whose name he didn't even know. But he'd always kind of recognized that they were crazy while he was doing them. The craziness had been part of their appeal.

When he'd kissed Monica last night, when he'd stripped naked and pulled her onto him, and come deep inside her while she'd come around him, he'd believed it was the sanest thing he'd ever done.

Quite possibly, the craziest thing he'd ever done was to trust Wayne MacArthur. If the guy had heroin stashed on his boat, Ty was going to have a hell of a time proving he didn't know about it. He'd also have a hell of a time convincing Monica of his innocence.

Her expression right now, her dark eyes still glistening, her head tilted slightly as she regarded him, her fingers still tense around her glass, told him she wasn't convinced of it now. He'd told her his story, and she clearly wasn't sure whether she bought it.

"I should find another place to stay tonight," he said, even though he couldn't imagine any place he'd rather be than next to Monica, his arms around her, his head nestled beside hers atop the plush down pillows on her bed. "I guess there are some motels down Route 1."

She continued to measure him with her gaze, her indecision visible in her expression. After a minute, she said, "We have some open rooms at the inn right now. We're booked pretty solidly from Memorial Day weekend on, but this week we've still got rooms."

"Okay." Apparently, her ambivalence would allow him to spend the night close to her, but not too close. Either that, or she wanted to fill the inn's vacant rooms. She was an executive there, after all.

She insisted she wasn't hungry for anything more, and the big bowl of chowder on top of the tasteless ham sandwich Nolan had scared up at the police station were enough to fill Ty's stomach. He paid the bill and they left the restaurant, which sat on a broad wharf jutting out into the sea. Further up the wharf, he saw the silhouettes of a couple of commercial fishing boats docked and rocking lazily on the gently rippling waves. No wonder the Lobster Shack had a big sign beside its front door reading "Fresh Fish Daily." He supposed the chef just walked down the wharf to the boats when they steamed into port and bought their catch right out of their nets.

Monica remained silent as she and Ty climbed into her car and she started the engine. He knew better than to disturb a woman when she was thinking things over, but the tension pinching her lips and shadowing her eyes bothered him. "Are you all right?" he finally asked.

She managed a faint smile. "I don't have the law breathing down my neck, so I guess I'm in better shape than you." The smile vanished when she added, "We're just so different, Ty. You bop around the country, doing this, doing that, tapping into your trust fund and moving on. I'm the opposite. I grew up here. My family owns a hotel. A place where people *stay*."

He was surprised to experience a twinge of...was it envy? The thought of actually *staying* somewhere seemed alien to him, probably because he hadn't really had a home since the accident. The house where he'd grown up in Pasadena had been sold and emptied after his parents died. His grandparents had sold or donated most of the furniture, too. Because he'd been in the rehab hospital at the time, they'd packed what they felt he needed—clothing, books, his baseball glove, his Discman and a few CD's—and discarded the rest. When he'd finally been released, he'd discovered all his other treasures—his comic books, his water pistol, his trading cards, the sea-polished rocks he'd gathered during trips to the beach with his parental grandfather, his Frisbee, his Swiss Army knife, the drawers full of silly junk that meant nothing to anyone else but everything to him...All of it gone. He'd lost his parents and he'd lost his belongings.

From that moment on, he'd never had a home. No wonder he never stayed anywhere for long.

Well, it looked as if he would be staying in Brogan's Point at least until he cleared his name and the cops decided he was no longer a person of interest. Glancing at Monica as she steered her car along Atlantic Avenue, the road paralleling the coastline through town, he was struck by the odd thought that even if he didn't like the reason he was trapped in Brogan's Point for a while, the thought of spending time here appealed to him.

Not that he expected to regain the intimacy he and Monica had shared last night. That had been a fluke, inspired by some alcohol consumption and an ancient rock song.

Even so, there were worse things in life than to be stuck in a pretty New England hamlet like Brogan's Point for a while. Maybe, after he met with the lawyer tomorrow morning, he could follow through on his plan to rent a bike and motor around the region. He wouldn't go far. He'd check in as often as necessary. It wasn't as if he had an electronic bracelet strapped around his ankle.

Monica turned onto the driveway of the Ocean Bluff Inn and parked in one of the empty spots in the lot. He hauled his duffel and laptop out of the back seat and followed her up the steps, across the broad veranda and into the building.

The lobby looked like something from a movie set his father might have worked on: old, solid furniture, brass lighting fixtures, cream-colored walls, genteelly faded rugs. The hotels he'd been to in Florida generally featured light, airy lobbies with sleek leather or wicker furniture, and planters filled with ferns and palms. Those hotels were painted swimming-pool blue or flamingo pink, and they had cool tile floors. This inn, with its warm woods and golden lighting, and the fireplaces he glimpsed in the rooms flanking the lobby, shouted that he was no longer in the tropics. There was a permanence about the décor and the building that housed it, a sense that if a hurricane ever did make it this far north, it wouldn't leave much of an impression on the inn. The place had lasted a long time, and would last a long time more.

He liked it.

"Hi, Kim," Monica greeted the young woman behind the counter. "My friend here needs a room for the night." She stumbled almost imperceptibly on the word *friend*.

The clerk didn't seem to notice. She ran an appreciative gaze over Ty, but he wasn't in the mood to be appreciated. If he couldn't spend the night with Monica, he wanted to check into a room, take a long, hot shower, and sack out. A night of uninterrupted sleep wasn't as appealing a prospect as a night bouncing around on Monica's mattress, but his body could use the rest.

Apparently sensing no reciprocal interest, the clerk tapped her computer keyboard. "Room 27 is open. So is Room 34. Twenty-seven is nicer," she told Ty. "It's got an ocean view. Thirty-four is up an extra flight of stairs and it overlooks the pool."

"If 34 is cheaper, I'll take it," he said. God knew what the lawyer was going to cost him. No sense burning any more money than he had to.

"Great. I'll need a credit card impression," she said, tapping some more on her computer. As worked, she turned her attention to Monica. "How's the mess at Rose Cottage?"

"Don't ask," Monica muttered. "Mess is definitely the operative term."

"Is it going to be fixed in time?"

"It has to be," Monica said, sounding exasperated. "The cottage is booked for Memorial Day weekend. If we've got to work night and day to get it fixed, we will."

The clerk swiped Ty's credit card and returned it to him, along with a reservation folder with "34" scribbled onto it and a key card tucked inside. Ty thanked her with a nod and stepped away from the reservation desk. "What kind of mess?" he asked Monica. They'd spent the evening focusing on him. It occurred to him that Monica had a life, too, and things might not be gliding a smooth course in it.

She sighed and shook her head. "A mysterious leak in one of the residential cottages. The plumbers haven't located it yet, even though they've torn apart the wall and a bathroom vanity."

"I can do walls," he said.

She peered quizzically at him.

"Plumbing is beyond me. But walls are easy."

"They can't be that easy. The construction crews here charge a fortune."

"I can help. As soon as the plumbers are done, I can do the walls for you."

She opened her mouth and then shut it. "You don't owe me anything, Ty."

He owed her everything, but even if he didn't, he'd lend a hand. "You've got a tight deadline. I'm just saying—if you need help, I can help."

A low, humorless chuckle escaped her. "If you're not in jail," she muttered.

He didn't take the dig personally. Grinning, he said. "Right. If I'm not in jail."

Eight

Caleb Solomon's office was a long walk from the Ocean Bluff Inn, but Ty could manage a long walk, especially after a quiet night spent in a comfortable bed. He'd awakened early, showered again—after a week of washing beneath the spitting, erratic spray of the Freedom's cramped shower, he appreciated the showers he'd enjoyed in both Monica's apartment and the cozy third-floor room at the inn, his current home. His clothing was wrinkled from having spent too much time rolled up inside his duffel, but at least some of the garments were clean. He donned fresh jeans and a button-front shirt, the most presentable apparel he'd brought with him, and after a breakfast of scrambled eggs and rye toast in one of the inn's dining rooms, he slung his laptop bag over his shoulder and hiked into downtown Brogan's Point for his morning meeting with his lawyer.

If the sign outside the colonial brick building that housed Solomon's office was any indication, the guy had two partners. "Chase, Mullen and Solomon, Attorneys-at-Law," it read, block letters on a classy brass plaque. Entering the building, Ty was assailed by the aroma of fresh coffee.

After the week he'd spent on the boat slugging down instant in the hope of a caffeine rush, fresh-brewed coffee was as much a luxury as showers with steady water pressure. The coffee at the inn had been good. This coffee would be good, too. Neither would be as good as the coffee he'd drunk in Monica's apartment yesterday morning, but that coffee had tasted wonderful because he'd been able to gaze at her while he'd consumed it.

Once Ty identified himself to the receptionist, he was led to a conference room and served a steaming cup of the beverage he'd smelled. He had barely settled into one of the chairs surrounding the oval mahogany table when Solomon entered. Like last night, he was wearing a suit and shirt with no tie—a navy blue suit this time, but it looked as rumpled as last night's suit—and he was toting his battered leather briefcase. Ty stood out of courtesy to the two women who accompanied Solomon: one a tall, too-thin woman wearing eyeglasses and carrying a laptop, the other an attractive blond woman in a silky beige suit that looked a lot pricier than Solomon's. She carried a yellow legal pad and a fountain pen. Solomon gave Ty's hand a shake, then introduced the women: "This is Annie Adler, a paralegal, who's going to be taking notes. And this is Heather Chase, one of my partners. She's got better connections in South Florida than I do."

Thank God for the trust fund, Ty thought as he waited for the women to sit and then settled back into his chair. Two lawyers were probably going to cost him twice as much.

And he hadn't even done anything wrong. It seemed ridiculous that he should have to hire two hot-shot lawyers to defend him when he was innocent.

They arranged themselves around the table, the paralegal fired up her laptop, and the receptionist brought in more coffee. Solomon didn't seem to need caffeine. He was already firing on all cylinders. "Here's what we've got so far. Wayne MacArthur does exist."

"Not on Google, he doesn't," Ty said. "I did a search for him last night, but I couldn't find anything. I've met him, though. He paid me."

"He could have been using a false name. He could've taken a powder. But fortunately, he didn't. He's still down in Key Biscayne. And he really does own a house up on the north end of Brogan's Point. I talked to a couple of his neighbors up here and they hardly know him. They said that when he's in town, he keeps to himself. The staff guy at North Cove Marina knows him more for his boat than for himself. They said he pays his bills on time and never causes any trouble."

"Has it occurred to anyone that maybe there *aren't* drugs on his boat?" Ty asked. "Like, maybe he's just a nice guy?"

"A nice, very rich guy who supposedly owns a few laundromats in Miami," Heather Chase said, giving Ty an expensive-looking smile—straight, white teeth framed by plump, glossy lips. "A few laundromats don't generate the kind of money that buys a fancy sail boat and two mansions."

"His houses are mansions?" Ty asked.

The pretty lawyer nodded. "His Brogan's Point house is valued at more than one-point-five million on Zillow. His house on Key Biscayne is closer to two-point-five million. And the boat."

"That still doesn't mean he deals drugs. Maybe he inherited his money or something. Maybe he's got a rich wife." Maybe his family had been wiped out by the spoiled, doped-up son of a movie-industry honcho who'd bought his silence with a trust fund.

A much bigger trust fund than Ty's. He couldn't afford four million dollars' worth of real estate and an ocean-worthy sailboat that clocked in at more than fifty thousand.

Heather Chase clicked uncapped her pen. "Where did you meet Mr. MacArthur?" she asked.

Ty named the Florida marina where MacArthur docked his boat in the winter.

"You work there?" she asked.

"I'm an independent contractor," Ty said. "When a luxury yacht needs work, they call me." At her questioning look, he elaborated. "Interior repairs. Woodwork. These yachts usually have fancy paneling, elegant dashboards, that kind of thing. Big-mother steering wheels, oak trimmed with brass. The wood gets dinged, cracked— you're on a boat in a storm, sometimes stuff shifts around and bangs up the paneling. Or the weather does a number on it. Or whatever. I work on houses, too. Carved banisters and newels. Inlays. Moldings. Built-ins. I do ordinary carpentry, too. But the custom jobs pay a lot more."

"So Mr. MacArthur knew about your work?"

"Jeff—the marina manager—put him in touch with me. Jeff knew I could handle a run up the coast. I've done a lot of sailing."

"You're a jack-of-all-trades," Solomon remarked.

"Just a few trades."

"You don't do windows?" Solomon joked. Ty drank some coffee. At Heather Chase's request, he provided Jeff's last name and contact information, as well as the names of some of the clients for whom he'd worked down in the Miami area.

"Have you ever heard Mr. MacArthur referred to as Mr. Smith?" Solomon asked.

"No."

"Anyone at the marina down there called Smith?"

"I don't know. There could be some boat owners." Ty shrugged.

"MacArthur never mentioned someone named Smith to you?"

Ty shrugged again. "If he did, I don't remember. I mean… Smith? It doesn't exactly leave an impression."

Solomon and his colleague exchanged a look. "All right," she said, pushing to her feet. "Let me see what I can dig up."

Ty and Solomon stood as well, waiting until she left the conference room before they resumed their seats. He might have despised living with his maternal grandparents in St. Mary's, Kansas, but they'd hammered good manners into his head. If his father's father had gotten custody of him after the accident, Ty would never have known he was supposed to stand when a woman entered or exited a room. He probably wouldn't have known the importance of tucking in his shirt and keeping his fingernails short and clean, either. His grandpa in California had never managed to master either of those skills.

"I've gotten some information from the police," Solomon told Ty as Annie the paralegal typed away. "Does the name Danny Watson mean anything to you?"

Ty frowned. Unable to think of anyone he knew by that name, he shook his head. "Should it?"

"He's the police informant. He was arrested a couple of weeks ago and charged with dealing. He'd been working on a fishing boat out of Brogan's Point, but apparently he had a nice little side business going. He told the police a major shipment of heroin would be arriving by boat from Key Biscayne, and then you sailed MacArthur's boat into port from Key Biscayne."

"That's all the cops have on me? Maybe another boat's heading up here from the Keys."

"Maybe. Everything the police have is circumstantial—although it was enough to get a search warrant."

"But they didn't find any drugs on the Freedom, did they."

"Not yet." Solomon dug around in his briefcase and pulled out a folder, which he opened. "Okay. This fellow, Danny Watson, said his supplier was named Smith, and the heroin was going to be arriving on a sailboat out of Key Biscayne sometime this week. Now, here's our problem. If the police go after MacArthur, he's going to say he knows nothing about any drugs and you must have smuggled the heroin without his knowledge. You're saying *you* know nothing about any heroin, and *he* must be smuggling it without *your* knowledge. It's a 'he said, he said' situation."

"Is there some way to trace the heroin? Like, to whoever MacArthur got it from?"

Solomon shook his head. "I don't know how MacArthur got his illegal cargo, and I'm not sure we need to know that. All we need to do is get your name cleared. We don't have to do the police's work for them."

Ty took some comfort in the understanding that his lawyer actually believed he was innocent. At least his words implied that he did.

"Are there people in Florida who can vouch for your character?" Solomon asked.

Ty provided a list of names: his neighbors, his landlady, clients, Jeff at the marina. Annie dutifully typed the names into the computer, her fingers fluttering, the keys tapping in a gentle tempo.

"How about up here in Massachusetts?" Solomon asked.

The only person who knew him here was Monica. And how well did she know him? They'd slept together—before they'd even known each other's names. Hardly a strong character reference: *He picked me up in a bar, we reconnected at my parents' inn, and we screwed our heads off.*

She'd found him this lawyer. Surely that meant something.

It didn't mean much. Just that she'd heard the desperation in his voice when he'd left that voice-mail message. That she'd come through for him because they'd had a good time in bed.

Solomon was staring across the table at him, his eyes as hard as polished black granite. "I haven't been here long enough to make a lot of friends," Ty said.

"Monica Reinhart contacted me on your behalf. I take it she knows you?"

Ty didn't want to drag her into his mess. "She did me a favor," he allowed. "A huge favor. I can't ask anything more of her than what she's already done." And if he *did* decide to ask more of her, it wouldn't be that she attest to what a fine, upstanding citizen he was. What he wanted to ask of her was that she open herself to him one more time. That she climb onto a bike behind him, wrap her arms around his waist, lean into his back, and ride away with him. He'd ask her to spend days with him, nights with him.

He'd ask her to trust him, to believe in him.

Hell. He wasn't a fine, upstanding citizen. He was a guy who roamed around the country and sailed the ocean, who traveled because if he ever stopped, he'd have to call wherever he was home, and he had no idea what home was anymore. He was a guy who knew how to fix things, how to build things, how to craft things, a guy who knew how to make a woman like Monica moan with passion.

But he couldn't force her to swear to Caleb Solomon, or to Ed Nolan of the Brogan's Point police department, or to anyone else, that Ty was a clean-living, law-abiding gentleman. As far as she knew, he was just...A wild thing.

If it weren't for that song, blasting out of an antique jukebox in a working-class bar, she wouldn't even know that.

—◊—

Monica pressed her cell phone to her ear and stepped outside Rose Cottage. Inside was a disaster: a gaping hole in the parlor wall, a displaced vanity in the second-floor bathroom above, plaster dust everywhere, and the plumber still hadn't found the source of the leak. Hovering over the workmen and wringing her hands wasn't doing anyone any good. Nor was wondering where Ty was, what he was doing, what was being done to him.

She needed a break. She needed sleep, thanks to the restless night she'd endured, a night smelling Ty's clean ocean scent on her pillow and remembering the heat and strength of his body, wanting that heat and strength and knowing she shouldn't want it. She needed perspective, sanity, a friend. "Emma?" she spoke into the phone as she stood on the cottage's front porch and sucked in the fresh, mild afternoon air—air that wasn't choked with white dust. "Are you busy?"

"I'm at the community center," her best friend said. "Getting things organized for the summer art program."

"Can you take a break? I'm going crazy."

Emma laughed. "I'm the head-case in our friendship. You're not allowed to go crazy. That's a rule."

"Then I guess I broke the rule," Monica said unapologetically. "Can you spare a half hour?"

"Sure. Wanna meet at the Faulk Street Tavern?"

Much as Monica would love to sip a glass of wine—or, more accurately, guzzle a bottle or two of something far more potent— she knew she couldn't do that while one of the inn's guest cottages was being dismantled in search of an elusive leak. But she could get a soft drink at the pub. "I'll be there in two minutes," she told Emma.

"I'll be there in ten," Emma responded before disconnecting the call.

Monica stepped back inside Rose Cottage, alerted one of the workmen that she'd be gone for a while but reachable via cell phone, and exited the building once more. At one time she'd loved Rose Cottage, hadn't she? At one time, water stains hadn't appeared on the cottage's pretty walls. At one time, the cottage *had* pretty walls—before the guys from Parnelli's had removed a large chunk of one of them.

Could they actually find the leak, fix it, and restore the building to its usual tidy state before Memorial Day? If they couldn't, what would Monica do with the bridal party scheduled to spend the holiday weekend in the cottage?

With that pending disaster swaying above her like the pendulum in the Edgar Allan Poe story, its lethally sharp blade descending closer and closer to her with each passing minute, why was she wasting an instant of her mental energy on Ty Cronin?

Because she was crazy, that was why.

Stuffing her phone into her purse, she strolled down the entry drive to Atlantic Avenue and south to Faulk Street. At two-thirty in the afternoon—she belatedly realized she'd forgotten to eat lunch—the tavern was practically empty. It was open for business, though. That was all Monica cared about.

She surveyed the room. Gus Naukonen stood at her usual station behind the bar, talking to Manny, her burly, good-natured second-in-command. They both turned to see who'd entered. "Hey," Gus greeted Monica, then indicated the unoccupied tables with a sweep of her hand. "Take your pick."

"Thanks." Monica crossed to the table she'd been sitting at the day she'd seen Ty, the day "Wild Thing" had blared out of the jukebox. She wasn't sure if the table was bad luck or good. She and Ty had had a spectacular night, after all. But nothing had gone right since then.

She'd barely taken her seat when Emma swept in, her red hair flying as if her scalp was on fire. When Boston University had assigned Emma Glendon as Monica's freshman-year roommate, Monica had wondered why. She'd had nothing in common with Emma, who had grown up the daughter of back-to-the-land hippies in northern Vermont and planned to major in fine arts. Yet they'd become instant friends. Monica had envied Emma's enormous talent, her energy, her lack of pretense. Emma had always said she admired Monica's stability and drive. Monica had known, even before she'd unpacked her boxes in their cramped Back-Bay dorm room, that she would be returning to Brogan's Point after college to help run her family's inn. Emma had known only that she wanted to paint. How she would support herself as she pursued her art had been a mystery.

She'd stumbled along, though, creating what she called "Dream Portraits" and scrambling for commissions and art students. Then, after she'd moved to Brogan's Point, she'd talked Nick Fiore at the community center into hiring her to teach art classes. And she'd met Max Tarloff, her high-tech gajillionaire, and they'd fallen deeply in love. Now she lived happily with him in his gorgeous glass-walled house overlooking the ocean, the two of them planning their wedding.

They'd fallen in love because of the jukebox. When Emma had insisted that a song the jukebox played had brought them together, Monica had been skeptical, even though she'd spent her whole life hearing Brogan's Point residents talking about the jukebox's magical powers.

Now here she was—the friend who was supposed to be sane, but who had been enchanted by a song from that same jukebox. Not enchanted—brainwashed. Hexed. Jinxed.

"Wow," Emma said, sliding into the booth facing Monica. "Either you've been emptying vacuum cleaner bags over your head, or you've got the worst case of dandruff I've ever seen."

Monica brushed her hands over her hair. A flurry of plaster dust swirled into the air around her. "The plumber is dismantling Rose Cottage in search of a leak," she explained. "It's a mess. My entire life is a mess."

"That can't be," Emma argued cheerfully. "Let me get you something to drink." She leaped back to her feet and headed toward the bar.

"An iced tea," Monica called to her.

Emma nodded, conferred with Gus for a minute, and returned carrying a beer for herself and a glass of chardonnay for Monica. Emma knew her friend's taste well.

"I can't drink this," Monica said as Emma set the wine glass down on the table. "I'm working."

"Not right now, you aren't. Come on, girl. One glass of wine isn't going to make you drunk."

On an empty stomach, one glass of wine might knock Monica out cold. As if Emma could read her mind, she returned to the bar and came back carrying a bowl of mixed nuts. "Okay," she said as she slid onto the banquette across from Monica and took a sip of Sam Adams. "What's wrong? And if you tell me you've gotten back together with Jimmy, I might have to beat you senseless with this bottle."

Monica shook her head and scooped a few nuts into her palm. "I will say my life was a lot saner when I was with him," she admitted, staring at the array of cashews, almonds, and walnuts in her hand, not quite sure what to do with them. Eventually, she remembered and tossed the nuts one by one into her mouth. Her stomach gave a grateful growl.

"Your life was stagnant when you were with Jimmy. It was stalled out. It was stale—"

"Okay. You've made your point." Monica sighed and washed down the nuts with a sip of wine. It tasted a hell of a lot better than iced tea would have. "No, I'm not back together with Jimmy. He still hasn't apologized to me for blowing me off when I made him that fabulous anniversary dinner."

"He always took you for granted. He's a jerk."

"Don't worry. Even if he did apologize—and he probably will, in a few days, when he decides he misses me…" Another sigh. "I'm done with him." Everything Emma had said was true: Monica's relationship with Jimmy had been stagnant. They hadn't been growing, moving forward, developing closer bonds. Jimmy was Jimmy. He was never going to change. And Monica *had* changed. "It's that stupid jukebox," she confessed.

Emma's eyes grew round. "What happened?"

"'Wild Thing' happened."

Emma listened as Monica told her about her acquaintanceship with Ty. Not everything, of course. She couldn't admit, even to her best friend, that she'd had sex with Ty before she'd even known his name. But she revealed that they'd spent some time together, and she was drawn to him, and he was the hottest guy she'd ever met. "But he's rootless. He roams around the country, always moving on. He's never been to college. He's repairs boats."

"That's cool," Emma said, her eyes still wide but glowing with approval.

"Look at me. I'm Ms. Straight-and-Narrow. What am I doing, mooning over some nomadic guy who repairs boats?"

"You're letting your hair down," Emma said. "Even if it's full of white crap."

Monica allowed herself a tiny smile, then grew solemn. "He's in legal trouble. I found him a lawyer and I'm trying to keep my distance. But..." She fell silent and took another sip of wine.

"But?"

"I believe he's innocent. I have no grounds to believe that. I hardly know him. But...I can't believe he's done what Ed Nolan thinks he's done." More accurately, she couldn't believe she could have made such rapturous love with a drug dealer.

At Emma's goading, Monica filled her in on the events of the past twenty-four hours. The boat Ty had sailed into the North Cove Marina, the police's suspicion that heroin was hidden somewhere on the boat, their assumption that Ty was connected to the heroin. The message he'd left on her work phone. Her scaring up a lawyer for him.

As if simply talking about him was enough to conjure him, the door swung open and in he walked. Although he was a good thirty feet away, she caught a whiff of his sea-breeze scent, and once again she felt bewitched. Even with no music pouring from the jukebox, she fell under its spell. Under *his* spell.

Emma traced the direction of Monica's gaze to the tall, broad-shouldered man standing just inside the entry, his jaw set, his sun-streaked hair windswept, his piercing blue eyes aimed at Monica. "Oh my god," Emma murmured. "He *is* hot."

Nine

He was hot, no question about it. Monica returned his stare, painfully aware of just how hot he was and wondering what he was doing at the tavern. Why wasn't he with the lawyer she'd found for him, or fleeing the jurisdiction, or whatever one does when one is suspected of being a drug dealer?

And why did she wish he'd race straight across the room to her table, sit down beside her, and wrap his arm around her shoulders, as if they were just any ordinary couple? Why did she yearn for something she didn't even understand?

Why did her imagination conjure the thrashing opening guitar chords of "Wild Thing," making her feel wild? She'd never felt wild with Jimmy. He might have been an asshole, but at least he was safe.

Was Ty safe? She didn't know. In some deep, dark recess of her soul, she didn't care. That scared the hell out of her.

After a long moment, he started toward her. He didn't race, but at least he walked in her direction. Some other part of her brain—not the part hearing a rock singer howl the song's simple lyrics—nattered that he was nothing more than a one night stand and she ought to forget about him. Yet she shifted on the banquet, leaving space for him to sit beside her, just in case that was what he intended to do.

He stopped at their table. "I've got a bike," he said.

She felt her eyebrows soar toward her hairline. "What?"

"A motorbike. Want to run away with me?" His lips weren't smiling, but his beautiful blue eyes glinted with mischief.

Emma cleared her throat. "Hi," she said. "I'm Emma Glendon. Monica's best friend."

Emma merited a genuine smile from Ty. "Hi," he said, extending his hand. "Ty Cronin."

Monica forced her mind back to his initial words. "You got a motorbike?"

"I rented it. Two helmets, if you want to take a ride."

Was she supposed to give him points for safety because he had two helmets? He could have a hundred helmets and still not seem safe to her. "Why did you rent a motorcycle?" she asked. The real question she wanted to ask was, *How big is that trust fund of yours? You've got huge legal bills looming in your future.*

"I need to be able to get around town while I'm here. I ride a bike in Florida."

"This isn't Florida."

"What I meant was, I've got a motorcycle operator's license. A bike is cheaper than a rental car. It uses less gas."

Oh, lord. He was a possible drug dealer-slash-biker. "Did the lawyer say renting a bike was a good idea?" she asked, then cringed. She sounded like someone auditioning for the role of his mother.

"The lawyer said I'm staying in town for a while. I need transportation." His gaze drifted to her wine glass. "Are we starting early today?"

"I've had a rough day."

"How's the plumbing problem at—what was it called? Flower House?"

"Rose Cottage," Monica said, surprised that he remembered her problems when he had far worse problems of his own. "They're working on it."

"I meant that, about helping with the walls if you need an extra pair of hands. It's the least I can do."

Because she'd found him an attorney? Because he was stuck in town and bored? Because he wanted to earn some brownie points before being carted off to prison? Because he was madly in love with her?

Scratch that last possibility from the list.

"Can I join you?" he asked.

"Sure," Emma said before Monica could decide whether she wanted him at the table.

Ty's gaze lingered on Monica for a moment. "Let me get something to drink. I'll be right back." He sauntered over to the bar. Even from behind—especially from behind—he was hot. Broad shoulders, long legs, taut buns, and those glorious windswept waves of hair.

Monica swallowed a sigh before glaring at Emma. "Here I am, telling you that letting him into my life was crazy. And now you're encouraging him to remain in my life."

"You don't need my encouragement," Emma argued gently. "With or without me, he's in your life."

He returned to their table, carrying a tall, frosty tumbler filled with a pale yellow liquid. "Lemonade," he answered Monica's unasked question as he placed the glass on the table with a quiet thump and then settled onto the upholstered bench next to her.

"I guess you haven't had a rough day," she muttered.

His response was a laugh. She was too edgy to share his laughter. Although he'd left a few decorous inches of space between them on the banquette, she sensed his proximity. His thigh seemed to exude heat. Her own thigh responded, her muscles tensing, silently begging her to edge closer to him, close enough for their hips to touch.

She didn't need the damned jukebox to cast its spell on her. Ty's nearness was enough.

Thinking about his legal problems ought to break the spell. "So," she said, "what does the lawyer think? Are you going to prison?"

"No."

Well, that didn't break the spell at all. It only elevated his appeal. She wasn't one of those women who fell in love with convicts and wrote them romantic letters while they were behind bars. She liked her men free, without criminal records.

Men? There had only been two men in her life: Jimmy and Ty. And Ty wasn't really in her life. He was just in her town, passing through. If not for this drug thing, he might have been halfway back to Florida by now, or heading off to some new address.

Ty didn't elaborate on his terse answer. Evidently, he didn't wish to divulge his lawyer's thoughts, at least not in front of Emma. And really, Monica wasn't sure she had a right to know his legal situation. It wasn't as if they were lovers. One night did not a relationship make.

Although he *did* phone her when he was in trouble. She was the one he'd reached out to.

She sipped her wine. It was a few degrees warmer than when Emma had first brought the glass to her, and she could taste its wheaty undertone. God, she was drinking wine at two in the afternoon, and sitting next to a man in serious trouble, a biker who might also be a drug smuggler—and even knowing all that, she wanted to jump his bones.

Monica Reinhart, the good girl, the organized, well-behaved, straight-and-narrow woman, had gone wild.

—⁂—

Ed didn't expect to see Tyler Cronin when he entered the Faulk Street Tavern at around two-thirty. He'd been on the go all day; he hadn't bothered with lunch. He deserved a cup of Gus's coffee. The station had a coffee maker, but the stuff that came out of it tasted like burnt oil. Gus knew how to make a lot of drinks, and her coffee deserved a spot somewhere near the top of the list.

He'd thought he would just stop by, tank up on her brew, flirt for a minute or two, and get back to work. Not that he was an expert at flirting, but he and Gus had been together long enough that she accepted his efforts with a smile.

However, there was the kid from Florida, Ed's prime suspect in the drug case, seated in a booth with a tall tumbler of something in front of him—and Monica Reinhart next to him. That red-head who'd talked her way into a job teaching art at the community center sat across from them, her hand wrapped around a brown beer bottle.

Ed continued straight to the bar, where Gus was counting change into the cash register and Manny was unloading dishwasher trays of glasses. Gus shot Ed a smile. "Coffee?"

She knew him well. "Yes, ma'am."

She shut the register door with her hip, strolled down the bar to her coffee machine, and returned carrying a mug with steam floating up from it. He allowed himself a moment to admire her long, long legs, then tipped his head in the direction of the one occupied table. "What's Monica Reinhart doing with that guy?" he asked.

Gus glanced over at the table and shrugged. "Having a glass of wine."

"What's he drinking?"

"Does it matter?" Gus asked, eyeing Ed curiously.

"Humor me."

"Lemonade."

All right. At least the bastard wasn't getting wasted. Even so, Ed didn't like the thought of Monica hanging out with him. She was a Reinhart. To call the Reinharts pillars of the community would be an understatement. They were the buttresses, the bedrock of Brogan's Point. Reinharts had been running the Ocean Bluff Inn for at least four generations. Ed knew Monica's parents. Everyone in town did— and everyone in town knew Monica, the sweet, pretty daughter who'd gone off to college to get a degree in hospitality management and then come back home to join her parents in operating their landmark hotel.

She shouldn't be keeping company with a guy who might be a drug runner.

Ed leaned toward Gus and murmured, "He's trouble. I don't think Monica ought to be having a drink with him."

Gus chuckled. "If anyone's leading anyone astray, it's her. She's the one with the alcoholic drink."

"I'm not kidding."

"Monica's a big girl. And Jimmy Creighton wasn't exactly a winner."

"You're saying she's a bad judge of character when it comes to men?"

Gus raised an eyebrow. "I don't know who he is," she conceded, jutting her chin in the direction of Monica's table. "He's not a local. But he seemed pleasant enough when he was here at the bar a couple of nights ago. Had a bourbon and a beer chaser, and made polite small talk with Margie Carerra, who was all over him like peel on an orange. And then a song came on the jukebox."

"Don't start with that nutty jukebox crap," Ed said, wincing at how judgmental he sounded. That people believed the myth of the jukebox's magical powers brought customers to Gus's establishment, so he would never debunk the legend. But it was bullshit. He knew it, and Gus knew it.

She shrugged again. "He heard the song, and Monica was sitting right at that table, staring at him. What happened after that is anybody's guess, but there they are, side by side."

"Monica's too sensible to fall for the jukebox thing," Ed said, then gave Gus a measuring look. "While the guy was sitting here at the bar with Margie, did he say anything interesting? Anything that made an impression on you?"

Gus opened the register drawer and resumed counting her bills. "Nothing much. He tolerated Margie's come-ons, turned her down without hurting her feelings, said he was just passing through and running an errand."

Running an errand. An illegal errand? Ed wished the search warrant had turned up the drugs. He was sure they were somewhere on that boat. Danny Watson, the low-level dealer he'd arrested, who was scared shitless about going to prison and was knocking himself out to be helpful to the cops, had insisted that a shipment was coming north from Key Biscayne on a sailboat. He'd said his last shipment had been brought up from Miami on a boat, too, and that he'd been informed the next shipment would be entering the area through the port of Brogan's Point. He'd said he'd been told some guy named Smith would connect with him once the shipment had arrived, but Smith could be an alias. Probably was. As common as Smith was reputed to be, Ed had never met anyone with that name.

Was Tyler Cronin Smith? Or did the Smith pseudonym belong to Wayne MacArthur, the guy Cronin claimed had hired him to sail the boat to Brogan's Point?

Unlike Watson, Cronin had lawyered up. Caleb Solomon was sharp. Ed wasn't going to get more out of Cronin than he already had, not without a deal on the table.

He sighed and drank some coffee. Its rich flavor boosted his mood. "I've gotta go back to work," he said, draining the mug, leaning across the bar, and dropping a light kiss onto Gus's cheek. "I'll see you later tonight."

"I'll be here," she promised.

He slid off the stool. "Tell Monica to watch her step," he said before turning to leave.

He shot Cronin a hard look as he passed their table. Cronin stared back. Cool customer, Ed thought. The guy looked as innocent as a newborn baby.

Ed still hoped Monica would be careful. He'd been a cop long enough to know that guys who looked innocent usually weren't.

Ten

"I have to go back to work," Monica said, polishing off the last of her drink. She skimmed a couple of almonds from the top of the bowl of mixed nuts and popped them into her mouth, as if they would absorb the wine she'd consumed. But she wasn't feeling light-headed. If she'd hoped the wine would dull her senses, it hadn't.

Just as well. She *did* have to go back to work. God knew what shape Rose Cottage was in.

Ty chugged down his lemonade and stood to let her out of the booth. "I'll take you," he said. He gave Emma a regretful smile. "I wish I could give you a lift, too, but—"

"That's okay," she assured him. "I've got my own bike. The kind with pedals."

The afternoon was balmy, the sky a rich blue with just a few wispy clouds trimming it like ribbons of lace. Ty escorted both women out of the bar. He and Monica waved Emma off on her bicycle, and then he led Monica to a small black motorcycle with enough chrome trim to make her retinas ache. What appeared to be a bike lock fastened two battered helmets to one of the chrome bars supporting the padded seat back.

It wasn't much of a seat back, she thought with a twinge of apprehension. If she sat there, and the bike lurched forward abruptly, would she tumble over backward and hit the road? And while she was worrying, what about the odds of her falling off the side of the bike if Ty took a sharp turn? Not that there were many sharp turns between the tavern and the inn.

Forget about sharp turns. What if a car hit them? On the motorcycle they'd be utterly exposed. No roll bars. No chassis. No shatterproof glass. No air bags. No seatbelts.

While she fretted, Ty unlocked the chain that held the helmets and handed her one. Surely this bubble-shaped blob of padded plastic wouldn't keep her from dying in an accident. It wasn't as if the magic jukebox had played a motorcycle song, like "Born to Run," when her eyes had met Ty's inside the tavern a couple of days ago. It wasn't as if the jukebox's magic extended to making people indestructible.

Ty shot her a grin as he strapped the other helmet onto his own head. His helmet was a glossy black, hers blood-red. Like the color her pulpy, smashed-in skull would be once they crashed.

He slung one long leg over the padded seat, then peered over his shoulder. "Climb on," he invited her.

Don't be a wuss, she scolded herself as she strapped her helmet on with faintly trembling hands. If they crashed and she died, she wouldn't have to deal with the wrath of the Kolenko bridal party when they arrived at Rose Cottage next week and discovered gaping holes in the walls and a mysterious leak drip-drip-dripping down the pipes from a second-floor bathroom.

Mustering her courage with a deep breath, she straddled the thinly padded seat behind Ty. She leaned back, testing the seat back and deciding it was, indeed, insufficient and she was sure to fly over the rear fender of the motorcycle and go splat on the pavement. Instead, she leaned forward. Not so far forward that her chest pressed into Ty's spine. Just forward enough that she didn't have to feel that skimpy seat back.

He started the engine, which emitted a dull rumble. The seat vibrated under her, and she lurched slightly as he shifted into gear and eased away from the curb. She gripped his waist—only to keep from falling off, she told herself. And it was only because her arms weren't that long that she tilted forward and rested her cheek against the broad, strong surface of his back.

She didn't know him. She didn't trust him. She'd slept with him for no other reason than that, as Emma had pointed out, he was hot. That and the fact that she'd been celebrating the conclusion of her relationship with Jimmy. And the jukebox.

And the truth that no other man—not even Jimmy, definitely not Jimmy—had ever made her entire being, body and soul, feel so alive, so hungry, so consumed by lust, merely by gazing at her. No other man had ever turned her on the way Ty did.

And one other truth: that for once in her life, Monica didn't want to be a wuss. She didn't want to play it safe. She wanted to be wild.

All right. So there were a whole lot of reasons why she'd invited Ty back to her bed the night after the jukebox had serenaded them with "Wild Thing." For all those reasons, she pressed closer to him, felt his hips nestle in the hollow between her thighs, and breathed in his now familiar sea-breeze scent. And let the motorcycle hum against her bottom.

He steered down Atlantic Avenue, cruising at a modest speed. Although he wasn't racing, the wind blasted against her body and tugged at the fringe of her hair sticking out below the edge of the helmet. He drove past the entrance to the Ocean Bluff Inn, and Monica shouted a half-hearted, "Hey!" Perhaps he couldn't hear her over the growling engine. Or perhaps he just chose to ignore her.

She wasn't about to hop off a moving motorcycle. So she slid her hands a little further forward, until her palms rested against his sleek abs, and closed her eyes, and enjoyed the wind and Ty's warmth and the throb of the engine against her bottom. Her fear dissipated as she settled into the pleasure of the ride. She realized that she could fall in love with motorcycles if she let herself—more accurately, she could fall in love with sharing a motorcycle with Ty.

Less than a mile north of the inn, he pulled into the parking lot of the North Cove Marina and shifted the bike into neutral. It sputtered once or twice, as if protesting having to stop, then settled into a muted grumble. Ty stared across the asphalt to the building at its end, and then beyond it to the docks that extended out into the water in a neat, whitewashed grid.

Monica gazed out at the boats, too: tall sailboats, their masts empty and their ropes clanging. Deep sea fishing boats, their canopied cockpits high above the decks and their stern brackets waiting for someone to wedge sturdy saltwater rods into them. Pleasure cruisers boasting more living space than her tiny apartment at the inn.

Ty twisted to view her. "The inn is too close to the bar," he explained. "I wanted to give you a little ride before taking you back to work."

He'd given her a ride, all right. Hugging him, feeling the heat of him between her legs, and being whipped by the wind and vibrated by the bike's motor, she'd experienced quite a ride, indeed. Ty's smile implied that he knew exactly what she was thinking, what she'd been feeling.

His smile faded as he turned to look out at the water again. Tracing the angle of his gaze, she realized what he was looking at: one sailboat bobbing in its slip, with yellow police tape draped around it.

That must be the boat he'd sailed up from Florida. The boat he'd used to smuggle drugs to Brogan's Point.

Assuming he was guilty.

She told herself she didn't care if he was, but she *did* care. She wasn't as wild as she wished, certainly not wild enough to shrug off the possibility that she'd made love with a felon two nights ago. That she'd made love with him, that she'd willingly, if hesitantly, climbed onto the back of a motorcycle with him, that she currently had her arms wrapped snugly around him. He could have taken her anywhere. He could have ridden out of town and out of the state with her, and held her as a hostage.

The thought sent a ripple of emotion spinning through her, part fear and part excitement. Oddly, the fear was not of Ty, but rather of her own excitement at the thought of being abducted by him. What would she have done if he'd simply kept riding while she clung to him, and crossed the state line into New Hampshire and on into Maine, maybe all the way to Canada? She would have been free of all her responsibilities, all the expectations everyone had of her. Free of her reputation as a good girl, a nice girl, a hometown girl. Free to love Ty.

Not that he'd given her any indication that he loved her, or that he would welcome her love. He could sweep her off to Canada and then dump her, pursuing his adventures as a fugitive without her, while she purchased a bus ticket back to Brogan's Point and resumed her role as the good, nice, hometown girl.

Stupid fantasy. She wrenched her mind back into the present. "Is that the boat you sailed here?" she asked, pointing to the boat tied up in police tape.

He pulled off his helmet and ran a hand through his hair, his gaze fixed on the ribbon-wrapped sailboat bobbing gently in its slip. "That's it. I wanted to see if the cops have completely dismantled the thing. For all I knew, it could be sitting in pieces in the parking lot."

"Why would they do that?"

"Because they're so damned sure there are drugs on the boat, but they haven't found any."

She frowned. "Then why are they so sure there *are* drugs?"

He shrugged. "They believe their informant more than they believe me."

She stared at the boat. Except for the police tape, it looked innocent. More innocent than Ty himself looked.

He looked...dangerous. Straddling a motorbike, the ocean breezes tossing his hair, one hand fisted around the motorcycle's handle while the other cradled his helmet. Dangerous, yes, but he didn't look *guilty*.

What did she know? She was a lousy judge of men. How long had she stayed with Jimmy, believing he would grow up?

"Well," Ty said, his voice emerging on a resigned sigh. He lifted his helmet back onto his head. "The boat's still in one piece." Another sigh, and he turned the handle, causing the engine to whine. "I'll take you to the inn now."

So much for being abducted and whisked out of the country. Monica wouldn't get to find out whether the world would stop spinning if she was forced to abandon her life in Brogan's Point. She would go back to managing the inn's maintenance and learning everything she needed to know about running the place. She would revert to being her staid, well-behaved self. No biker-chick life on the lam for her. She told herself this was a good thing, but she wasn't quite convinced.

He took the drive back to the Ocean Bluff Inn at a slower pace. She treasured the minutes with him, her arms circling his waist, her legs sandwiching his hips. It didn't matter how sensible she tried to be, how good a girl she was, how dangerous Ty was. She wanted him. She wanted to be wild with him. And she shouldn't.

At the entrance to the inn, he cut the motorcycle's speed to a crawl and rolled up the driveway to the visitors' lot. She immediately spotted one of the guys from Parnelli's Plumbing standing on the veranda, talking to another man. The plumber had on a Parnelli's polo shirt, dark green with the company name and logo stitched into the fabric on the left side of his chest. The other man wore a long-sleeved plaid shirt and khakis. He was tall and thin, with a narrow nose and a border of neatly trimmed dark hair surrounding his bald spot.

Her father. Damn.

She loved her father. She'd been blessed to be born to two devoted, hard-working parents. But she didn't want her father to see her climb off the back of a motorcycle being driven by a guy suspected of a crime.

Too late. Her father spotted her, turned from the plumber and scowled. "Monica?"

Reluctantly, she dismounted and tugged the helmet off her head. "Hi, Dad. I just took a quick break. I've been at work since seven-thirty. It's crazy over at Rose Cottage. I needed a few minutes, that's all." She doubted her father cared about her taking a brief break during a long, difficult day. What he cared about—what caused his brow to sink more deeply into a frown—was that his precious daughter had been the passenger on a motorcycle driven by Ty Cronin.

Her father said nothing. He just watched her, disapproval ooz-ing from him.

Ty removed his helmet and climbed off the bike, as well. He seemed to sense that some diplomacy was called for. "Mr. Reinhart?"

Her father glowered at him.

"Tyler Cronin." He perched their helmets on the motorcycle seat and approached the steps to the veranda, his right hand extended. Monica remembered the first time he'd scaled those steps. She'd been sitting on one of the Adirondack chairs, mourning the death of her relationship with Jimmy, and suddenly there Ty had been, her wild thing. And she'd brought him back to her bed.

She told herself the heat in her cheeks was due not to a blush but to the wind's having chafed them during the ride. "Ty is a friend," she said, realizing how feeble that sounded. Her father had spent his entire life in this town, as had Monica. He knew who her friends were.

"Monica mentioned the situation in that cottage," Ty said. "I'm a carpenter. I thought I'd check it out, see if I could help get things back in shape once the plumber is done." He shot a quick smile at the guy from Parnelli's, who seemed just a bit too interested in mon-itoring the tension between Monica and her father. Not only did everyone in a small town know who was friends with whom, but they also knew who was pissed at whom—and they generously shared that knowledge whenever the opportunity presented itself. She could just imagine him telling all the guys at Parnelli's that the boss's daughter, Boss Junior, was spinning around town on the back of a motorbike driven by a stranger, and the boss was not a happy man.

"We have contractors we use," Monica's father said tightly.

"That's fine. I just thought I'd have a look." Ty gave her father a dazzling smile, but apparently it did not have the same effect on her father as it had on her. She was impressed by Ty's poise, though. He didn't seem at all rattled about being scrutinized and judged by the father of a woman he'd slept with just a couple of nights ago.

He probably didn't care what Monica's father thought of him. He'd be gone soon enough, anyway—back to Florida or to jail.

Lacking a better idea, she took her cue from him. "Come on, Ty," she said. "I'll show you the cottage." Before her father could intervene, Monica led Ty around the building. Once she was sure they were out of her father's range, she said, "Thanks."

Ty laughed. "I can't imagine why he didn't welcome me with open arms." As relaxed as he seemed, he peered over his shoulder to make sure they weren't being followed. "Is he going to come after me with a shotgun?"

"As far as I know, he doesn't own any guns."

"Phew." Ty mopped his brow with an exaggerated swipe of his hand, then surveyed the pool patio at the rear of the main building. The grounds crew had arranged lounge chairs and tables on the decorative slate surrounding the pool, although the chairs weren't wearing their cushions yet, and the tables weren't equipped with their sun umbrellas. That would all be taken care of next week, in time for the holiday weekend guests. The pool was filled, its water reflecting both the pool's blue walls below and the sky above, reminding her of the vivid, shimmering blue of Ty's eyes. "Wow, this is nice," he said, shifting his gaze from the patio to the acreage beyond, the azaleas blooming, the trees dotted with new leaves, the cottages nestled into the landscaping and the tennis court visible behind Hydrangea Cottage.

Monica used to appreciate the inn's beautiful grounds more when she hadn't been in charge of maintenance. Viewing them through Ty's eyes reminded her of how lovely the resort was. The cottages were homey white clapboard structures with small porches and peaked roofs. The lawns were a lush green, much healthier than they would look in a few months, once the summer heat had parched the grass. Her family and their staff worked hard to keep the place beautiful. The Ocean Bluff Inn was a destination, after all, not just a rent-a-bed at the end of a highway exit ramp.

She led Ty to Rose Cottage, which appeared deceptively intact from the outside. Inside, the parlor looked as bad as it had when she'd left to meet Emma an hour ago. The large rectangle of plasterboard that had been cut out of the wall lay on the floor; the hole exposed a skeleton of vertical beams, wiring and pipes. The furniture that usually stood in front of that wall had been moved to the other side of the room and left in a jumble of chairs, tables and ottomans. Thumping noises penetrated the ceiling from above, where the plumbers were apparently busy tearing apart the second-floor bathroom.

"Oh, this looks good," Ty said, crossing to the gaping hole. Monica eyed him skeptically, certain he was being sarcastic. But he actually seemed serious. "They did a neat job. Didn't mess with the I-beams, even though that left them a lot less space to access the pipes."

"This does not look like a neat job to me," Monica said, noticing the plaster dust scattered across the rug like confectioner's sugar.

"Trust me, it is." Ty ducked to peer inside the hole, then straightened up. "It'll be easy to fix. Fit the drywall back in, seal it, paint it. The only thing that's going to take much time is waiting for the plaster to dry. And the paint. The actual work'll be nothing."

"Really? Nothing?"

"A couple of hours of labor. Maybe not even that. Then waiting for stuff to dry." More thumping prompted him to glance up at the ceiling. "I don't know what the bathroom looks like. If you've got tile work in there, fixing that could be a pain in the ass."

"The plumbers removed the sink and vanity."

"All right, so that'll take a little time to replace. They'd have to hook up the sink. Putting in the vanity, though…Another couple of hours. You'll be fine."

Monica thought about the contractors the inn had always used. They never told her something could be done in a couple of hours and she'd be fine. They definitely never told her the actual work would be nothing. If they admitted that, they wouldn't be able to charge as much.

"The plumbers will probably reinstall the vanity. They'll have to hook up the sink, anyway," Ty said. "All you need a carpenter for is the walls. Patch them, paint them. I could do that for you in an afternoon."

She stepped back and regarded him, confused. Was he looking for work? Hoping she'd hire him? Did he need the money to pay for his lawyer, or the room he was renting in the main building? He had a trust fund, didn't he?

Evidently, he was able to read her mind. "I'd do it for free," he said.

"Why?"

He shrugged. "It's what I do. I enjoy it. Besides, I'm stuck here in town, anyway."

Stuck. Given an opportunity, he would have departed by now. He would have hopped on that motorcycle and headed...somewhere. Somewhere that wasn't Brogan's Point.

His gaze softened, his smile losing some of its brilliance but deepening as he lifted a hand to her cheek. He cupped it, his palm warm and strong against her skin, and then slid his fingers into her hair. "I'd do it for you," he said, then tipped her face up as he lowered his mouth to hers. His kiss began gently enough, but swiftly deepened, his tongue probing her lips, demanding entry. She gave it willingly, leaning into him, wrapping her arms around his waist, thinking that as fun as it had been to hug him while perched behind him on the motorcycle, embracing him face to face was much better. Embracing him while his mouth was conquering hers was much, much better.

She felt swamped by need, by yearning, by every sensation he'd awakened her the night he'd made love to her. How could she have deprived herself of him last night? Knowing he was under the same roof as she, just two floors separating them...What strange willpower had kept her from racing up the stairs to his room, or begging him to sneak downstairs to hers?

The strong muscles of his chest pressed into her breasts as he slid his free arm around her waist. His hand crept down to her bottom and guided her hips to his. She could feel the hard swell of his erection through her slacks and his jeans. His low groan implied that he knew she was as aroused as he.

A loud thump from above jolted them apart. A breath escaped him, half a sigh, half a laugh. "Wrong time, wrong place," he murmured.

Monica struggled to regain her bearings. What if, instead of a noise from the plumbers upstairs, they'd been interrupted by her father?

What if? She was twenty-seven years old. She could be with Ty if she wanted. She could do the unexpected. She could swoon over a sexy guy—and kiss him as if her life depended on it. "Figure out a right time and a right place," she said, pleasantly surprised by her own bravery. "I'll be there."

Eleven

When she returned to her office at the end of the day and saw the message light on her phone flashing, she knew the caller would not be Ty. They'd exchanged cell phone numbers before parting outside Rose Cottage. Given her father's apparent disapproval of him—or of his motorcycle, or of his having spirited Monica away from her work for a brief respite that afternoon—she thought it best that Ty not contact her on her business phone.

She lifted the receiver, punched in her code, and listened to the message: "Hi, sweetie. It's Mom. Let's have dinner tonight. We need to catch up."

Great. Her disapproving father must have informed her mother about their wild daughter straddling the back of a motorcycle and clinging to a tall, buff, sexy stranger. "Sure," Monica said. She might be a wild daughter, but she was also a dutiful one. "What time?"

"Just come on up whenever you're done for the day," her mother said. "I'll see you soon."

The apartment where Monica's parents lived occupied about a third of the top floor of the inn's main building. Growing up there, Monica had always known her home was a bit unusual—her friends had yards to play in, while she had acres and acres of resort property but couldn't organize kickball games or invite her playmates to splash in the pool if guests were using it. On the other hand, she and her friends used to love racing up and down the fourth-floor hall, playing hide-and-seek among the buildings or in the woods surrounding the cottages, and hanging out in the kitchen, where the Jerry and the other chefs would sneak them leftover desserts.

And no one expected them to be prim and quiet on the inn's private beach.

The apartment itself was spacious, filled with odd nooks and unexpected closets. Monica's old childhood bedroom, tucked beneath the eaves, featured an upholstered window seat wedged into a dormer window that overlooked the pool patio and the cottages beyond. Monica had spent many lazy hours curled up on that window seat, a book open in her lap while her daydreams carried her off. She'd imagined herself running the inn someday, ruling over all that acreage, all those buildings. All that history.

Her mother had furnished the apartment with pieces removed from guest rooms that had been renovated and furnishings from the public rooms once they no longer served their purpose. As a result, the rooms contained a hodgepodge of mismatched pieces, faded rugs, and a few antiques in need of tender loving care. But as eclectic as its décor was, the place was always clean and tidy. There were definite advantages to having a housekeeping staff at one's disposal.

Monica and her parents also had the dining room chefs at their disposal, but her mother enjoyed cooking and made frequent use of the small, outdated kitchen located at one end of the apartment, overlooking the driveway where it snaked around the side of the building to the staff lot. No stainless-steel appliances in that kitchen. No granite countertops. No sub-zero freezer or trash compactor or Viking range. But the stove, the refrigerator, and the sink worked, and that was adequate to feed a family of three.

When Monica arrived at the apartment, she found her mother in the kitchen, filling a large pot with water. "Pasta with clam sauce," her mother announced. "Louie picked up a ton of fresh clams down at the dock this morning. I asked him to buy some extra for us." Louie was the inn's sous-chef.

Monica nodded and kissed her mother's cheek. Her mother looked youthful in a pair of capri slacks and a Red Sox T-shirt, her hair tied back into a ponytail. Then again, her mother always looked youthful. Monica hoped she'd inherited her mother's smooth-skinned, energetic beauty, but she feared she took after her father more. At least she didn't have a bald spot like his.

Within a minute, her mother had armed her with a sharp knife and a pile of vegetables for a salad. While Monica rinsed the romaine and tomatoes, her mother chatted about the early summer bookings and shared some gossip. "Guess who was in this morning to discuss booking a wedding here?" she asked, then didn't wait for Monica to answer. "Nick Fiore, from the community center. He's thinking of a December wedding. Since most of the guests live in the area, he isn't worried about the weather. And this place can be so gorgeous in the winter. Warm and cozy in the main function room, while pristine white snow is piled up on the other side of the windows. Fires in all the fireplaces. It would be beautiful."

Monica hoped her mother wasn't leading toward mention of the lack of an imminent wedding in the Reinharts' immediate family.

"But here's the funny part," her mother continued. "Nick's fiancée—Diana something? They met when she was here checking out the place as a wedding venue for herself and some other fellow."

"I remember." Monica smiled and nodded, still bracing herself.

A good thing, too. "Speaking of weddings," her mother said as she peeled a couple of garlic cloves. "What's going on with you and Jimmy?"

"We broke up," Monica said.

Her mother nodded. She'd probably already heard gossip. She and Gus Naukonen were friends, and while Gus was pretty tight-lipped, she might have mentioned something to Monica's mother. "You've broken up before."

"This time it's for good."

Her mother turned her attention back to the pearly, teardrop-shaped cloves. As she minced them, the room filled with the tangy scent of garlic. "You've been with him a long time, sweetie. Do you really want to throw all that away?"

"I've been with him too long." Monica kept her attention focused on the tomato she was slicing. "We weren't growing. We weren't growing closer. We were just going along, same as always, in a rut. It's time for something new."

"Something new wouldn't happen to be riding a motorcycle, would it?"

Monica believed her mother truly did want to have dinner with her. But the real reason for this invitation was now clear—and it was what Monica had suspected. Her father must have informed her mother about Monica's new "friend."

Rolling her eyes, she swallowed the sarcastic whine that threatened to color her voice. "Mom," she said as calmly as she could. "I'm an adult. I'm allowed to make friends without checking in with you and Dad about it."

"Oh, I love that you're making friends," her mother agreed. "But riding on a motorcycle? Isn't that kind of dangerous?"

The real danger wasn't the motorcycle, Monica thought. It was Ty. His bedroom eyes. His seductive smile. His ability to make her toss caution aside.

And his possible criminality, added a small, nagging voice inside her skull—a voice that sounded uncomfortably like her mother's.

"Dad met Ty," she said, pleased that her tone remained level, neither defensive nor hostile. "He's a nice guy. He's in town for a few days. He's going to help me with Rose Cottage. He's a carpenter, and he says he can repair the wall once the plumbers are done there."

"Even though he's just a tourist? Why would he want to do that kind of work if he's only here for a few days?"

Monica couldn't very well tell her mother that he was stuck in Brogan's Point because he was under investigation for smuggling drugs into town—drugs no one had found, so they might not even exist. Nor could she tell her mother that Ty's desire to work on Rose Cottage's walls might be related to the fact that he and Monica had spent an orgasmic night together in her bed. "He enjoys the work," she said, assuming that was pretty close to the truth. "And...he's a good friend."

"A very good friend in a very short period of time." Her mother poured some olive oil into a skillet and added the garlic. More mouthwatering aromas plumed into the air. "If he's that good a friend, maybe we should invite him for dinner."

"We can think about it."

"I mean now," her mother said. "Louie gave me way too many clams. Does your friend like clams?"

—⁓—

"I'm sorry," Monica said. "I know this is last-minute, but my mother wants you to join us for dinner."

Ty turned off the motorcycle engine and digested Monica's words. He had decided to explore Brogan's Point a little, cruising around the winding, tree-lined streets, journeying along the waterfront well south of the marina and the inn and the restaurant Monica had taken him to for chowder last night. He'd set his cell phone on "vibrate" and stuffed it into a front pocket of his jeans. In his hip pocket, the phone's vibrations would melt right into the vibrations of the bike's engine against his butt. He'd never detect an incoming call.

He had to keep his phone close at all times, in case Caleb Solomon needed to reach him with news about his legal predicament. But the truth was, he was far more eager to hear from Monica. They hadn't figured out their plans for tonight yet, although when he'd departed from that flower-named cottage at the inn, he'd done so with the assumption that those plans would include hours spent naked and sweaty and gasping for breath. Just kissing her for a few seconds in the cottage had turned him on like a light—the sort of blinding light stadiums relied on for night games. He'd glowed with it, blazed with it. If there hadn't been workmen banging around upstairs, he would have dragged her onto the sofa across the room from the broken wall and done the naked, sweaty, gasping-for-air thing with her right there.

When his cell phone vibrated against his thigh, he pulled it out, saw who the caller was, grinned, tugged off his helmet, and shifted into neutral. When he heard Monica's invitation, he shut the bike's engine off completely. "Dinner?" he asked. "With your parents?"

"Spaghetti with clam sauce. It's delicious the way my mother makes it, if you like garlic."

"I like garlic," he said, although his mind was not on food. It was on Monica. And her parents. Christ, he hardly knew her, and now he was supposed to have dinner with *her parents?* "I got the impression your father wasn't my biggest fan," he muttered.

"The invitation came from my mother. I'm in her apartment now. In another room," Monica added, although she lowered her voice slightly. "You can say no if you want."

Gazing out at the tranquil water lapping against a pebbly stretch of coastline, he mulled over the invitation. He wanted to say no, but he wanted to be with Monica even more. And he did like garlic. "What time?" he asked.

She gave him the details, assured him he didn't have to dress formally, and thanked him. After stuffing his phone back into his pocket and wedging his helmet back on, he ignited the bike's engine, pulled a U-turn, and steered back toward the heart of Brogan's Point. The wind coming off the ocean mixed with the stronger wind blasting his chin and neck below the helmet's eye shield. It carried a pleasant trace of warmth. Not the furnace heat of southern Florida at this time of year, but definitely a hint of summer.

The road paralleling the coastline wasn't clogged with vehicles, but he shared the pavement with enough cars to have to remain below the speed limit. This must be what passed for rush hour in a small New England town, he thought.

He didn't mind the traffic. He needed to think.

Why had he agreed to have dinner with Monica's parents? The obvious answer was that he wanted to have dinner with Monica, and accepting her parents' invitation was the only way he could accomplish that. But Ty didn't trust obvious answers.

More than spending mealtime with Monica, he realized that he wanted to prove her father wrong. He didn't know exactly what her father thought of him, whatever it was, Ty suspected it wasn't good. He wanted to turn the old man around. It was a challenge. It would be fun to prove to Mr. Reinhart that Ty knew to spread his napkin across his lap and chew with his mouth closed. His grandparents drilled good manners into him during those stultifying years in Kansas.

It was more instinct than any brainwashing on his grandparents' part that guided him into a parking space when he spotted a florist shop. Survival instinct. Bringing Monica's mother some flowers might earn him her approval. He reminded himself that he didn't have to go out of his way to impress the Reinharts; they weren't going to be a part of his life for very long. Sooner or later, he'd be exonerated and allowed to return to Florida. But for as long as he was stuck in Brogan's Point, he intended to spend time with Monica, and if bringing a smile to her mother's face made that easier, he'd do it.

Five minutes later and fifty dollars lighter, he strapped a bundle of flowers wrapped in green tissue and protective cellophane to the back seat of the bike and continued up Atlantic Avenue, past the downtown shops, past the rows of modest three-story row houses squeezed shoulder-to-shoulder along the sidewalk across the road from the sea wall, past larger houses with broad green lawns, and onto the driveway leading to the inn. He parked in the visitors' lot, carefully gathered the flowers from the back seat, and jogged up the porch steps into the main building and up two more flights of stairs to his third-floor room. The inn had an elevator, but he needed to burn off some nervous energy. Stairs were good for that.

In his room, he checked his watch. He had time for a very quick shower, and after tooling around on the bike—and poking around the ravaged wall of the cottage, which he could see from his window—he felt a shower was called for. A shave. A fresh shirt, which was unfortunately wrinkled from having spent too much time crammed into his duffel bag. When he'd packed for the sail, he hadn't expected to be spending multiple days in Brogan's Point.

He'd noticed an iron and board in the room's closet. Screw that. He wasn't going to knock himself out just to present himself to Monica's parents in a pressed shirt. At least the damn thing was clean.

After his shower, his hair was wet, and he debated whether it would be more gauche to arrive at Monica's parents' apartment late, or to arrive on time with wet hair. He toweled his hair as he best he could, slapped on some aftershave, grabbed the flowers, and climbed one more flight of stairs.

Judging by the placement of the door, the apartment consumed a full third of the fourth floor. He thought of his apartment back in Miami—a one-bedroom on the second floor of a square lemon-yellow building overlooking a noisy side street. No balcony, but the building's stairwell was open-air. Landscaping consisted of a couple of squat, sickly palm trees flanking the entry. He rented month to month, which he preferred to a lease. Wherever he lived, he liked knowing he could take off the instant he felt the time to move on had arrived.

He pressed the doorbell, then raked a hand through his hair. Still damp. He should have taken the time to dry it. A drawstring sack hanging from a hook in his room's bathroom held a compact hair drier. It would have taken only five minutes, and—

Why was he so concerned about making a good impression on Monica's parents?

The challenge, he reminded himself, catching a sweet whiff of the bouquet's perfume.

The door swung inward. Seeing Monica, he forgot about the flowers, about making a good impression, about everything except the way he'd felt kissing her a few hours ago, the way he'd felt bedding her a few nights ago. Just one look at her smooth, mink-black hair, the elegant angles of her face, the slender grace of her body, her tentative smile as she gazed up at him…He reflexively reached for her, and she took a discreet step back and said, in a clear, firm voice, "Come on in. My parents can't wait to meet you."

That sure put a damper on his lust. Her father had already met him, and Ty was sure the guy would have been happy to wait a nice, long time before having to meet him again. As for her mother, Ty didn't know.

"I brought these for your mom," he said, joining Monica in the entry to the apartment. The floor was a burnished hardwood—oak, he'd guess—covered with a patterned rug. Amber lamps added to the fading daylight that seeped through the windows of the living room beyond the foyer. As Monica led him into that room, the scent of the flowers was overpowered by the aroma of garlic drifting from the kitchen.

Monica's father was working the cork out of a bottle of wine beside a formal dining table in an alcove off the living room. The cork gave with a gentle pop, and he set down the bottle and shot Ty a smile that looked forced. "So we meet again," he said.

"It's a pleasure," Ty said, extending his right hand and then realizing he was holding the flowers in it. With a grin, he shifted the flowers to his left hand, freeing him to shake hands with Mr. Reinhart.

Her father seemed taken aback by the flowers. "How thoughtful," he said, then called into the kitchen. "Cheryl? Tyler is here and he's brought you flowers."

"Flowers!" Monica's mother bounded out of the kitchen. Monica hadn't been kidding when she'd told Ty this would be an informal gathering. Her mother was dressed in clothes suited for an exercise walk on the beach, or maybe for spending an hour cooking pasta with clam sauce, heavy on the garlic. The smile she gave Ty was a much more genuine than her husband's, and her eyes widened at the sight of the flowers. "Oh, they're lovely. How sweet of you. Monica, can you get a vase from the breakfront?"

The next few minutes were a jumble of activity and instructions and food being carried to the table. "Don, honey, give the salad a final toss," she commanded her husband. "Monica, is there room on the table for the flowers? Maybe put them on the credenza for now. The bread is in the oven...where's the bread basket? Go ahead and pour the wine, Don."

Ty stood out of the way, watching the Reinharts moving in a smooth choreography, transporting the meal from the kitchen to the table. The dishware looked old, heavy cream-colored porcelain with a textured border. The table cloth was thick, the furniture solid and classic. In spite of the fact that the apartment was part of a hotel, the atmosphere was one of permanence. This was not just a residence. It was a home.

It was Monica's home, or at least the home where she'd grown up. For a brief, crazy moment, Ty experienced a twinge of envy. She had two parents. They used endearments when they addressed one another. They anticipated one another's moves and offered assistance. There was an intimacy in the way they interacted. Nothing he could identify, but he sensed it.

Had his parents been that way? When he thought about them, his memories shimmered with warmth. They had loved him. They hadn't been wealthy, but they'd been rich in affection. And it had all ended so suddenly. He hadn't felt any sort of permanence since then—not until he'd set foot inside Monica's parents' apartment.

Their home. *Her* home.

Twelve

"So, this inn has a private beach?" Ty asked once they'd finally extricated themselves from Monica's parents' apartment.

The dinner hadn't gone badly. Monica had had a moment of anxiety when Ty had shown up with his hair a tangle of long, damp locks, but he'd smelled so good—at her insistence, a few years ago, the inn had upgraded the courtesy bottles of shampoo and conditioner the housekeeping staff placed in the bathrooms, and now she was personally reaping the rewards every time she caught a whiff of his freshly washed hair's spicy fragrance. And bringing her mother flowers had been such a thoughtful gesture.

But mostly, things had gone well because, to her amazement, Ty and her parents had gotten along splendidly. Her parents hadn't been too nosy with their questions, and he'd been relaxed and generous with his answers. He'd told them about his carpentry business in Florida, the fine detail and finishing work he was known for both in boat restorations and in the luxury residences he worked on. He described the hand-carved newel post he'd created for the bridal staircase in the mansion of a well-known fashion designer, and the teak cabinetry he'd constructed for the yacht of a hedge fund manager. He didn't mention his rootlessness, but he did tell her parents that this was his first visit to New England, which gave them the opportunity to sing the region's praises. They were in the hospitality and vacation business; they loved telling everyone how magnificent New England was.

Ty had complimented Monica's mother's cooking. He'd sipped his wine. He'd insisted he was stuffed but still managed to accept a second cube-shaped chunk of tiramisu—baked downstairs in the resort's kitchen, Monica knew, but she kept her mouth shut when her mother allowed Ty to believe she herself had made the rich dessert. Monica's father was slightly less captivated by Ty than her mother was, but he'd treated Ty cordially and opted not to comment on the motorcycle Ty had been driving when he'd chauffeured Monica to the inn earlier that afternoon.

Finally, by eight-thirty, they'd made their escape. In the hallway outside her parents' door, Monica had wanted to hurl herself into his arms and kiss him senseless in gratitude. She realized she hadn't known him long enough to predict how he'd weather a dinner with her parents, but he'd been a true gentleman, wet hair notwithstanding.

And of course she wanted to kiss him senseless just because. Because he was Ty. Because sitting across the table from him for the past two hours had allowed her to gaze into his crystalline eyes, to imagine the solid sculpture of his torso beneath his loose-fitting shirt, to brush her feet against his under the tablecloth. Because being within ten feet of Ty—hell, being within ten miles of him—turned her on.

But she exercised restraint as they descended the stairs together. After such a filling meal, she appreciated the exercise. She'd appreciate another kind of exercise even more, but before she could drag him back to her apartment, he asked her about the beach.

"A small private beach, yes."

"Let's go look at it."

A bit of fresh evening air might cool her off, which wouldn't be such a bad thing, she thought as she led him down the final flight of stairs into the inn's lobby. The last traces of daylight colored the sky a pale lilac, interrupted by a few smudgy purple clouds. From the veranda, she escorted him along the path of crushed seashells that circumvented the guest lot and cut through a small garden of shrubs to a plank stairway that led down to the sand below. Long strands of beach grass covered the dunes.

A couple with a toddler in tow were on the beach. They rolled a plastic ball back and forth across the sand, and the little girl charged after it on her stubby legs, shrieking with laughter. The ocean was calm, the breeze gentle. Ty bent over to yank off his sneakers. "This is beautiful," he said, offering a hand to Monica so she could lean on him while she removed her shoes. The sand was chilly against the soles of her feet. Summer hadn't baked it yet.

She supposed it *was* beautiful. She was used to this beach, especially during the off season, when it wasn't crowded with guests of the inn. She was used to gathering here with her school friends, huddling beneath blankets on the sand on cold nights and racing barefoot along the water's edge on warm nights. She and Jimmy used to make out in the small, protected cove, and argue here. It was simply a part of her world, like the veranda and the dining room's tiramisu and every other aspect of growing up inside a classic old hotel.

Viewing the beach and the gray-green ocean beyond it through Ty's eyes made her appreciate it more. "You must go to the beach pretty often in Florida," she said.

"Not as much as I'd like." After stashing his shoes and hers beneath the stairs, he took her hand and strolled out onto the sand. "I haven't done much surfing since I left California. How's the surfing here?"

"It's not bad if there's a hurricane off shore," she told him. "We get big waves then."

"I bet." His eyes glowed. "Surfing during a hurricane. That must be fun."

Maybe, if you thought you were immortal. Ty was a daredevil. He'd probably love tackling the huge rollers that crashed into shore when a storm tore up the coast. Monica had never even attempted to surf. She'd always thought it seemed too dangerous.

Ty stopped and bent over to pluck an object out of the sand. Straightening, he handed it to her—a smooth brown oval of beach glass. She loved beach glass. How had he known? And how had he spotted the polished chip of glass in the waning light?

"Thank you," she said, closing her fingers around the treasure. She wanted to rise up on tiptoe and kiss him, but the presence of the couple and their giggling young daughter inhibited her. Unlike Ty, Monica wasn't fearless. Public displays of affection—even on a private beach—made her uncomfortable. She'd need a bit more wildness to shed her innate modesty

"So," he said, his fingers laced through hers, his gaze focused on the horizon, a growing a little less visible as the evening light continued to wane. "Why did your parents invite me for dinner?"

A blunt question, and it deserved an honest answer. "My father saw me on the back of your motorcycle. My mother heard I'd broken up with my old boyfriend. Clearly they thought further research was warranted."

He smiled at her wry remark, then glanced down at her. "Did I have anything to do with breaking you and your boyfriend up? Because, I mean—if a woman is with another guy, I keep my distance."

"No. We had already broken up when I met you." Just a day earlier, but Ty didn't have to know that. The break-up had had nothing to do with him. "How about you? Do you have a girlfriend in Florida?" Or, God forbid, a wife?

She didn't realize she was holding her breath until he said, "Nope. Same rule for me. I don't want to be on either end of a cheat."

Her lungs emptied with a sigh of relief. Ty might be wild, he might be footloose, he might be reckless and rootless and too sexy for her sanity. He might even be a criminal. Yet she sensed a moral core to him. Drugs or no drugs, he would not cheat on a woman.

A cold drop of water tapped her nose. They weren't that close to the ocean's edge, and the breeze wasn't strong enough to have carried sea spray across the sand onto them. She glanced up and realized that the encroaching darkness was only partly due to the sunset. Those purple clouds had expanded, rolling up the coast.

Another drop struck her cheek. From a few yards away, the voice of the woman drifted toward her and Ty: "Uh-oh! It's starting to drizzle."

"Uh-oh!" the little girl echoed, then giggled. "Uh-oh!" The man scooped up the child, who let out a bubbly laugh as he hoisted her onto his shoulders. "Uh-oh!" she bellowed. "Uh-oh!"

Monica considered rushing back to the stairs, but her feet seemed pinned to the sand. Or else she was pinned by Ty's gentle clasp of her hand. He seemed in no hurry to escape from the rain.

The couple and their daughter grinned at Monica and Ty as they jogged past, heading straight for the stairs. Another raindrop struck Monica, and another, and still she couldn't imagine seeking protection. Running indoors would be the safe, sane thing to do. She might not be daring enough to surf through a hurricane, but surely she could stand in the rain.

Ty gazed toward the stairs, watching the family escape from the beach. Then he turned back to Monica, lifted his hands to her cheeks, and cupped her face. The kiss she'd yearned for outside her parents' apartment—and inside it, and every moment since Ty had kissed her at Rose Cottage—arrived, and she welcomed it eagerly.

The fragrance of the gentle spring shower mingled with the ocean's briny perfume and with Ty's scent, clean and spicy and powerfully male. They kissed as the raindrops peppered them, kissed as the waves hissed and whooshed against the sand, kissed as their clothing grew damp and clung to their skin. Kissed as Ty lifted his hands to her hair and threaded his fingers through the damp locks. Kissed as he rocked his hips to hers, as she felt his hardness. Kissed as she wrapped her hands around his waist and chased his tongue with hers, and felt herself becoming wet in places the rain couldn't reach.

"You make me crazy," he whispered, tilting her head back and grazing the skin beneath her jaw.

You make me sane, she thought, but only clung more tightly to him, probing the taut muscles of his lower back through his soggy shirt.

He dipped his head lower, nibbling a path along her sternum. The sky had grown even darker, clouds obliterating the moon. He pulled his hands from her hair and unfastened a few buttons of her shirt, opening it far enough to expose her bra. He tugged the cups downward, freeing her breasts, and nuzzled them, first one and the other, and then the hollow between them as his thumbs brushed her nipples.

Her legs trembled, strength draining from them as all her energy centered on where Ty was kissing her, touching her—and where she wanted him touching her. She moaned, and he released her breasts and tucked his hands around her bottom, lifting her off her feet. She wrapped his legs around his waist and he carried her toward the stairs.

She tried to calculate the distance between the beach and her bed. She tried to collect her wits enough to consider buttoning her blouse, in case she and Ty encountered anyone between here and there.

Apparently, he thought the distance to her apartment was too great. At the stairs, he turned and settled onto a lower step, holding Monica in his lap, her legs still around him. His mouth remained on hers, hot and hungry.

"Ty," she whispered.

He worked open the fly of her slacks and slid one hand inside, under the elastic of her panties. He found her, soaked and swollen, his thumb playing over her, his fingers plunging.

She choked out a cry. She was coming, here on the hard wood steps to the beach, on Ty's lap. She was coming, and he wasn't with her, and she couldn't stop writhing against him, couldn't stop the sensations from crashing through her with more force than the surf during a stage-five hurricane.

She didn't need the thrill of surfing. She had this. She had him.

As the deep, wrenching spasms subsided, she leaned against him, struggling to breathe. He kept his hand where it was, calming, soothing. When her heart finally stopped its galloping pace and her respiration slowed, she murmured, "Wow."

"Yeah." She couldn't see his face, but she could hear his smile.

The rain fell quietly around them, against them. She rested her head on his shoulder and tried to think of anywhere she'd rather be. She came up blank.

As if he could read her mind, Ty said, "I like this place. I like the inn. I like the beach." He brushed a light kiss on her forehead. "I like these stairs."

"At the moment, so do I." At last she pulled back. Her shirt, saturated from the rain, weighed heavily against her skin. Her hair dripped down her back. Ty looked as waterlogged as she felt. "Open your fly."

"That's okay, Monica, I—"

"Open it." She tugged at his belt, but her hands were shaking. Her soul was perfectly steady, however. She felt sure of herself. She felt wild.

Ty must have seen her determination in her expression, because he dutifully unzipped his jeans. She reached inside and he sprang free, warm and steel-hard. She stroked the length of him, then bowed and opened her mouth over him.

A ragged groan escaped him as she took him in. He was warm, salty, silky. Large, yet he didn't choke her. She'd never much liked doing this with Jimmy, but he'd loved it and she'd accommodated him. With Ty, though—it felt right. He tasted wonderful. She was driven by the need to make him as delirious with pleasure as he'd made her. The need, the desire, the excitement. Rain beat down on her as she swirled her tongue over his tip and then down the length of him. She tightened her lips. He groaned again.

It didn't take long before he was gone, pulsing into her, his fingers fisting in her hair. Feeling his climax and hearing him groan again turned her on as much as his caresses had.

God, yes, she liked these stairs.

And she liked being wild.

Thirteen

The next day he worked on the wall in Rose Cottage.

He would have preferred to spend the whole day in bed with Monica. After that crazy, amazing interlude on the beach, they'd raced back to her apartment, as wet as shipwreck victims by the time they'd reached her door at the end of the back hallway. Wet was fine with Ty, though. What else could you do when your clothing was soaked but strip that clothing off? No more than fifteen seconds after Monica had turned the bolt to lock them inside her apartment, they'd been naked, toweling each other off before they tumbled onto the bed and went at it for real.

He wouldn't mind being shipwrecked with her. Stranded on a remote island, living on coconuts, bananas, fish, and sex. Yeah, he could enjoy that.

But he also enjoyed the comfort of her bed, the cozy thickness of the comforter, the plush down pillows. He could imagine spending every night in Monica's bed and waking up every morning with her in his arms, her velvety skin pressed against his, her silky hair tickling his chin. He could imagine doing this for a long time.

That wasn't like him. He never did *anything* for a long time. He'd known women—known them longer than he'd known Monica—and had fun with them, and then parted ways with them, always amicably, always with good wishes and pleasant memories. The women he'd been with always knew going in that he wasn't a forever kind of guy, or even a long-time kind of guy. The women he'd been with didn't have parents who'd invited him for dinner.

That was another weird thing. He'd liked Monica's parents. He'd liked having dinner with them.

Imagine growing up in a spacious, elegant apartment in the resort where your family worked. Imagine returning to that resort as an adult and living in another, smaller apartment in the same building. Imagine having roots as deep as a pine tree's, anchoring you to a place you loved. And knowing your parents were there, eager to meet your friends, to make sure those friends were good enough for their daughter.

A gut-deep pang of longing seized Ty. He'd known something like that as a child, known his parents adored him, known a feeling of permanence, a sense of home. But it had all been snatched away from him. He'd eventually come to believe that surviving the accident was all the compensation he was going to get in exchange for having lost his parents—and since it was all he was going to get, he made sure it was all he needed.

But a home, a real home, a soul-deep knowledge that you belonged somewhere...Man, that would be sweet.

He gave his head a shake to clear it and surveyed the equipment he'd gathered from the maintenance building on the premises. Monica had brought him there and told him to help himself. Surveying the shelves, he'd felt like a kid in a toy store. So much gear, so many tools, all of them well maintained and neatly stored.

Back in Florida, he'd strap his tool box to the back of his Rebel and motor over to a job, and hope that everything he'd ordered for the job showed up by the time he needed it. At the Ocean Bluff Inn, everything was already at hand: sacks of plaster; trowels; a bucket to stir the mud, as construction guys called wet plaster; a ladder; a drop cloth; paint; brushes; rollers; stirrers.

Imagine living in a place that had everything you needed—and every*one* you needed. Imagine knowing that place was *your* place, feeling it in your marrow. Never wanting to leave.

Another sharp shake of his head, and he set about to work, unfolding the drop cloth to protect the hardwood floor beneath the hole the plumbers had cut into the wall. They'd finally located and repaired the leak in a pipe that extended from the second-floor bathroom sink down to the cellar of the cottage. It had warped the bathroom floor slightly upstairs, but Ty assumed the floor would settle back down once it had dried thoroughly, and the vanity would cover any water stains left behind.

The plumbers had done a neat job when they'd opened up the parlor wall, cleanly slicing the drywall and setting the piece they removed aside to be reused. He'd be able to cheat a bit, smoothing the mud into the drywall so he wouldn't have to extend the patch too far beyond the perimeter of the cut. He'd need to paint the entire wall, though. Possibly the entire room. He'd have to see how the paint dried, whether it matched up with the other three walls, how many coats it would take to cover the patch.

Monica had told him not to knock himself out. She had a maintenance staff who could do the painting. But they were busy overseeing other tasks in the run-up to the resort's big summer season. Besides, Ty wanted to do this—not just for her, but because… Because this was her home, and he wanted to leave his mark on it.

Before patching the hole, he reached inside and smoothed out the insulation, which had been shoved aside when the plumbers had been searching for the leak. The fleecy strips of pink fiber felt dry to him, and they settled back into place around the pipes. He used the flashlight app on his phone to inspect the floor in the space between the inner and outer walls, to make sure no one had dropped anything there. Workmen sometimes left tools behind, or pocket change, or rags. Once the wall was sealed, any junk left behind would be trapped inside the wall forever—or until the next leak, when the wall got cut open again.

No junk. No treasures, either. No wads of cash, no jewelry, no stolen artwork.

No drugs.

As he troweled the mud onto the wall, smearing and smoothing, smearing and smoothing, his mind revved into high gear. If someone wanted to stash heroin somewhere, they could do worse than to hide it in the hollow behind a wallboard. If someone wanted to stash heroin on a boat, to have the drugs transported north without the boat's captain-crew-passenger knowing it was there…

The Freedom didn't have a lot of empty space behind its walls. Its design was streamlined and efficient. Every cubic inch that wasn't filled with gear was accessible for storage. The outer seats lifted up on hinges, and beneath them were storage bins. The space under the sleeping bench in the cabin provided more storage space. The galley was equipped with a mini-fridge and a microwave running off a small generator, and a few cramped cabinets in which Ty had stored utensils and food. The only area that didn't open up for storage, as far as Ty knew, was the panel behind the toilet in the head. The only purpose of that panel was to allow a plumber access if something went wrong with the pipes.

No one would be stupid enough to secrete a shipment of drugs where there were pipes, right? As Monica had learned the hard way, pipes developed leaks. A leak could destroy that illicit cargo, unless the drugs were wrapped up really well, in waterproof layers of plastic or canvas.

Last he'd heard, the cops hadn't discovered any heroin on the Freedom. Some clown had sworn to them that heroin had been carried to Brogan's Point on the boat, but as far as Ty knew, Nolan and his fellow officers of the law hadn't found it. If they had, Ty wouldn't be plastering a wall right now, and he wouldn't have spent last night doing sweaty, X-rated things in bed with Monica. He'd be behind bars, charged with drug smuggling.

But what if there *was* heroin? It might be behind the toilet, in the one region of the boat Ty hadn't become intimately acquainted with during his week-long sail, the one place no one would think to look. The one place no one *could* look if he didn't pry the panel off.

Ty finished spreading the mud on the wall, then stepped back and inspected his work from several angles to make sure it was perfectly smooth. Fortunately, last night's rain had ended and the air was dry. The plaster would dry in less than a half hour.

He wiped his hands on a rag, then carried his tools into the kitchenette off the parlor, washed and dried them. Returning to the parlor, he studied his work, and imagined the space behind the wall. He pulled his cell phone from the pocket of his old jeans and punched in the number of Caleb Solomon's law office.

The receptionist put him through. "No news," Solomon informed him, then contradicted himself. "I take that back. Detective Nolan told me the police down in Key Biscayne have been monitoring your buddy, Wayne MacArthur. He's bought a plane ticket to Boston, arriving Saturday afternoon."

"Is that good or bad?" Ty asked.

"Good. He's coming up here. Nolan can turn his attention to him. Maybe he'll retrieve his heroin, assuming it even exists, and the police will catch him red-handed, and he'll confess. Wouldn't that be nice?"

Sure, it would be nice. It wasn't going to happen, though. "I had this thought," Ty said, then hesitated. Was he nuts even to mention it? "If there's heroin on the boat, I think I know where it might be hidden."

Solomon didn't say anything for a moment. "All right. This could go one of two ways. One way, the police decide you're so helpful and cooperative, they stop suspecting you. The other way, the police say, 'Of course you know where the heroin is hidden. You transported it here.'"

"The thing is, I never saw drugs on the boat. I never had a clue there were drugs on the boat. But if Wayne was moving them up to Brogan's Point, he wouldn't have had to tell me about them. All he needed me to do was sail the boat—and hide them someplace where I wouldn't find them. I think I've figured out where that place might be."

"Okay." Solomon thought some more. "Don't do anything. Let me talk to Nolan and get back to you."

Ty thanked the lawyer, then thumbed the disconnect icon and stuffed his phone back into his pocket. Restless, he stepped outside the cottage. From its front porch spread a vista of soft, green grass, well-tended flower beds bright with azaleas, tulips and crocuses, and trees lush with new spring leaves. The swimming pool spread across the flagstone patio, its bright blue practically a mirror of the cloud-less sky. Comfortable-looking lounge chairs and tables furnished the patio, and beyond that the inn's main building sprawled like a New England palace—white clapboard, black shutters, sloping slate roof.

Squinting, he could guess which window belonged to Monica's apartment. His own apartment down in Florida wasn't much big-ger, but he didn't spend that much time in it, anyway. There were always parties, bars, people hanging out on the beach, women issu-ing invitations. That apartment didn't feel like home. He'd never expected it to.

Why did Monica's apartment feel like home to him? Why did he want to stay there?

Why did the thought of clearing his name, turning in his rented motorcycle, and flying back to Miami depress him?

He turned and reentered the cottage. The plaster already felt dry. He planted a can of paint on the drop cloth, used a screw-driver to pry off the lid, and reached for a stirrer. When his cell phone rang, he pressed the lid back onto the can, straightened and answered. "Nolan wants to meet with us at the marina," Solomon said.

—⁂—

Ed had told Caleb Solomon to have his client down at the North Cove Marina at four o'clock. The boat had been sitting there since the day Cronin had sailed it into the slip, impounded but not exactly under lock and key. The Brogan's Point police force didn't have the manpower to keep a guard stationed beside the boat twenty-four-seven.

If Cronin knew where the drugs were on it, he could have slipped past the police tape under cover of darkness, sneaked on board, removed the stash and tossed it into the sea. Losing a few hundred thousand dollars of smack would hurt, but not as much as a conviction.

If Cronin was just the courier, of course, he wouldn't be losing a few hundred grand. He'd already gotten his payoff from MacArthur. So dumping the smack would have been the smart move—if he wanted to avoid prosecution.

But he'd sworn he was innocent. And volunteering to help the police wasn't the sort of thing a guilty guy would do. At least not unless he was truly Machiavellian. Cronin seemed smart, but he didn't strike Ed as a shrewd schemer.

In any case, it was only three-thirty, which gave Ed a half-hour to kill before he met Cronin and his lawyer. Well, twenty minutes. It would take him some time to get from the Faulk Street Tavern to the marina.

The tavern was nearly empty, as it usually was at this time of day. At night, you had to elbow your way through a mob to reach the bar. But mid-afternoon, the only patron in the room was Carl Stanton, slumped on a stool at the far end of the bar, staring blankly into a glass of something alcoholic. Carl started his drinking early and ended it early—because Gus made sure to end it for him.

Ed once asked Gus why she even bothered to open as early as she did. She said she usually made a few bucks around noon—some folks were determined to drink their lunches—and she liked the quiet afternoons. They gave her and Manny a chance to check inventory, set up, prep the snacks she served in the evenings, and wait the occasional table. When Gus had begun her career at the Faulk Street Tavern, she'd been a waitress. Within a few weeks, the owner of the place had become smitten with her; within a few months, they'd been married. She'd learned the business when she wasn't raising her sons, and when her husband died, she'd slid smoothly into the role of proprietor and boss. But she still knew how to take an order and wield a tray. Waiting tables brought her back, she told Ed, made her feel young again.

She was plenty young enough, as far as he was concerned. But then, he was the guy smitten with her now. One of these days, he'd get her to marry him. He'd proposed a few times, but she always shrugged and said she saw no need for the piece of paper. It wasn't as if they were going to be having any kids together, and merging their finances would only complicate matters for their families after they died.

He spotted her behind the bar as soon as he entered the tavern. She was as tall as a high-fashion model, and just as appealing to him, although she always laughed and shook her head when he complimented her appearance. "I'm going gray," she'd remind him, but he liked the threads of silver glittering in her short, tawny hair. He liked the angles of her face, the faint lines crinkling the corners of her eyes. He liked what she had under her clothes, too, but she got embarrassed whenever he mentioned that. Not embarrassed enough to deprive him of the pleasures of her body, but embarrassed enough to blush and shove him away and tell him he was embarrassing her.

She was reading something on a computer tablet as he strode across the room, but glanced up as he neared the bar and shot him a smile. "Coffee?"

"You know me too well," he said, grinning and settling onto a stool.

She filled a mug with steaming coffee and slid it across the bar's polished surface. Hot, black, and unsweetened, the way he liked it. Then she glanced at her tablet, tapped a button, and gave her full attention to him. "My wine distributor's offering some serious discounts," she said, gesturing toward the device. "I'm stocking up."

Ed nodded.

Gus filled a second mug with coffee, blew lightly on the surface and took a delicate sip. The information about her wine distributor's sale was more than she usually volunteered. She was a listener, not a talker, and a patient listener than that. If someone wanted to chat with her, she'd wait until he launched into a conversation. Silence didn't bother her. She had the perfect temperament to be a bartender.

"I'm heading down to North Cove Marina in a few," he told her. "I'm supposed to meet with that kid and his lawyer. The kid thinks he knows where the drugs might be stashed on the boat."

Gus took another sip. "If he smuggled the drugs, it makes sense he'd know where they were."

"Exactly."

She gave him a canny smile. "But he didn't smuggle the drugs, so he only *thinks* he knows where they are."

"That's his story." Ed took a slug of coffee. "If he shows me the drugs, what do I do? Arrest him or thank him? Or both?"

"He didn't smuggle the drugs," she said with surprising certainty.

"Don't be swayed by that mellow beachcomber attitude. The boy is trouble."

"You're sure of that, are you?"

"Yeah, I'm sure of that. He's roaring around town on a motor-cycle and hitting on Monica Reinhart. A nice, sweet girl like her—he can't give her what she wants. He's only passing through town, unless he winds up passing through the criminal justice system. What's he messing with her for?"

Gus said nothing for a moment, then: "Maybe *she's* messing with *him.*"

Ed's eyebrows shot up so fast his forehead ached. "What?"

"Maybe she's the wild one."

"Oh, come on. Monica Reinhart? Probably the only member of her generation who's never gotten a speeding ticket or a warning for underage drinking. Hometown girl. The sweetheart of Brogan's Point High. The daughter of the Reinharts of Ocean Bluff Inn."

"All of the above," Gus agreed. "But...she's got a wild streak."

Ed snorted. Gus was pretty talented when it came to reading people, but so was he. He had to be. That skill was a necessary part of his job, just as it was part of hers. "I just hope the Cronin kid doesn't break her heart," he said.

"If you arrest him, maybe you'll be the one breaking her heart."

"Or saving her from a really big mistake." He checked his watch, drained his cup and stood. He shot a glance down the bar to Stanton, then leaned across the bar and murmured, "Take his keys."

Gus patted the pocket of her apron. Ed heard the jingle of keys and smiled. "I've got his wife's number on speed-dial."

"He ought to get into treatment."

"I've recommended it a few times." She eyed Stanton and sighed. "His next refill is coffee, straight up."

"Then he's a lucky man. You make the best coffee in town." Ed brushed a kiss against Gus's cheek, turned, and sauntered toward the bar, wondering if Cronin was going to convince him of his innocence, the way he'd apparently convinced Gus.

Fourteen

Caleb Solomon was already at the marina when Ty motored into the parking lot and shut off the bike's engine. A few vehicles were parked in the lot above the docks, one of them the glossy black Beemer he'd seen his lawyer climb into the evening he'd rescued Ty from Detective Nolan's interrogation at the police station. He saw no police cars in the marina lot, though.

He took comfort in the fact that Solomon was prompt. Clearly, Solomon thought following up on Ty's hunch about where the drugs were hidden on the Freedom was a good idea. Or else he'd wanted to get to the marina early to keep an eye on Ty, to make sure he didn't say or do the wrong thing.

Ty was paying the guy by the hour—by the minute, probably. If he showed up at the marina early, those extra minutes would appear on the bill he presented to Ty once this shit was over. But if he cleared Ty's name, every penny would be worth it.

Solomon emerged from his car as Ty walked toward it. Once again, the lawyer had on a suit—and a tie, this time, although the knot was loosened and his shirt's collar button unfastened. Even so, Ty felt grungy in his old jeans and a gray T-shirt. He'd managed to slap the first coat of paint on the parlor wall he'd repaired, but as it dried, he'd acknowledged that he'd need to add a second coat to cover the patch adequately. The other three walls of the cottage parlor would require a coat of paint, too, to match the repaired wall. He could get the rest of the painting done in the evening, if this meeting didn't take too long, and it if didn't end with him in handcuffs.

He'd rather spend the evening with Monica than painting a room in the resort cottage. But getting the cottage back into shape before the first guests arrived was more important than his own pleasure. The second-floor bathroom needed some touching-up, too. The plumbers had reinstalled the vanity under the sink, but the walls had a few dings.

If Ty *did* wind up arrested by the end of the afternoon, Monica's regular maintenance staffers could finish fixing the cottage walls. But Ty wanted to do it. He believed in completing what he'd begun. More important, restoring the cottage meant a lot to Monica. He wanted to be her hero.

He shook the lawyer's hand. "You know the drill," Solomon said. "Don't touch anything unless I tell you it's okay. Don't say anything without my permission."

Ty nodded.

"I'm not sure how this is going to play," Solomon said, "and when you're a lawyer, that's a problem. We like to know our destination before we take the first step."

Ty nodded again. "I'm *not* a lawyer," he said. "I just—if I'm right about this, I want the drugs gone. I like this boat. I lived on it for a week. I got to know it inside and out. And I don't want drugs on it. It was my home, you know?" At least it had felt like a home to him back when he defined home as wherever he happened to be sleeping that night.

"What if you're wrong?" Solomon asked him. "What if we don't find the drugs?"

"Then there are no drugs on the boat," Ty said. He meant it, too. As he'd said, he knew the boat. There was no other place drugs could have been stashed on it without his having stumbled upon them.

"All right. Let's see how it goes. At the very least, you're winning points with the cops for being helpful. There's Detective Nolan now." He motioned toward the police cruiser turning off the road and into the parking lot.

Within a minute, the three of them were down on the dock, approaching the slip where the Freedom was tethered. Before Solomon could request it—before Ty could even think of it—Nolan handed Ty a pair of latex gloves and snapped a second pair onto his own hands. "You're not going to be touching anything, are you?" Nolan asked Solomon.

The lawyer smiled and shoved his hands into his trouser pockets. "I'll try not to."

Ty considered pointing out that every surface of the boat was likely already covered with his fingerprints—except, of course, for the space behind the toilet in the head, where he believed MacArthur would have hidden the drugs if there were, in fact, drugs on board. Ty knew that the absence of his fingerprints in that space wouldn't exonerate him. MacArthur could have stashed the drugs there and Ty could still be convicted of transporting them. But he appreciated that Nolan didn't want him adding his fingerprints to anything incriminating they might find behind the crapper.

Once he'd maneuvered his hands into the tight elastic gloves, he followed Nolan onto the boat, ducking under the yellow police tape. "I've got to get some tools," he said, climbing down into the cabin and lifting one of the benches. Beneath it was the storage bin where he'd stashed a small tool chest, in case he'd had to perform repairs on the boat while he'd been sailing it north. He knew where every storage bin on the boat was, and what was inside each one. Flares over here. Spare life vests in that compartment. Oatmeal and saltines in the galley cabinet. Canvas for patching sails folded neatly in that container. None of them contained any illegal drugs.

"What makes you think you know where the drugs are?" Nolan asked as Ty unlatched the tool chest and pulled out a couple of screwdrivers.

Ty obediently turned to Solomon, who nodded his permission to answer. "*If* there are drugs on board, this is the only place I can think of where they'd be," he told the cop. "It's the only place Wayne could have hidden them where I wouldn't find them. When Wayne hired me to make this run for him, I told him I could handle any sort of repair on the boat except a plumbing problem. I don't do plumbing. It's beyond me. So there's no way I'd open the panel behind the toilet."

"What would you have done if there *was* a plumbing problem while you were out at sea?" Nolan asked.

"I'd bring the boat into dock," Ty said.

"And then some plumber would come to repair the plumbing problem, and he'd find the drugs. Assuming they're where you think they are."

"Wayne told me he'd had the plumbing serviced a week before I was scheduled to sail. He's got a top of the line commode, the kind that treats raw sewage so it can be emptied at sea. That kind of toilet demands regular servicing, so I guess he'd taken care of that. He said if I had a plumbing problem, I should phone him from wherever I was moored and he would deal with it. But he swore to me there wouldn't be a problem."

"And there wasn't?"

"Lousy water pressure for the shower, but I expected that. It's a boat." Satisfied that he had the right size screwdrivers, he crossed to the cramped head. He'd forgotten how small it was. A few nights at the Ocean Bluff Inn—either in his own guest room or in Monica's apartment—had completely erased his memory of the inconveniences of living on a sailboat. He loved sailing, and when you were doing something you loved, you could ignore the fact that the bed you were sleeping on was really just a thick cushion on top of a hard bench, and the doorway into the cabin was low enough that if you didn't duck, you could knock yourself unconscious on the door frame. And that the bathroom was the size of a coffin and carried a faint whiff of mildew.

Ignoring the stale odor, he hunkered down in front of the toilet. The access panel behind the seat was stained the same color as the surrounding wall, camouflaging it so it was barely noticeable. The screws holding it in place were Philips-head, and Ty got to work with one of the screwdrivers. He could feel the cop and his lawyer behind him, even though he couldn't see them. The cop was close enough that Ty could practically sense the inch of air between their bodies pressing on his back. Did Nolan think he was going to do something stupid, like swallow the drugs if he found them? Or unearth a gun stashed inside the wall and blow the cop away?

Back off, he wanted to shout. *I'm doing you a favor here. Your idiot crime scene guys should have pulled off this panel.* But he knew he had to remain polite. He was doing Nolan this favor in the hope that Nolan would do him an even bigger favor: cross him off the suspect list.

As each screw came loose, he slid it into the chest pocket of his T-shirt so it wouldn't get lost. After removing the final screw, he eased the panel off the wall. Then he pulled out his cell phone, clicked on the flashlight app, just as he'd done at the cottage earlier that day, and took a peek inside.

Below the pipes that snaked out the back of the bowl, he saw two white bricks wrapped heavily in plastic. He sighed, edged back, and handed Nolan his phone. "Have a look."

Nolan squatted down beside him—hard to do in the confined space—and peeked into the opening. "Shit," he muttered.

Was Nolan disappointed? Sorry that Ty had found what his own officers couldn't? Ty peered up at Solomon, who shrugged, evidently as bewildered by the detective's curse as Ty was.

If anyone should be cursing, it was Ty. He'd just provided Nolan with the evidence the guy needed to slap those handcuffs on Ty's wrists.

Nolan reached his gloved hand into the opening and pulled out first one brick and then the other. He produced a plastic bag from his back pocket, slid the bricks carefully into it, folded down the edge and pressed an adhesive strip to seal it. Then he pulled out a pen and scribbled his name and the date and time across the seal. "These will have to go down to the state crime lab for testing," he said as he stood. His knees announced his age with a few clicks; he winced as he slowly straightened his legs.

"Yeah," Ty said. "It could be baking soda or something." Actually, it looked a little like the plaster powder he'd stirred into mud for the cottage wall earlier that day.

"But let's assume the obvious for now," Nolan said, his craggy face etched into a pensive frown. "I've got to take you in, Mr. Cronin. Sorry, but I have to."

Solomon clicked into high gear. "He's just handed you your case, detective. Without him, you had nothing. Now you can nail MacArthur to the wall. You should be thanking Tyler."

"Thank you," Nolan said, sounding surprisingly genuine. "I've still got to bring you in."

Ty knew he'd run the risk of arrest when he removed the panel. But if MacArthur was shipping illegal drugs—and using Ty as his unwitting delivery boy—Ty wanted the son of a bitch hung out to dry. He wanted him caught, convicted, and locked up for good.

"Look," he said. "I was in the middle of a repair job at the Ocean Bluff Inn. The room needs a coat of paint. Can I go back and finish that, at least?" Starting work on the bathroom upstairs was probably out of the question, but maybe the cop would let him get the parlor back into pristine shape, with no water stains or visible patching. "One hour, two tops. Then you can arrest me."

"I wish I could say yes." Nolan again sounded as if he really meant it. "And I'm not going to arrest you yet. First we have to find out whether this—" he lifted the evidence bag "—is baking soda. Then we'll see where we stand."

"My client is innocent," Solomon insisted. "Regardless of what the lab says."

"I hope so. But you know I can't let him go free while we get this stuff tested. If it's heroin, he could be long gone by the time the lab is done with it. For all I know, he could be setting MacArthur up by leading me to the evidence. Then he'll do a vanishing act and leave MacArthur to take the fall."

"I'm not that smart," Ty protested.

"Yes, you are," Nolan said. "So. I'm going to bring you down to the station and hold you without charging. We can hold you for seventy-two hours, by which time Mr. MacArthur will be in town. In the meantime, we'll get the lab to expedite the testing on this. I'll talk to the DA and the DEA guy down in Boston, and we'll see what we can do."

What they could do was keep Ty from finishing his work at the inn. What they could do was keep him from spending the night with Monica.

They could also keep him from returning to Florida. But that didn't bother him nearly as much.

"DEA?" he asked.

"Drug Enforcement Administration," Nolan explained. "In a case like this, they get involved."

Wonderful. A federal agency was now "involved," to use Nolan's euphemism. It seemed as if everything Ty did—even being helpful and finding the drugs for the cops—only pushed him deeper and deeper into a hole. Now he was going to have to cool his heels at the police station. For seventy-two freaking hours. While Rose Cottage still needed work. While Monica…

Hell. Once he returned to the police station, once he got locked up inside a holding cell, once the DA and some drug enforcement guy in Boston piled on, Monica wouldn't want anything to do with him. He knew he was just a fling for her, an experiment, a rebound dude after she'd ended things with her longtime boyfriend. But a second spell in the police station was probably more than she could tolerate.

Nolan thought Ty was smart. But Ty knew Monica was the smart one—smart enough to wash her hands of someone just passing through town. Someone who couldn't finish a repair job he'd promised her. Someone who couldn't seem to stay out of trouble.

Fifteen

Where was he?

Monica entered the Rose Cottage parlor and gazed around. The wall that had had a gaping hole in it that morning was now intact, smooth, and painted. But the room's other three walls were a slightly darker hue, and a ladder, tools, and a drop cloth cluttered the floor. The furniture huddled at one end of the room as if the chairs, sofas and tables were conferring on a football play.

Ty clearly wasn't done with the repair. But he was gone.

He'd said he would call her that afternoon, and like a lovesick teenager harboring a crush on the cutest senior in the school, she'd checked her cell phone dozens of times throughout the day. Maybe he'd left a message. Maybe he'd sent a text. Maybe she'd turned her phone off by accident, and that was why it hadn't rung. But no, the phone was on and it was working—and she had no missed calls, no messages. So, when she'd finally finished her other work, she'd abandoned her office and strolled past the pool and across the lawn to the cottage.

Which was empty. No plumbers. No workmen. No Ty.

Trying to ignore the knot of anxiety in her gut, she exited the cottage and circled around the main building to the guest lot. No motorcycle.

She took a deep breath and willed her eyes not to fill with tears. If he'd left, he'd left. He had never promised he would stay. He'd told her he was rootless and restless, not the kind of man who settled down. He was a wild thing, after all. She had never imagined that she could tame him. She'd never let herself dream that far into the future.

Why wouldn't he leave? It wasn't as if he'd been arrested. No bail money would be sacrificed if he took off. And good-byes could be so awkward, so painful. Why not just go while the going was good, turn in his rented motorcycle, cab down to Boston and fly back to Florida, where he could live until he decided it was time to move on again, to find some other town, some other woman, some other ocean to sail.

It would have been nice of him to finish his work on Rose Cottage, though.

Her phone abruptly trilled inside her purse, and like the lovesick schoolgirl she'd feared turning into, she felt the dark weight of hurt and anger lift off her heart and the sky open up, as bright as heaven. *He's calling! He's calling!* Pulling the phone out, she checked the caller-ID on the screen and saw his name. *It's him! He called!*

She took a deep breath to steady her nerves. Aware of how devastated she'd been when she'd thought he was gone, she cautioned herself not to be too thrilled that he *wasn't* gone. Sooner or later, he *would* be gone. She couldn't let herself want him so much.

But for now, just for this evening, she could let herself experience a moment of giddy joy. She pressed the connect button and lifted the phone to her ear. "Ty?"

"This is his attorney," came an unfamiliar male voice. "Caleb Solomon. He asked me to call you."

So much for giddy joy. The weight returned, heavy with foreboding. "What happened? Is he all right?"

"Things have gotten complicated," the lawyer said. "Drugs were found on the sailboat."

"Oh." What did that mean? What did it imply? Had Ty smuggled the drugs to Brogan's Point, after all? Was he as guilty as the police seemed to think?

What was the opposite of giddy joy? Whatever it was, that was what she was feeling now.

"He's being held at the police station for the time being, while the DA decides whether to charge him."

One sliver of her brain took a step back and assessed the lawyer's words. It seemed bizarre that Monica Reinhart, a well-behaved, by-the-book woman should be having a conversation about drugs and criminal charges with the attorney of a man with whom she'd recently enjoyed torrid sex, a man with whom she was this close to falling in love.

The rest of her brain clamored with panic, curses, a crazed blend of fear and hope. "So…he hasn't been arrested?"

"Not yet."

"I'm coming down to the police station," she said. "I need to see Ty."

The lawyer said nothing for a minute, and then, "Okay. I'll be here, too."

He hadn't told her not to come. He hadn't told her to give up, to accept that her hot blond lover was heading to the big house, the pen, up the river—whatever people called prison these days. What did she know about prison, anyway? Just what she'd viewed in old movies. *The Shawshank Redemption. The Green Mile. The Rock. Dead Man Walking.*

The infatuated-schoolgirl swooniness rose up inside her again. No matter that Ty was in trouble. No matter that Ty *was* trouble. He would have told his lawyer if he didn't want to see Monica. The lawyer would have urged her not to come—or he wouldn't have even called her. But he'd called, and when she'd said she would come to the police station, he'd said okay. She was going to see Ty. Even if he was a criminal. Even if he was the most dangerous man she'd ever known. Even if he could break her heart—because he had a hold on her heart in a way Jimmy never had.

She headed straight for her Subaru, cranked the engine and steered down the winding driveway to Atlantic Avenue. She didn't notice the ocean to her left, the waves curling onto the shore as the tide came in. She didn't notice the ocean's perfume, the scent of home. She didn't notice the puffy clouds rolling across the late-day blue of the sky, the steady stream of cars carrying workers home from their jobs, the pedestrians ambling down the sidewalk along the sea wall and savoring the view. She kept her eyes on the road ahead of her and her mind on her destination: Ty. In trouble.

Brogan Point's police station was a squat brick building down the street from the community center. The local police department had no need for anything huge or state-of-the-art. Most crime in town was petty: shoplifting, vandalism, underage drinking, the occasional scuffle. The closest the town had ever come to a murder in her lifetime was when Nick Fiore was convicted of attempted murder of his father. Nick had been a couple of years ahead of Monica in high school, and she'd never believed he was capable of such a crime. But his father had somehow gotten critically injured—the rumor in school was that Nick had beaten up his father because his father had been beating up Nick's mother—and he'd been diverted into the juvenile justice system, and everyone had been deeply shaken.

But Nick was still in town—according to Monica's mother, he was considering having his wedding at the Ocean Bluff Inn—and one of his closest friends in town was Ed Nolan, the police detective. Mr. Nolan was a fair man. Monica hoped he'd be fair with Ty.

More than that, she hoped Ty was innocent. She yearned to believed he was. But…she didn't really know.

She parked and entered the building. Behind a counter in the front room, a plump middle-aged woman in a uniform held a hand up to halt Monica, as if the officer was on a street corner directing traffic. "Can I help you?"

"I'm here to see…" What was Ty's attorney's name? Monica had hired the guy for Ty. She sifted through her memory until she recalled it. "Caleb Solomon. He's a lawyer—"

"Monica, yes," Caleb Solomon called out as he entered the room, his stride brisk and determined. His suit was slightly wrinkled, his tie loosened, his jaw shadowed by a day's growth of beard. He sent the uniformed officer behind the counter a mildly flirtatious smile that caused her to grin girlishly, and then joined Monica. "Let's talk," he said, taking her elbow and ushering her to a scratched wooden bench that stood against a pale green cinderblock wall. Once they were seated, he leaned toward her, speaking in a low voice. "Tyler came up with a good guess about where the drugs might have been hidden on the boat. A very good guess, as it turned out. He, Detective Nolan and I boarded the boat and found the drugs."

"Then he did a good thing. Why is he being arrested?"

"He hasn't been arrested. The police have the right to hold him without charging him for seventy-two hours. They're expediting a test on what Tyler found to make sure it really is heroin. Then I think they're planning to plant a decoy package—something that looks just like the drugs—in the same place on the boat. The boat's owner is flying into Boston Saturday—that's tomorrow, I guess," he added, checking the date on his watch. "The police will monitor him and see if he goes to the boat to retrieve the drugs. Then they'll arrest him."

"And they'll let Ty go?" she asked hopefully.

"Maybe. Maybe not. That the boat owner would retrieve the drugs doesn't necessarily exonerate Tyler."

"But he showed the police where the drugs were," she said.

"Which could indicate that he knew all along where they were. It doesn't clear him, Monica."

She sighed. Tears stung her eyes and she batted them to keep from sobbing. "What would clear him?"

"The boat's owner could. A Mr. Wayne MacArthur. He has a house here in Brogan's Point. Are you familiar with him?"

The name meant nothing to her. She shook her head. "If he has a house here, he doesn't stay at the inn. Is there any chance he'd clear Ty?"

Caleb Solomon shrugged. "We could hope he'd blurt out that Tyler had no knowledge of the drugs. But that's not likely. Drug dealers are rarely that honest and accommodating."

"What if Ty could get him to say something? Could the police put a wire on him?" If what she knew about prisons came from old movies, what she knew about police investigations came from TV cop shows. On those programs, the police often wired someone and then sat in a van, eavesdropping on the chatter until someone said something incriminating.

The lawyer smiled. "Ty suggested that himself. The police said no. They want to keep him under lock and key for now."

"Then I'll wear a wire," Monica said.

"What?"

"I'll do it. They can wire me. I can…" She thought for a moment. "I can pretend I want to buy some of his drugs. What kind of drug are we talking about?"

"We believe it's heroin. The crime lab will ascertain that. But you wearing a wire?" He considered the idea, winced, and shook his head.

"Why not? I could talk to the guy. I could get him to admit Ty knew nothing about the drugs." If she could ride on the back of a motorcycle, if she could go down on Ty on a beach in a rain storm, she could wear a wire.

"I don't know. It could be dangerous," the lawyer warned.

Monica smiled. "I can do it," she said.

—⁂—

Ten minutes later, Monica, Caleb Solomon, Detective Nolan and Ty sat around a table in a gray, windowless interrogation room. "No," Ty said emphatically.

"I'm telling you, I can do this," she insisted, trying hard to ignore her ghostly reflection in the mirror attached to the wall across from her. "I know how to act. I starred in a play in high school."

They all stared at her.

"*You Can't Take It With You.* I played Alice."

"I know that play," the lawyer said. "Isn't Alice the sweet young daughter? The only sane person in the family?"

Monica conceded that her portrayal of the only character in the play who wasn't wild had been a bit of type-casting on the director's part. But she'd proven in that production that she could act. And she'd acted patient with and tolerant of Jimmy all those years when he'd treated her like reliable old car, able to get him where he was going and easy to forget once it was parked in the garage.

Maybe all the years she'd been such a good girl were an act, too. Maybe she'd always been a little wild at heart, and she'd been performing a role all along. Closing her eyes, she heard the crashing guitar chords that opened the song she'd heard on the Faulk Street Tavern's juke box barely a week ago, chords and a gravelly, growly voice. *Wild Thing.*

"Let me do this. I'll tell the guy I want to buy some drugs from him."

"Does he sell directly?" Caleb Solomon asked. "It seems to me he hires other people to handle the grunt work. Sometimes in ignorance." He gave Ty a meaningful look.

"He had a local guy selling for him," Detective Nolan said. "A kid named Danny Watson. He worked on one of the trawlers out of port, and he sold drugs on the side. He's under arrest, though. He was the one who tipped us off about MacArthur's drugs. Only he said the guy's name was Smith." He, too, sent Ty a meaningful look. "Unless *you're* Smith."

Ty issued a long-suffering sigh. "I'm not Smith. I don't know who the hell Smith is. I don't know who the hell Danny Watson is, either." He turned to Monica, addressing her as if no one else was in the room. "I don't want you to do this," he said. "I've already told the cops I'll wear a wire and talk to him. There's no reason for you to get involved."

"I already am involved," she said.

His gaze tightened on her, his dazzling blue eyes so intense she could practically feel the heat of them on her cheeks as he searched her face. He must have figured out what she'd meant when she said she was involved: not involved with his legal issues. Involved with him.

Involved.

In love.

And she would help to clear his name, and then he'd leave.

Yet she couldn't *not* help. "It could go the other way, too," she pointed out to Detective Nolan and Caleb Solomon. "This Mr. MacArthur—or Mr. Smith—might wind up saying something that would prove Ty was guilty."

That possibility seemed to please Detective Nolan. He clearly believed Ty was complicit in the drug dealing. If there was a chance Monica could help to prove that, he would want her on his team. "All right," he said. "Let me talk to the DA and start the paperwork. As soon as we hear back from the crime lab, we can get this process rolling." He pushed back his chair, the wooden legs squeaking against the linoleum floor, and stood.

"Can I have a few minutes alone with Monica?" Ty asked, glancing from Detective Nolan to Caleb Solomon.

The lawyer turned to Detective Nolan. "He hasn't been charged," he reminded the policeman. "Give them a few minutes."

Detective Nolan pressed his lips together in disapproval, but started toward the door. He waved in the direction of the mirror and said, "I'll be keeping an eye on you."

Ty waited until the men left the room, shot an annoyed glance at the mirror, and then reached across the table and gathered Monica's hands in his. His touch turned her on, but more than that, it moved her. There was something sweet and gentle and protective about it.

"I don't want you to do this," he murmured.

"Why? Don't you want to nail that bastard?"

"Of course I do. But not if it puts you in danger."

"You'd rather rot in jail?"

"Than put you in danger? Yes."

His answer was so forthright, she fell deeper in love with him. Miles deeper. Light-years deeper.

She reminded herself once more that he was going to leave. If she was successful at getting the boat's owner to admit that Ty had nothing to do with the drugs, Ty would be released, free to go. Free to travel to wherever he wanted to live today, or tomorrow, or a week from now.

It didn't matter. She loved him. She would do what she could to exonerate him.

More than that..."I *want* to do this, Ty," she said. "Not just for you. For me."

"Why? Jeopardizing your safety—how is that good for you?"

"I heard the song," she said, struggling to find the words to explain. "At the bar. 'Wild Thing.' It—I don't know. It made me wild. It set me free. *You* set me free. And now I can set you free."

He studied her face, his hands tightening around hers, his thumbs brushing her wrists. The caress sent shivers of longing up her arms and into her heart. She wanted to climb over the table, settle in his lap, wrap her arms around him and kiss him until they were both gasping with pleasure.

But Detective Nolan and Caleb Solomon were watching them through the one-way mirror. So she only gave his hands a squeeze in response and said, "Trust me."

Sixteen

It wasn't that he didn't trust her. It was that he didn't trust MacArthur, or Nolan, or some guy from the Drug Enforcement Administration, or anyone else who could place Monica in danger if he made the slightest mistake.

And Ty could do nothing to protect her. He was stuck in this ugly holding cell. Not exactly luxury accommodations like what he'd had at the Ocean Bluff Inn—a room he'd used ridiculously little, since he'd spent most nights in her apartment. He should have brought her to his room for a night. He wondered if she'd ever experienced a night as a guest in her family's establishment. He wondered if sex with her would be different in a different bed. It sure as hell had been different on those wooden steps leading down to the beach.

His groin twinged with arousal. Not much he could do about that. He leaned back against the chilly wall behind the bench in the holding cell where he was seated, and where he would have to sleep. Did Nolan and his law-enforcement buddies honestly think Ty would flee the jurisdiction if they released him? If he'd intended to split, he could have been gone days ago. Why would he have first helped them find the drug stash if he planned to do a disappearing act?

Whatever. Caleb had told Ty the police could legally hold him without charging him. So here he was, being held.

He and the lawyer had reached the first-name stage. Caleb had even stopped back at the cell after he, Monica, and Nolan conferred with the guy from the DEA, and when Caleb had reappeared, he'd been carrying a large waxed-cardboard container of clam chowder from Riley's and a plastic spoon. This chowder wasn't as good as the stuff he'd had with Monica at the Lobster Shack, but it was a shitload better than the sandwich of bland meats and limp lettuce a uniformed officer had brought him. What had she called it? A grinder. Stupid name. In Florida, they'd call it a Cuban sandwich, and it would taste much better.

Not that he cared. He didn't have much appetite, anyway.

He heard the faint buzz of the fluorescent light fixture illuminating the corridor outside his cell, and the low din of voices yakking in the precinct room down the hall. Were they talking about him? Talking about Monica? Filing the paperwork that would allow her to wear a wire and walk into the lion's den?

How could he let her do that?

How could he stop her?

Why was she willing to take such a huge risk for him? Was it all a game to her? An extension of her high school theater experience? A big adventure?

Damn. *He* was her adventure. He'd taken her for a spin on a motorbike, and now she was getting to go undercover on a drug bust. File under: Big excitement for a small-town girl. Why else would she do this risky thing for him, when she knew he wasn't going to stay in Brogan's Point? He was her fling, her brief vacation from her sane, sober life.

In the distance, he heard a telephone ring. The sound triggered another memory, a song suddenly blasting through his skull: *Wild Thing*. He didn't believe in magic, let alone that a song or a jukebox could be magic. Yet that song...As the lyrics said, it made Monica's heart sing. Maybe Ty's, too.

He just hoped that, if she got the okay and wore the wire and had her walk on the wild side, her heart would still be singing when it was all over.

—⟋⟍—

She'd wanted to call her best friend, Emma, and share this with her—but she couldn't. If she'd wanted to tell her parents—which she definitely did *not* want—she couldn't. She couldn't discuss what she was about to do with anyone other than Detective Nolan and the man from the Drug Enforcement Agency office in Boston.

They had drilled her on everything she needed to know: Danny Watson had been Wayne MacArthur's local dealer until his arrest a few weeks ago. He'd been the one to tell the police that there would be drugs on the boat Ty had sailed up from Florida, only he thought the boat belonged to someone named Smith. Wayne MacArthur had taken a flight from Miami to Logan Airport that morning, and had landed shortly after noon. Both Ty and Danny Watson had provided the police with MacArthur's cell phone number. Monica sat with Detective Nolan and the DEA agent in a small, quiet office in the police station, and she phoned MacArthur, setting her cell to speaker-phone.

"Hello?" His voice was gruff and gravelly. A smoker, she guessed.

"Mr. Smith?" she asked. Having Mr. Nolan and the DEA agent seated so close to her made her self-conscious. Seeing them distracted her. She closed her eyes.

"Who's calling?"

She didn't want to give her name—or a false name—so she ignored his question. "I got your number from Danny Watson. I used to, like, get my stuff from him? But I guess he's not available or something?" She wanted to sound vague, young, different from who she really was.

"Where are you?"

"I'm in Brogan's Point. And...like, I'd really like to get some stuff." She added a slight tremor to her voice, the desperation of a drug addict, or so she hoped. "Danny said you could help me?"

He muttered a curse that she sensed was directed at Danny Watson, not at her. "Yeah, sure. It'll have to be later, though. I'm not even at my house yet."

"Do you want me to come to your house?" she asked, opening her eyes and exchanging a glance with the men huddling around the desk where she sat.

"No. Not my house. Meet me—" he paused for a moment, apparently thinking "—in the parking lot of the North Cove Marina. Nine o'clock tonight. If you're not there at nine, I'm leaving."

"Nine o'clock. Okay. Thank you." She again tried to infuse her voice with desperation, tempered with abundant gratitude that this wonderful drug dealer was going to save her from the agony of heroin withdrawal.

She heard a click, and then the DEA agent leaned across the desk and pressed the disconnect button on her cell. "Very good," he said.

A man on the far side of middle age, he looked oddly formal in a pressed gray suit and burgundy tie. Detective Nolan was dressed for a Saturday, in a polo shirt and khakis. Monica had already figured out what she'd wear that night: old jeans, sneakers, and her hoodie. She doubted MacArthur would recognize her—surely he hadn't attended the high school's production of *You Can't Take It With You* a decade ago, and he'd never been a guest at the inn—but with her hair flopping in her face and the hood of her sweatshirt covering her head, she'd be practically anonymous.

The DEA agent was still holding her cell phone. "You understand, there's no wire involved," Mr. Nolan explained. "We have to add an app to your phone, and it will record everything. You'll have it in your pocket, you'll turn on the speaker, and we'll hear and record everything. Much safer than wiring you."

"Okay."

"We'll be parked about a block away in an unmarked van. We'll hear everything you have to say. If you feel you're in danger, say the word 'crazy.' Say, 'You're crazy,' or 'This is crazy,' or 'I must be crazy.' We hear that word, and we'll swoop in and extricate you from the situation. Do you understand?"

"Yes."

"*Crazy*," he emphasized.

Monica nodded. She got it. She wasn't stupid. Maybe these officers of the law thought her eagerness to do this was proof that she *was* stupid. Or else they just thought she was crazy.

She wasn't, though. She was determined. Motivated. Tired of being demure and doing what was expected of her. Just wild enough to believe she could save Ty.

—⁓—

She arrived at the parking lot of the North Cove Marina at ten minutes to nine. Even though it was a relatively short walk from the inn, she drove there, slowing a block away from the marina's entry when she spotted a nondescript van parked on a side street. In the nighttime gloom, she couldn't tell the van's color—some dark hue, maybe burgundy or brown—but the headlights flashed twice, the signal Ed Nolan had told her to watch for. She flashed her headlights twice in response, then continued to the marina.

Only a few cars were parked in the lot, scattered across the otherwise vacant asphalt. She didn't know if any of them belonged to Wayne MacArthur, but she assumed he would come in a car. She wanted to be in a car, too. She wanted to have a way to escape quickly if she needed to—she doubted she could outrun the average man, but her Subaru could get her back to the van in a matter of seconds, if need be. She also liked the protection her car offered—steel and shatter-proof windows. Standing all alone in the dark lot would make her too vulnerable.

Near the ramp down to the dock, she spotted Ty's rented motorcycle, its abundance of chrome trim glinting in the silver glow of a bright lamp attached to the building, just beneath an eave. The building's windows were dark. The bike looked forlorn, abandoned. She was definitely all alone.

As she'd been instructed, she spoke in a normal voice. "I'm in the parking lot now. I don't see anyone here."

Her backups in the van signaled that they'd heard her by sending a signal through her phone, which vibrated in the breast pocket of her shirt for a couple of seconds. She'd stashed it there so it would be closer to her mouth and better able to pick up her conversation with MacArthur.

Her gaze drifted back to the motorcycle. What a shame that Ty was paying a daily rental on it when he couldn't use it. She'd taken the liberty of packing his belongings in his room at the inn, moving them downstairs to her apartment, and checking him out. She hoped that wasn't too presumptuous of her. Not that she expected him to move in with her when he was finally sprung, but she saw no reason for him to be paying the inn's hefty nightly rate while he was living rent-free as a guest of Brogan's Point's finest. If he wanted a room at the inn once he was cleared and granted his freedom, she would find him one. The reservation crunch wouldn't begin until Memorial Day weekend, six days from now.

Beyond the motorcycle, beyond the building, she counted the boats and slips, trying to recall which was the one Ty had sailed to Brogan's Point. The police had removed the yellow tape surrounding the impounded boat so as not to tip MacArthur off. All she could see in the uneven radiance from the spotlight on the building and a moon smeared with thin clouds was a forest of masts, silhouette-black, swaying gently as waves rocked the sailboats. All she could hear was the quiet whoosh of the wind and the clanking of hooks and rings against the masts. It was such a familiar sound to her, she hardly noticed it.

She did notice a shadow moving along one of the docks. She checked her watch: nine o'clock. The shadow moved toward the building. Definitely a man. A tall, limber man carrying a small duffel bag. He strode up the sloping gangplank, heading for the parking lot. "I think this is him," she said, and after a second, her phone vibrated against her chest.

She raked her hand through her hair to tousle it, then pulled the hood of her sweatshirt over her head. She'd circled her eyes with gobs of black eyeliner, figuring she ought to look, if not skanky, at least not like the clean-cut, well-groomed woman she was. Once her hood was firmly in place, she eased open her car door and swung her legs out. She moved slowly, cautiously. She didn't want to startle the guy. He might have a gun or something. He was a drug dealer, after all.

He stepped into the wide oval of light shed by the lamp, and she suppressed a smile as she studied him. *He* was the clean-cut, well-groomed party at this rendezvous. He wore a tailored shirt, khakis, and deck shoes. The duffel he carried appeared to be leather. His hair was too short to blow in the breeze rising off the water. His face was square, his features symmetrical. He looked like the sort of man one might run into at a prep school reunion.

"Mr. Smith?" she asked, remembering to speak in a slangy, jangly way, her voice as disheveled as her hair.

He continued toward her, moving in determined strides. She dug her hands into her hoodie's pockets and hoped she looked like a helpless junkie. The few roles she'd played in high school drama club productions didn't qualify her for an Equity card, but she remembered how to create a character from the inside out. For the next few minutes, she had to believe she was a drug addict eager to buy dope. She had to live it.

"You're the girl I spoke to on the phone?" he asked.

She nodded. "Thanks so much for meeting me. I would've taken care of this with Danny Watson? But I couldn't. He was..." She shrugged.

"Yes. He is," MacArthur said, choosing to be as vague as she was about his local distributor's fate. He moved out of the light, but her eyes had adjusted enough to the night's gloom that she could make out his crisp, genteel features. She inched a few steps closer to him. The closer she stood to him, the more clearly her phone would pick up his voice. "I don't believe you told me your name," he said.

"It's Mary."

"Mary what?"

"Mary Smith."

He hooted a laugh, one sharp syllable that quickly melted into the air. He didn't seem amused, though. His eyes were dark and hard. "Don't tell me we're related."

"I don't think so." She fidgeted with the tie string of her hood. "So Danny gave me your number, but he also told me some other guy was bringing the stuff here on your boat?"

"Danny told you that?"

Was she implying that Danny Watson—with whom she had never exchanged a single word—had told her things he wasn't supposed to reveal, or couldn't have known? Would MacArthur stop believing her because he knew Danny would never have said such a thing? She plunged ahead, ignoring her tap-dancing pulse. "Like, I didn't want to have to bother you. And this guy brought your boat up a week ago, so I thought, like, maybe he could help. I'm trying to remember his name. It wasn't Smith, I know that."

"Tyler Cronin," MacArthur said. "Did you talk to him?"

Had she—Mary Smith, the ditzy druggie—spoken to Ty? Would it be better if she had or if she hadn't? She didn't know. Saying the wrong thing would ruin everything. "Well, like, I *tried*," she said, then trailed off.

"So you didn't talk to him?"

Taking a chance, she shook her head.

"Good," MacArthur said.

Her heart raced just a little less. She'd guessed right.

"He couldn't have helped you," MacArthur said. "He's just some kid I hired to sail my boat so I wouldn't have to kill a week bringing it north myself. He doesn't know anything about this." He lifted the bag slightly.

Was that good enough to clear Ty? She wasn't sure. "This? You mean the smack? He didn't know it was on your boat?"

"How did *you* know it was on my boat?"

Shit. She'd said the wrong thing. Just because MacArthur had told her to meet him at the marina didn't mean he'd taken the heroin off his boat. She knew he had, thanks to the police—or at least, she knew he'd taken something that looked like the heroin from his boat, assuming they'd replaced the real stuff with something innocuous. But if she was just a junkie named Mary Smith, she couldn't know for sure that he'd just stepped off his sailboat with his illegal merchandise in his bag.

She had to extricate herself from this possible misstep. "I thought that was what Danny said? That you bring the stuff up on your boat?"

"Danny's an idiot," MacArthur said. "But yes, this is how I start the season. Fill my boat with precious cargo and bring it north."

"And that dude who sailed it up here for you—Tyler Whatever, not Smith? He couldn't have sold me some, huh?"

"He knows boats, but he has nothing to do with this. How much do you want? I'm not used to small transactions."

"Small transactions are all I can afford," she said, laboring not to smile. Surely Detective Nolan and the man from the DEA got what they needed. *He has nothing to do with this.* "Two dime bags," she said meekly, prying the twenty dollar bill the police had given her out of the hip pocket of her too-tight jeans. "That's all I got."

MacArthur made a face. "Jesus. I'm dealing with kindergarten here." He poked around in his bag, pulled out a block of something wrapped in plastic and a zip-lock bag. He settled these items on the hood of her car, eased open a corner of the plastic wrap and poured some powder into the bag. Was that the right amount? Monica had no idea how much heroin twenty dollars would buy.

"Here," he said, taking her money and handing her the bag. He regarded her for a moment, his expression softening. "How would you like to get your stuff for free?"

She widened her eyes, hoping she was doing a credible enactment of delight. "Really?"

"With Danny indisposed, I need someone to help with distribution. I'd give you a list of a few customers, you'd deal with this dime-bag shit, and I'd pay you with free dope."

He was asking her to deal for him. She hadn't counted on that. The script she'd used to prepare for her performance didn't include this scene. "I don't know," she hedged. "I mean, like, it's against the law."

"Your standing right here with me now, handing me that twenty dollar bill in exchange for two dime bags, is against the law, sweetheart. This would just be a temporary thing, anyway, until Danny clears up his problems. And you look so sweet and innocent. No one would suspect you of anything."

"I don't think so, Mr. Smith. I just—"

"You needed me and I came through for you. Now I need you."

"I'm sorry." She shook her head. "I just don't think I could do that." Like hell she couldn't. Right now, she felt as if she could do anything. Buy heroin. Perform on Broadway. Rule the world. Save Ty.

Abruptly, MacArthur clamped a hand around her arm. He was a lot stronger than she'd expected, his grip iron-tight despite his polished, gentlemanly appearance. "Listen, Mary—I can't be standing in parking lots dealing out dime bags. That is just not going to happen. If you want to get stuff from me again, you're going to have to help me out. This is not a negotiation, honey. This is me telling you."

Her arm hurt. He was bruising her. He was too close. Too threatening. She blurted out, "What are you, crazy? Let go of me!"

She hadn't even thought about the word. She'd just said it. *Crazy.* He gave her a fierce shake and her head jerked. "Listen to me. You'll be perfect. You won't get caught."

"No."

He snatched the bag of heroin from her hand. "Bitch. I'm doing you a favor, meeting you like this. I ought to kill Danny just for sending you my way. Pain-in-the-ass—" And then he fell back, wide-eyed, as glaring blue lights flashed across his face. Monica sprang free from him and turned in time to see the dark van and two police cars tear across the parking lot, screeching to a halt just a few feet from Monica and MacArthur.

"You bitch!" he screamed, reaching for her again.

She sprinted away, colliding with Detective Nolan as he and several uniformed cops swarmed around MacArthur. She tripped over his foot and went down, sprawling on the asphalt. Loose pebbles tore at her palms.

Detective Nolan halted and bent over to help her.

"I'm fine," she said, pushing off the ground and swiveling to sit. Detective Nolan looked so worried—but he shouldn't be. She *was* fine. She'd nailed the bastard. She'd engaged in an undercover drug deal, she'd said the word *crazy*, she'd done things she had never, in her wildest dreams, imagined doing.

She'd slept with a stranger. She'd fallen in love with him. She'd saved him.

The air blinked bright blue and dark, bright blue and dark with flashing lights. MacArthur raged and ranted. Uniformed officers shouted at him and wrestled him into handcuffs. And all Monica heard were the bold, wailing opening chords of a song: Wild Thing.

She'd made everything groovy, as the song said. She knew for sure. She was a wild thing.

Seventeen

Ty couldn't stay. The reasons multiplied and blurred in his mind, but the bottom line was, he had to leave.

All his stuff was in Florida. He had an apartment there. His Honda Rebel. Clients. Contacts. A flourishing career.

Brogan's Point had become a holding cell in a police station. It had been a place where he'd been suspected of crimes. A place he didn't belong.

Mostly, he couldn't stay because of Monica. Because she'd risked her life for him, and scraped her hands, and he felt guilty. He'd caused her pain.

She didn't seem to mind that she'd gotten injured that night in the marina parking lot. When he'd seen the scabs on her palms, she'd laughed and told him they didn't hurt. She'd laughed when he was released from the holding cell, too. She'd laughed and flung her arms around him and said, "Wow! It was so exciting, Ty! You should have seen me. I was amazing!"

He had no doubt about that. As far as he could tell, she was always amazing. She was smart and gorgeous and successful, and in her spare time she could extricate a guy from a tricky legal situation more effectively than his high-priced lawyer could—a lawyer she'd found for him.

He owed her too much, and she didn't seem interested in collecting on that debt. She was too thrilled about her excellent adventure.

He didn't want to be an adventure for her. He wasn't sure what he did want, but it wasn't this—to hang around her quiet little town, doing odd jobs for her at her family's resort and being beholden to her.

Besides, he never stayed anywhere for long. Now seemed as good a time as any to leave.

Caleb had told Ty he would mail a bill, and Ty could do whatever he had to do with his trust fund for the payment. Ty turned in his rental bike, and through some convoluted wrangling, Monica found a ride for him to Logan: the fiancée of her best friend's boss at the community center shuttled back and forth to Boston on a regular basis because her family and the antiques dealership she worked for were located there. Diana was an amiable, bubbly young woman who insisted that driving Ty to Logan Airport was no hardship. "This is what I love about small towns," she said. "Everyone helps everyone else out."

Maybe that was why Monica had done what she'd done—small-town helpfulness.

It didn't matter. He couldn't stay. He wasn't sure he even knew how to stay.

—⚌—

Florida was unbearably hot. Even with the air conditioner blasting in his apartment, he felt as if he might melt. The building's open staircase and pastel stucco walls seemed alien to him. The palm trees dotting his street seemed as if they'd been dropped into place from another planet. Even the Atlantic Ocean smelled different here. It smelled warm and soupy.

It took him three days to decide he couldn't stay here, either. This wasn't home. He hadn't really had a home since the day his parents died. He'd had places where he'd lived for a while, but no home. He wasn't even sure what home was, but when he spoke the word, shaped his mouth around it, his mind conjured images of a quiet, private beach, a cool breeze, a cool rain. Clam chowder in a rough-hewn dockside restaurant. Parents who wanted to meet their daughter's friend and make sure he measured up, even when the friend knew damned well he didn't.

He thought of Monica. Her dark, silky hair. Her sleek, slender body. The heat of her surrounding him, holding him deep inside her. Her courage. Her sensibility. Her knowledge of who she was and where she was headed. And those blinding sparks of wildness that flashed through her, captivating him. Making him ache with wanting her.

Fortunately, he rented his furnished apartment month-to-month, so he didn't have to break a lease. He packed up the belongings he considered worth saving, borrowed a neighbor's pickup and drove the boxes down to the marina where he repaired boats and where, for better or worse, he'd met Wayne MacArthur. For worse, because he'd gotten pathetically snagged in a web of legal problems. For better, because he'd met Monica.

At the marina, he asked the manager to store the boxes for him until he called with an address to ship them. Ty insisted on giving Jeff money to cover the shipping costs and compensate him for his trouble. Then he strapped what he could—some clothing, his laptop, a couple of good books—to the back of his Rebel and hit the road, heading north.

—ɯ—

Sun streamed through the window in Monica's tiny office down the hall from the inn's lobby. She was glad the room was small, just as she was glad her apartment was minuscule. Too much space made her keenly aware of how alone she felt.

The hotel was packed. Rose Cottage looked beautiful—a few guys on the maintenance staff had finished what Ty had begun, repainting the parlor and touching up the second-floor bathroom—and the cottage was now filled with the Kolenko wedding party. Every room in the main building was filled, too, although now that the Monday of the three-day Memorial Day weekend had arrived, people were starting to check out. During the week, the place wouldn't be packed, but next weekend promised to be as busy and profitable as this past weekend. Weddings were booked for every weekend through the end of August. Romance floated through the air like a sweet perfume.

She ought to be thrilled. Her parents were. The accountants were. The guests were, too.

But she was wistful. Melancholy. Feeling like an idiot.

She had known Ty would leave. He'd told her he would. She'd accepted that. Loving him despite the knowledge that he wasn't the sort of man who stuck around and committed to a place, a life, a woman...It had been risky, but Ty—and the moment they'd found each other while the magic jukebox cast its spell over them—had compelled her to take that risk.

She didn't regret it. She just wished that the end of the song didn't make her want to weep.

Her phone rang—a direct call, not through the front desk. She answered. "Hello?"

"Hey, baby!"

Jimmy. She wasn't in the mood to speak to anyone right now, but on the list of people she wasn't in the mood to speak to, Jimmy surely ranked in the top three. "Hello," she said grimly, hoping her tone would deter him.

"Listen, I got a great deal for you. A brand-new Focus, no money down. Great mileage. Automatic everything."

"I'm happy with the car I have, thank you."

His voice lost its salesman edge. "I heard that guy you were fooling around with has left town. No hard feelings, babe. Let's move on."

She wondered how he'd heard she was fooling around with a guy—which hardly described what she'd been doing with Ty, but the point wasn't worth debating. In a small town, no one had secrets, she supposed. He could have picked up gossip about her from anyone.

"I've moved on," she assured him.

"I'm sorry about the anniversary thing, okay? Let me make it up to you. How about dinner tonight? I hear the Ocean Bluff Inn serves great food."

"No."

"Come on, honey. We're past that bump in the road, right? I let you take your walk on the wild side."

"Wrong song," she told him.

"Huh?"

"Nothing," she said. "You said no hard feelings, and I agree. You said let's move on, and I agree with that, too. Let's move on, Jimmy."

"How about, let's move *in*," he improvised.

"No." No song connected her to Jimmy. No magic. She wasn't the person she'd been when they were a couple. That all seemed like another lifetime, another world. A world so safe it had nearly smothered her.

She was a different person now. The scabs on her palms had healed, and her heart…It would heal, too. Like any muscle, it would wind up stronger because of what it had endured. Scar tissue was tough.

"All right, well, just think about it," Jimmy said. He was a car salesman, after all. Car salesmen never took no for an answer. Even after you walked out of the showroom and drove away, they still believed they could sell you that shiny new Ford Focus.

"There's nothing to think about," she insisted. "I'm going to say good-bye now. Take care." She lowered the receiver gently into the cradle, not wanting the last thing he heard from her to be the bang of a phone slamming. She and Jimmy had a history, and they would always have that history. Some good times. Some not-so-good times. But it *was* history. Not the present. Not the future.

She didn't want to think about her future, because Ty wasn't going to be a part of it. Right now, the present was making enough demands on her, anyway. She swiveled in her chair, turning her back to the window and studying the schedule on her computer screen. Had she hired enough college kids for the summer? Their school calendars meshed well with the inn's, at least at the beginning of the summer. The hotel had hired a dozen girls to supplement the regular housekeeping staff, and half a dozen boys to supplement the grounds crew. That struck her as terribly sexist; why couldn't boys vacuum floors and scrub toilets? Why couldn't girls push lawn mowers and clean the pool? They could, of course, but the girls always applied for housekeeping jobs and the boys always applied for grounds-crew jobs. Gender politics notwithstanding, Monica couldn't force people to apply for jobs they didn't want.

Her phone rang again. Sighing, she lifted the receiver and said, "No. I'm not going to think about it."

"Monica?" The voice belonged to Kim Seaver, the front desk clerk.

"Oh—sorry," Monica said. "I thought it was someone else calling me. What's up?"

"There's somebody here who wants to see you."

"An irate guest?" *Please, no. I'm not in the mood.*

"He's not a guest. He says he wants a job."

"It's not Jimmy, is it?"

Kim laughed. "No. Can I send him back?"

Monica glanced again at the staff schedule on her monitor. Maybe it was a liberated young man who wanted to clean rooms this summer. She should encourage him. "Sure."

Less than five seconds after she hung up the phone, he swung into her office. Windblown. Sunburned. Covered in road dust.

Sexier than any man had a right to be.

"Ty?"

He was wearing faded jeans, thick-soled boots, and a dark blue T-shirt that had seen better days. A leather jacket was hooked around his index finger and slung over one shoulder. He filled her doorway, looking relieved and worried and…She sighed again. Unbearably sexy.

He gazed at her, silent. She saw a motion in his neck as he swallowed.

"You want a job?" she asked.

"Yeah. Maintenance. Repairs. You know I can do that. I won't leave any jobs unfinished, either."

"I thought you went back to Florida."

"I couldn't stay there anymore. It's not my home."

"It's not?"

He swallowed again. His eyes took her in, so blue, so intense. "No, it's not. You're not there."

Now it was her turn to fall silent. He ventured into her cramped office, one step at a time until he was an inch from her desk. She'd never thought of her desk as particularly large, but now that expanse of furniture between them seemed enormous. She wanted it gone. She wanted nothing between them, nothing but love.

She rose and circled the desk to him. He opened his arms and she stepped into them. For a long moment, they just held each other. Then he leaned back. "I'm serious. Hire me. I'll be the best maintenance guy you've ever had."

"I don't doubt it," she said, "but I can't hire you. I don't have an opening for someone with your expertise. I could use you on a contract basis for special projects—"

"That'll be fine."

"You could advertise your services as a freelance contractor. You'd make a lot more money than I could pay you, and I'm sure people around here would be happy to hire you." She paused, then added, "We've got a lot of boats in Brogan's Point."

"Right."

He still hadn't smiled. He looked so wired, so focused. "When did you get into town?" she asked.

"Five minutes ago."

She could smell the road and the wind on him. "Did you—ride your motorcycle?"

"Yeah."

"All the way from Florida?"

"I wanted it here with me. This…" He took a deep breath. "This is where I want to be. This is home, Monica. This town. This place. This part of the ocean." He bowed his head and touched his forehead to hers. "This woman. You. My wild thing."

"If you stay here, you might get tamed."

Finally, he allowed himself a small, hesitant laugh. "That's not going to happen."

"Oh." She smiled. "Good."

"So. I'm here. To stay," he emphasized. "To have a home."

She tightened her arms around him, tilted her face to his, and kissed him. A long, deep, wild kiss. A kiss that would have lasted forever if she didn't have to breathe.

But she did. She pulled back, inhaled, and smiled. "You make my heart sing," she said.

He returned her smile and quoted the song's best line: "I love you."

—⟁—

About the Author

USA Today bestselling author Judith Arnold knew she wanted to be a writer by the time she was four. She loved making up stories (not exactly the same thing as lying) and enjoying the adventures of her fictional characters. With more than ninety published novels to her name, she has been able to live her dream. Four of Judith's novels have received Reviewers Choice awards from *RT Book Reviews,* and she's been a multiple finalist for Romance Writers of America's RITA Award. Her novel *Love In Bloom's* was named one of the best books of the year by *Publishers Weekly,* and her novel *Barefoot in the Grass* has appeared on recommended reading lists at hospitals and breast cancer support centers. Married and a mother of two, Judith lives near Boston in a house with four guitars, three pianos, a violin, an electronic keyboard, a balalaika and a set of bongo drums. You can learn more about her at her website: www.juditharnold.com.

www.ingramcontent.com/pod-product-compliance
Lightning Source LLC
Chambersburg PA
CBHW051430260626
47162CB00001B/28